TRUE *of heart*

by

MARTHA KEYES

Dedicated to Gina.
Thank you for being my life twin.

Preface

DUKE ORSINO
What dost thou know?
VIOLA
Too well what love women to men may owe:
In faith, they are as **true of heart** *as we.*
My father had a daughter loved a man,
As it might be, perhaps, were I a woman,
I should your lordship.

Twelfth Night, William Shakespeare

Retellings are a difficult balance to strike, to say nothing of attempting a Shakespeare retelling. In my mind, this entire series straddles the line between "inspired by" and "retellings," though I'm not certain anyone really knows where that line falls. In any case, I have tried to take some of my favorite elements of the original play—in this case, *Twelfth Night*—and give them a Regency twist.

This book had an extra challenge above and beyond those that come with retellings. Writing about a woman who dresses up as a man and goes about society undiscovered was no small task. I took courage, though, when I discovered the true story of Dr. James Barry (1789-1865) who, it was discovered at death, was in fact a woman who had managed to go through medical school and live over fifty years as a respected doctor, with almost no one the wiser. So often, truth is stranger than fiction.

Whether you are a lifelong Shakespeare fan or have never read (or enjoyed) one of his works, I hope you will enjoy this twist on *Twelfth Night.*

Chapter One

Philip Trent, Viscount Oxley, sorely regretted the rash promise he had made to marry when he turned thirty years old. It was the type of idiotic thing one did when one was sitting comfortably at the age of three-and-twenty, naïvely believing that, not only was thirty an eternity away, but that one would be infinitely wiser—almost a different creature entirely—when that time *did* arrive.

Philip's friend, Julius Finmore, had never been one to tiptoe around unwelcome subjects. "A month to woo *and* marry a bride," Finmore said.

They held glasses of punch in their hands, watching from the outer walls of the ballroom as couples skipped up and down the set together.

"No, no." Philip swallowed the last bit of his punch and placed it on the silver tray of a passing footman. "I never said *by the time I turned thirty*—merely that I would marry *when I was thirty*. It is a vital distinction, and it gives me an entire year."

Finmore leveled him an amused glance. "Afraid, are you? You're not usually one for putting off unsavory tasks, Ox."

Philip smiled. "No, that is generally *your* domain, isn't it?" The thought of marriage wasn't exactly *unsavory*. Merely unsettling. But unsettling or no, it was his duty. And, if his father were still alive, he wouldn't have hesitated to say as much.

According to him, thirty was the perfect age for marriage —"enough time to see a bit of the world but not so much time that a man gets too attached to his independence," he had always said.

Finmore smiled widely but shook his head of sandy blond hair. "I am merely a man who enjoys his...entertainments."

Yes, Finmore certainly enjoyed his entertainments. Women, horses, cards. Philip didn't envy his friend's debts, but he *did* sometimes envy his ease with women. Gentlemen often referred to him as Shark Fin, an allusion to his ability to steal any woman from any man with the stealth of a shark.

"Well," Finmore said, putting out a hand to display the couples dancing. "Which one will it be? There's hardly a soul missing among the eligible women in London tonight. If you want a woman fit to become Lady Oxley, this is as good a place as any to decide. Why not choose one? What about Miss Conroy?"

Philip shook his head. Her name *was* on the list of candidates that sat in the drawer of his desk, but there was a neat line through it. There was a hint of instability about Miss Conroy if the scandal her elder sister had caused was any indication.

"Miss Welland, then," Finmore offered.

Philip shook his head again. Miss Welland was stable enough, but her family came from new money. Philip's father would never have approved.

"Lady Eliza."

Ancient family but no money.

Philip's father had made it clear what type of woman he expected Philip to marry: good family, wealthy, poised, free of scandal, and kind.

Well, Philip had added that last one.

Finmore turned to him, frowning. "Go on, then. Do you already have someone in mind?"

Philip's gaze flickered over to where Miss Rebecca Devenish stood on the far end of the ballroom. His eyes had found her the minute she'd walked in, hand elegantly holding up the side of her lilac gown.

Still lilac. He was beginning to think she might never put off mourning entirely. And while he wasn't precisely tripping over himself in a hurry to the altar, he couldn't court her very well while she held men at arm's length.

She was everything a woman needed to be to fill the shoes of Philip's mother. He had watched her carefully since she had begun attending events again, though she never participated in the festivities. He had never seen her show anything but kindness to those who approached her, and it was that which had finally tipped the scales in her favor. He trusted that his observations indicated an even-keeled disposition—someone his father would approve of but who wouldn't subject Philip to the hurt his mother had caused her family in private.

Finmore didn't miss the direction of Philip's glance. "Ah," he said with a knowing glance. "Right. Of course you would choose the one woman you cannot have."

Philip scoffed. "Cannot have?"

Finmore cocked an eyebrow at him. "I have watched your oh-so-captivating transformation from strong, capable viscount to clumsy, blubbering idiot in the presence of women. Like you, she has the pick of the Town, and I'm sorry, Ox, but she doesn't seem to be interested in you."

Of course Finmore would have noticed what was a source of severe frustration to Philip. Miss Devenish didn't seem to care overmuch about Philip's title or wealth or even his appearance, which was generally thought to be well above the average. She treated him just as she treated every other man. He had hope, though, that once she was no longer in mourning, and once he made his intentions known, that would change.

He swallowed uncomfortably at the thought that his hope might be an unfounded one. But he said nothing, merely watching as Miss Devenish and her father exchanged smiling remarks to one another. Her hair gleamed in the candlelit ballroom, arranged as it was in undulating twists and currents, like freshly poured honey. Her cheeks had that healthy, rosy glow that something artificial like rouge could never achieve. She was certainly not unpleasant to look at.

"I believe she does it to torture everyone," Finmore said, eyes narrowed as he watched her. "Coming to events like this, I mean, and refusing to dance and make merry. I imagine it gives her a sense of power to hold everyone's attention and keep the *ton* on its toes, waiting for her to arrive in anything but half-mourning. I cannot think her brother would wish her to mourn him for this long. Only a tyrant would."

Philip didn't believe anything of the sort about Miss Devenish. Finmore, while very capable with women, held a great deal of cynicism toward them. Philip admired Miss Devenish's devotion to her brother, even if he had a hard time understanding such familial affection.

Finmore took a drink. "In any case, you will need help wooing her."

"Wooing her?"

Finmore raised his brows. "Yes, wooing her. What reason have you to think she would favor your suit over any of the others?"

Philip shifted uncomfortably. He wasn't arrogant, but one didn't grow up a Trent of Oxley Court without a certain awareness of one's desirability.

Finmore chuckled, seeming to take Philip's silence as answer enough. "No, Ox. You have your work cut out for you, I'm afraid. Miss Devenish wants to be swept off her feet by someone who knows how to charm."

"By which I am to understand that I lack such a skill?" Philip knew he did. But he didn't like the thought that anyone else knew it —even a friend as close as Finmore.

Finmore clapped him on the shoulder. "Yes, Ox. Yes, you do. You are one of those fortunate men who has the luxury of ignoring the art of flattery because you have so many other means of attracting women. Oh, don't look at me like that, as if I was conveying staggering news. You may be a Nonesuch in every other category, but everyone has their Achilles' heel, you know. Luckily for you, it is a skill that can be learned."

Philip crossed his arms across his broad chest and laughed. "And you propose to teach me, I take it?"

Finmore smiled. "No, I haven't the patience *that* Herculean task would require."

"It is just as well. I need a wife, not a reputation as a rake."

Finmore chuckled softly and lifted a brow as though a thought had occurred to him. "Perhaps what you need is someone like the Swan."

A passing woman sent a coy look at Finmore over her splayed fan, and he gave her a half-smile in return.

Philip stifled an eye roll at the silent exchange.

"The Swan?" Philip adjusted his cravat, more curious than he cared to let on.

The young woman sent another glance over her shoulder at Finmore, and his eyes remained on her as he responded. "Yes. Something I heard from McQuaid the other day. Apparently he accompanied his mother to some small town outside of London and discovered a self-proclaimed genius in the art of love—this Swan figure. McQuaid ascribes his success with Miss Curran to heeding the Swan's counsel. I can find the man's address if you'd like. Apparently, he runs an advice column in the local newspaper."

Philip waved his hand dismissively. "No, no." Surely he wasn't so hopeless as *that* with women. He sincerely hoped not.

Finmore shrugged. "Suit yourself. But I can promise you, Miss Devenish won't be won by a man without any address, be his family and title ever so ancient. Her parents have promised to let her choose her husband, and she is too sentimental to marry purely for convenience. You might simply set your sights a bit lower. Any other woman in the room would have you willingly—oaf that you are." He clapped Philip on the shoulder with a smile. "I'm for the card table. Join me?"

Philip shook his head, but Finmore seemed to have anticipated the response and was already on his way out of the ballroom. Philip watched his friend disappear into the pockets of people between him and the doorway. *The Swan*. He scoffed silently. He needed no such help.

His eyes roved around the ballroom, finding Miss Devenish again. He wasn't entirely sure what love felt like, but he didn't think it was what he felt toward her. Nervous? Certainly. Awed? Why, yes. But he had chosen her for logical reasons, not sentimental ones. Love had little to do with marriage in a family like his. It was a strategic alliance. It was safer *not* to be in love, in fact. Love was a slippery, unpredictable thing. It was chaos and vulnerability, and Philip enjoyed neither. He would rather be in control of himself.

He spun the signet ring on his finger for a moment, tugged down on his coat, and made his way over to the far side of the ballroom. With every step closer to Miss Devenish, his heart beat a little more quickly. Devil take Finmore and his words—they were making Philip nervous, and he hated being nervous. It was as if, the moment he finally *wished* to please a woman, all of his good sense and confidence deserted him. How some silly swan was supposed to help that, Philip couldn't at all see. The man would have to be very skilled indeed to affect Philip's heart rate.

Besides, he well knew what he had to recommend him—he merely needed to ensure Miss Devenish understood it too. His suit was the logical choice, and she was too smart to ignore such considerations for such a fickle thing as romance.

It wasn't until the final steps toward her that he felt the sensation of his throat closing off, as if he'd tied his cravat for the neck of a five-year-old. No doubt the Swan would simply tell him to push through such a silly feeling—hardly anything he didn't already know.

"Good evening, Mr. Devenish. Miss Devenish." His voice sounded small and pathetic, reminding him of the way it would squeak as a child whenever he spoke to his mother.

Miss Devenish curtsied, and her father bowed, both smiling amiably upon him.

"I know you are not dancing, Miss Devenish. I only wondered if you might desire me." Philip cleared his throat, and his eyes grew wide as Mr. Devenish's brows went up slightly. "That is, what I meant was, I wondered if she might desire *to take a turn about the room* with me." He swallowed the massive lump in his throat, wishing he could disappear. Apparently, his throat hadn't closed off quite enough to prevent him from saying ridiculous and humiliating things. "I would be happy to procure a glass of lemonade for you as well, Mr. Devenish."

Mr. Devenish smiled but shook his head, nudging his daughter along with a hand on her back. "Go on, Rebecca. I shall be quite content to stay right here until you return."

She took Philip's offered arm with a polite smile that made his tongue feel too large for his mouth. He hated the uncertainty—not knowing what to say or how to please. It brought back too many unpleasant memories.

As they threaded through the room toward the refreshments, Philip noted the various men whose eyes rested hungrily on Miss Devenish. He was grateful that the task of navigating through the crowd prevented him from needing to speak to her.

They passed by Sir Allan with one of the Chesford twins on his arm, and Sir Allan sent Miss Devenish the type of intimate glance that caused Philip to set his jaw. Miss Devenish returned the glance with a smile then addressed herself to Philip.

"And how are you this evening, Lord Oxley?" Her voice had a deep, pleasing quality to it that made her sound dignified and more mature than her twenty years.

"Very well, thank you," he said, glancing at the different glasses on the table and wondering whether he should offer her lemonade, ratafia, or punch. Everything he did seemed to carry great significance—as if the drink he offered Miss Devenish might determine whether or not she would receive his addresses. His hand hesitated between the lemonade and the ratafia.

"Lemonade will do, thank you," she said. "I can never refuse a fresh batch on the occasions where it's offered. So often it is made with powder now, and I do prefer it fresh squeezed." She smiled gratefully as she took the glass from his hand.

Seeing an opportunity, Philip took it. "I am pleased to know that you like it. We always serve it fresh at Oxley Court, so you will feel quite at home—*would*. Would. You *would* feel quite at home if —that is—"

Miss Devenish looked bereft of speech, blinking at him wordlessly.

"Ah, Miss Devenish." An unwelcome voice spoke from behind them, and Philip shut his eyes in consternation before turning toward it, at which point he was subjected to the theatrical bow of Finmore who, evidently, had changed his mind about the card table.

Miss Devenish curtsied to Finmore who met Philip's gaze with a humorous glint in his eyes.

"I thought," Finmore said, donning his most charming smile, "that you might enjoy seeing the magnificent ice sculpture that has just been put on display. I believe they are serving flavored ice at the table, which I imagine you will enjoy even more than *that*." He indicated the glass of lemonade in her hand.

"Ices?" she said with a hint of curiosity reflected in her blue eyes.

Finmore nodded. "I would have brought you one, but I thought you might wish to choose between the flavors—a lemon and a parmesan, I believe."

Finally finding his tongue, Philip interjected. "My apologies, Finmore, but I told Miss Devenish's father that I would return her to him, and she hasn't even had the chance to taste the lemonade she holds."

Finmore's eyes gleamed with mischief. "I promise to return her to her father directly after visiting the ice sculpture—I have a matter I wish to speak with him about, in fact. But we shall let the lady decide, of course." He looked to Miss Devenish with an attitude of patient confidence, and Philip suppressed the desire to throw a glass of lemonade in his friend's face. Finmore was proving his earlier argument, and Philip well knew it.

Miss Devenish glanced up at Philip, a hint of apology in her eyes. "I confess I have been wishing to try an ice, and I can only imagine how much I shall like it flavored with lemon. But of course, I shouldn't wish to abandon you, Lord Oxley."

He was fairly certain that abandoning him was *precisely* what she wished to do.

He managed a small chuckle. "Not at all. I cannot speak for the lemon flavor of ice, but the parmesan is very enjoyable. I imagine Finmore intends to ensure you a taste of both—he is always *so very* giving of himself—so I shall leave you in his capable hands."

Miss Devenish's mouth broke into a smile, and she handed her glass of lemonade back to Philip before taking the arm proffered by Finmore, dipping into a curtsy, and thanking Philip.

"Oh, and Oxley," Finmore said, guiding Miss Devenish away from the refreshments. "You might take a look at the ice sculpture when you have a chance. I imagine you will enjoy it. It is carved in the shape of two swans." And with that Parthian shot, Finmore escorted his stolen charge gracefully through the ballroom, not even sparing a backward glance for Philip, who stood with two glasses of untouched lemonade in his hands.

Chapter Two

Philip pressed the seal stamp onto the hot wax of the letter sitting on his desk. He set the letter on the pile of those already sealed and stamped, straightening them so that the edges all lined up.

The library in his London townhouse was but a fraction of the size of the one at Oxley Court. It housed a respectable number of books, but it fell far short of the towering shelves of his country estate's grand library—the accumulation of centuries-worth of books, acquired by the five Viscounts Oxley who had come before him.

He glanced up, grateful that here, at least, he didn't have to gaze at the looming portrait of his mother on the wall. The painting was every bit as large and imposing as the room that housed it, and the artist had managed to capture the similarly grand presence of the subject—her clear, perceptive gaze, her regal posture, as though she looked down from a throne onto her kingdom below. He preferred not to have her eyes watching him while he conducted his business.

Philip wondered if she would be proud of what he had done with Oxley Court—the way he was managing everything. He had been working tirelessly at it since his father's death six years ago. He thought she at least would be pleased with his selection of Miss

Devenish for a wife. But perhaps he was wrong. He never had been able to accurately judge what would please her.

He had few memories of his mother, but they were all wrapped up in the same feeling: the wish for her approval and the uncertainty of obtaining it. He could still remember picking a bouquet for her, setting each bloom in a neat pile on the grass as he had taken turns selecting the most exemplary flowers. He had been so certain she would be pleased. She loved flowers, and she had been thrilled with the last bouquet he had brought her. He didn't remember what she said when he handed her the offering, only the way she had barely glanced at it, ordering one of the servants to take it away and ensure Philip had a bath. He could still remember how confused he had felt at her reaction.

There was a knock on the door, and Philip shook out of his daze, inviting the servant inside. A footman came in with a silver salver, on top of which sat two notes, apparently sent by the penny post. "These arrived with the morning post."

"Thank you, Stephen." Philip took the letters in hand, and the footman bowed and left.

He watched the servant's departure with a slight frown. He had found that his servants responded best to him when his expectations were high and his approval expressed readily. He doubted his mother had been one for praising the servants. Miss Devenish at least would manage the household capably *and* kindly.

He opened the first piece of correspondence—a simple invitation to an al fresco party to be held in a week. Miss Devenish would be there, he imagined.

The thought of her made him feel slightly warm about the gills. He had made a complete fool of himself the other night. Seeking the counsel of the Swan was sounding a bit less ridiculous now.

He glanced down at the unopened letter in his hand and recognized the stamp on the back as Finmore's. He sighed as he broke the seal.

Ox,

If you're feeling a bit humbler today:

The Swan
Office of The Marsbrooke Weekly
High Street
Marsbrooke
Your servant,
Fin

Philip stared at the address for a full minute, his mind working, his pride rearing its head, even while his sense of duty swatted it back down. Little though he liked to admit it, he needed help. It was a humiliating realization. Someone in his shoes shouldn't need assistance making a match. And Finmore was right—he could have paid a visit to any number of fathers in Town and received nothing but resounding "yeses" to an offer of marriage.

But he didn't want them. It was Miss Devenish he wanted—he wanted her gentleness as much as he needed everything else she possessed.

When Philip understood what was expected of him, he found it quite easy to meet those expectations. He merely needed to find out what it was Miss Devenish wished for in a husband. And for that, he required help. What if this Swan fellow was just what he required? No one—not even Finmore—need ever know Philip had employed his services. He could pay for discretion. Just one meeting to help him get ahead of the other suitors. That was all it would take.

With a determined breath and a setting of the jaw, he put down the letter and pulled a sheet of foolscap toward him.

Chapter Three

Ruth Hawthorn's forehead wrinkled in concentration as she summed the numbers in the neat column on the paper before her. She squinted harder to block out the sound of little feet clomping and creaking on the wooden floor outside the room she shared with her sisters. She didn't even look up as she dipped the quill, wiped the excess on the edge of the ink pot, and brought it back to the paper before her, scratching the sum at the bottom of the column.

She sat back with a sinking heart. "It seems impossible, but I am quite sure it is correct." She looked up at the maid beside her, who leaned over, frowning at the paper as well. Ellen had been with the family when they had entertained every family in the neighborhood —and now, when they could barely feed themselves. She was one of just two servants they had been able to keep on since the death of Ruth's father just over a year ago. If things continued as they were, they might be obliged to let Ellen and Lucy go, too.

Ellen stood straight, setting her hands on her wide hips and jutting out her lips in a determined gesture. "I shan't buy any meat for this week, miss. That will save a good amount, though I know how Master Christopher loves his mutton."

Ruth hurriedly checked the numbers again, but it was no use. The sum was correct.

She set the quill back in its stand. They had hardly any money left and still far too much time until more would come at quarter day —the small amount from the jointure Ruth's mother received. Thank heaven her father hadn't managed to lose that too. Ruth knew too well how much he had regretted his well-intended investment scheme to feel any anger toward him. She could manage a life of poverty better if he were still here.

Ruth's stomach writhed with guilt as she stared at the drying number on the paper. She wasn't accustomed to managing finances, and certainly not in the way they were now obliged to do, stretching every last farthing. She rubbed her forehead harshly, staring at the paper, as if she could will the numbers to change by looking at them.

Ellen put a soft hand on Ruth's shoulder. "Let me go see what we still have in the kitchen, miss. Perhaps we can make do for the rest of this week without buying the usual things."

Ruth nodded absently. As Ellen opened the door to leave, the volume of children's voices heightened, only to fall again as the door shut with a loud creak.

But it hadn't even been a full minute when the door opened again and the chaos of running children erupted in the room. Ruth continued to stare at the paper before her, hardly flinching when two children bumped up against her, one wrapping her arms around her leg, the other tugging on her arm as their urgent voices complained in disharmony. She tried to focus, but the voices became louder, pressing in on her thoughts.

"Stop!" Ruth cried, sliding the chair back and rising so that both children were obliged to unhand her. She put a finger to her temple and shut her eyes, forcing herself to draw in a deep breath. She looked down at her five-year-old sister Joanna, who looked stricken at Ruth's outburst, tears beginning to fill her sweet eyes. George's chin was trembling, his lower lip sticking out in a way that made her forget for a moment that he was three years old—his crying face had wrung her heart ever since he was an infant, and now more than ever, as he tried in vain to control it.

She sat back down, heart aching fiercely, and put out her arms. "Come, my loves. I am sorry for yelling." Both George and Joanna walked into her arms, and she pulled them to her tightly, planting a kiss on both heads. She loved all of her siblings dearly, but these two had come to depend upon her since their father's death in a way that had earned them a particularly warm corner of her heart. "Will you forgive me?"

George sniffed, but the corner of his mouth turned up in the beginnings of a smile—one that still struggled against his quivering chin. "'Course," he said. Joanna nodded with a smile more sure than her brother's.

"I'm hungry, Ruthie." George cast his large eyes up at her pitifully. The water from his unspilt tears still hovered precariously in the wells of his wide brown eyes.

"Come, Georgie," Joanna said, tugging on his arm. "You know we have to wait till dinner."

Ruth swallowed down the emotion in her throat at the thought of George's hunger. "What do you say we make some banana muffins? I saw an overripe one in the corner by the pots."

Both George and Joanna's mouths split into smiles, and they nodded vigorously.

"Go tell your brothers and sisters," Ruth said. "I only need five more minutes, and I shall come help."

The two children skipped out of the room, Joanna holding onto George's hand.

Ruth let out a breath as the two of them disappeared, her smile fading with their voices. She would have to tell her mother of their circumstances, but she dreaded it. Her mother wasn't meant for such a hand-to-mouth existence as they were now leading. None of them were, in truth. But her mother had married a gentleman and, as much as she tried to accept their new situation with equanimity, it was obvious that she was unhappy. It was no wonder. Losing a husband and a fortune in one blow was more than anyone should have to bear.

Ruth stood from her chair and looked around the room for her apron. She was still wearing it. Of course. Where was her mind going?

She brushed impatiently at the hairs escaping the simple, loose knot in her long hair—she had never been good at doing it herself, and she hadn't the time to devote to it now anyway—and put a smile on her face to go make banana muffins with the children.

The windows that let onto the street were open, bringing in the sounds of the bustling town of Marsbrooke, and releasing both the warmth from the stove and the scent of fresh banana muffins. Ruth's younger siblings—all but Topher, though he would take issue with the word *younger*—munched contentedly on the treats, while her mother was lying down for a rest upstairs in the relative quiet that reigned when all her children's mouths were at work. She was always so tired nowadays, as if when they had lost the money, she had lost her energy along with it.

Ruth and Ellen declined to take muffins for themselves. Ruth's stomach grumbled, but she could wait to eat until dinner.

The door opened, and Ruth's twin brother Topher walked in, his soft golden curls ruffling slightly with the breeze that blew in with him. For siblings who had shared so much of their existence, the two of them shared little in common by appearance.

Topher shut his eyes, breathing in the smell in the kitchen. "I thought I smelled your banana muffins from halfway down the street, Ellen." He strode over to the basket, unfurling a pair of spectacles, which he set on his nose before taking the last muffin in hand. He bit into it with a sigh of pleasure.

"You've got glasses!" eight-year-old Sarah cried, stating the obvious.

Topher tipped the glasses down his nose to stare at her through them teasingly. Ruth snatched them off his nose, inspecting them. Her first impulse was to chastise him for such a purchase, but she knew his eyes had been bothering him for some time now when he read, and she didn't want to discuss it in front of the children.

"And where have *you* been?" Ruth asked, handing the glasses back to him. Joanna reached for them, though, and set them on her face with delighted giggles.

Topher wagged his eyebrows at Ruth, swallowing down a mouthful of muffin. Topher was always energetic and good-humored, but he seemed to be in an especially happy mood today. He reached into his neat blue coat—conspicuously out of place in their humble kitchen—and pulled out a small bag of jingling coins, dropping it onto the wooden table, which sat unevenly on the floor below. "My best go of it yet!"

Ruth's eyes widened, and she plucked the bag from the table, yanking her brother's arm and pulling him into the small parlor that led off the kitchen. She shut the door behind them. "You can't be serious, Topher," she hissed. "Is that smuggling money?"

He nodded, wiping at the crumbs around his mouth. Smuggling was Topher's way of putting off the unpalatable task of choosing what occupation to pursue. She couldn't blame him too much. All his life, he had believed he would be inheriting Dunburn.

"You know we need it," he said.

"Yes, but the last thing I want is for Charlie to get wind of it. You know how he idolizes you, and who knows what mischief he would get up to if he found out. He thinks himself fair grown, for all he's only thirteen."

Topher seemed to sober at that. "You're right. I shan't speak of it in front of him again. We will simply tell him it's money from the Swan."

Ruth sighed. "That's hardly better." She thumbed the coins through the rough burlap. "And we certainly don't make this much from the Swan."

"Ah," Topher said, reaching into his coat. "Speaking of which, we have some post."

Ruth's lips drew into a thin line at the sight of his waistcoat. "Is that new?"

He pulled out three letters and glanced down at his waistcoat, a bright blue satin with embroidered green clocks. "I thought my success worth a little splurge." There was a hint of defensiveness in his voice.

"Well, it is hideous." She tugged the letters from his hand and brushed her flour-speckled hair away from her face. "You cannot continue to dress as though we still lived at Dunburn, Topher. We barely have enough to eat, let alone to waste on foppishness." She tried to soften her words with a teasing glance as she broke the seal on one of the letters.

"Allow me." He straightened his spectacles and took the letter back, walking over to the light of the window. "He thanks the Swan for *his*"—Topher sent her a smirk—"helpful advice on the topic of gaining an introduction to a woman and begs us to address in the following column how a man might go about wooing a woman whose heart is already given to another." He grimaced at Ruth.

She folded her arms and leaned against the wall. "Apparently he is *not* a careful reader of the column, or he would already know our answer to such a question. We are *not* in the business of stealing hearts—only—"

"—cultivating love in hearts that are unattached. Yes, I know," he said impatiently, taking the other two letters from her. He opened the second one. "This fellow wishes to express his profound thanks, feeling that he owes a great part of his success to the Swan, having lately become betrothed to a lady who will go unnamed out of respect to her privacy. Signed, J. McQ."

Ruth smiled. "I love those ones."

Topher narrowed his eyes at the last one, rubbing a finger along the crimson wax seal on the back. "Very fine indeed."

Ruth walked over and peered over her brother's shoulder. The seal was an ornate crest with a large O in the middle. Topher glanced up at her in annoyance. "A man's sister shouldn't be able to see so easily over his shoulder."

"Even an older sister?"

He scoffed and tore open the letter. "Older by all of five minutes."

"An inch for every minute," she teased.

He sent her an annoyed glance. "You are *not* five inches taller."

She smiled and stepped away so she could listen as he read the letter, chewing absently on the tip of her thumbnail.

His eyebrows knit together, and he held the letter up, staring at Ruth. "He wants an in-person consultation."

Ruth stared back. "What?" She took the letter from him and ran her eyes over the masculine but neat script. Her eyes widened. "Twenty pounds? He's offering twenty pounds for an hour?"

Topher's shoulders lifted, and his lip quirked at the side. "Can't put a price on love, can you?" He watched her, and she returned her eyes to the letter. "We shall accept the request, of course," he said.

Ruth looked up. "Of course? Of course *not*."

"What? Why not? Twenty pounds, Ruth! We need it. And it's only an hour."

Ruth stared at her brother incredulously. "Yes. In person! No doubt it has escaped your notice, but I am *not* a man, and I think that should become very apparent over the course of an entire hour."

"Would it, *Henry*?"

She punched her brother in the arm. Every now and again, he called her by the name their parents had chosen for what they had hoped would be twin boys. Her larger-than-average height did nothing but add fuel to the fire of his teasing, but she knew he resented being the shorter of the two.

Ruth had never explicitly stated that the Swan was a man, but she hadn't been terribly disappointed when people made the assumption. It was better for business, after all. And it was why, even when she accompanied him to the newspaper office, she always had Topher deal with the owner, Mr. Jolley. But she wondered whether the man had his suspicions.

Topher rubbed his arm. "Of course this 'O' fellow would see you were a woman, but what if it wasn't you who went?"

Ruth laughed. "What, *you*?"

"Why not?"

She folded up the letter and handed it to him, directing a baleful stare at him. "There's a reason I write the advice and not you, Topher. *I* am the one Papa taught. *I* am the one whose advice keeps *The Weekly* paying for the column. *I* am the one whose counsel creates success stories like that of this McQ." She nodded at the second letter.

"And I merely handle the correspondence," he said in a childish voice. "I *know*. But it's only for an hour, Ruth. Surely you could teach me enough of the basics to give good account of myself to Mr. O. Just think—twenty pounds for a mere hour!"

Twenty pounds *was* a significant amount. She imagined how it would change the sum on the paper upstairs and chewed on her lip. How much were her scruples worth? "But it feels so...so...vulgar."

"I hate to be the bearer of bad news, sister, but"—he motioned to the bare parlor—"we *are* vulgar now."

"Topher!" she cried. "Not vulgar. We may be poor, but it is not the same thing at all."

He shrugged. "Fact is, we need money—and we need it sharpish. If you won't respond to the fellow, *I* will."

Ruth's eyes widened. She wasn't entirely proud of her venture as the Swan, but neither did she want to trust Topher with the reputation she had taken care to cultivate.

He noted her reaction and grinned. "What? You don't believe me capable? Think I don't know how to win over hearts?"

Ruth gripped her lips together and took the letter from his hand. She ran her fingers over the broken seal, feeling a fluttering of nerves at the thought of agreeing to something so new for the Swan. It was so easy to write a weekly column, hiding behind paper. This was uncharted territory. "How should I know what you're capable of when you refuse to talk to me at all about your own romantic ventures?"

"I tell you as much as you tell me." He sat on the chaise longue and rested one ankle over the other. The elegant piece of furniture belonged in the low-ceilinged room as much as Topher's waistcoat did. It was one of the few pieces they'd brought with them from

Dunburn. Ruth would have preferred two wooden chairs, honestly. She hated the unwelcome reminder—comfortable as it was—of all they'd had to leave behind.

"That is only because I have no romantic ventures to speak of," she said. "And don't even begin to pretend the same is true for you. I am not stupid."

She *had* dreamed of romance. But that had been before all of this. The prospect of her own love story was yet another thing she'd had to leave behind at Dunburn. Love was a luxury she couldn't afford. Now she merely helped other people find it.

A knock sounded on the parlor door, and Ellen appeared in the doorway. "Shall I reheat last night's soup, miss? If we wish for something else, I will just need to make a short trip to the market before dinner."

Ruth didn't respond right away, keeping her eyes on the maid. This would be the third night in a row they'd had the soup. She could already hear George's whining. She glanced at Topher, who indicated the coin bag on the parlor table with a significant raising of an eyebrow.

"Give her one of the coins." Ruth swallowed as Topher obediently took a coin from the bag and handed it to the maid. "See what you can find with that, Ellen."

The maid nodded and disappeared.

Ruth stared at the door for a moment then sat down in the seat at the escritoire. "Let's respond to this 'O' gentleman, then."

The Hawthorn children wouldn't have soup five nights a week if Ruth had anything to say to the matter.

Chapter Four

Mrs. Watts had chosen the perfect spring day for her al fresco party. Birds chirped happily, the skies were streaked with thin, white clouds, and people trailed steadily into the gardens of Redditch House.

Philip glanced at the newest arrivals, hoping to see Finmore. It was a foolish hope—Finmore would no doubt stroll into the party twenty minutes before the end. He was rarely out of bed before eleven on a Saturday, and he could never abide being rushed.

Reasoning that the one place Miss Devenish was sure to go was the refreshment tables, Philip positioned himself on the outskirts of the food tents, speaking with whoever addressed themselves to him, all the while keeping an eye on her. He was obliged to wait for some time, as, by all appearances, she was approached by every eligible man in attendance, some even bringing her offerings from the table so that Philip doubted she would even *need* to come there for herself.

On all this attention her father looked with a watchful but not unkind eye. He seemed to be in little doubt what a treasure his daughter was.

Just now, her petite hand was being bowed over by Robert Munroe, a man nearly old enough to be her father. And yet, she still accorded him the same polite smile as she did every other man. She seemed to show no preference at all between the dozen men who had greeted her. It was what Philip so liked about her—and also the thing which made him worry so for his own prospects.

When she finally arrived at the refreshment table, Philip's legs were fairly begging him to sit down or walk about, but he took the few steps over to the table and then feigned surprise.

Her father greeted him and then excused himself as he was addressed by a man behind Philip.

Philip smiled at Miss Devenish, but she was selecting a tart and seemed not to notice. "I see you come to the table with the same goal as me," he said. "Sampling the lemon tarts before they have all been consumed." He bit into one of the tarts.

Miss Devenish raised her brows. "Oh. I thought I saw you eating one just a few minutes ago. You have been standing here for quite some time, so I imagined you'd had the opportunity to sample nearly everything you could wish to."

So she *had* noticed him. If he hadn't just been caught in a lie, the realization might have been more gratifying. Feeling an explanation was called for, he said, "Oh, well, that is—" Crumbled lemon tart crust from his mouth flew onto Miss Devenish's lovely lavender dress.

Philip's hand shot up to his mouth, eyes wide. He hurriedly chewed and reached for his handkerchief before continuing to speak. "I apologize, Miss Devenish. Allow me." He began to reach his hand out, only to realize how entirely inappropriate it would be for him to remove the piece of tart from the fabric between Miss Devenish's bosom and shoulder. "Here," he said, thrusting the handkerchief at her.

She took it, and Philip looked away while she removed the offending chunk of lemon curd. "I am not normally so clumsy," he said with an uncomfortable laugh that would convince no one.

She smiled up at him. "It is no matter, my lord." She seemed to hesitate with the handkerchief in hand, as though unsure whether to return it to him.

He waved a hand. "No need to return it to me. You may keep it."

She thanked him genuinely, slipping it into her reticule.

"Rebecca," her father said, coming up to them. "Mrs. Birch is in Town and was hoping to speak with you. I have just seen her arrive."

"Ah." She looked out onto the grounds. "Yes, I see her." She smiled up at Philip kindly. "If you will excuse us. Good day, my lord."

Philip sighed as he watched the Devenishes walk off, reliving every agonizing moment of the past two minutes in such vivid detail that he was hardly aware when someone came up beside him.

"You'll have to do better than that if you mean to have her." Finmore reached for one of the sweetmeats on the tiered tray beside them. "Of course, one should take care when generalizing, but I am tolerably certain that women tend to regard being spat upon with disfavor."

"It was hardly done intentionally," Philip said, a bite to his voice. Finmore would never commit such an error.

"I'm afraid that, in something as delicate as the pursuit of women, such a distinction is rarely appreciated. Why you cannot show a little humility and ask for some help is beyond me."

Feeling unbearably hot, Philip removed his hat, sliding his hands along its rim as he considered whether to tell Finmore of his upcoming meeting with the Swan. But Philip didn't want to give him the satisfaction of knowing he had taken his advice. He could be unbearable sometimes. "Thank you, Fin. But no."

Philip's pride—the thing that told him he was capable of anything he set his mind to—balked at admitting he would be employing the services of a stranger to aid him in something that should have been easy for him to accomplish. But he clearly needed that assistance.

That and to stay far away from lemon tart.

Chapter Five

Ruth's heart pounded as she approached the door to her house. She put an anxious hand up to her neck, feeling how it prickled her fingers, and tightening her bonnet ribbons. A silly gesture, of course. At best, it would delay the inevitable.

She straightened her shoulders. It was done, and it hardly mattered. All that signified was the money she carried in the pocket of her pelisse. Not as much as she had hoped for, but it would afford them the post-chaise to London. Topher had insisted they had an image to maintain, and she couldn't deny he was right. Who would wish to take love advice from someone arriving on the stage or the Mail Coach? Thank heaven they didn't live far from Town.

She opened the creaking door, slipping into the kitchen so that her back faced whoever might be sitting at the table.

Her legs were quickly enveloped in a pair of small arms, and she smiled as she reached down to pick up George. "Hello, my love!" She planted a wet kiss on his cheek, causing him to crinkle his nose and wipe at it with the back of his hand. His eyes widened as he peered under the lip of her bonnet.

"Your hair, Ruthie!"

"What of it?" She put him down on the floor and avoided the gazes of her siblings.

George pointed at her head. "It's all gone."

Ruth forced a laugh. "Not all of it, silly!" She paused a moment. But this was as good a time as any other, and she tugged at the ribbons before pulling her bonnet off. Her neck felt naked, and she reached a cupped hand to the back of her head, her heart startling again at the mere inches of hair, cropped close to her head, much like Topher's, only much straighter and darker.

Gasps sounded from every single one of her six siblings, accompanied by wide-eyed stares of horror.

"Ruth!"

"Now she *really* looks like a boy!"

"Shh! She does *not*."

Heat rose into Ruth's cheeks. She knew it was just teasing, but what she didn't know was how much truth lay behind it.

Topher was the only one who had yet to say something, and he walked over wordlessly, putting a hand to Ruth's short, dark hair then looking at her for an explanation.

She lifted her shoulders with the best nonchalant smile she could muster. "You may go hire our chaise now."

Topher's cravat moved up and down as he swallowed. "You ninny," he said softly. "What were you thinking?"

"It's not much, but between this and a bit of what you earned the other day, it should get us there and give us enough for lodgings."

"Hire a chaise?" their brother Charlie said. "To where?"

"Ruthie and Topher are going to London!" Joanna said excitedly as she came up to them. "Aren't you?"

Ruth nodded, taking her sister's grubby hand. "We are indeed."

"Sophia said that women go to London to make a smart match. If you do, shall we be able to go back to Dunburn?"

Ruth opened her mouth to respond, but she was overruled.

"She can't make a match like *that*." Ruth's eight-year-old sister Penny pointed at her hair, nose wrinkled. "She looks too much like a man."

"She's not strong enough to be a man," said an affronted John, Ruth's ten-year-old brother. "Plus, she's got girly eyes. Just look how long her eyelashes are."

"Yeah, almost as long as *yours*," Charlie said with a jab at John.

Topher shooed the young ones away with both hands, telling them to go wash up for dinner, and Ruth busied herself with removing her pelisse, not wanting to meet her brother's eye. She was secretly bruised by her siblings' comments.

But it didn't matter how she looked, as long as her siblings had food on the table and opportunities to better themselves.

Topher walked over to her and put an arm around her shoulders. "We don't deserve you, Ruthie." He ruffled her hair with a teasing hand.

Ruth could see her mother eying her close-cropped hair with a sort of wistful sadness, and she hurried to put on her bonnet. She had been trying not to think about her hair since cutting it. In many ways, it was a welcome change. Ruth had always been impatient with her hair—particularly when she was young and Topher was already outside playing, while she had to sit and wait for her hair to be tamed. She merely needed to think of her current hairstyle as a childhood dream finally realized.

The door opened, and Topher walked in, wearing the finest pieces of clothing he owned. "The chaise is waiting for us at The Red Lion. We should go."

Ruth nodded, swallowing the lump of nerves in her throat.

"Will you bring me back a doll, Ruthie? Oh, please." Joanna grasped her hand and looked up at her with so much hope Ruth could hardly bear it. "Sophia said that her doll was made specially in London."

It had been more than a year since Joanna had seen her friend Sophia McCausland, but she had a very good memory.

Ruth crouched so she was at eye level with her sister. "We shan't be in London for very long at all, my love." She tucked a hair behind Joanna's ear, watching as the girl nodded bravely, eyes filling with tears. "I will keep an eye out, though." She wrapped Joanna in a full embrace and then rose to bid her mother goodbye. Her protestations against Ruth and Topher's plans had been milder than expected. She obviously knew they needed the money, even though it meant her children stooping to levels that pained her.

Ruth kissed her mother on a floured cheek. "Goodbye, Mama."

"Hurry, Ruth," Topher said, still standing in the open doorway, his packed belongings at his feet, and a sealed letter in hand. Their younger maid Lucy stood quietly by, holding Ruth's portmanteau.

"Are you certain you can spare Lucy?" Ruth asked her mother.

She nodded and put a hand to the pieces of hair peeking out of Ruth's bonnet. She rubbed a short lock between her fingers. "Ellen and I will manage. She and Lucy took some time to prepare things for the week last night. And Charlie has already promised to help where needed. I feel easier knowing you have someone with you. I wish I could chaperone you myself, as it should be." Ruth had already considered that option, but George couldn't be deprived of both Ruth and his mother simultaneously.

"We shall be back before you know it."

Topher kept a quick pace on the way to the inn where the post-chaise awaited, only slowing for a quick stop in the offices of *The Marsbrooke Weekly* to deliver the column for the coming week. Ruth and Lucy waited, keeping watch over his portmanteau and valise as he delivered the paper. Ruth frowned at her brother's belongings.

"Surely you don't need all of that for a short stay in London," Ruth said as he picked up the valise.

"You yourself said we have an image to maintain, didn't you?"

She raised a brow at him. "You were the one who said that. Why in the world would you need two hats? Or two pairs of boots?"

He looked astounded. "I cannot wear my riding boots with my Wellington. You must surely see that."

She didn't at all see it, but she held her tongue, feeling it to be wasted energy—and not wishing to spend hours in a carriage with a moody Topher.

By the time they arrived at The Red Lion, the horses were fidgeting, their muscular haunches gleaming in the springtime sunshine.

Ruth stopped in the inn yard and stared at the equipage, biting her lip and hardly noticing when the postilion took her portmanteau and set it on the platform. She was certain this had not been what her father had in mind with all he had taught her about love.

"Come, Ruthie," Topher said, gesturing to her from the steps of the chaise. "Let's not dilly dally."

He was anxious to get to London. Their father had fallen ill just as Topher was meant to accompany him to Town for the first time on business—the same business that had gone terribly awry soon after. Ruth couldn't help wondering how much of Topher's desire to meet with Mr. O was simply a wish to see however much of London he could. She couldn't blame him for wanting an escape.

Topher stepped back down to the ground, coming over and putting a hand on her arm. "What is it?"

She shook her head, watching as the postilion assisted Lucy onto the seat behind the rear wheel. "Nothing." She smiled. "Just my missish scruples again. I can't rid myself of the notion that what we are about to do is not very genteel."

Topher cocked a brow. "Have you not been telling me to stop dressing as though we were genteel?"

"No, I have been telling you to stop dressing like a fop." She elbowed his bright waistcoat, from which a pocket watch chain dangled—a pocket watch chain with no pocket watch at the end. But only Ruth and Topher knew that.

She couldn't deny he looked much more *ton*-ish than she did. They would certainly appear to be in better circumstances than they were, and that was best for business. They needed Mr. O to be content with their services, and Topher would inspire more confidence attired as he was.

Ruth thought of Joanna's request for a doll and grimaced. She couldn't give the girl a doll, but she could ensure that they returned home with twenty pounds. Perhaps it was time for Ruth to take a closer glance at some of the men who lived nearby—the baker's son always had a ready smile for her when she passed the bakery. It was not the type of match she had envisioned for herself, but it might serve well enough. At least Ruth would no longer be a drain on her family's precious resources.

She sighed.

"Where were you last night?" Ruth asked as they passed the last houses on Marsbrooke's High Street.

Topher lifted his chin, but she didn't miss the infinitesimal pull at the corner of his mouth—the smallest of smiles at whatever memory her question had conjured. She knew her twin better than he realized.

"Out having clandestine meetings with women?" she teased.

"Wouldn't you like to know?"

"I don't know if I *would*." She settled into the squabs.

"I'm not a dashed loose screw, Ruth." He shifted with annoyance in his seat. "I just don't want your love advice."

She put her hands up to convey her innocence. "I wouldn't presume, though how you think to convince others to take my advice when my own brother disdains it, I don't know."

He sent her a suspicious sidelong glance. "It's better this way. Don't ask, don't tell. My business is my own. Your business is your own."

"Fine," she said. He had never forgotten the time Ruth had offered a critique of his approach with women.

The journey to London only required two stages, providing limited time for Ruth and Topher to discuss some important details of their escapade.

"I have been giving it some thought," Ruth said, "and I think you should give a different name. To protect the identity of the Swan, of course, but even more so to protect Mama and the children."

Topher considered this with a slight frown.

She clutched her hands tightly in her lap, recognizing in her brother the same hesitation she felt at the deceit. But they couldn't afford for people to discover the identity of the Swan. She couldn't imagine people would be as keen to take the Swan's advice if they knew who was behind the column. They needed the money it brought in every week, and she didn't want her younger siblings associated with it. "The last thing our family needs is more scandal and less money, and that is what we would get if it became known that I am the one behind the Swan. You can keep your given name, but perhaps you might go by Franks instead of Hawthorn. Being Mama's maiden name, it isn't *so* far from the truth, and I think that the closer we can keep to the truth, the easier it will be."

Topher nodded, brow still wrinkled. "Very well, but it is only an hour meeting, Ruth."

"I know..." She trailed off, and they fell into a somber silence.

The change of horses was made quickly, Ruth and Topher not even stepping down from the chaise for refreshments. They would need every last farthing to hire lodgings in Town, particularly since they would need two rooms instead of one.

Earning twenty pounds was turning out to be quite expensive.

Chapter Six

As Philip arrived home from an errand to his tailor, he frowned at the presence of his sister's carriage being driven from the front of his house toward the stables. Alice delighted in stopping by unannounced. Philip only hoped she had brought the children with her and left her husband behind.

He handed his coat and hat to his butler upon entering, cocking an ear and smiling slightly at the sound of his nieces' muffled giggling.

"Lady Tipton is in the drawing room, my lord," the butler said. "Along with the Misses Tipton and their nurse."

"Thank you, Draper. I suspected as much." Philip glanced in the mirror and straightened his cravat. "And Sir Jon?"

The butler shook his head, a knowing glint in his eye. He was not overly fond of the man, either. "No, sir. And I hope you don't mind, but I took the liberty of asking that a small platter of meats and cheeses be prepared for the Tiptons. And a few biscuits for the girls."

"Very good."

The butler had a soft spot for the little girls, much like Philip did, and they had come to expect something sweet from him whenever they visited.

Philip strode toward the drawing room and paused before opening the door. The high-pitched voices of his nieces sailed through the small gap between the French doors. He put a hand on both doorknobs and, as quickly as he could, threw the doors open with an "Aha!"

Little shrieks of terror, accompanied by frantic scurrying to hide, morphed quickly into hand-muffled giggles of delight as Philip entered the room. He smiled at the view of two curly heads of hair disappearing behind the sofa. The edge of one dress, betraying the hiding spot, was snatched and concealed by a small, chubby hand.

"Good heavens, Philip," Alice said with a hand to her chest. "Do you frighten all of your guests to death, or am I simply unlucky?"

Philip dipped to kiss his sister on the cheek then crouched and stepped softly around the side of the sofa.

"I cannot understand why—"

Philip silenced his sister with a finger to his lips and was met with an annoyed sigh. "I could have sworn," he said loudly, "that there were two little girls here when I entered, but I see no sign of them anywhere."

More muted giggles came from behind the sofa.

He tiptoed two more steps then swung around to the back, causing another eruption of shrill screams.

Their nurse, Mrs. Morris, smiled benevolently from her position near the windows. But, seeing her mistress's expression, she stepped forward. "Now, girls, you know your mother can't abide screaming."

Alice's eyes were closed, her fingers pressed to her temples. "Why you must needs encourage such behavior is beyond me, Philip."

Philip scooped up Mary with one arm and Anne with the other, bending down so that they rested on his knees. "Kisses!" he demanded. "Or I shall tickle you until your guts come out!" They hurriedly wrapped their arms around his neck and pressed their soft little mouths to his cheeks before scrambling out of his arms, away from the threatened tickling.

"Good gracious, Philip," Alice said. "I am trying to teach the girls how to be proper ladies, and here you insist upon making them screech like monkeys and speaking unseemly words like"—she glanced at the girls, who were being shepherded by Mrs. Morris, and put up a hand to shield her mouth—"*guts*."

Philip chuckled, pouring himself a glass of brandy from the liquor cabinet. "My apologies, Alice, but I have a role to fill, you know."

"What? Corrupting influence?"

"No." He sat down on the arm of the chair across from her and took a swallow of his drink. "The fun uncle. Every child needs one." Mary and Anne especially needed it. They shouldn't grow up thinking that every man was like their insufferably rigid father. Marrying Sir Jon Tipton may have been strategic for the Trents, but it had not improved Alice. With each passing year, she became more and more like her husband, making Philip wish that his father had not forbade her from marrying the man she had loved, be he ever so plain a mister. Did Alice ever regret complying with their father's demands?

She smoothed her skirts. "I thought you were going to say the bachelor uncle, and between you and Roger, I think we have that *well* covered."

Philip declined to respond to this, merely setting his glass down on the short table in front of him and reaching for a piece of cheese from the platter. Their brother Roger was far too young to be thinking of marriage yet, but he knew that to say so would invite a retort from Alice about Philip *not* being too young.

Seeming to accept that he didn't intend to oblige her by responding, Alice proceeded. "Do you *ever* intend to marry?"

"Of course," Philip said, sending a mischievous sidelong glance at the girls, who were now seated primly on the settee ten feet away, hands folded in their laps. They both tried to stifle smiles.

"But *when*? And to *whom?* I can tell you that I am quite happy to offer a few suggestions of women to be considered, Philip, for I am a very good judge of character, you know."

Having eaten two large holes from his piece of cheese, Philip held it up to his eyes, eliciting delighted but muffled laughs from Mary and Anne.

"This is *serious*, Philip," Alice said. "You must choose your wife wisely, for not every woman is fit for the role. I was thinking the other day that Victoria Munroe might suit very well."

Philip held up his hand. "Thank you, Alice. But I do not require your assistance in this matter. I have things well in hand." He *would*, at least.

Alice raised her brows, the beginnings of a hopeful smile on her lips. "You have already chosen someone, then? Who is it? I do not mean to doubt you, Philip, but you haven't Father or Mother to guide you now, and I think I might be a great help if—"

"Miss Devenish," Philip said, hoping it would silence her.

Alice blinked, staring at him for a moment before speaking. "Miss Devenish...well, yes. I say, Philip, that is a *very* good choice, and one I hadn't even considered somehow—perhaps because she is still in mourning. Though, why any woman should mourn her brother's death for an entire year and more, I cannot understand."

Philip's mouth drew into a half-smile, and he crossed his feet at the ankles. "How long precisely should I expect you to mourn *my* death? A week?"

She attempted to suppress a smile. "Oh, no. I should give you two or three, I imagine, providing you weren't in my black books."

"You flatter me, Alice."

She sent him an arch look. "So, when are we to anticipate the news of your betrothal? Have you spoken to her father?"

Philip was conscious of a mixture of annoyance and embarrassment at his sister's assumption. "I can hardly court her properly when she is still in mourning, can I?"

Alice tipped her head from side to side. "Not in the strict sense of the word, perhaps. But much can be accomplished through your regular interactions, you know. You can certainly take action to ensure she isn't snatched up by someone else when she finally *does* put off those dreadful half-mourning colors. Though, I must say, they complement her beauty nicely."

"Unfortunately, you are not the only one to take notice of that. She has a dozen men lined up to pay their addresses to her."

Alice tugged on her glove unconcernedly. "She would be a fool to choose anyone but you."

Philip wished he could feel so confident on the subject, but he imagined his sister would think differently if she had seen him launching half-chewed lemon tart at Miss Devenish the day before.

He was quite ready to bid Alice farewell an hour later when she led Mrs. Morris and her daughters out onto the street where their carriage awaited. He would have gladly kept his nieces for the afternoon, but he wasn't fool enough to ask such a thing of his sister. She was particular about whom she allowed to care for her children, and she clearly thought Philip's influence undesirable.

So, he embraced his nieces in the entry hall of his townhouse, reveling in their sweet scent and wet kisses.

"Will you come visit us at our house soon, Uncle Phil?" Four-year-old Mary looked up at him with her wide, brown eyes.

"You must," Anne said, sounding much older than six. "For Mama gave us a new tea set, and we should like to have you over one of these afternoons."

Philip executed a flourishing bow to match Anne's formal invitation. "I should be honored."

"We shall be so pleased." Anne performed a careful curtsy in return then hurried off to the carriage where her mother sat waiting.

Philip sighed and waved a hand as the door to the carriage shut. Would that all women were as easy to please as his nieces.

Chapter Seven

The business of arranging for rooms at The Three Crowns was taken care of by Topher, who managed to acquire them a pair with an adjoining door—a request Ruth had made. She wanted to attract as little attention as possible, and being obliged to step out of her room to communicate with Topher was likely to attract more notice than she cared to elicit. Being in London without a proper chaperone was already grating on Ruth's sense of propriety. But these were desperate times, and, like love, propriety was a luxury.

They had been at the inn all of ten minutes when Topher knocked on the door between their rooms. She opened it to find him hat in hand, hair arranged in a decent imitation of the Windswept style.

Ruth blinked at him. "Where are you going?"

"Out." He straightened his cravat with one hand.

She opened her mouth to respond, but he hurried to speak. "Now, don't spoil my fun. You know how long I've been meaning to see London. Besides, the meeting isn't for two days. Plenty of time."

"But we need to go over the lesson to prepare you," she said incredulously. "This is the entire purpose of our coming, Topher."

"Stop fussing, Ruthie," he said. "I shall be back before you know it, and I promise I shall work my hardest to ensure I am prepared. I may not be as smart as you, but surely I am not so slow that I require two full days of preparation for one single hour."

She said nothing, having no other argument against his plans than a nebulous mislike of them.

He glanced at her hair and smiled mischievously. "You might even come with me, you know. You could blend in quite well now with that hair of yours."

She made an attempt to kick him in the shins, but he jumped back in time to avoid her, laughing. "Heaven knows you brought enough clothing for the both of us," she said.

"You could do with a bit of relaxing," he said. "You've become so stiff, and we're in London, for heaven's sake."

Ruth forced herself to relax. She *was* stiff. But the stresses of life had made her thus. "I need to compose something for you to study tomorrow. *One* of us should take this seriously, at least." She was teasing him, but she felt the familiar hint of resentment at the freedom Topher had. He would no doubt be out till all hours of the morning then sleep late, spend an hour looking at what she had spent all afternoon drawing up, and waltz into Mr. O's lodgings with not a care in the world. And, most infuriating of all, he would likely handle the meeting just fine, despite his lack of preparation.

"Suit yourself," he said, stepping back into his room and setting his hat at a jaunty tilt atop his head. "How do I look?" He put his hands out to his sides with a charming smile. He *was* handsome, Ruth had to admit. He looked the part of the Swan.

"Ridiculous enough to attract far too much attention. We are *trying* to remain inconspicuous. Please remember that. And don't forget that you are Mr. Franks." She glanced at his new pair of glasses, sitting next to the wash basin. "Don't you need your glasses?"

"They're only for reading, silly. And I won't be doing any reading where I'm going. Believe me."

She bit back the desire to ask him why he had felt it necessary to spend precious money on glasses he barely needed, but she refrained. He looked so much like a boy again in his excitement to see

London, and she couldn't find it in her heart to smother it. "Where *are* you going?"

He smiled and shrugged. "Wherever the wind blows me. Watch over Ruth, Lucy," he called into the other room, where the maid was still unpacking Ruth's things.

The door shut behind Topher, and Ruth stared at it for a moment before turning away.

The next morning, as Philip was partaking of a hearty breakfast, Draper presented Philip with a letter from his steward.

Philip read it with a deepening frown then a raising of the brows. The bulk of the letter was devoted to the subject of Philip's housekeeper, Mrs. Hines, whose mother had apparently fallen ill and was now in need of constant care.

Mrs. Hines herself was nearing her retirement, though she adamantly maintained she wouldn't retire for another five years. She was a stubborn woman—to which accusation she had always replied, "Stubborn as an ox of Oxley Court, my lord." Philip had a special place in his heart for her.

He sighed as he folded up the letter. He would have to make the journey to Oxley Court to handle things—and soon. He wanted to ensure that there was no chance of Mrs. Hines being absent if her mother took a sudden turn for the worse, and he knew her well enough to know she would resist the steward's efforts to make her see reason. Stubborn as an ox, indeed.

His meeting with the Swan, though, was set for two days from now. He would simply have to ask that the meeting be moved up. He could leave directly after, and his journey to Oxley Court would give him time to process what he learned from the Swan. Not procrastination. Just mulling things over.

He hardly knew what to expect of the Swan, but in his mind, he envisioned a Casanova-like figure, with an almost ethereal handsomeness. He wondered how many women the man had wooed—and what he would think of someone like Philip, who had been too busy managing the estate for even the lightest of flirtations. At least that was the excuse he gave himself.

And now he needed to win over one of the most desired women in London. The entire future rode upon his success.

Whatever the Swan looked like, Philip sincerely hoped he could help him.

Ruth woke to the familiar sounds of town bustle through her window. She blinked sleepily and pulled the covers over her head in her usual futile attempt to block out the noise. She missed the peaceful chirping of birds at Dunburn.

Topher would have no trouble snoring through the shouting of merchants and the clopping of hooves. She should be grateful *she* couldn't hear his snoring, thin as their walls were. Topher's "snorting" was something John complained about at least once a week.

Ruth threw the covers over and slipped her feet onto the cold wooden planks, reaching for her wrapper and walking to the small, handheld mirror on the wash basin. She turned her head from side to side, smiling slightly at her hair. A few rebellious hairs stuck up in the back, but it was certainly nice to wake without something resembling a rat's nest at the back of her head. She had never been a particularly dainty sleeper.

She fingered the short locks of brown hair, wondering how long it would take them to grow out again. Penny hadn't been wrong when she declared that Ruth wouldn't make a match with her hair that way. She knew of fine women who managed with such coiffures, but they had money and status to support them in their daring. Ruth had neither.

Leaving her appearance for more important things, Ruth looked over the lesson she had prepared for Topher to study, feeling a fluttering of nerves. She hoped it was what Mr. O was looking for. She had a great fear that he would claim it was all common sense and refuse to pay them.

Lucy brought a tray of toast and tea from the coffee room for Ruth's breakfast, which Ruth partook of at the small, ill-balanced writing desk by the window as she went over the lesson notes.

Multiple times, she resisted the urge to knock on Topher's door, wishing to explain something in the lesson, but she had no desire to wake the sleeping beast yet. He was not at his best in the morning, and he still hadn't come back by the time she guttered the candles at one in the morning.

Lucy returned an hour later, holding a letter. "This came by way of a private messenger," she said. "The boy awaits a response below-stairs, I understand."

Ruth frowned slightly. It must be from Mr. O. He was the only one who knew of their presence or location in Town.

"Thank you, Lucy. I shall call for you when I've composed the response."

Sure enough, she saw the familiar seal on the back as she took the letter in hand. Her heart dropped for a moment as she considered whether Mr. O might have decided against the meeting after all. He had been clear in the letter that had followed their acceptance of the rendezvous that he wished for complete discretion—and he trusted that the twenty-pound rate would cover it.

Perhaps he doubted their discretion and was regretting his request to meet. She hurried to read the missive.

Dear Swan,

I hope that your arrival in town has been without mishap and that you are comfortably installed at The Three Crowns. Regrettably, I have had some unforeseen but urgent business arise, which requires me to leave town as soon as possible. If it is feasible, I ask that you meet me today at your earliest convenience. Please respond to inform me whether or not the change is acceptable to you. If it is not, no matter. I will send word when I have returned in a week's time. Please forgive me for the inconvenience.

Your servant,

O

Ruth's eyes grew large as she read the note. *At your earliest convenience?* Or *in a week's time?* She sprang to action, tipping over the chair in her rush to knock on Topher's door.

"Topher!" she hissed, knocking insistently. "Christopher!"

There was no response from within and, cursing her brother's deep sleep, she lifted the latch and pushed the door open, stopping short in the doorway.

Topher's bed lay empty, unslept in, his portmanteau still sitting open on the bedcovers, just as it had been when he had left the afternoon before.

Ruth put a hand to her chest, trying to contain the deafening pounding of her heart. She stepped back and out of the doorway to escape the feeling of the walls closing in around her. It wouldn't be the first time Topher had failed to return after a night of gallivanting, but he had been much more reliable since they had left Dunburn. Had London made him forget how different life was for them now? Besides, where could he possibly have slept?

She put her hands on her head and shut her eyes. Why, of all days, had he chosen this one to revert to irresponsibility? Or was he perhaps in trouble?

She lowered her hands slowly, forcing herself to breathe calmly. Undoubtedly, he had merely had too much to drink and had taken refuge in one of those haunts Ruth had only heard about in the form of cryptic remarks from the men in her life. She shuddered slightly.

The more she thought about it, the more she felt certain that Topher would return soon—likely with a splitting headache. She would box his ears when he did, and then she would go over the lesson with him on the carriage ride to Mr. O's and pray that his performance met expectation. He had assured her when he left that he would return in no time at all.

She sat down, her chest still rising and falling more rapidly than usual, and composed a short but civil response, conveying the Swan's intention to call upon the gentleman that day once he was apprised of the address at which he should present himself. She bit nervously at a nail as Lucy took the sealed letter to give to the waiting messenger.

What if Topher *didn't* return in time? Mr. O had mentioned that the meeting could be postponed, but that would be impossible. They hadn't enough money to continue paying for rooms at the inn for another week, nor to go home and return in a few days' time.

Ruth paced the length of the two rooms, back and forth, back and forth.

She should never have agreed to allow Topher to go out the evening before. She had felt it intuitively but had chosen to relent to his cajoling. It had been an idiotic idea of his—only marginally less idiotic than his suggestion that she join him in whatever foolhardy mischief he decided to get up to. As if she could have masqueraded as a man.

She stilled before the bed in his room, a frightening idea presenting itself to her as she stared at the open portmanteau, clothes folded neatly inside.

It was utterly mad. An idea fit only for Bedlam. Besides, Topher's clothing likely wouldn't even fit her. She was taller and thinner than him.

With a shaking hand, she reached for the shirt folded on top of the clothing pile. Topher had worn all of his finest clothing on his outing the night before, but what remained was still in excellent condition. He was particular about his clothing to a fault. She had teased him a time or two about becoming a valet. But Topher didn't want to be a valet. He wanted to *employ* a valet.

Deciding it couldn't hurt to simply try, she pulled the shirt over her head and turned toward the mirror on the wall. Her shoulders weren't quite as broad as her twin's, but the shirt fit surprisingly well, even atop her muslin dress. She stared at herself in the mirror, unsure what to think of what she saw there. The shirtsleeves hung strangely from her arms, accustomed as she was to close-fitting gowns and gloves. She *did* look quite a bit like a man, though—that is, if she didn't regard the skirt of her dress showing below the hem of Topher's shirt.

The realization was equal parts lowering and encouraging.

She hurriedly pulled the shirt back over her head. She *couldn't*. Of all the ungenteel things to do, masquerading as a gentleman was surely at the top of the list. It was ludicrous and offensive and brazen.

And yet...what other option did she have? The meeting was the difference between hunger and security.

She rushed over to the bell and tugged on it. Time was running out, and Mr. O expected the Swan's arrival as soon as possible. Anytime, she might have his response with his address, and she hadn't the slightest idea where Topher was.

Curse Topher!

She stopped in front of the mirror, forcing her mind to focus. She had three options.

Option one—send word to Mr. O canceling the meeting altogether—demonstrating an inexcusable variability of character that would undoubtedly ruin any chance of his future business.

Option two—wait for Topher to arrive, hoping that he would do so before it was too late to call upon Mr. O, while also courting the risk of missing the meeting altogether if he *didn't* return in time.

Option three—dress in Topher's clothing for a simple, hour-long meeting from which she would emerge with twenty pounds.

The answer seemed fairly clear, but it terrified her. She couldn't return to Marsbrooke empty-handed, worse off than when they had left. She hadn't cut her hair off for nothing, after all. Besides, unlike Topher, she needed no studying to conduct such a meeting—at least not any studying for the part of the Swan.

In her impatience, she had already donned a pair of stockings and pantaloons when the door opened. She whipped around, knowing in her mind that it would be Lucy, but unable to stifle the hope that it was Topher.

"Oh," Lucy said in a mortified voice, lowering her head. "Pardon me, sir, I mistook the room."

She began to bow herself out, but Ruth called out to her. "Lucy! It's me."

The door opened slowly, and Lucy's head reappeared, eyes

widening as she looked upon Ruth. "Good gracious heavens," she said, hurriedly closing the door. "What in heaven's name are you doing, miss?"

Ruth lifted one knee at a time, feeling the way the pantaloons hugged her legs as if they were a second skin. She felt naked and exposed, and yet....contained. It was the strangest feeling in the world.

"Isn't it obvious?" Ruth said, trying for a lightness she was far from feeling. "I have transformed into a swan." She gave a tremulous smile.

Lucy stood with her mouth agape, eyes running along Ruth, from short hair to stockinged feet.

Ruth shed her pretended nonchalance. "Did you really believe me to be a gentleman when you first walked in?" She wasn't even sure what answer she should hope for.

Lucy closed her mouth. "Yes, miss. But I only looked at you for a moment, and now, of course, I recognize you."

Ruth bit her lip, reaching for the Hessians Topher had left in favor of his other boots. "But if you didn't already know me, should you suspect me to be a woman dressed in a man's attire?"

Lucy looked at her with narrowed eyes. "I don't think so, miss. It would be a strange thing to assume, though, wouldn't it?"

Ruth nodded. It was true. And she was counting on it. Who would be foolish enough to dress as a man? The sheer audacity and unlikelihood of it would protect her from discovery—and ruin her if she *were* discovered. "We must hurry. I need you to help me with these boots. I think they shall be a bit large on me, but better large than small, I suppose."

Lucy insisted upon wrapping Ruth's chest tightly in the fabric of an extra cravat to flatten her bosom, tucking the end underneath when she had finished. Between the two of them, they managed to tie a simple but decent cravat—nothing Topher would approve of, of course—and brush Ruth's hair forward in a style that added to her masculinity. She watched as her feminine attributes dwindled and nearly disappeared.

Ruth worried her lip. "What about my voice?"

Lucy tilted her head from side to side. "It would be nice if it were a bit lower."

"More like this?" Ruth had to duck her chin slightly to change the pitch of her voice.

Lucy cringed and shook her head. "Too obvious."

"Yes, I think you are right. It would be hard to maintain for an hour, too. What about this?" She made only the slightest adjustment to her voice, intentionally speaking in the lower tones she normally used, leaving out the high ones. It felt strange not to make use of the full spectrum of her voice, but she could do it for as long as it was required of her.

"Much better," Lucy said. Her mouth twisted to the side as she looked Ruth over, clucking her tongue. "But those eyelashes, miss."

Ruth couldn't help laughing. "Shall I just burn them off with a candle? I am starting over with my hair. I suppose I may as well start fresh with my eyelashes, as well." She leaned toward the mirror, grimacing at the long, dark lashes that framed her eyes. They *were* rather feminine, but, for all her joking, she wasn't brave enough to burn them off. She had known plenty of men with long, dark lashes, but she wished they could be hidden all the same.

She shot up, her gaze darting to the bedside table where Topher's glasses sat. She hurried over and picked them up, pulling the rims out and setting them upon her nose. She blinked and her lashes brushed against the lenses. The room had gone fuzzy, the objects before her suddenly undefined. It was disconcerting, to say the least, and she found her eyes blinking in a failing effort to refocus her vision. "Good gracious. And these *help* Topher to see?"

"To read, miss. Are they awful to look through? They *do* hide your lashes just a bit, and they certainly add to the disguise. But if you are tripping all over everything, it won't do."

"No, no. I can see." She tipped them up to unobscure her eyes and then set them back in place. "It is just...hazy. I can't see any detail at all, but it will do well enough for a short meeting." She had to imagine the full effect of the glasses on her appearance, but she could see enough to know that it solidified her disguise, and Lucy confirmed it.

Ruth would never be considered a Corinthian, of course, with her lean build, but she no longer looked like a woman either—just a youthful man.

An inn servant brought a letter to the room, and Ruth had Lucy retrieve it, too terrified to face anyone yet in her disguise. As Ruth read the address given by Mr. O, the last hopes she had for Topher's return fluttered away. She was on her own.

"You look like Master John, miss," said Lucy, handing her Topher's top hat.

That she looked like a ten-year-old boy was hardly encouraging, but the thought of her younger siblings gave Ruth a dose of much-needed courage, and she set Topher's top hat atop her head. The final touch made her feel different enough that she had to think she looked even more convincingly so.

But she didn't have to convince herself. She had to convince Mr. O.

Chapter Eight

The simultaneous thrill and trepidation of being utterly alone made Ruth's hands shake and her skin tingle. She looked through the window of the hackney carriage, wishing she could properly see the sights passing by, but too terrified to remove her glasses.

After living in Marsbrooke for a year, London felt enormous. Topher could be anywhere. She said a quick prayer that he was safe, wherever he was in that large town.

She slid her gloved hands across her pantaloons nervously, wondering whether she would be used to their tight fit by the end of her meeting with Mr. O. She had to continuously remind herself that, despite feeling as though she was walking around entirely indecent, she wore the usual clothing of a gentleman.

She had been certain that the jarvey would see through her the moment she approached the hackney stand, shouting her secret out to everyone in the street. But he had not. In fact, he had treated her with respect and deference and not shown any inclination to look at her with anything but passing interest—at least not that she could tell through the blur of her glasses. No one would have reason to question her if she could only persuade herself to act normally.

She didn't know London well enough to understand what Mr. O's address conveyed, and the thought only heightened her nerves. Brook Street sounded harmless enough, but Ruth was painfully aware that she was very much a fish out of water, with little idea of what social sphere her client orbited other than what she had gleaned from the ornate seal on his letters and his manner of writing. Perhaps they had been too ready to trust this man.

By the time the hackney reached Brook Street, though, it was apparent to Ruth that Mr. O's lodgings were located in a fashionable part of Town. The warm brick building façades and the carved white stonework around the windows—all blurry through her lenses—left little doubt of it.

The hackney finally came to a stop, and Ruth took a moment to breathe deeply and utter a prayerful plea for help, only to realize that perhaps God was not terribly eager to assist her in impersonating a man. She could only hope he would forgive her deceit in the name of saving her family.

The jarvey opened the door, and Ruth waited for him to extend a hand of assistance. He was not looking at her, though, and it was with a jolt that she realized he would not be assisting her down. She hurried to step down on her own and handed him one of the precious few coins remaining to her before making her way up the three steps to the address Mr. O had given in his short response.

She waited a moment before pulling the bell, hoping to slow her heart rate from a gallop to something more like a canter. But its speed only increased with every passing second.

Twenty pounds. For George. For Joanna.

She tugged on the bell. There was no turning back now. Not unless the butler recognized her deception immediately and sent her on her way, that was.

But, while the man who opened the door looked her over with the practiced rapidity of a seasoned butler, he was kind enough in his question: "How may I help you, sir?"

Sir. That final word was like a draught of liquid courage to Ruth's fraying nerves. "I believe your master is expecting my call." She sent a glance around to ensure no one else was within earshot, but there was only one other solitary equipage in the street. "He knows me as the Swan."

"Very good, sir," the butler said, opening the door wider to allow Ruth in. He offered to take her hat and gloves, which she gently refused. She wasn't yet confident enough to remove the hat. He looked at her strangely but said nothing.

The interior of the house was grand indeed—something not even her glasses could obscure. It was far more spacious than the front had given her to believe. The butler led her through the entry hall and down a corridor while Ruth tried not to marvel at her surroundings. She needed to give the impression that this was nothing out of the ordinary, that she was accustomed to assisting wealthy clients.

"Just in here, sir," the butler said, taking the doorknob in hand. "He awaits you in the library. Allow me one moment to inform him of your arrival."

Ruth inclined her head, and, when the butler turned away again, allowed her eyes to bulge. Mr. O must be quite well-to-do—perhaps she should have assumed that from the fact that he was offering twenty pounds for one paltry meeting.

The butler cleared his throat. "The Swan here to see you, sir."

"Very good, Draper. Send him in, then." The voice was deep and firm—and young—and it sent a rush of relief through Ruth, who had known a moment of misgiving, wondering if she would be obliged to instruct a septuagenarian on how to woo his third wife.

The butler moved from the doorway. "He is ready to see you, sir."

Ruth swallowed and smiled, resisting the urge to tug on her cravat. How in the world did men survive with veritable nooses tied about their necks day in and out? The realization that she might well *end* in the noose did nothing to allay her nerves.

It would be a miracle if she survived the next hour.

Philip looked up at the young man who stood in the doorway and frowned. "You can send in your master. Thank you." He glanced back down and straightened the pile of letters in front of him.

"My master?" The voice made the man sound even younger than he looked. Eighteen perhaps? And one of those unfortunate souls who had to wait an eternity for their voices to lower.

Philip sighed impatiently, rising from his seat. He would already have to delay his journey home until the morning, when he had been hoping to go a few stages before nightfall. "I was under the impression that I would be meeting with the Swan himself. Does he generally delegate such meetings to his assistants?"

The young man cleared his throat, color slightly heightened. "I apologize for the misunderstanding, sir. *I* am the Swan."

Philip stared, and silence filled the room until an incredulous chuckle broke through his lips. "*You* are the Swan?" This little fellow? The one with glasses and an ill-fitting coat? The one who looked like he might belong as a footman in Philip's house?

The first flash of annoyance crossed the young man's face. "I apprehend that this is a humorous revelation to you, sir."

Philip laughed softly again. "I confess it is." It occurred to him that he had been had. This was a prank. Of course! "Finmore put you up to this, didn't he?"

"I haven't any idea who Finmore is, sir," the Swan said. "I am here to offer the services you requested. You *did* wish to see me for an hour, did you not?"

Philip's smile faded, and he hesitated. The young man was in earnest. He considered lying and sending him on his way. But he hated to lie. "Yes, I did. I merely hadn't expected..."

The young man's eyebrows rose, a challenge apparent in his eyes, even through the thick lenses that covered them.

Philip knew a brief moment of hesitation at the show of unexpected confidence. The young man held himself well, at least. Well, then. If he wanted the truth, Philip would give it to him.

"I hadn't expected a child," Philip finished. He couldn't possibly accept love advice from this babe in arms. It was humiliating enough to ask for help in the first place. But from this bespectacled lad?

The young man stood still for a moment then bowed. "Very good, sir. I bid you good day."

"Wait," Philip said, a strange and annoying curiosity getting the best of him.

The Swan paused with his hand on the door knob.

"Just how old *are* you?"

He didn't turn. "Twenty, sir. Not that it is any of your business."

Philip's brows went up. He didn't know whether to applaud the boy's spirit or take offense. He certainly wasn't used to people standing up to him. Besides Finmore, of course. But how in the world could one offer love advice at the age of twenty?

"Forgive me. It is just that I can't imagine what you might have to offer on this...topic. You have barely had time to see any of the world, much less become an expert in the domain of love. Have you even kissed a woman? Other than your mother, I mean." It was a low blow. And he regretted it almost instantly. But his own pride was a bit wounded, not to mention the disappointing destruction of the hopes this meeting had raised in his breast.

The Swan turned his head, a mocking smile on his lips. "You mock me, sir. But you would do well to remember that it is *you,* not I, who offered to pay a man twenty pounds for love advice. So, you tell me which one of us is the more pathetic figure."

Philip's jaw hung open, and the Swan disappeared through the door.

Philip's shock lasted but a moment, and he hurried around the desk and after the young man. Why, he hardly knew. Something inside him told him that there was more to the fellow than met the eye. He had stood up to Philip, and that counted for something, surely, in a world full of toadeaters. He could at least give the Swan a chance to prove himself—or to prove Philip right, more likely. Philip couldn't deny the curiosity he felt at what type of advice the twenty-year-old could possibly have.

"Wait!" Philip said, going after the retreating figure—so thin and youthful—of the Swan. He was certainly not the Corinthian Philip had been expecting.

The Swan didn't wait, but Philip hurried up beside him and took his arm. "Please, wait."

The Swan turned, looking at him through those ridiculous glasses perched atop a nose with flaring nostrils. His gaze flicked to Philip's hand grasping his arm, and Philip released it.

"I am sorry," Philip said. "I was rude."

"Insufferable," said the Swan. His eyes and his jaw—entirely free of any hair—were hard.

Philip chuckled, his pride somehow softening at the unapologetic response. "Insufferable *and* rude." He grimaced. "It is a bit humiliating asking for help, and I've never been particularly good at swallowing my pride. But I would ask for another chance from you, if you will give it to me." He put out a hand in a gesture of goodwill.

The Swan stared at him, then down at his hand, then up at Philip again. And all the while, Philip waited, feeling like a fool as his hand hovered in the air. He deserved this, no doubt, but he didn't know whether the man's hesitation was revenge or simply uncertainty about continuing the business relationship.

Finally, he reached out and grasped Philip's hand.

Philip smiled, feeling relieved. "I shall add a couple of shillings to your payment to cover my rudeness."

"And insufferableness." There wasn't a trace of humor on the young man's face, aside from a slight twinkle in his eye. But it might have been the light from the library windows reflecting on his glasses.

Philip nodded with a chuckle, leading the way back toward the library. "That too."

"I believe the accepted rate is a half sovereign."

No, Philip hadn't imagined the twinkle. There was even a half-smile to accompany it now. He indicated the chair at the desk in an invitation for the Swan to take a seat. "Ah. The price has risen since I last checked. I had better be more judicious in my insufferableness."

"Perhaps we can agree upon a discounted rate for the extra fees you will undoubtedly accumulate over the next hour. I wouldn't want the cost of this meeting to be prohibitive."

Philip grinned widely. By Jove, he was already glad he'd gone after the fellow.

Chapter Nine

Ruth couldn't see the man across the desk from her. Not properly, anyway. She could see a dark head of hair, a set of full eyebrows to match, and a ready smile—or more ready now than it had been upon her arrival, at least.

And she could sympathize with the change, for she felt similarly about him. His reaction upon discovering that she was the Swan had boiled her blood. She had come to the swift conclusion that some things were simply not worth twenty pounds, including the insufferable blob of a man before her. All the pent-up emotion of cutting her hair, leaving her family, creating a lesson she felt confident Topher could deliver, and then risking everything by dressing in her brother's clothes—it had all spilled over in the form of a terrible insult to Mr. O.

A terrible insult that she hadn't regretted in the least—until he had come after her and apologized. But the instant the man had shown a bit of humility, she had begrudgingly begun to like him.

Mr. O leaned back in his seat. "Thank you for coming, and on such short notice. I am not in the habit of asking such things, but I am obliged to return to my estate in Devon for a matter of business that requires my own personal attendance. I hope you can forgive the highhanded gesture,"—he paused—"What *is* your name?"

"Miss Ruth—" She froze, stopping herself. Confound habit! How had she overlooked the issue of her name? She had been far too consumed with her appearance and her anger and her worry over Topher to consider such a detail. She hadn't anticipated giving her name at all, in truth. But Mr. O was waiting politely for her to continue, not seeming to have noticed her slip. She hoped that Miss Ruth had sounded like a mumbling Mister Ruth, at least.

She scrambled to undo her error, reaching for the familiar.

"Mister Henry Ruth, sir." Her conscience squirmed at the untruth, and she wondered if God would abandon her entirely, so lost to sense of right as her actions showed her to be.

She calmed herself with the assurance that it was only for an hour, and it was as much truth as it was lie. Anxious to move to another topic, she continued. "Tell me, then, sir—"

"Oxley. Call me Oxley."

Ruth inclined her head. "Tell me, Oxley. What help do you wish for from me? We have but an hour, and I would like to ensure we use that time in the manner most helpful to you."

Oxley sighed, looking down at his clasped hands with a frown. "I am not entirely certain what help I need, to be quite frank. All I know is that Miss Devenish seems to regard me just as she regards all of her other suitors."

"Miss Devenish," Ruth repeated, wondering what the woman was like. "And how does she regard all of her other suitors?"

"With polite disinterest, I suppose."

All the subtleties of human expression were dulled through Ruth's foggy lenses. It took every ounce of her concentration to note the wry lift to the corner of Oxley's mouth. "And what reason have you given her to regard you otherwise?" She tried to keep her voice on the lower end of what felt natural to her.

Oxley blinked—she was fairly certain, at least—and Ruth raised her brows.

"What do you mean?" he asked slowly.

Ruth shrugged. "If she has multiple suitors, why *should* she choose you, of all of them?"

He let out a soft laugh, a pleasant sound, deep in his chest. Ruth hadn't known that a laugh could *sound* attractive, but there it was.

"What?" she said. "Why do you laugh?"

He folded his arms in front of his wide chest. "You have trapped me. If I say the truth, you shall think me more insufferable than ever."

"I'm afraid it is too late for that," Ruth said with a smile. "Might as well tell me the truth. I shan't be able to help you much without it. Why *do* you think—Miss Devenish, was it? Why should she choose you?"

There was a pause. "Very well. Frankly, then? Because of the triad."

"The triad?"

He reached out and brushed off the edge of the desk. "That is what Finmore calls it. Title, wealth, and—if I am to believe others—a pleasing appearance."

Ruth had to stifle an overpowering desire to tip her glasses down and inspect the man in front of her to verify the last part of his claim. What sort of title did he hold, anyway? Had he mentioned it in their communications and she had overlooked it? She took a moment before responding. "Well, I was wrong."

"Wrong?"

"You *do* seem more insufferable than ever."

He laughed. "No doubt you feel you have deduced already why Miss Devenish seems not to prefer my suit. By the time the hour is over, your bill of service will have risen so steeply that perhaps I shall be reduced to a"—he paused—"a dyad?"

Ruth looked at him significantly. "And that might be for the best, for then you wouldn't be able to rely upon such factors in your pursuit of Miss Devenish. In fact, let us leave *all of it* for now. Imagine for a moment that you had no title, no wealth, and no"—she fumbled for a moment—"no beauty that woman should desire you. Why *else* should she choose you?"

Oxley's mouth twisted to the side, and silence ensued.

Ruth took in a large breath. "I see. Allow me to ask a different question. Why have you chosen *her*?"

He cleared his throat but said nothing, and Ruth raised a brow. "Is she also possessed of the triad?"

His head tipped from side to side. "Not exactly, but close enough."

Ruth blinked at him. "Am I correct in understanding, then, that this is *not* a love match you seek?"

"No," he said.

"No," she repeated, her heart beginning to drum nervously in her chest.

There was a pause. "Surely love needn't be a factor in every marriage," Oxley said.

"Certainly not, but I admit that I am at a loss to understand why you would engage *my* services if that is not your motivation or goal." Why, oh why, had she not asked more questions of him through correspondence? To understand the situation better before lopping off her hair and making this foolhardy journey to London?

How was she to instruct a man in love when love was not his object?

Philip hesitated for a moment at Ruth's words. He hadn't anticipated that the Swan would take issue with the situation. Perhaps twenty pounds hadn't been generous enough. "I suppose I thought that, if anyone could help me, it would be you. Is that not what you do? Help men win women over?"

Ruth let out a gush of air through his nose. "Yes, but only when love is a factor in the equation. Generally, the people who seek my help are in love with a woman and merely need my assistance in fostering reciprocal sentiment. In your situation, there seems to be love on neither side. If you seek a marriage of convenience, your time is better spent addressing yourself to Miss Devenish's father, is it not?" He smiled slightly. "I cannot imagine it would be too difficult to have his approval, given the triad."

Philip shook his head. "Her father is too fond of her to force her into a match. He will let her choose for herself once she puts off mourning."

Ruth frowned. "She is in mourning?"

"Yes, for her brother. For over a year now."

"A year?" Ruth said incredulously. He waved the news aside. "Never mind that. The fact is, my methods are meant to encourage love. They are not really fit for anything else."

Misgiving filled Philip. "Are you not willing even to try? Surely what I am asking of you is *less* complicated or difficult than what you are accustomed to."

Ruth opened his mouth only to then shut it. He looked at Philip consideringly. "Do you know why I chose a swan to represent me, sir?"

Philip shook his head. He hadn't really considered the matter, but it *was* a curious choice.

Ruth adjusted his glasses, pushing them up higher on his nose. "Not many animals choose a mate for life, you know. But many swans do. They are romantic creatures—they even go through a grieving process if their mate dies, and many will remain single for the rest of their lives if that happens." A little hint of a smile drew up the corner of his mouth, and his eyes became slightly unfocused. "My father loved them. He used to take us to Prior Park in Bath, where the same two swans were nearly always on the lake. We would sit on the grass and watch them float around together. My father was fascinated by the bond between them, by what drew them together. He held the same fascination with what draws two humans together." Ruth's gaze moved to Philip. "I chose a swan because I want to help draw people together. I want to foster the type of love that grieves loss like a swan grieves it."

Philip was silent, staring at the strange young man before him, who spoke with the wisdom of someone much older than his twenty years. He couldn't help feeling drawn to the picture Ruth painted—a love match. But everything Philip knew about love contradicted the image of two gentle swans, gliding along the placid waters of a pond together.

Love was unpredictable. It was unreliable. And—perhaps most importantly—it took second place to duty.

He frowned. "This love you speak of—it is not something with which I have personal experience, and I cannot think it wise to spend time waiting for it—to leave everything up to chance. What if, when it *did* strike me, it was sentiment for someone entirely unsuitable? I owe my family a duty." He shook his head. "Call it what you will, Miss Devenish is the one woman I feel confident I could marry. I hold her in high regard, certainly. I would not wish to marry her if that were not true. And, in some ways, that seems a more sure foundation upon which to build a marriage than something as volatile as love. In any case, I cannot pretend to something that I do not feel."

"Volatile," Ruth said softly, as if to himself. He met Philip's gaze. "Do you even *wish* to fall in love?"

Philip stilled. *Did* he wish to fall in love? Sometimes he thought he did—to be loved thoroughly, to be desired and appreciated. To feel all those things for someone else.

But to *fall* in love. The phrase itself sounded unpleasant. Someone like Ruth would undoubtedly have him believe that what awaited him at the bottom of such a fall was soft and desirable—like a plush feather bed.

Reality was less rosy, though. Falling wasn't enjoyable. Philip spent a great deal of his energy avoiding falls and mistakes—and the inevitable pain that resulted from them.

But what if love was the only thing that could win over Miss Devenish?

"You think you could *make* me fall in love?" The thought made his heart trip and stutter in a tangle of fear and hope.

Ruth studied him for a moment. "I can guarantee nothing, and I certainly can't force you into anything you are set against. But I believe love to be the natural result of certain circumstances, and my purpose is to promote such circumstances. If you hold Miss Devenish in high regard, as you say, I think it likely that your regard might turn to something even more rich and fulfilling."

Philip rubbed the top of his signet ring pensively.

Ruth was watching him curiously, eyes enlarged by the thick lenses of his spectacles. "As I mentioned, I have no experience with marriages of convenience. With such an aim as that, I cannot help you. But if you are open to changing the way you approach Miss Devenish, to developing real and lasting attachment to one another, I could instruct you on how to go about it."

Real and lasting attachment. Attachment had its risks, but it sounded much less threatening, much more controlled than *falling in love*.

He set his jaw. The fact was he wasn't going to marry Miss Devenish without some assistance—not with the utterly ridiculous things he was saying and doing in her presence when left to his own devices.

"Very well," he said, setting his hands on the desk. "What must I do?"

A look of relief and appreciation crossed Ruth's face. "Very good. First, then, I must know what you admire about Miss Devenish. Forget the triad or whatever she happens to possess that makes her a good candidate for a marriage of convenience. I imagine there are a number of women who might fulfill such requirements. So, tell me: why Miss Devenish?"

Philip tilted his head to the side, frowning slightly. "Her kindness, I suppose."

Ruth clasped his hands together, smiling. "Her kindness. That is promising. *That* is what I would like for you to focus on. Not the triad." He shot Philip a look full of meaning. "She stood out to you, and now we must make you stand out to her."

Chapter Ten

"You spat lemon tart on her?" Ruth covered her amusement with a hand. For some reason, she felt particularly feminine when she laughed. But Oxley didn't seem to notice.

"I did." Oxley narrowed his eyes, but she thought she saw the hint of a smile through her glasses. "What, do you think Miss Devenish disliked it? I thought you might congratulate me for setting myself apart from all of her other suitors."

"Well, it is not the recommendation *I* would have given, I admit...."

He smiled. "You are beginning to regret accepting a mere twenty pounds now, aren't you? Little did you know how I would challenge you."

She laughed. Oxley's sense of humor—his ability to laugh at himself—was, quite frankly, charming. He was not the haughty man she had met upon her arrival. If only Miss Devenish could see this side of him, surely Ruth's work would be easy.

"The truth is," Oxley said, "I transform into a blubbering, clumsy fool near Miss Devenish—around any woman I desire to impress, really."

Ruth was unable to stifle a smile. "I admit, I should dearly wish to witness this for myself. I find it hard to imagine." She didn't *really* know what the man looked like, but his voice alone boomed with confidence. It was not the voice of a man with two left feet.

He gave a wry chuckle. "I like to meet expectations. I am generally quite good at it. But I haven't any idea what women expect from me, and apparently in such a situation, I am overtaken by an irrepressible impulse to underwhelm. It is why I have generally avoided such situations in the past."

"Unless lemon tart is involved," Ruth said.

He smiled. "Best to set the standard low, is it not?"

She tapped her mouth with a finger. "You might be onto something with that. Now it will be all the easier to ensure that you leap over that standard with ease." She cocked a brow at him. "I hereby forbid you from eating lemon tart in Miss Devenish's company."

Oxley's mouth stretched wide in a smile. "Fair enough. I don't particularly like lemon tart, truth be told."

Ruth itched to take her glasses off for a clear view of him. She hadn't anticipated how maddening it would be to have such a vague idea of what he looked like. It was strange to know someone's voice before their face—to get a glimpse of a personality before ever meeting eyes. Perhaps he was not as attractive as he sounded, though he *had* mentioned his appearance as part of the infamous triad.

"What do I do, then, Master Swan? How do I leap over the low standard I have set? I can see no rhyme or reason to any of it. What pleases one woman displeases another."

"Certainly there is both rhyme *and* reason to it."

One of his thick, dark brows went up. "By all means, enlighten me."

She stared at him thoughtfully, resisting the impulse she felt to rub at her eyes to better see him. It was like awaking bleary-eyed from sleep, with eyes that never adjusted to the world. Her head was beginning to ache from the effort to make sense of the indistinct shapes which surrounded her. She missed her vision terribly, and it was hard to breathe in the tight wrap around her chest.

"I should clarify," she said. "You are right to an extent. Love is more than logic. That doesn't mean that logic and reason play no part in it but rather that they fail to account for *every* part of it. But, if I were to show you the closest, most simple representation of what I have come to believe about love..." She glanced at the stack of paper near Oxley. "May I?"

"By all means." He handed her a piece of foolscap and slid the ink well toward her.

It wasn't until she had the paper and quill in hand that she realized how difficult it would be to write when she could barely see. She cleared her throat and nudged her glasses farther down her nose, tipping her head so that she could see the paper over the top of the silver rims.

The clear lines before her—the texture of the paper, the sheen of the wet ink at the edge of the quill she held—were like a breath of fresh air to her exhausted eyes.

She wrote the word *love* on one side of the paper, followed by an equal sign. "While love looks a bit different—sometimes significantly so—from one couple to another, there are certain elements that I believe must be present in order for it to flourish. Much like a plant needs proper soil, sunlight, and water. Remove any one of those, and it will shrivel rather than grow."

On the other side of the equation, she wrote *time + sacrifice x connection.*

Oxley was watching her quill scratches carefully, but he rose from his chair and came around the desk to stand beside her, putting his hand on the back of her chair.

"Hm," he said. "It is nice to see it laid out so rationally, but the ideas within the equation are still nebulous to me, I admit. *Connection,* especially."

Ruth nodded. "Thankfully, I have an equation for *that*, too."

"An equation within an equation. We soon reach the limits of my mathematical capabilities."

She chuckled and wrote *love=time + sacrifice x (honesty + listening + humor + vulnerability).* "As I said, this is greatly simplified, and certainly there is an element in the romantic love described in poetry that no amount of skill in logic or math can generate. But without this equation, I don't believe that romantic love can survive long." She tapped the quill on the paper gently. "This is the type of love that endures."

"That is quite the equation," he said. "You have clearly given this much thought. But what do you mean by *vulnerability*?"

She sent him a sympathetic grimace. "It means exactly what you think it means: being willing to be hurt."

She thought she saw his throat bob. Of course, no one liked to be hurt, but she couldn't help wishing she had a bit more time to discover what it was that caused Oxley to stand there silently, staring at the word like it might jump off the page and bite him. What caused such a sturdy man to fear something most people sought after so doggedly?

"Like many things in life, love cannot be won or given without risk. It cannot be taken forcefully." She thought for a moment. "You mentioned that you transform in the presence of Miss Devenish and forget how to conduct yourself. At the risk of causing offense, may I suggest that it is perhaps because you are too focused on yourself."

He laughed, but she pressed on. "Perhaps you are too concerned about what Miss Devenish is thinking about you, when you *should* be concerned with how she is feeling, what sort of a day she has had, what amuses her—things like that. If you are too preoccupied with your own image, you have no time to forge real connection."

He was quiet, still hovering over her shoulder, and she hoped that it was a good sign—that she had made him think. She felt the hairs on her neck stand on end as he leaned down further to run a finger along the equation. He smelled faintly of amber. She swallowed and forced herself to focus, embarrassed by the way his proximity was affecting her—this man whose face she hadn't even seen.

She glanced over her glasses at the clock on the shelf opposite them, behind the desk. Their hour was almost up. How in the world was that possible? She doubted she had even helped him at all. She had certainly not earned twenty pounds.

Oxley followed her gaze and grimaced.

"I can stay a few extra minutes," she reassured him. And she found she didn't mind the prospect.

"You are certain? I just have two or three more questions, I think. This equation is very helpful." His gaze returned to it, and she took the opportunity to glance up at him over the rim of her glasses.

She stilled. Clear as day—blessedly clear—she could see the truth of one part of the triad: Oxley *did* have a pleasing appearance. His forehead was furrowed in concentration just now, and she could see the line of his jaw, the way it ran rigid and straight before suddenly angling upward toward a head of rich brown hair. She could see his lashes, the rim of dark brown around his iris, and his full brows—no wonder she had been able to see them even through the spectacles.

"The listening piece of this—can you expound upon that?"

She pushed her glasses back up the bridge of her nose, reluctantly ending the clarity of her vision and its object, and smiled. "Never listened to a woman, have you?"

He gave a soft snort.

"I am only teasing," she said. "Listening might be seen as the counterpart to vulnerability, I suppose. If you wish to continue with our theme of mathematics, I would advise that listening consume around eighty percent of your time with Miss Devenish and talking a mere twenty percent." She scribbled the number eighty above *listening*. "You ask questions—her likes, dislikes, preferences—and you listen *carefully*"—she shot him a significant look—"to her answers. As acquaintance turns to friendship and friendship to love, the percentage will even out a bit. But it should never, ever reverse. As you progress, you begin to shift what you ask and share toward things of a more personal nature. If you insist upon diving in too early, or, conversely, if your conversation never penetrates the surface, you risk putting a woman off entirely."

He stood up straight, taking in a deep breath and putting a thoughtful fist against his mouth. She itched to remove her glasses and regain the crisp view she'd had.

He said nothing, brows still wrinkled in a deep frown.

"I no doubt sound like a madman," Ruth said. "I am used to having time to compose my words for the advice column. I am afraid I am not so practiced in explaining it verbally."

He shook his head. "No, it isn't that. In fact, it makes perfect sense. I have never seen anything regarding love portrayed so rationally or so clearly. It is just...I am beginning to realize how very far I have to go; how very much I have to learn." He directed his gaze at her but said nothing for a moment. "What if I hired you? To continue your services, I mean."

She stared, throat constricting, heart accelerating. She opened her mouth to demur, but Oxley continued.

"I would pay you more, of course. A handsome sum if you engaged to help me—to explain things in more detail"—he nodded to indicate her equations—"and to be here for my continuing questions. I could put into practice what you teach me, and you could correct me—teach me how to be less insufferable."

She could only imagine how the blurry half-smile he wore might look without her spectacles on. Perhaps it was for the best that she couldn't see it clearly. "But..." How could she phrase her refusal? For there was no doubt in her mind that she *should* refuse. The alternative didn't bear considering.

"I am leaving tomorrow," he said. "But I shall return Saturday, and we might resume then. You could stay for a couple of weeks—two or three. I think you'll agree that I need every moment possible if I am to avoid making an utter fool of myself."

"*That* I cannot deny," she said with a smile. How could she agree to more of this, though? Her head was aching doubly, both from the way the glasses gripped her head and from the way her eyes struggled to make sense of the world around her.

He had said he would pay a handsome sum. What exactly *did* he consider a handsome sum? Surely it couldn't be enough to justify the expense of two rooms at The Three Crowns for another three weeks.

She sighed and shook her head. "I am afraid I cannot agree to it."

"Two hundred pounds."

Ruth sucked in a breath of surprise, and her cheeks grew warm. Two hundred pounds?

He watched her, and she was certain he saw her resolution waver.

How could it not? She had come to London for twenty pounds. Would she leave two hundred on the table? She took in a fortifying breath. "I could never accept such a sum, particularly not when my advice holds no guarantees. You might well be paying me for nothing."

"Of course I understand that. Even if your advice was perfect, my execution of it might be lacking—in fact, it is bound to be. But your time and wisdom is valuable to me, all the same. Shall we say two hundred for your time and three hundred if I find success?" He smiled. "A little incentive for you not to hold anything back."

She swallowed, staring at him as refusals and acceptances warred on her tongue. She couldn't accept such an offer. But how could she refuse it?

"I wouldn't consign you to staying at The Three Crowns, either," Oxley said. "I know the place, and it isn't fit for more than a night or two. You could easily stay here."

Oh, heavens. That was the last thing they needed—for Ruth to stay at a bachelor's establishment.

It was outrageous. And so very needed. She thought of Joanna and her pleas for a doll like Sophia's. With two hundred pounds, they could easily afford a little doll, to say nothing of the more important things they had been going without recently. "That is generous, indeed, sir. But I cannot stay *here*."

"Why not? There is plenty of room, I assure you."

She hesitated then smiled slightly. "You value your privacy, sir. Well, so do I." It would be nigh on impossible to maintain her disguise if she was living under the same roof as Oxley, aside from the unfathomable impropriety of it.

She thought of Topher, and her stomach clenched. Was he safe? None of this would matter if something awful had happened to him. Though, if something awful *hadn't* happened to him and he had forced her into this situation for no good reason, she would be tempted to *do* something awful to him. "I am traveling with my colleague, as well, and we couldn't impose upon you in such a way."

Oxley frowned. "It is not an imposition. I am offering it freely. But if you prefer not to stay here, you might just as easily stay at my uncle's. He lives in Upper Brook Street, just through Grosvenor Square."

Ruth said nothing, wringing her hands in her lap. How was she to explain why it was impossible? Staying with Oxley's uncle was only marginally better than staying with him—not when she would be obliged to keep up such a disguise. It was simply too much.

Oxley was watching her carefully. "He won't be returning to Town for another six weeks, but he always keeps staff on hand. He is the kindest of fellows, and I can assure you he would be happy to have someone in his townhouse while he is away. Particularly if you intended to keep his horses exercised."

There was that half-smile again.

She was stuck. If she refused, she would forgo two—perhaps three—hundred pounds and give offense to Oxley. And for reasons she had no desire to inspect more closely, she was reluctant to offend him.

If she accepted, though, she would be forced to continue in her disguise for heaven only knew how long.

An idea occurred to her. A third option.

"What if it was my colleague—Mr. Franks—who stayed in Town to assist you?" She could teach Topher what he needed to know, couldn't she? In all truth, she wasn't sure. It was one thing for him to manage an hour-long meeting with someone—and clearly, he hadn't even been able to manage *that*. It was another matter entirely for him to spend weeks teaching material that came from Ruth's head and experience.

Oxley shook his head and sat on the edge of the desk beside her, folding his arms. Another hint of amber wafted toward her. "No, Ruth. I am afraid that this offer extends only to *you* and your personal services. I admit that I had grave doubts about your abilities when you first walked into this room—I hadn't thought I would be taking advice from an infant"—he smiled provokingly, or at least that is what Ruth imagined—"but you have managed to make me feel not only comfortable but *hopeful*. I don't wish to start over with someone new, and I certainly don't desire to humiliate myself in front of yet another person. Your colleague is welcome to stay with you at my uncle's, but I want *you*, not him."

Ruth swallowed. He wanted *her*. Or at least who he thought she was. Could she do it? Or, perhaps more to the point, could she *not* do it? How in the world could she return home, knowing she had left such a sum behind?

She needed time. And space, too. It was too difficult to think clearly with Oxley so near and her head pounding.

"Allow me the day to think on it," she said. "I cannot in good conscience accept the offer before conferring with my colleague." Ruth thought Topher was more likely to throttle her neck if she *rejected* the offer without conferring with him.

Oxley nodded once. "Very well. Send me word by this evening. I leave tomorrow, and I shall need to send a message to my uncle and his staff if"—he smiled—"*when* you decide to accept my offer."

Ruth had the feeling that, if she had taken off her glasses right then and seen the full power of Oxley's smile, she would have been powerless to say anything but yes.

Chapter Eleven

By the time Ruth arrived at The Three Crowns, she was a bundle of nerves, and her head felt like to split. She had removed her glasses during the hackney ride, hoping that it would relieve the vise gripping her head. And while this had certainly provided a welcome reprieve from the obscured vision she had been obliged to endure for the past two hours, her head continued to pound.

Her one consolation was the twenty pounds in her coat pocket. Twenty-one, actually. She smiled as she entered the inn. Despite her protestations that she had only been teasing, Oxley had insisted she take the extra sovereign.

She hurried up the inn stairs and into her room, immediately rushing over to the door which adjoined her room to Topher's and flinging it open.

She breathed an enormous sigh of relief at the sight of her twin, squinting as he picked up the note she had written to inform him of her whereabouts in case he returned while she was out.

Her relief was short-lived, though, soon giving way to anger. "*You!*"

Topher turned his head and reared back at the sight of her. "What the devil?"

Ruth took off the top hat she wore and flung it at him. "What the devil indeed!"

He caught the hat and set it on the table. His blinking shock shifted, and he folded his arms across his chest, looking Ruth up and down. His shoulders began to shake.

Her anger flamed, and she fumbled with the knot at her neck. "You may as well get out all of your laughs, for I assure you, I mean to strangle you with this *blasted*"—she slid the last of the fabric from around her neck and flung the cravat at him—"torture device!"

He covered his mouth, but his eyes were watering with laughter. "I am sorry, Ruthie. I really am. I only laugh because you *do* make a half-decent gentleman."

Two hours ago, those words would have allayed her fears; now, they rankled. For all she was glad she had not been discovered in her disguise, she didn't *want* to look like a man.

"Where in the devil have you been?" she flung at him. "You nearly ruined us!"

His eyes had widened at her words, a hint of approval in them.

"What?" she challenged him. "If I must dress like a man, surely I am also permitted to *speak* like one. And you have only yourself to blame."

His shoulders lifted in defense. "I thought the meeting was for tomorrow."

"It was!" She plopped down upon his bed, setting herself to the task of removing her boots. "Did you not read the note? Oxley was obliged to move it up a day."

He had picked up her note again, but his head shot up. "Can't read a thing without my glasses."

"Here." She handed him the folded spectacles in her hand, but he was looking at her strangely.

"Did you say Oxley? As in *Lord* Oxley? As in the viscount?"

She stared at her brother, doubt assailing her. Had she just acted a deception upon a viscount? He *had* said he was titled, but she hadn't thought much of it. "I...I...I don't know."

"Gad, Ruth!" Topher ran a hand through his hair. "Did you really go to the meeting impersonating a man?"

Ruth yanked off a boot, her hackles rising. "I did. You left me no other choice. I shouldn't have been obliged to do anything so frightfully inappropriate if *you* had only kept your word and been here this morning!" She threw the boot at him, and he caught it with both hands.

"How was I to know that the man would move up the meeting?" He glanced over the boot, rubbing at a spot on the toe. "I thought that I would have plenty of time for study this evening and tomorrow morning."

Ruth said nothing, only letting out an annoyed huff through her nose. She wanted to throttle him. "You might have at least *told* me you had no idea of returning last night. We could have spared ourselves the expense of your room at least."

He set the boot down on the floor. "And perhaps I would have if it had been my intention." His cravat was too high to tell for certain, but Ruth thought she saw him flush slightly. "I made a friend, and he was good enough to let me stay with him, just two doors down from the evening party I attended. My mistake was in sampling too much of the brandy he had on hand. Didn't even crack an eyelid open until past noon."

Ruth narrowed her eyes at him. "How in the world did you manage to gain admittance to an evening party when you don't know a soul in Town?"

Topher avoided her eye, taking up the boot again and busying himself with rubbing the smudge. "I met the friend *before* the party, though I shan't tell you more than that, for you shall only look severely at me and ruin what turned out to be a perfect evening." His hand paused on the boot, eyes glazing over slightly, while the hint of a smile formed on his lips.

"Topher," Ruth said suspiciously. "Did you meet a friend? Or did you meet a woman?"

He looked up, the fond smile fading, and this time she was certain that his face was redder than usual. "You know the rules, Ruth. You mustn't ask."

"And I shouldn't if you weren't endangering the real purpose of our time in Town."

He set the boot down again with a thud. "Well, it's done! You've gone already, haven't you? So I *didn't* ruin it. You have the twenty pounds." A shadow of doubt crossed over his brow. "Haven't you?"

She didn't respond right away. He deserved a bit of suspense after all he had put her through. "I do." She chewed her lip for a moment, anticipating his reaction when she told him the rest.

He shrugged. "Then that's that! No need for more of your lecturing."

"Perhaps."

He looked strangely at her. "What do you mean *perhaps*?"

"We have a decision to make." She sighed, pulling off the second boot and placing it on the floor gently. She already knew what he would say. "Oxley wants me to continue helping him."

"He wants you to—you mean *you* as in you the gentleman?"

Ruth nodded. "Until the end of the month. In exchange for two hundred pounds."

Topher gaped, mouth hanging open, eyes round as dinner plates. "Two *hundred* pounds?"

She nodded, not meeting his gaze. "Three hundred if he finds success in his aims."

"*Three* hundred?" He ran a hand through his hair.

She could already see the light in Topher's eyes—the possibilities her words had sparked in him. Reluctantly, she gave up the last bit of information. "And lodgings."

His gaze shifted to her, curious. "Lodgings where?"

Ruth stood and began pacing. "Upper Brook Street. The empty townhouse belonging to his uncle. He plans to come to Town sometime next month—well after we will have left."

"By Jove, Ruth! That's capital!" He grabbed her hands, forcing her to stop and look into his face, blazing with joy. "When do they expect us, then? And why are you looking like that?"

"I told Oxley I would send him word of my decision—that I needed to discuss the matter with my colleague."

He dropped her hands and hurried to the writing desk, pulling out a piece of paper and thrusting a quill toward her. "You have discussed it with me thoroughly and will very gladly accept his offer." He pulled out the chair in an invitation for her to sit.

She pushed the quill away. "Topher, you aren't thinking. Do you understand what this means?"

"Yes!" he said on an incredulous laugh. "I do! Lodgings in the best part of Town, more time to enjoy London, and three hundred pounds to bring home to Mama. Easiest answer in the world. Come on, then." He tried to nudge her toward the seat, and she resisted.

"Oh, yes," she said waspishly. "It is all well for you, isn't it? *You* aren't the one who must deceive Oxley—or feel the pressure of helping him win a woman. For you this is merely a well-paid holiday. No doubt, you will gallivant around Town day and night, leaving me to hope and pray that I am not discovered, while you flirt and make merry. How should you like it if you were obliged to dress as a woman for weeks? A bit less, I imagine!"

Her anger seemed to bring Topher back down to earth, and he took her hand in his again. "Of course I shan't leave you to yourself. I *do* hope to see more of Town—of course I do. I can't possibly sit inside day and night, can I? But I shall support you and be here to guide you—in the art of masculinity." He executed a deep bow.

It *was* quite elegant, but Ruth merely folded her arms, refusing to smile.

"Listen," he said leaving off his teasing again. "I know you are angry with me, and I can't say that I blame you. I would not have gone out if I had known the way of things. But, in the end, I think that it is all for the best, really."

She scoffed, but he continued. "Just think! If I had gone to see this Oxley fellow, with my half-baked understanding of things, and if he had requested my continued help—which is not a given, mind you—then we *would* be in the suds, for I wouldn't know *how* to continue helping him. Rehearsing can only take one so far. But now, all is well, for you are fully equipped to carry out the task. And only think what a relief it will be to Mama when we write home to tell her what has happened—and what we will bring home with us."

There it was. The thing that Ruth couldn't ignore. The reality of two—or perhaps three—hundred pounds. It was food in George's adorably round belly. It was a doll for sweet Joanna. It was books for Charlie and John to study, now that their understanding had surpassed the ones they had been able to keep. It was a new pair of shoes for Mama to replace the ones that were wearing through on the balls of her feet.

But it was in exchange for a lie. If the reality of what two hundred pounds could buy for the Hawthorn family was one side of the coin, the other side was the reality of Ruth's deception—the man she would be misleading, even if it *was* in pursuit of his best interests and hers. Mutually beneficial. Was it better to risk her family's well-being or to mislead a man while helping him?

Her family couldn't do without food. But Oxley need never know of her deception—not if she took care not to give herself away. If she could do it for an hour, she could do it for longer. The way was paved. And besides, she had *already* deceived him. It wasn't a choice between deceiving and not deceiving—merely between continuing the deception or ceasing it.

And then there was the little matter of the attraction she felt to him—the fact that she *wanted* to see Oxley again. That alone told her she should refuse his offer. But how could she let such a ridiculous, girlish fancy deprive her family of such a sum? She couldn't. She simply couldn't. This was about so much more than her. And it was business.

"Fine," she said, lifting her chin resolutely and taking a seat in the chair. Her hand shook as she removed the top of the ink pot and dipped the quill in it.

Topher clapped her on the shoulder. "Bless you, Ruth! You shan't regret it! And neither shall Oxley." There was a pause. "I wonder if he would be willing to pay half in advance?"

Ruth sent her brother a glare from her position, hunched over the letter. "Well, you shall have to continue wondering, Christopher Hawthorn, for I have no intent of asking him such a thing."

Chapter Twelve

Philip was just sitting down to dine when a letter was brought by the last penny-post of the day. By now, he recognized the Swan's handwriting—or Ruth's, rather. He smiled slightly at the sight of it. It matched the man—lean and youthful.

He opened the letter, feeling a bout of nerves at the thought that it might contain a refusal. He had known he was out of his depth with Miss Devenish, but he hadn't realized just how near he was to drowning—or that he could be taught to swim—until the meeting with Ruth that afternoon.

He breathed an audible sigh of relief as his eyes ran over the words *happy to accept.* Thank heaven.

It was a risk, keeping the services of Ruth, of course. He was placing his trust in someone he hardly knew and, if the man wasn't as trustworthy as Philip had taken him to be, it would mean humiliation on a level Philip had never experienced. He would make it clear in his response that he still required complete discretion.

No one could ever discover he was using the Swan's services—Miss Devenish least of all—but not even Finmore. Philip well knew how easy it was for one confidant to innocently take his own confidant—or two—and before one knew it, what had begun as a secret was common knowledge and appearing in the betting books at White's. It was exactly how his mother's liaisons had changed from a private family affair to *ton* gossip.

But he didn't think Ruth would serve him such a trick. Philip had seen the way Ruth's eyes had widened behind his spectacles at Philip's offer. It would be foolish for the man to throw it away by breaking his word. Three hundred pounds was a neat sum, certainly. But it would be well worth it if Ruth helped him win Miss Devenish. It was an investment.

Philip knew a bit of impatience to begin. Understanding of a subject that had long troubled him was finally within his grasp. He had to admit, too, to a certain amount of curiosity regarding Ruth. The man was an enigma. How did such a young man—and one whose appearance made him difficult to take seriously—come by his knowledge and wisdom?

But the journey to Oxley Court couldn't be helped, and Philip wasn't one to shirk his duty.

When she and Topher had first transferred their belongings to Sir Jacob's townhouse in Upper Brook Street, Ruth had been uneasy. She had visions of the master of the house returning to Town prematurely and finding Ruth attired in her wrapper and shift. Her worries were slightly eased when she discovered that she and Topher would be inhabiting spare bedchambers rather than those of the master, and once she had instructed that Lucy be the only servant to enter her bedchamber when she was at home, she was able to relax. She needed one space at least, be it ever so small, where she had no need to pretend.

Lord Oxley's note—for Topher had confirmed that it was indeed the viscount Ruth was helping—had assured them that his uncle was apprised of their presence in his townhouse and would be thoroughly offended if they refused to make use of his carriage and horses. And as Ruth considered her situation, she had to admit that some adjustments to her wardrobe needed to be made, which would require her venturing forth from the house.

Spectacles were the first item of business which needed addressing. While the prospect of having a crystal-clear view of Lord Oxley's pleasing countenance was as appealing as it was dangerous, Ruth simply couldn't continue wearing her brother's glasses. It would be to court clumsiness and hamper her ability to do what she had been hired to do—a chance she couldn't take. If she was going to earn hundreds of pounds, she needed to be entirely devoted to Lord Oxley's success.

When she and Topher sallied forth from Upper Brook Street to visit the nearest optician in Sir Jacob's carriage, she felt on edge, once again fighting the near certainty that she would easily be identified as an impostor. She was no longer wearing Topher's glasses, which had come to feel like a secret weapon of sorts—the keystone of her entire disguise. But they arrived at the optician's and were greeted by the bespectacled shopkeeper, who gave no indication that he found anything amiss in Ruth's appearance.

He immediately took her over to his collection of quizzing glasses, his bristly gray brows rising when she told him that she needed a pair of full spectacles—preferably ones with regular glass in place of lenses.

"But why?" He blinked at her through thick lenses of his own, which made his eyes appear like those of an insect.

Ruth hesitated, realizing how ridiculous her request sounded.

"For our sister, sir," Topher interjected. "She has the silliest obsession with spectacles. She saw the ones I wear for reading, you know, and we promised her we should bring her a pair of her own, though she has no need for them. What eight-year-old does?" He put a hand on the optician's shoulder with a charming smile. "But you know what silly flights of fancy women take into their heads at times."

Ruth shot her brother an annoyed glance, and the optician chuckled, leading them over to his collection of spectacles. "I have just one pair with 'blanks,' as I call them. They were only ever meant to be for display, and I'm afraid the glass is set in the least popular pair of frames we carry. They have sat now for nigh on a year." He picked up a pair of glasses with bulky frames of a chocolate brown. "Made of horn, these ones, and a very dark horn it was, as you can see. Most people prefer the less conspicuous silver frames."

Ruth felt Topher's shoulders shake beside her, his hand covering his mouth as he looked at the frames.

"Thank you, sir." Ruth took the pair and set them on the bridge of her nose. She breathed a silent sigh of relief as she set the earpieces in place. They didn't squeeze her head like Topher's had. And how glorious it was to look through plain glass! The fact that her vision was framed in a blurry, dark oval due to the combination of narrow lenses and thick frames was certainly not ideal, but she would become habituated to it quickly, no doubt.

The optician offered her a handheld mirror, and she startled slightly at the sight of her face in the reflection. The spectacles certainly couldn't be described as unobtrusive, but she was pleased —and displeased—with the way they added to her masculinity. They would draw the attention away from her lashes, at least—indeed, it was impossible to even see they existed if she set the spectacles slightly down on the bridge of her nose. The frames would draw all the attention, and better she look a fool than be suspected a woman.

She glanced at a pair of daintier, silver frames with a wisp of envy. She would certainly look more like a woman in those.

But that was not her aim, no matter how much her silly vanity begged her to embrace her femininity in the company of Lord Oxley. Indeed, it was the very *opposite* of her aim.

"I shall take them," she said, handing the horn rims to the optician.

She traded a few coins with the man and pulled Topher away from a particularly ornate gold quizzing glass frame, bidding the shopkeeper adieu.

Their next stop was a tailor, who was able to provide Ruth with a shirt, a waistcoat, and pantaloons—not tailored to her measurements, but good enough for her needs. Topher encouraged her to buy a pair of boots and a hat as well, from the shops down the street, but she refused. "I shall just use yours."

Quite predictably, Topher took issue with this.

"Oh, do stop," Ruth said. "You will never need two pairs of boots or two hats at once. We cannot spend *all* the money we have earned, Toph. We will need much of it for tips and other miscellanea, I imagine."

She spoke with eyes slightly downcast as they walked from the top to the bottom of St. James's, aware that she was the only woman on the street. There was something terrifying and enlivening about it that engendered within her two irreconcilable desires: one to gawk at everything around her, and the other to shade her eyes in case she should see something indecent.

But her successful ventures shopping and the fact that no one had stopped her to question her presence in that haven of masculinity breathed life into her confidence—and she needed every bit of it if she was to help Lord Oxley.

"You ought to go out on your own, you know," Topher said after spending some time offering suggestions of how to appear and act more masculine—how to bow, how to sit, how to walk. "I'd lay odds you'll enjoy it." He seemed anxious to shed her company, and Ruth knew that she needed the boost in confidence that would come from practicing what she had learned from Topher. The more she could practice before Lord Oxley came back, the better.

Topher was spending all the time he could away from Upper Brook Street, in the company of his new friend, Robert Rowney, who was apparently more than happy to lend Topher the necessary clothing to enable his attendance at two more formal Town events, one of which Ruth suspected to be a masquerade or a ridotto. She hadn't the willpower or mind space to pay much heed to Topher's shenanigans, aside from her frequent request that he be wise and not draw attention to himself.

The animation in his eyes and his disposition to smile and tease even more than usual let Ruth know that he regretted coming to London not in the least. He was living out a lifelong ambition, while

Ruth was stumbling through an impossible dream which might well prove to be a nightmare.

She debated between riding and walking through the Park and finally settled on the former. She doubted that riding for leisure was as common in Town, but if Lord Oxley wished to go out on horseback at any point, she would rather that her first experience riding cross-saddle *not* occur in his presence.

She was a capable rider, and she had vague memories of riding astride as a young girl, but the experience of swinging her leg up over the saddle was strange after so many years. It was all Ruth could do not to betray to the groom how utterly unnerving it was, or how insecure she felt in the large, man's saddle.

Brook Gate gave nearly instant access to the Park from her street, but Ruth took her mount up and down Upper Brook Street twice in an effort to ensure she was comfortable on the horse and saddle before entering the Park. Her pantaloons chafed at her legs. It felt strange to slide around in the saddle, and she had to exercise great control to remind herself not to squeeze the poor horse with her legs in an effort to feel more secure. The last thing she needed was to draw attention to herself with a gallop through the Park because she had given her mount an unintentional signal.

Brook Gate brought her onto a wide expanse of green grass, where people rode horses, walked in groups of two or three, and slowly rumbled down the dirt lanes in open carriages. She inhaled the park air, a sense of newfound freedom coursing through her and making her feel light and adventurous, even as her heart pattered nervously. She was completely anonymous here. It was precisely what she had dreamed of as a child—the liberty she had always begrudged Topher.

During their meeting, Lord Oxley had mentioned that Miss Devenish made a habit of walking in the Park each afternoon, and Ruth had chosen her destination with that in mind. She hoped she might spot her, this woman Lord Oxley was so determined to win over. It shouldn't be too difficult, given that Miss Devenish would be wearing half-mourning colors.

Sure enough, Ruth hadn't to wander the Park for long before she spotted her, and her heart dropped with an annoying thud the moment she did. Ruth had assumed that someone as eminently eligible and handsome as Lord Oxley would only choose a woman of equal beauty. And so he had. Where Lord Oxley was tall, muscular, and dark, Miss Devenish was elegant, fair, and of perfectly regular height. Surely it was little wonder that *any* man would be enamored of such a woman.

Her beauty was unparalleled, but Ruth couldn't help wondering what Miss Devenish the woman was like. Was she kind, as Lord Oxley had said? Was she shy? Was she truly inured to Lord Oxley's charms?

Miss Devenish was flanked by a friend, and a maid stood slightly off from the two young ladies while a gentleman held Miss Devenish's hand in his. He looked to be in his late thirties, and his conversation did not seem to be entirely welcome, based on the way Miss Devenish was attempting to extract her hand. A group of older people stood a dozen feet away, engrossed in conversation, and Ruth wondered if Miss Devenish's father was perhaps among them.

An idea occurred to Ruth, and she slowed her horse to a stop in the middle of the lane, swinging herself over and down to the ground, with a heart that thudded violently against her chest at her own audacity. But the more she knew of Miss Devenish, the better she could help Lord Oxley.

"Ah," she said, striding over with as much jovial masculinity as she could muster. "Miss Devenish! What an unexpected delight to meet you here."

Ruth kept her eyes trained on Miss Devenish, who gazed at her with an expression of bemusement and uncertainty, while the gentleman rose from his hunched position and allowed Miss Devenish's hand to drop. He looked less-than-pleased at the interruption.

"Forgive me, sir," Ruth said with the most confident and amiable smile at her disposal, "but I simply couldn't pass by without greeting Miss Devenish. What has it been, three years, since we last met?" She held Miss Devenish's gaze purposefully and was relieved when a glint of understanding lit the woman's eyes. She wasn't all beauty and no brains, then.

"Has it been three?" Miss Devenish said. "I rather thought it had only been two."

Ruth laughed and shook her head. She had watched enough men flirt to know what one might say in response. "It is too cruel of you to say so. I had hoped that time passed as slowly for you in my absence as it does for me in yours. But no, no. It has certainly been three. Though even two years would feel like an eternity away from that smile, I confess." She bowed over her hand gallantly. "I must hear how you have fared since we last met." She put out an arm. "Will you walk with me? You and Miss...?"

"Parkham, sir," said the young woman. She, too, was beautiful, with kind eyes and a bit more timidity in her demeanor than Miss Devenish.

Ruth executed a bow and smiled. "Miss Parkham."

"We should be happy to, of course." Miss Devenish looked at the other man with an apologetic smile. "Please do excuse us, Mr. Munroe. I wish you a pleasant afternoon."

"Of course." Munroe gave a stiff bow, sent a glance at Ruth full of promised retribution, and excused himself.

Ruth watched him walk off for a moment, hoping she would never have occasion to see him again, then turned to the young women with an apologetic smile. "You will have to forgive me—it was very presumptuous of me to interject myself and act as though I knew you. But I couldn't help feeling that perhaps Mr. Munroe's attentions were not precisely to your taste."

Miss Devenish glanced in that man's direction. "You apprehended the truth of it, sir. My father is nearby"—she glanced over her shoulder at the group of middle-aged men Ruth had remarked upon arriving—"but he saw an old friend and has all but forgotten me, I think. Thank you for your kindness."

Ruth inclined her head. "It was my pleasure, I assure you. And now, I shall leave you to enjoy your walk in peace. Miss Devenish.

Miss Parkham." She touched her hat and turned back toward her horse, blessing Sir Jacob's groom and the excellent training that kept the horse standing in wait rather than cantering across the Park with his newfound freedom. Ruth had already drawn more attention to herself than she had hoped to.

"Sir! Sir, wait," Miss Devenish said.

Ruth turned, brows raised.

"You needn't go just yet," Miss Devenish said. "You must at least tell us whom we have to thank for the kindness."

Ruth took a few steps back toward the women. "Ruth. Henry Ruth." He bowed again. "At your service, ladies. But it was no trouble at all."

Miss Devenish smiled. "I must admit, I wasn't entirely sure what to think of it when you approached us, for I was certain that I didn't know you. I have quite a good memory for faces, you see, and I worried that perhaps you were taking advantage of the situation to gain an introduction, though I imagine that sounds quite arrogant of me to say."

Miss Parkham interjected. "It wouldn't be the first time it has happened. Men will go to great lengths to gain an introduction to her. They have little respect for her privacy." She nodded to indicate Miss Devenish's mourning clothing.

Ruth smothered the question that rose to her thoughts: if Miss Devenish desired privacy, why did she make a habit out of strolling through the Park at the most popular time of day?

"You are in mourning, Miss Devenish?" asked Ruth.

She nodded. "For my brother. He died last March."

Ruth frowned. "I am terribly sorry to hear that. You must have been close with him."

Miss Devenish and Miss Parkham shared a glance. "We were as close as most siblings near in age, I think." She leaned in toward Ruth. "Truth be told, though, sir, I have found it somewhat convenient to continue my period of mourning. It gives me a bit more control over whose attentions I am obliged to entertain. Mr. Munroe happens to be one of the more aggressive gentlemen who refuses to be put off by my situation."

"I see," Ruth said, wondering how Miss Devenish regarded Lord Oxley's attentions. Was she using mourning to ward him off as well? "But does this not inhibit you from accepting the welcome attentions of gentlemen, as well?"

The young women shared another glance, and Miss Devenish's cheeks turned a shade rosier. "You perceive the problem well. Though, in truth, it was never an issue until recently. It is the reason that I have decided to put off mourning soon."

"In time for the Walthams' masquerade," Miss Parkham said with an energetic clasping of the hands.

Ruth's brows went up. She hoped that this boded well for Lord Oxley. Perhaps spitting lemon tart on Miss Devenish hadn't been such a disaster after all. She wished she could inquire further, but it would be too forward after such a short acquaintance.

"Well, Miss Devenish. I wish you every success with whatever gentleman was fortunate enough to inspire such a change. I am afraid I have an engagement I must rush to now, but it was a pleasure to meet both of you."

She bid the young women farewell and swung herself up over her horse, feeling quite pleased with the fluidity of the motion. She wasn't struggling nearly as much as she had feared in her charade as a gentleman.

Chapter Thirteen

Ruth read the note brought around to the townhouse in Upper Brook Street on Saturday with a gush of nerves. Lord Oxley had returned, and he wished to meet as soon as Ruth was available—that very evening if possible.

The thought of spending the evening with him made her heart knock about—something she was certain owed only to the very novel prospect of being alone with a gentleman in his home at such a time of day. She would have felt the same way no matter the identity of the gentleman in question. Her silly attraction to Lord Oxley in those brief moments when she had seen his face had been a ridiculous reaction. It had only taken a few days for her to come to that conclusion. *Of course* he was more attractive through clear vision than he had been as the nebulous blob she had seen through Topher's glasses.

But when she arrived in Brook Street that evening, the sight of the viscount was enough to make her knees wobble—enough that she glanced down at them to ensure the sensation wasn't visible. Dresses could hide shaking knees in a way pantaloons could not.

Through her new spectacles, Ruth had seen dozens of men walking and riding about Town over the past few days, and there was simply no denying it: none could compare to Lord Oxley—the viscount who believed she was a man. Who believed she was *the* man who would help him win over Miss Devenish.

And it all made perfect sense. In physical beauty, wealth, and status, Lord Oxley and Miss Devenish were equals. If any two people were meant for each other, surely it was them.

It should make Ruth's work easy enough. Theoretically.

Lord Oxley smiled widely upon her entrance, and her heart stuttered slightly at the welcome sight. He wore no coat over his broad, muscular shoulders, and his hair was slightly disheveled, a lock draping across his forehead. His brows went up as he rose from his seat in the drawing room. "What in heaven's name are those?" He strode over and narrowed his eyes, inspecting Ruth's face so shamelessly that she blushed.

"What, are these meant to intimidate me?" He touched the rim of her glasses, and she pulled back, afraid he might remove them.

She took one step back, reining in her reaction. "*Do* they intimidate you?"

He chuckled, folding his arms across his chest. "No, I am afraid they do not. They remind me too much of a panda. Perhaps you should change your name. Do pandas mate for life?"

"Pandas?"

"Yes. Exotic creatures that live in the Orient? They look much like bears but with white faces and large, black circles around their eyes." He nodded to indicate her. "Much like you."

She wasn't sure how she felt about being likened to a beast. She was still trying to come to terms with looking like a man. "And *you* look like a...a..."

"Greek god?" he suggested, though his mouth trembled.

She pursed her lips, annoyed that his playful suggestion was near the truth. "No," she said flatly. "But if you insist on Greek mythology, Narcissus seems an apt choice."

He grinned. "What happened to the other spectacles?"

"They were giving me headaches," she answered honestly.

Oxley gripped her by the shoulder and ushered her toward the small fire in the grate. "I am glad you are here. I admit I had worried you might have thought better of your decision to stay in Town. I am happy to be wrong." With a smile, he indicated a large chair by the fire for her to sit in.

Fiend take that dashing smile! Perhaps she should have brought Topher's glasses, after all. A continuous headache might be worth regaining the fuzzy Lord Oxley rather than this clear view of him.

She gave herself a mental slap. This was the man who was paying her *two hundred pounds* to help him win over another woman. He was a man who knew what he wanted. And he wanted Miss Devenish.

"Always happy to prove you wrong, my lord," Ruth said genially.

Lord Oxley looked at her with a raised brow as she took her seat. "I thought I told you to call me Oxley."

"You did," Ruth acknowledged, reveling in the softness of the chair. "But you failed to mention that I should be calling you *Lord* Oxley. All this time my colleague and I had been referring to you as *Mr. O.*"

He chuckled. "Well, that was by design. I hadn't any idea how discreet you were when I was corresponding with you. And once I met you, it seemed silly to stand upon ceremony. Besides, I *did* tell you I was titled, didn't I? And paid you a half sovereign for the honesty. But I do like *Mr. O.* I certainly prefer it to *sir* or *my lord.* Brandy?"

Ruth shook her head, fumbling for an excuse. "No, thank you. It is my policy when meeting with clients to keep a clear head on my shoulders." Oxley was regarding him with a slight frown, and Ruth saw that he required more than her flimsy excuse. "While I am sure that my appearance gives every indication that I could drink any man under the table, I am afraid the truth is otherwise."

Lord Oxley laughed, and Ruth throttled her heart to prevent it from soaring at having elicited such a pleasant sound.

"You may not be able to drink as much as I with your smaller build," Lord Oxley said, "but I imagine you experience some benefits to make up for it. The lack of need for shaving, for instance?"

Ruth smiled. "Indeed. You would be astounded if you knew how much time and money I save."

"Ah, yes. Behold me consumed with envy." More dashing smiles.

"How was your journey home?" she said, steering the conversation to safer avenues.

He disposed of himself lazily in his chair. It was strange to see a gentleman so relaxed in her company. She was accustomed to formality in the company of the opposite sex. But she liked seeing Oxley this way.

"The journey was pleasant enough, though it feels good to stretch my legs after all that time in the coach."

She had so many questions—where *was* home? Did he prefer it to Town? What kind of master was he? Perhaps she would learn it all in the next couple of weeks. "Well, I tried to make good use of my time while you were away, and I was fortunate enough to come upon Miss Devenish in the Park the other day."

Lord Oxley narrowed his eyes at her. "Stolen her from me already with your equation, have you?"

How in the world could Miss Devenish resist that little hint of a smile on his lips? Wealthy viscount or no, the man was charming, and even more so because he wasn't doing it on purpose. He had no one to impress here. And he apparently thought himself in danger of losing a woman to Ruth. Ah, the irony.

"You have nothing to fear from me there—I promise you."

Lord Oxley tilted his head to the side. "You were unimpressed by her, then?"

Ruth chose her words carefully. "Not at all. I quite understand why you have set your sights on her. My own tastes are merely different from yours."

He looked thoughtful. "And if they were not? If you had fallen under Miss Devenish's spell as so many other men have, would you feel yourself duty-bound to decline helping me any further?"

It was such a nonsensical question, given the truth, that Ruth hardly knew how to answer. "I am quite capable of separating business and personal interests." It was more of a wish than anything, but it needed to be true, and she was glad for the accountability that saying it provided her. The entire topic was dangerous ground, so she shifted the conversation. "But I did learn some things of interest while speaking with her and Miss Parkham."

"You *spoke* with her?" Lord Oxley said, sitting forward and staring at her with wide eyes, as if she had admitted to abducting Miss Devenish.

Ruth shrugged. "Yes. What of it?"

"What *of* it? It is the very thing I have called upon you to help me with, and yet you say it as if it were the most natural thing in the world—especially given that you've never been introduced to her. How did you manage it?"

Ruth was hard pressed not to laugh at the wonder in his eyes. "Without spewing lemon tart on her, thankfully, but it was a near miss."

Lord Oxley dipped his head and held up his glass. "I felicitate you. You have successfully and irrefutably demonstrated your qualifications as the expert," he said. "But really? How *did* you manage to gain an introduction?"

"Through unconventional tactics, I admit. I saw an opportunity and took it. She clearly had no desire to be kept in conversation with the gentleman speaking to her, so I interjected myself on the pretense of knowing Miss Devenish. I wondered if she might not send me on my way, but she was clever enough to play along until the man accepted defeat and left her be."

Lord Oxley sighed. "She has a number of determined suitors."

"That is good news, I think."

He raised his brows incredulously.

"Miss Devenish seemed not to relish this man's attentions at all, and if he continues to be assiduous in them, it may provide *you* with the opportunity to be cast in the role of deliverer."

Lord Oxley stared at her. "You are far too wise for someone of twenty."

She smiled. "I discovered another piece of useful information:

Miss Devenish plans to put off her mourning in time for the Walthams' masquerade, whatever and whenever that is."

Philip blinked. "You are a wealth of information. The ball is in two and a half weeks. Did she give a reason?"

"Apparently it was inspired by the fact that mourning is inhibiting her ability to pursue further acquaintance with a gentleman." Ruth wagged her eyebrows.

His jaw shifted thoughtfully. "Will you stay until the ball, then?"

Two and a half more weeks. With Oxley. For at least two hundred pounds. "If it is what you wish," she said warily.

He nodded. "It is. But of course I shan't compel you to stay." And then he smiled in a way that compelled her.

She took in a breath. "No compulsion necessary. I shall stay until then. I thought tomorrow at church might be a good opportunity for you to put into practice some of the things we discussed earlier this week."

Lord Oxley sat forward, resting his elbows on his knees and swirling the liquid in his glass. "That means attending at St. James's." He grimaced. "Very well. At least there is no threat of lemon tart." His words were humorous, but by the way he didn't meet her gaze, she suspected that he felt less confident than he sounded.

"No, indeed. And it is a chance for you to heed the advice I gave you on asking questions and listening. You can ask her opinion on the sermon, for example, and then employ the eighty-twenty rule we touched on."

She watched him grow more tense. What in the world had happened to make the man so ill-at-ease in front of women? He had every reason to walk into a room and approach any woman present with full confidence, and yet he was a bundle of nerves at the mere mention of asking something as harmless as an opinion on the church service.

For some unaccountable reason, it made Ruth like him all the more. She had always thought confidence the key ingredient in winning a woman over—the thing that could overcome deficiencies in wealth or appearance or even status. But as she looked at Lord

Oxley, his lack of it only drew her to him. She wanted to understand it—to understand him.

"You are nervous," she said.

He set his glass down on the table next to him and ran his hands down the legs of his pantaloons. "I told you. I am always nervous in the presence of Miss Devenish."

"Why?"

He threw up his hands in the air helplessly. "I don't know how to act, I suppose."

"Why act at all?" Ruth said. "I imagine that, if Miss Devenish could see you here, talking with me as you have been for the last quarter of an hour, she would like you very well indeed."

"But this is entirely different."

"Is it?" What would he say to know that he had been speaking to a woman this entire time with no awkwardness whatsoever? She wished she could tell him—perhaps it would increase his confidence. But it would also destroy his trust in her—and any chance of receiving the two hundred pounds her family so desperately needed. Or, heaven willing, three hundred.

"Certainly it is. I don't even need to think to carry a conversation with you. It is completely natural." He sighed. "It is different with Miss Devenish. And with women in general."

It was foolish to feel hurt by a man saying it was easy to converse with her. It should have been a compliment. And yet it stung.

"You needn't change yourself merely because you are in the presence of a woman. Talk to her as you have to me. Remember what I said about forgetting yourself and focusing on her." Ruth sat forward so that their faces were on the same level and looked him intently in the eye.

Good gracious heavens, as Lucy would say. He was close enough that she could see the light sprinkling of freckles across his nose. Close enough that she could smell the brandy—whether in his glass or on his breath, she didn't know, but she knew an impulse to get nearer to determine which it was.

She clenched her jaw. It was time to focus. "This is where the blessed combination of asking questions and abiding by the eighty-twenty rule comes in. The more questions you ask of her and the more you listen carefully to her answers, the less you will need to scramble for conversation. I am not here to teach you how to become a different person to appeal to Miss Devenish. I am here to help you break down the barriers both you and Miss Devenish have constructed—whether consciously or not—to recognizing the best in one another."

He swallowed and nodded. "And if I still manage to sabotage things tomorrow at church?"

"Then we get up and try again the next day."

He let out a large breath laced with brandy then shot her a significant look. "You are coming with me, of course."

"That I am most certainly not." Ruth sat back.

"Why not?"

"Have you need of a nursemaid to hold your hand throughout the ordeal, then?"

Lord Oxley seemed to consider that. "Perhaps it *is* just what I need."

Ruth laughed, heart fluttering briefly at the thought of holding his hand. "You had better spit an entire batch of lemon tarts at Miss Devenish than do that."

Something much like a snort escaped Lord Oxley. "I shall never live that down, shall I? Besides, it was not a *batch* of lemon tart. It was a mere...morsel."

"How very appetizing you make it sound." Ruth stood up and took a book from the nearby shelf. "Whatever it was, I am *not* coming to church with you." The last thing she needed was to spend more time with Lord Oxley than was absolutely necessary.

"Three hundred and twenty-five pounds."

Her head snapped up.

Lord Oxley was smiling mischievously.

"For heaven's sake, no!" Ruth snapped the book shut. "Besides being insufferable, you are utterly incorrigible."

His eyebrow went up. "Three hundred and fifty, then?"

She drew her lips into a thin line. "You would bribe me to go to church?"

"No," he said, feigning deep offense. "I am *paying* you to be on hand for any emergencies that might crop up." He put a hand over his heart and closed his eyes. "I rely upon you to help save me from myself."

"I thought you wished to be discreet."

"And I do."

"Then it can hardly be conducive to that goal to appear at church with the Swan."

He narrowed his eyes at her. "Do others in Town know of your work as the Swan?"

She shook her head.

He looked relieved and gave a shrug. "Then there is no danger of it. You come as my friend Henry Ruth, and no one need know how we became acquainted."

She held his gaze. He made it sound so simple. But there was nothing simple at all about this game she was playing.

He put his hands palm to palm, looking at her with a pair of pleading eyes that obliterated any resolve she had remaining.

"Fine," she said in amused annoyance. "I will go with you. And I shall bring my"—she caught herself—"my colleague too. But only if you stop attempting to pay me more. I want none of your sacrilegious bribes. We agreed upon two hundred for my assistance, three hundred if you find success."

Lord Oxley inclined his head penitently. "A small price indeed to save a pathetic, helpless man like myself."

Ruth was beginning to wonder whether she might be the one who needed saving when all was said and done.

Chapter Fourteen

Philip fumbled with his cravat, let out a frustrated groan, and tore the piece of cloth from his neck, tossing it onto the floor to join two other crumpled ones. It wasn't as if Philip had never tied his own cravat before, but this morning both his fingers and the cloth refused to cooperate. He was sorely regretting giving his valet the morning off.

He dropped his arms to his sides, letting his muscles rest from the exertion of smoothing and adjusting the neckcloths. He looked at himself critically in the mirror. He had selected a simple blue waistcoat, but he was beginning to think it a bad choice.

A soft knock sounded on his door.

"Yes?"

"Mr. Ruth is here, my lord," came the reply.

Ah, good. Ruth would be honest with him about his clothing.

"Send him up," Philip said. "I require his help."

"Very good, my lord."

He squinted at his shirt in the mirror. Was that a stain? He looked down and, sure as anything, a yellow blotch stared back up at him.

With a sigh of annoyance, he undid the buttons of his waistcoat, tugged it off, and threw it on the bed next to a similar one of crimson satin, then undid the button at his throat and pulled his shirt over his head.

"Lord Oxley?" Ruth's voice came through the door, a hint of hesitation in it.

"Come in, Ruth." Philip strode over to the door, opened it, and walked back over to the armoire to pull out one of the neatly folded shirts from a pile. "Thank heaven you've come. *You* can choose between the red and the blue waistcoat. For the life of me I can't—" He stopped.

Ruth stood in the doorway, regarding him with wide eyes.

"What?" Philip said, feeling sudden dismay. Had he a stain on his pantaloons as well? He glanced down, but his pantaloons were the one article of clothing he felt confident in. "Is it my hair?" He turned toward the mirror, brushing softly at a tuft of hair that had moved from its place. "I gave my valet the morning off, and I have never regretted something so profoundly." He turned back to Ruth. "Well? What is it, man?"

Ruth swallowed and blinked. "Nothing. It is just...I have never seen a dandy in his natural habitat. It is fascinating."

Philip scoffed and pulled the shirt over his head. "A dandy! That's rich. I have never in my life been called that."

Ruth's brows went up, and he nodded at the pile of cravats and the waistcoats on the bed. "You certainly seem to meet some of the criteria."

Philip finished buttoning the shirt at the throat and sent him an unamused glance before holding up the waistcoats. "Red or blue?"

Ruth looked at him carefully, eyes switching between his face and the waistcoats. "Red."

Philip hurriedly shrugged into the waistcoat then reached for a new cravat. "Perhaps I should have *you* tie it. My fingers seem to be covered in butter today."

Ruth laughed. "No, Narcissus. I shall come with you to church, but I must draw the line somewhere, and I think tying your cravat is well beyond that line."

"Hadn't any idea what you were getting yourself into when you accepted my request, did you?" Philip tucked the end of the cravat through itself and glanced at Ruth through the mirror.

Ruth shot him a look full of meaning. "You have no idea."

On the walk to Piccadilly, Philip asked question after question of Ruth, who patiently answered and expounded upon each answer.

Philip couldn't help but chuckle as he looked over at the young man, laboriously explaining the proper use of eye contact to hint at his interest in Miss Devenish.

"In the beginning, you cannot afford anything but the briefest of exchanged glances when you are not directly speaking to one another. Hold her gaze too long before she has given you encouragement that she looks favorably upon your suit, and you will only succeed in making her feel supremely uncomfortable. Better too short than too long in this case."

"I must trust you, no doubt," Philip said. "I can only imagine you see the world quite a bit more clearly than I with *these*." He plucked the spectacles from Ruth's face, and Ruth scrambled to get them back, wresting them from Philip and setting them back on his nose.

Surprised at the vehemence of Ruth's reaction, Philip put his hands up in a display of innocence. "I never knew a man to be so attached to his glasses. You must be the only man under the age of sixty who wears them all the time."

"Well, not all of us are blessed with the triad," he said the last word with feigned reverence.

"Perhaps not," Philip said, eying the spectacles with amusement. "But you might have chosen a pair of glasses a bit less...obtrusive. You bring new meaning to the phrase *making a spectacle of oneself*. Or is this your method of being noticed? Perhaps you *should* let me borrow them today."

"Don't veil your eyes," Ruth said. "Let Miss Devenish see them clearly. They are one of your best features."

Philip chuckled, a half-smile bringing up the side of his mouth. "You positively unman me with your flattery, Ruth."

Ruth sent him an annoyed glance through the thick rims of his glasses. Why was it so entertaining to tease him?

"When there is but one good feature to capitalize upon, I feel myself duty-bound to point it out," Ruth said. "Now, as I was saying, when you are speaking directly to Miss Devenish, you should hold her gaze clearly as she speaks. Let her see that your attention is on her."

Reaching the gates of St. James's, they followed behind a middle-aged couple into the churchyard.

The vicar stood just inside the church doors, and he greeted Philip with a raising of the brows. "Lord Oxley," he said, voice loud enough to carry for many feet around them. "How good of you to join us. I hope this is the turning over of a new leaf and that it means we shall begin seeing more of you. I am always devastated to see your empty box each Sabbath. God is pleased when a lost sheep returns to the fold."

Philip smiled civilly. "Thank you, Mr. Gibson."

"I encourage you to listen carefully to today's sermon, my lord," said the vicar.

Philip gave a nod and pulled Ruth's arm to force them both into the church.

"You shock me, Oxley," Ruth said, covering his mouth in a failed attempt to stifle a laugh. "I hadn't any idea you were a prodigal."

Philip eyed the vicar with disfavor as they proceeded into the church. "Is it any wonder I stay away?"

"No," Ruth said. "Though I confess I am impatient to hear what the subject is for today's sermon. Or does the vicar say that to everyone who attends?"

They slipped into the Trent family box pew. "No, he does not. He seems to feel that every call to repentance is tailored for me."

The sermon was, as it would have it, on vanity, something that Ruth found extremely amusing. He found it incumbent upon himself to send Philip a stern, pointed glance each time the vicar mentioned the word, mouthing "Narcissus" on one occasion. Instead of the usual frustration and annoyance Philip felt at the vicar's singling him out, he was hard put not to laugh.

As soon as the sermon ended—complete with a final inclining of the vicar's head in Philip's direction—Philip and Ruth left the pew.

"Is she here?" Ruth asked, eyes casually searching the crowds.

"Yes." Philip had found her easily enough. "She doesn't generally stay long after the service."

"Well, then." Ruth shot him a significant look.

But Philip wasn't obliged to go in search of Miss Devenish. Her eyes were roving over the groups of churchgoers, as though searching for someone in particular. When her gaze landed upon Philip and Ruth, she smiled in surprise and began to make her way over, trailed by her friend Miss Parkham. It was Ruth she had her eyes trained on, though, and Philip had to admit he was impressed. So, the man knew what he was talking about, after all.

"Mr. Ruth," said Miss Devenish with a friendly smile. "What a pleasure to see you here. And you, too, Lord Oxley."

Philip felt a small nudge from Ruth, who addressed himself to Miss Parkham.

Philip cleared his throat and smiled at Miss Devenish. "What did you think of the sermon, Miss Devenish?"

She looked at him with a suppressed smile. "It was very...severe." She laughed softly. "I believe Mr. Gibson was directing his words at me."

Philip smiled and shook his head. "Oh, no. You may rest easy. He as much as told me that he chose it for my benefit."

She tilted her head to the side wonderingly. "Did he really?"

He looked down and nodded, then, remembering that he was supposed to be meeting Miss Devenish's gaze squarely, brought his head up and looked her in the eye.

Her smile wavered. "What? What is it?"

"What? Nothing."

"Oh," she said, blinking. "I thought you meant me to understand something by the way you looked at me just now."

He shook his head quickly, heat rising in his neck. "No, no." He laughed uncomfortably and looked to Ruth, who was still conversing with Miss Parkham. He searched his mind for what Ruth had told him the night before and on their walk to the church. He was to listen carefully—but Miss Devenish wasn't saying anything to *listen* to right now—and he was to ask questions.

But she wasn't looking at him. Her eyes were again roving over the crowds in the church.

"Are you looking for someone?" That was a question, wasn't it?

"Oh, no." She returned her eyes to him, smiling again. "Merely ensuring my mother knew my whereabouts."

Silence reined again, and Philip caught Ruth's eye with a significant look. Ruth nodded, and the four of them parted company, just in time for Miss Devenish to be approached by Mr. Munroe. Munroe's eyes seemed to linger on Ruth as he spoke with Miss Devenish.

Philip breathed his relief at no longer being obliged to come up with questions or conversation. A slight wave drew his attention. "Ah, here are my sister and nieces. Mr. Gibson would have done better to direct his sermon at *her*."

Chapter Fifteen

Ruth watched with an increase of nerves as a woman, flanked by her two daughters, approached them. The woman held herself with the same natural confidence as her brother and was regarding Ruth with an evaluative eye, and Ruth could only imagine what her impressions might be. Would a woman be more likely to recognize her real identity?

She straightened and tried to hold herself in a more masculine way.

"Uncle Phil!" cried out one of the girls, rushing over to him and wrapping her arms around his knees. Ruth was reminded of Joanna, and she felt a little pang at the vague likeness.

"Mary," said Oxley's sister in a severe whisper, pulling the child's arm. "You mustn't run in the church. Nor assault your uncle when you see him."

Oxley bent down. "Your mother is right, of course. We shouldn't run in the church. Mr. Gibson is *very* strict, you know. But if we went outside..." He wagged his brows.

The girls both grinned and nodded, and Ruth thought it might be in Oxley's best interest if Miss Devenish could see him interacting with his nieces—and in Ruth's best interest if *she* was never allowed to witness it again.

"Ah, how thoughtless of me," Oxley said, rising to a stand. "Alice, allow me to introduce you to my friend, Mr. Henry Ruth. Ruth, this is my sister, Lady Alice Tipton."

Ruth bowed to Lady Tipton.

"And these"—Oxley tweaked a curl on both of his niece's heads—"are the most beautiful women in all of London, Miss Tipton and Miss Mary Tipton."

"You state the obvious, Oxley." Ruth bowed even more deeply, smiling conspiratorially at the little girls.

"Were you just speaking with Miss Devenish, Philip?" Lady Tipton said, glancing in that woman's direction.

"Yes," he said. "Only for a moment, though."

"And you let Mr. Munroe steal her out from under you?" Lady Tipton made a *tsk* sound. "He is hardly fit competition for you, but one cannot blame him for trying. She is such a taking thing." She tilted her head to the side as she regarded Miss Devenish. "Perhaps you could do with a bit of help. I could—"

"Thank you, Alice," Oxley said, with a speaking glance at Ruth, "but that won't be necessary. Come, girls. Let us go outside for some fresh air." He took his nieces by the hand and looked down at them with a smile that ached somewhere in Ruth's chest.

Lady Tipton walked close behind her brother, and Ruth hesitated before following along, unsure whether she should walk beside Lady Tipton or behind her.

"Did I understand correctly from Draper that you let Mrs. Hines go?" Lady Tipton asked of Oxley as they emerged into the sunlit outdoors.

"Yes," he said over his shoulder.

"But I thought she wasn't meant to retire for another few years at least."

"She wasn't. But her mother took ill, and she was needed at home."

"Poor thing. But might you not have simply given her a leave of absence? For now you must pay her a pension *and* hire a new housekeeper besides."

Oxley sent her a look of annoyed incredulity. "After over thirty years with our family, I think she has more than earned it."

"Perhaps you are right. Besides, what Oxley Court needs is a *real* mistress." She raised her brows significantly as Miss Devenish walked by.

Ruth managed a forced chuckle. She had never seen Oxley Court, but the name itself conveyed grandeur, and Miss Devenish certainly looked like the type of woman meant to be mistress of a grand place.

"Girls, it is time to go," Lady Tipton said suddenly.

Cries of injustice were raised, but Lady Tipton insisted. "You may play with Uncle Philip another day. Come now."

Ruth felt bemused by the sudden demand and looked to Philip, whose expression was one of resigned disappointment.

Lady Tipton took her daughters by the hand and, as an older matron approached, inclined her head stiffly. "Good day, Aunt Dorothea."

The matron greeted her and stopped the girls to give them each a little piece of sugar candy, eliciting a tight-lipped expression from Lady Tipton, who pulled insistently on her girls' hands and led them out of the churchyard.

"She hates when you do that," Philip said.

His Aunt Dorothea smiled fondly as she watched the girls leave. "I know. She hates everything I do, though."

Philip chuckled. "I think she merely resents how you treat her husband."

She gave an unconcerned shrug. "She should have married Mr. Vickers. Better a man in humble circumstances than an unbearable one like Sir Jon. Now, who is this?" She was looking at Ruth.

Oxley turned toward Ruth. "This is my friend, Mr. Henry Ruth. Ruth, this is my aunt, Mrs. Dorothea Barham."

Ruth executed a bow and smiled at the intriguing woman before her, dressed in a blue pelisse as colorful as the magenta dress below it. The lines on her face gave her a good-humored look even when she was not smiling.

Mrs. Barham surveyed Ruth with an evaluative but not unkind eye.

When they bade her goodbye a few minutes later, Philip watched her go with a fond gaze much like Mrs. Barham had worn as she watched her great nieces leave.

"She likes you," he said. "No doubt it was the glasses. She loves anything that flouts expectation."

"*Or*," Ruth said, "perhaps it was my undeniable charm."

Philip looked at Ruth for a moment then shook his head. "It must have been the glasses." He elbowed Ruth playfully, and she nudged him right back harder.

"Tell me, then," Ruth said as they made the journey on foot back to Brook Street. "How did your very *brief* conversation with Miss Devenish go?"

Oxley sighed. "It was going well for the first twenty seconds, I thought. But then I fear I frightened her while trying to heed your advice to look her in the eye while speaking with her."

Ruth laughed. "Perhaps I am doing more harm than good with my counsel."

"No, no. I asked her a question and even managed to make her laugh with my response before bungling it."

Ruth clapped her hands. "Bravo! You have leapt ahead to a new lesson entirely, then. We haven't yet touched on humor, but in truth, I hardly think you stand in need of the lesson."

"You consider me amusing, then?"

"Well, you certainly make *me* laugh." Ruth took the opportunity to look in the opposite direction in order to hide the warmth in her cheeks.

"Perhaps your standards are too low," Oxley said.

"I imagine that would be apparent to anyone who saw me in your company," Ruth said, unable to avoid glancing at him to see how he took the teasing.

He was smiling widely, and Ruth looked away hurriedly. Many

more of these moments with Oxley, and she would be in serious trouble.

They came upon Oxley's house, and he stopped. "When do we next meet?"

"I am at your disposal," Ruth said, wishing it wasn't so very true.

"You may as well come dine with me tonight, then. And what of your colleague? Was he not going to join us at church today?"

Ruth chuckled. "Yes, he was. But when the time came to leave, he was still abed, and I hadn't the energy to force *two* prodigals to church. I wouldn't be surprised if he isn't yet awake."

"Well, he is welcome to come to dinner tonight as well."

"Oh," Ruth said with a slightly nervous laugh. "You needn't worry about him. He will be little enough help. He handles more of the business side of the Swan."

Oxley gave her a funny look. "Did you not offer his services in place of yours at one time?"

Ruth opened her mouth then showed a smile full of clenched teeth. "I did. But surely you cannot blame me."

"Why? Because of how awful I was to you when we first met?"

Ruth laughed, thinking what things would be like if he had accepted such an arrangement—or if he hadn't come after her when she tried to leave.

"Well," Oxley said, "we needn't discuss business tonight. We can leave that for tomorrow instead."

Ruth sucked in a breath and nodded. She wasn't sure she wished to share Oxley with Topher—or to risk Topher's saying something that might undo them.

When she arrived back at Upper Brook Street a few minutes later, Topher was partaking of breakfast in his room.

"Ah, there you are." He scooped a forkful of egg into his mouth. "Looking very dapper in that waistcoat, aren't you?"

Ruth sat down on the edge of his bed, letting her foot swing as it hovered above the floor. "You missed church."

"I did. Had a late night."

"Have you had anything *but* late nights since we arrived in Town?"

He grinned and took a sip of coffee.

"Where were you this time?"

He set the coffee cup down and wagged his eyebrows. "Getting us more business."

Ruth stilled. "More business? What do you mean?"

"Mark Kirkhouse." Her brother stabbed the last bit of egg with a fork, ate it, and gulped down another swig of coffee.

"You are joking," she said.

He shot her a funny look. "Why should I be? You are meeting with him tomorrow at his lodgings for dinner."

"Christopher Brandon Hawthorn! What in heaven's name were you thinking?" She stood up and shook her head vehemently. "No. No, no, and no. Absolutely not."

He reared back. "What do you mean *absolutely not?* He is expecting you—relying on you, even. The man is besotted, Ruth, and he just needs a bit of advice from someone to inspire him with confidence. He's willing to pay five pounds for it. Easiest thing in the world for you."

She folded her arms and shook her head again. "I cannot do it, no matter how easy. We came here to help Lord Oxley, not to take on more clients."

"We came here to make money, Ruth. *That* is why we're here. Gad, why are you so upset when I've found another opportunity for us?"

Her chest rose and fell quickly, and she took to pacing the floor. "Don't you see, Topher? Every person I am forced to spend time with increases the likelihood of my being discovered. And if I *am* discovered, rest assured we shan't have *any* of the money we are expecting. Besides, I assured Lord Oxley of our discretion. How can I possibly maintain that if word gets around about the Swan, as it inevitably will if I take on more clients?"

Topher's hands were up, inviting her to calm down. "Very well, very well. I see what you mean. I hadn't thought it through carefully, and I am sorry. But I assure you, Kirkhouse is no gabster, and I can't very well tell him 'never mind' now. I shan't seek out any more clients, but surely you can help just the one man? He is a friend,

Ruth. And from what he has said, this girl he's fallen in love with is near to being forced into a marriage with some slimy fellow that's more than twice her age."

Ruth clenched her eyes shut for a moment. She was overreacting. The thought of disappointing Oxley terrified her. Whether it was because it meant risking the two hundred pounds or because she had come to place such value on his opinion of her, she didn't know. She didn't want to know.

"Ruth," he pleaded. "If you refuse, it will not only hurt my reputation but that of the Swan as well."

Ruth chewed her lip. If Topher had already told Mr. Kirkhouse of the Swan, the damage was already done. "Just this *once*," she said.

Topher nodded quickly. "Of course."

"I mean it, Topher. No more. I would rather return to Mama with a sure two hundred pounds than have ten clients like Mr. Kirkhouse who put it all at risk."

He nodded quickly. "You are right, of course. It was thoughtless of me. But I do think you will like Kirkhouse when you meet him tomorrow. And this girl he's taken such a fancy to. She's a sweet thing. I'm not the expert, of course, but I think what Kirkhouse needs is just a bit of a nudge, really—something to give him the confidence to declare his feelings, since I am fairly certain that she would accept him if she was sure he returned her regard." He stood and went over to ring the bell. "And now, I must get ready. Rowney and I are going riding in the Park."

"Oh, of course. Sunday afternoons are the time to be seen, aren't they? And it's such a nice day today. Perhaps I shall come with you."

Topher looked so aghast at the suggestion that Ruth couldn't help laughing.

"Embarrassed of me, are you?" She cocked a brow and lowered her glasses to look severely at him. "Even in your own clothes?"

Topher scoffed. "I can't decide whether to admire or bemoan the fact that you are confident enough to go to church in Piccadilly wearing *those*." He nodded to indicate her glasses.

Ruth chuckled and took them off to inspect them. "They are

rather hideous, aren't they? But they serve their purpose, I think." She sighed, collapsing the spectacles. "Very well, I shan't come with you—to save your pride. But Lord Oxley has extended us an invitation to dine with him this evening if you care to come."

Topher's brows shot up. "The viscount? Invited me to dinner? By Jove! Yes, yes. I shall make sure to be back in time. How are things going with that, anyway?"

"Well enough." Ruth had little desire to delve into things with Topher—especially not when he was so uncommunicative about his own dealings. Her feelings were becoming a confusing jumble, and, much as she loved her brother, she had no desire to discuss it with him. "You mustn't forget, though, that to him you are Mr. Franks."

Topher nodded, already pulling out his attire for the day, his mind no doubt consumed with which style of knot would show to best advantage in the Park.

Chapter Sixteen

Dinner with Ruth and Franks was a pleasant, laughter-filled affair for Philip. In fact, it had been some time since he had laughed so much. The two men seemed to have known each other from time immemorial and to thoroughly enjoy embarrassing one another by relating experiences to Philip, the telling of which was always challenged and amended by its subject. Franks was the more gregarious of the two and Ruth the wittier.

True to his word, Philip refrained from talking about any business. It was refreshing to leave thoughts and talk of such things behind for an evening, like relieving a weight from his shoulders.

When the two men left, Philip's house felt suddenly bereft, the stark quiet making Philip frown. He felt a slight pang of envy, knowing that Ruth and Franks were able to continue the spirit of the evening together. Philip had friends, of course—people he liked and enjoyed happening upon in Town. And he and Finmore had known one another for an age. But it was different. Just how it was different, Philip couldn't quite put his finger on. But it was.

Or maybe he was merely imagining it.

When he strolled into Brooks' the next day, he saw a number of the people he considered friends, Finmore among them. Finmore was often to be found at Brooks', though what money he had to gamble with these days was an utter mystery to Philip.

"Ah, there you are, Ox," Finmore said, motioning him over to the whist table where he sat. "Hoped I'd see you here today." He scribbled some words on the piece of paper in front of him and handed it to the man across from him.

"More vowels?" Philip said, taking a seat next to rather than across from him to make it clear he hadn't come to play. He wasn't going to encourage Finmore's recklessness.

"Heard you went to church yesterday," Finmore said, gathering the cards.

"I did."

"Who's this Ruth fellow you were there with?"

Philip scoffed lightly. "Having me followed, are you?"

Finmore's half-smile appeared as he shuffled the cards into a neat pile. "The movements of the Viscount Oxley are always a matter of interest and discussion."

Philip stifled a sigh.

"So. Who's this odd youth you've taken under your wing?"

Philip felt a strange protectiveness rise up in him, one he brushed aside. Ruth was capable of defending himself—he had made that clear quite quickly. In fact, Philip rather thought he would enjoy seeing Finmore attempt to take Ruth on in a battle of wits. Ruth's appearance was certainly deceiving. And little did Finmore realize that it was Ruth who had taken Philip under *his* wing, in a way. What would he say if he knew that Ruth was the very Swan he had encouraged Philip to apply to for help? The thought brought a smile to Philip's face. But as entertaining as it might have been, he didn't wish for Finmore—or anyone—to know he was receiving such help.

"He is a friend I hadn't seen for some time."

"Hm. Munroe seems to have developed a distaste for him. Called him an *unlicked cub*."

Philip let out a snort. "Munroe is a fool. I might safely decide my friends based purely on those he dislikes and my enemies on those whose company he frequents."

"It seems as though Ruth cut him out with a woman or some such thing."

Philip smothered his surprise. Was Ruth courting women while in town? It would only be natural, of course, but somehow it seemed unfair that Ruth should know everything about Philip's romantic interests while Philip knew nothing of Ruth's. He had found a friend with whom he could speak freely and wished that Ruth felt the ability to do the same.

An unwelcome thought accosted him: he was *paying* Ruth to be his friend.

"I shall have to convey my compliments to Ruth when I next see him," Philip said. "Munroe could do with a bit of humbling. Besides, Ruth won't be in town for long, so Munroe can be at ease." Philip would miss Ruth when he left.

Finmore grunted, seeming to have lost interest in the subject already. "And how do you fare with Miss Devenish? I understand she has been seen more than once in the company of some gentleman. And looking quite cozy with him."

Philip frowned. "Who?"

Finmore shrugged. "Just idle talk I heard. Miss Devenish's movements are a matter of as much interest as yours, you know."

Philip did know it. And it didn't make him feel any better. Particularly if Miss Devenish was keeping company with someone new.

When Philip met Ruth on horseback that afternoon for a ride, his brow was still set in a slight frown.

"Is something amiss?" Ruth asked as they turned their horses down Rotten Row. It was too early in the day for many people to be found in the Park, so they had the lane almost to themselves.

Philip let out a breath and relaxed his face. "Nothing. Just something I heard today."

"What is it?" Ruth asked. "You can talk to me, you know." He smiled. "You *are* paying me to be discreet."

Philip's muscles clenched, but he managed a chuckle. "Very true."

"Well, then?" Ruth prodded. "What has you frowning?"

"It very well may be nothing, but apparently Miss Devenish has been seen more than once in the company of a gentleman. I was wondering if it might not be the reason she has suddenly decided to put off her mourning."

Ruth's forehead wrinkled. "Someone you know witnessed this, then?"

Philip shook his head. "Just hearsay. It wouldn't be the first time there were untrue rumors about Miss Devenish."

Ruth looked at him with a cock to his brow. "Rumor or truth, we must help Miss Devenish see what is obvious to anyone with a pair of eyes and a brain: she couldn't marry a better man than you."

Philip chuckled, though he was secretly touched by Ruth's words. "Perhaps you should offer your spectacles to Miss Devenish to help her see that."

Ruth shot him a feigned glare then laughed. "I am in earnest, though. She would be fortunate to call herself your wife, with or without the triad." He looked ahead. "Either way, I think we need to change our approach a bit. What you and Miss Devenish need is time for a real conversation, one where you can delve a bit deeper than is possible during two minutes at the church."

"I think I can only manage two minutes at a time without making a fool of myself."

Ruth shook his head. "It is merely a matter of momentum. Once you discover a topic upon which you and Miss Devenish agree—or some topic with which you both have experience—you will see how your conversation begins to flow. Are you aware of any topics on which she feels strongly?"

Philip pursed his lips. "You will think me stupid, no doubt, as I have known Miss Devenish for some time now, but I cannot say that I know much about her."

"Then we must rectify that. I have only met her twice, but I think I can surmise a few things from those short encounters. And, adding that together with what we know about human nature, I think we might come up with a few topics of conversation that are likely to draw her out of her shell."

Philip shot him an impressed look. "Let us have it, then. What have you gathered about Miss Devenish?"

Ruth made a pensive expression. "You mentioned that her father is too fond of her to force her into a marriage she doesn't wish for. Is she as fond of him as he is of her?"

"I believe so," Philip said. "She tends to stay near her father rather than her mother when the three of them attend events together."

"And the brother whose death she mourns, were you acquainted with him?"

"A bit, yes."

Ruth shrugged. "Why not ask her more about him?"

Philip frowned. "Is it wise to bring up such a painful subject? Might that not upset her?"

There was a pause. "In my experience, when people lose someone they love, the pain is enhanced when they feel they cannot speak of the loved one for fear of making others uncomfortable."

"In your experience...." Philip said slowly.

Ruth glanced at him. "Yes. I find joy in speaking of my father—in remembering him. It feels like honoring him, I suppose. But perhaps I am an anomaly."

Philip rarely spoke of his own father, but he couldn't say that it caused him any pain. "Were you very close with him?"

Ruth smiled with a hint of nostalgia. "Yes. Yes, I was. He is the one who taught me almost everything I know about love—I wouldn't be the Swan without him."

"How do you mean?"

Ruth's smile grew, though his gaze was trained on the space between his horse's ears. "I accompanied him every day to the Pump Room in Bath for the last year of his life. He hated drinking the waters, but I could never convince him that it would be better to drink the glass in one draft and be done with it. He insisted upon taking his time—a sip here and a sip there. Every single day was the same, and we would pass the time with a game—one he created to distract himself from his illness and the unsavory waters, I think. We would observe those who came and went during our hour there, taking particular note of the interactions between the men and women. My father would ask me questions, and we would make predictions." The nostalgia in his smile was tangible. "Did I think Miss Brownsword and Mr. Lovell were in earnest, or were they merely flirting? Would Mrs. Hewitt and Mr. Horton make a match of it? If so, when? Things like that, you know. He was nearly always right in his predictions—and he helped me see the subtleties of human interaction and their importance."

Philip felt a sting of envy. He had admired his father—his determination, his dedication to his position—but he had never shared anything with him like what Ruth described.

"What of you?" Ruth asked.

"My father would have consigned the Pump Room and its waters to the devil, I think."

"For good reason! I imagine the devil might send the waters right back, though. Vile stuff, isn't it?"

"It is," Philip said.

"And what of your mother?"

Philip frowned. "I can't say, really. She died shortly after giving birth to my brother. I was only five, so I have few memories of her."

"Few memories, but not none. What *do* you remember, then?"

Philip glanced at Ruth. Would he think ill of Philip knowing what he thought of his own mother? Somehow he didn't think so. "I admit that my memories often conflict with one another. When anyone else speaks of her, it is with near-reverence, though."

"It is customary to idealize the departed. I find myself doing it with my father. I loved him dearly, but he had his flaws, just as we all do. What did *you* think of your mother?"

Philip was grateful for Ruth's words. It wasn't wrong to recognize the faults of one's parents. "I found her...perplexing. Difficult to understand or predict. I remember sneaking from my bedchamber one evening and watching as she and my father greeted guests at Oxley Court. She was magnificent—so elegant, her face wreathed in smiles. She emanated warmth and grace. It was like watching a stranger, in some ways." He smiled wryly. "I must have been a disappointing child, for she was often cross with me. Or perhaps I was merely too sensitive."

Ruth was looking at him with a considering gaze. But there was no shock in it, neither was there pity. Only thoughtfulness.

"Perhaps not," Ruth said. "Children are quite perceptive, I think. They often see through façades more easily than adults—undeceived by words. They have very good memories for feeling, too. My own sister Joanna is five years old, and I do not exaggerate when I tell you that she remembers times when I lost my temper nearly two years ago. She is expecting me to bring her home a doll, and I can only imagine how long her memory will be if I fail to do so."

"Ah, yes," Philip said, thinking of his nieces' recent invitation to tea and what would happen if he failed to keep the appointment. "One offends children at one's peril."

"Indeed," Ruth said. "The Lord must have had personal experience when he said it were better for a man to have a millstone hanged about his neck and drown in the depths of the sea than to offend a child."

Philip laughed heartily, feeling a bit of his somberness depart.

"You must draw Miss Devenish out," said Ruth. "Let her see that you are someone she can speak with frankly, just as you've done with me."

Philip frowned. "I cannot imagine holding this sort of conversation with her."

Ruth sent him a look of commiseration. "That is the risk of love, I'm afraid. And friendship, too. The meaningful ones cannot be had without some peril. If you wish to make Miss Devenish feel safe confiding in you, you must take the chance of confiding in *her*."

Philip clenched his teeth and let out a hissing noise.

"I suspect the barrier is in your mind. If you think of Miss Devenish as your potential future wife, you will always feel immense pressure on your behavior. Perhaps you need to let go of that for a moment. Think of her first as a potential friend, a woman you would like to understand better—and speak to her as such."

"But that is just it," Philip said. "I *don't* speak to my friends about such things." The thought of confiding anything in Finmore was almost laughable—only less so than the thought of Finmore confiding in *him.*

"But you've spoken it to *me.*"

Philip let out a laugh, and it had a caustic ring to it. "Yes, and I am paying you two hundred pounds for the service, aren't I?" He glanced at Ruth, and his smile faded as he noted the hurt in the man's eyes.

"I am sorry to hear you think that."

There was a short pause, and Philip felt sick inside at the thought that he had hurt his friend.

"In any case," Ruth said, "it may initially cause you some discomfort to share your personal experience, as it is not something to which you are habituated. But I suppose you shall have to decide whether the ability to discuss meaningful subjects together is something you value in a wife. If you do, it seems wise to pave the way for it now. If not, then you may simply limit your conversation to more mundane topics. But if Miss Devenish has her pick of suitors, the bond that is forged through such connection will undoubtedly influence whatever decision she makes."

Philip sent a sidelong glance at Ruth, wondering if he had truly offended him by his comment. There was a slight crease to Ruth's brow, and Philip regretted his words. He tried to lighten the mood—to recapture the easy understanding between them. "You mean to say that, with enough practice, I shall find it quite natural to tell even my deepest secrets to the hackney driver?"

"Hardly," Ruth said. "I fear it is never *easy* to share that which is personal with someone else—there is something within each of us that simultaneously craves it and fears it—but it certainly comes more naturally between some people than it does others. When people speak of *falling in love,* I think it is generally *that* to which they are referring—the sort of connection between kindred spirits that is inexplicable yet undeniable."

There was experience in Ruth's words, and it brought to Philip's mind what Finmore had said about Ruth cutting out Munroe with a woman. "Have *you* felt such a connection?'

Ruth glanced at him, and Philip didn't miss the wary look in his eye. "I don't know."

Philip narrowed his eyes. "Did you not just say it was undeniable?"

"I did," he said, staring straight forward. "I had always thought it to be something felt either by both parties or neither. That was not the case for me. Or perhaps I mistook the feeling." Ruth glanced at him with a quick, tight smile.

"Someone in London?"

Ruth nodded but said nothing more, and Philip didn't resist when he shifted the focus back to Miss Devenish. But he couldn't help wondering if he was being rash in his decision to marry. If he married Miss Devenish, was he forgoing the chance of ever experiencing what Ruth spoke of? Was it that which Miss Devenish wished for?

What if he couldn't give it to her?

Chapter Seventeen

Ruth's mood was morose as she arrived back at Upper Brook Street after her ride with Oxley. She felt her own methods working against her—with every minute she spent in Oxley's company, with every question she asked him and every answer she gave to *his* questions, she felt cords binding her to him more tightly. But the thought of trying to break free—the knowledge that those cords would snap at some point, whether she wanted them to or not—left her future feeling bleaker than ever.

She went through the door at Upper Brook Street with a sigh on her lips. There was no way but forward. Her heart might be in tatters at the end of all this, but at least her family would be well-provided for. Surely that was worth any sacrifice. It was a goal that transcended her own happiness.

"There you are!" Topher said, his jovial voice at odds with the somber humor she was in. "Were you with Oxley, then?"

"Yes," she said, tugging off her gloves. "And where are you going?"

"The Park," he said, plopping his hat atop his head.

"Again?"

He nodded, smiling.

An hour after Topher's departure, Ruth had cleaned up and was on her way to meet Mr. Kirkhouse at his lodgings. Traipsing about the town unattended had become quite natural to her, and she relished in the freedom, even as she lamented her own lack of respectability and the knowledge that the liberty was only temporary.

Just as Topher had said, Mr. Kirkhouse was a likable fellow. He welcomed Ruth with a flash across his countenance of the same surprise Oxley had shown—but unlike Oxley, Kirkhouse said nothing. He must have trusted Topher—or Mr. Franks, as Ruth had to remind herself to refer to him.

Ruth didn't know whether to be happy or dismayed when Mr. Kirkhouse revealed that it was Miss Parkham he was in love with. When Ruth admitted that she was slightly acquainted with her by virtue of Miss Devenish, Mr. Kirkhouse's expression lit up, and he spent the next few minutes enumerating her best qualities. He was captivated by her but a victim to self-doubt. Miss Parkham was widely admired, and Kirkhouse felt undeserving.

Ruth asked him a number of questions to gain a sense of whether Miss Parkham returned his regard, and she felt satisfied that she did indeed do so. She offered him encouragement and advice, eliciting profuse thanks from him as she went on her way. She was genuine in her wishes that he experience success in his suit and invited him to send her a note if he needed any further advice.

With less than two weeks until the Walthams' masquerade, Ruth encouraged Oxley to seek out Miss Devenish as often as he could—within reason. She offered to ride with him to the Park, feeling it would seem a less pointed encounter if they came upon Miss Devenish together. Ruth hoped she might accomplish a few of her own tasks while she was there—discovering whose company Miss Devenish had been keeping and speaking with Miss Parkham to gauge her interest in Mr. Kirkhouse.

To Ruth's satisfaction, both women—accompanied by Miss Devenish's mother—were seen walking along the Serpentine River.

"What do you know of Miss Parkham?" Ruth asked of Oxley when they spotted the women.

Oxley glanced at her, the hint of a knowing smile on his lips. "A fair amount. Why do you ask?" He cocked a teasing brow.

Ruth laughed. Oh, the irony of it all. "I was merely curious. She seems to be in company with Miss Devenish every time I see her."

"Yes, they are cousins, you know. Miss Parkham's own parents died years ago, and she is the ward of her grandfather. Mrs. Devenish is often tasked with her chaperonage. I believe her parents left her with a tidy sum."

As they approached the women, Ruth couldn't help feeling that Miss Parkham was needlessly overshadowed by her cousin. They were both eminently eligible young women, but Miss Devenish seemed to have an edge in both wealth and beauty, besides possessing a more confident demeanor than Miss Parkham. It was little wonder that either of them should be admired by marriageable gentlemen.

Mrs. Devenish was pleased enough to cede her charges to Ruth and Oxley, taking a seat on the nearest bench where she could fulfill her duties with less exertion. After their initial greetings, Ruth deftly captured the attention of Miss Parkham, leaving Miss Devenish to Oxley, determinedly ignoring the little pinch of regret she felt. This was her purpose in Town. She had no other, no matter what her heart would have her believe.

Ruth had only been speaking with Miss Parkham for a matter of minutes when the young woman glanced down the lane which followed the river and began blushing and averting her eyes. A quick look in that direction told Ruth all she needed to know—and brought a silent wave of relief over her. It was Mr. Kirkhouse, approaching in his curricle.

"Ah, it is Mr. Kirkhouse," Ruth said, waving him down from a dozen yards away. "Do you know him?"

"Yes," Miss Parkham said, cheeks infused with pink.

"He is the best of fellows, isn't he?" Ruth said.

Miss Parkham offered an embarrassed, muttered agreement with

Ruth's words, but there was no mistaking the mutual admiration as Mr. Kirkhouse slowed to a stop beside them, alighting from the equipage and handing the reins off to his tiger.

Ruth remained with the two of them for a moment, ensuring that the conversation was off to a good start, before excusing herself to ask Mrs. Devenish a question. She stepped back, a satisfied smile on her face as she looked at the two couples. And if her heart panged as she watched Oxley and Miss Devenish laugh, she hardly regarded it, choosing instead to address herself to Mrs. Devenish on the wrought-iron bench beside the lane.

They spoke for a few minutes, allowing Oxley time to gain the momentum Ruth had spoken of earlier. Oxley glanced over at Ruth, the smile on his face reflected in Miss Devenish's expression, and Ruth gave him a subtle nod. On the ride to the Park, she had advised that he make an effort to end the conversation with Miss Devenish at a high point—to leave her wanting more. How anyone could leave Oxley's company *without* wanting more was admittedly a mystery to Ruth.

She hadn't been able to speak with Miss Devenish alone, but it was just as well. Oxley seemed to be making headway with her, and that was more important than any unverifiable rumors. She still couldn't fathom that a woman could be anything but a welcome recipient of Oxley's attentions.

They bid the women and Mr. Kirkhouse farewell, untying their horses from the nearest posts, and following the route of the Serpentine.

"Well, that went much better than I could have hoped for," Oxley said, wearing the smile of success. "Your advice about focusing on making a friend of her rather than a wife bore fruit. I even succeeded in making her laugh two or three times."

"Yes," Ruth said. "I noticed."

"I mean to make you proud as a pupil," he said, sending her that charming smile that sent her heart into her throat. "Good day, Munroe."

Ruth's muscles tensed as she met eyes with Mr. Munroe, and she didn't miss the hint of a sneer that pulled at his lip.

"Good day, my lord," Mr. Munroe said, inclining his head at Oxley. His gaze returned to Ruth.

"You are acquainted with Mr. Henry Ruth, are you not?" Oxley asked.

"Yes," Munroe said. "What interesting company you choose to keep, Oxley." His contemptuous smile made Ruth's heart beat more quickly, and she was glad that she had met Munroe in Oxley's company. She felt safer with him. It was unfortunate that he came to find her with Miss Parkham and Miss Devenish again, though. She had the sense that he regarded her as some type of competitor. If he only knew....

"And now," said Munroe. "If you will excuse me, gentlemen, I see some acquaintances." And with a tip of his head at Oxley and the merest flicker of his eyes at Ruth, he continued on his way toward Miss Devenish and Miss Parkham.

Ruth felt her neck and cheeks warming at Munroe's treatment of her—and at the knowledge that she didn't reflect well upon Lord Oxley.

Oxley looked over his shoulder in Munroe's direction. "He sees some acquaintances? More like victims. If only we had been ten minutes later in our arrival, I might have saved Miss Devenish from his attentions. Miss Parkham, too."

Ruth glanced at him, wondering if he felt the same jealousy over Miss Devenish that Ruth did over him. "Surely Munroe doesn't consider himself a real candidate?"

Oxley sent her a look full of meaning. "Oh, I assure you he does. For both Miss Devenish and Miss Parkham. He was a friend of Mr. Parkham's before the man passed, and it was fairly well-known that he intended to have Miss Parkham to wife—until he met Miss Devenish, that is. Somehow, he now feels he has a claim to both women, with Miss Parkham being the contingency plan if he is unsuccessful with Miss Devenish."

Ruth's stomach sank. Of all the people in London, she had managed to involve herself with the two women Mr. Munroe wanted.

"I see you have been so unfortunate as to incur his displeasure."

"Yes," Ruth said. "I told you how I came upon Miss Devenish in the Park and how I stepped in. It was *his* conversation I cut short by pretending an acquaintance with her. He was far from pleased."

Oxley chuckled. "No, I am sure he was not. The man has a volatile temper—he cannot abide being crossed."

Ruth ignored the misgiving she felt. If she could manage to have everything in order between Miss Devenish and Oxley by the Walthams' masquerade, she and Topher could return to Marsbrooke where she would be able to put Mr. Munroe's dislike of her aside—and hopefully her fast-growing feelings for the viscount. "He certainly seems to think less of you after seeing me in your company."

"All the more reason for you to accompany me anywhere I might happen upon him. There is something terribly satisfying about irritating Munroe. And he makes it so easy." Oxley looked at her. "Does his dislike worry you?"

She forced a smile. "A bit, if I am being quite honest. I am not accustomed to people taking notice of me—for good or ill."

"Even with *those* spectacles?" Oxley said with his teasing smile. He was trying to set her at ease, and the gesture warmed her heart. But he didn't know about Kirkhouse and Miss Parkham, and the thought of what he might say if he did know was like a bucket of cold water from the Serpentine on her heart. They had never explicitly stated that Ruth could not take on other clients, but Oxley certainly wouldn't have appeared with her in public if he had any idea that she would be recognized by anyone as The Swan. She fervently hoped that Mr. Kirkhouse was as discreet as Topher had assured her he was. Perhaps she should have said something to him explicitly.

Oxley seemed to notice that she was still anxious, and his face took on a more serious expression. "Munroe is one of those small men who is always in search of someone to bully. The more you show him any fear, the more you play into his hands. There is no love lost between Munroe and me, either, but he knows I won't stand for his harassing."

Ruth smiled wryly. "I rather think the triad is at play there. He would be a fool to attempt bullying you."

"Perhaps so, but Munroe has underestimated you, and I hope you will ensure he realizes it the next time he attempts to make you feel small."

They approached the fork in the lane, one route curving around and skirting Kensington Gardens, the other cutting through the center of the Park toward Oxford Street.

"I have some business at the silversmith's," Oxley said. "Join me?"

Ruth wanted to. She would have spent every moment of the day in his company if she could have. But she was not so lost to sense that she imagined such an approach was in her best interests. Her time with Lord Oxley should be restricted to business. She needed to take the rest of the day to remind herself of that—to refocus her mind and her heart on her purpose.

"I would that I could," she said, entirely in earnest. "I told Franks that I would sit down with him to go over some papers." It wasn't a full-fledged lie. She and Topher *did* need to go over things together—Topher needed a reminder of their purpose as much as she did. Whether her twin could be found at home was another matter.

Oxley nodded. "When do we next meet, then?"

"Tomorrow?"

Oxley grimaced, though a hint of a smile lightened the gesture. "I am afraid I have a longstanding engagement—tea with Anne and Mary."

Ruth smiled as she remembered watching him with them at the church. "Ah, yes. Well, I would never encourage you to court their displeasure by crying off. Friday, then?"

Oxley nodded, and they bid one another farewell. Knowing she wouldn't see him for two days, she knew a bit of regret at having refused the invitation to accompany him to Oxford Street.

She followed the lane past the deer pound and Kensington Gardens, her brow furrowed. Having so few acquaintances in Town, she wasn't obliged to stop or even greet anyone on her ride, despite it being the fashionable hour and full of smartly-dressed ladies and gentlemen. She was at her leisure to observe those around her—and to feel keenly just how different was the world she was currently living in.

Surrounded by such opulence and gaiety and living in Upper Brook Street, just a stone's throw from the Park, it was easy to forget the life she had come from, as if the year she had spent in Marsbrooke was the temporary situation rather than this short time in London. But the truth was, Ruth and her family couldn't even afford a doll imitating the style of the women she was riding by, much less live the lifestyle of such women.

But there was little use lamenting what couldn't be helped, and surely she wouldn't trade George's wet kisses for a life in Town, even were it a possibility. She was an impostor here in every way imaginable.

She froze, hands jerking at the reins slightly. Her horse tossed its head and danced skittishly as a phaeton approached, and Ruth absently nodded her apology at the driver and the woman beside him as they whipped by. She blinked and retrained her eyes at the cause of her distraction.

But there was no mistaking the waistcoat, nor the shade of lavender of the woman's dress, partially concealed though the couple was by the little copse of trees they stood within.

Chapter Eighteen

Nor was there any mistaking the way Topher held Miss Devenish's hand within his, clasped up by his chest in a manner that left little doubt of their relationship. Far from repulsing Topher's intimacy, Miss Devenish was looking up into his eyes, a shy smile on her lips. A quick glance told Ruth that Miss Parkham and Mrs. Devenish were walking together, ahead of Topher and Miss Devenish, who seemed to have stopped when they came upon the obliging grove of trees.

Ruth pulled at the reins, slowing her horse to a bare walk, unable to take her eyes from the scene before her as panic welled inside her. All of Topher's time away from Upper Brook Street, his abnormally good humor, his unwillingness to tell her anything of his activities during their stay in Town...was *this* truly what he had been at? Courting Miss Devenish?

How foolish Ruth had been to assume his good humor was merely a result of being in Town! She should have noticed before what she saw now, clear as day: the flush of infatuation.

She swung down from her horse, tugging it along with her as she swallowed down the bile rising in her throat.

"Franks!" she said as she came upon them.

Their heads whipped around, and unwelcome surprise immediately shadowed Topher's eyes.

"Mr. Ruth," said Miss Devenish, showing far less embarrassment than Topher. "We meet again."

Ruth forced a smile. "Indeed. It is always a pleasure to come upon you, Miss Devenish." That was certainly an untruth in this situation, but Ruth wasn't so angry to realize that Miss Devenish bore no blame here. "I am afraid I have to spirit Mr. Franks away from you, though. We have an engagement that we cannot forgo." She resisted the impulse to seize her brother's arm and perhaps drag him behind her horse through the Park.

Topher looked at her warily but nodded. "Just so. I must have lost track of the time. Allow me to accompany you back to your mother and Miss Parkham."

"No," Ruth said blankly. Realizing how authoritative she sounded, she forced a brittle-sounding chuckle. "It looks as though they are waiting for you, Miss Devenish." She nodded to indicate where the two women stood twenty yards distant.

Ruth and Topher both executed their bows, and Miss Devenish sent the latter a smile that made Ruth's stomach plummet to the ground. Heaven help all of them. She didn't dare consider the ramifications of what she had just witnessed.

When Miss Devenish had disappeared, Ruth swung around toward her horse. Her jaw was so tightly clenched, she didn't know if she could have spoken even if she wanted to. As it was, she had no desire to treat everyone at the Park to the display Topher would be subjected to when they arrived back in Upper Brook Street.

He seemed to sense that trouble was brewing and forbore speaking with Ruth. Everything within her pushed her to ride the remainder of the way at a gallop, but Topher was on foot, and she had to content herself with keeping a pace that forced him to take long strides, interspersed with a few skips here and there to keep up.

She said nothing as she handed the horse off to the groom, and maintained her silence as they walked up the three steps to the townhouse, nor did she say a word as they scaled the stairs inside. Not until the door closed behind them in Topher's bedchamber did she turn toward her twin.

"Have you lost your senses?"

He sighed and pulled off his hat. "*I know*, Ruth. She is so far above my reach that it seems like madness! But she *loves* me. And I love her."

Ruth tossed her hat onto the bed and rubbed her forehead harshly, not trusting herself to say anything even approaching civility to her brother. She felt trapped in a nightmare.

"I wasn't even aware you were acquainted with her," Topher said, "but if you are, I imagine you understand why I feel the way I do."

Ruth whipped around, staring at him with round eyes and knit brows. "*Acquainted* with her? What kind of fool's prank is this?"

He blinked at her. "Prank? I assure you it is no prank. I am in earnest, Ruth. And I should think you might understand now why I didn't wish to tell you of Rebecca. Only look how you are reacting."

"Rebecca?" She covered her eyes with both of her hands, groaning. Her anger reared its head again, and she let her hands drop to her sides. "Topher, you can never see her again." She stared at him with as much force as she could muster. "Ever. Do you understand? Go back to Marsbrooke if you cannot muster the discipline for such an arrangement, but you *cannot* continue seeing her."

His brow blackened. "I cannot, can I? You would have me abandon the woman I love—and who loves me in return?"

She was momentarily bereft of speech. "And *you* would risk everything I am working toward for a woman who doesn't even know your true name?"

He looked away. "I am going to tell her. She will understand. She loves me for who I am—not for my name."

"Does she? Does she know that you haven't a penny to your name and have taken to smuggling to help feed your family?"

"She won't care. She doesn't care about money, Ruth. She is better than that."

Ruth scoffed. "So you shall tell her, shall you? And will you tell

Oxley as well? Will *he* be so understanding? For I can assure you that it is *you* and not I who will tell him."

Topher shot her an annoyed glance. "Of course I shan't tell Oxley. It is none of his business."

"None of—" Ruth stared at her twin, uncomprehending. "He is paying me two hundred pounds to help him win her over! No doubt you wish for me to continue on as usual, defrauding him of his money while my own brother pays his addresses to her?"

Topher's face went pale, his eyes round, as though he was staring at a ghost. His cravat bobbed. "You mean Miss Devenish is the woman Oxley wishes to marry?"

"Of course she is!"

His head shook slowly from side to side in horror.

Ruth stared at him, trying to understand his reaction—there was no acting or artifice in it. "You...you mean to say you didn't know?"

"No! No. I was certain that...I...I...you must not have said her name."

"Surely I have!" But she was not sure. They had spoken little of the specifics of Oxley's situation. Topher was rarely at home to speak with. And now she knew why.

Topher shook his head again. "I swear I never knew, Ruth, I..." Grief began to dispel the horror in his eyes, and he slumped down upon his bed, eyes unfocused.

Ruth forced herself to take a deep breath. Topher *hadn't* intentionally undermined what she was doing with Oxley. It was a mistake.

A terrible mistake.

She sat down beside him and put a hand on his back, speaking softly. "I am sorry, Topher. I am. But you *must* end things with her."

His jaw hardened, and his nostrils flared. "I cannot."

Ruth's hand dropped, and anger warmed her blood again as she shifted to face him. "You can, and you must. I did not make all of these sacrifices only for you to—"

Topher let out a caustic laugh. "Sacrifices? *Sacrifices?* You aren't sacrificing anything! You are in love with Oxley, Ruth! I'm not so blind I couldn't see that after five minutes at his house with you."

Heat seared Ruth's cheeks. "I am not. He is a friend. It is business."

Topher raised a brow at her. "Well, which is it? You may be deceiving Oxley, and you may be deceiving yourself, but you aren't deceiving me."

"It doesn't matter." Ruth turned her body and jerked at the cravat around her neck, mortified to find that tears had sprung to her eyes. "The fact is, I cannot have Oxley any more than you can have Miss Devenish. For a dozen reasons."

"She loves me, Ruth," Topher said, rising to a stand so that he looked down at her.

Ruth rose to face him. "I don't care." Her chest heaved.

"No," Topher said, disgust and rage on his face. "You *don't* care. You cannot have your precious viscount, so you want me to be as miserable as you are." He whirled around and walked toward the escritoire, kicking at one of the legs.

All at once, Ruth's energy withered. She slumped over and let her head fall into her hands. Her spectacles dug into the bridge of her nose, and she tore them off, tossing them on the bed and rubbing at the area. "I don't wish you to be miserable, Topher. You say Miss Devenish loves you, but does she *know* you? Does she know that you are poor?"

He swallowed and looked away.

"You wear a disguise just as I do, Topher. And, kind and good as her heart may be, she will not marry a poor man, especially one who has deceived her. Her family won't allow it. I spoke to her mother only today, and while they will let her choose her husband, there are limits to how far that boundary extends. We are well outside of those limits."

"Her parents like me," Topher said. But she could hear the doubt in his voice.

"Of course they do. They would be foolish not to—you are charming and kind. But, while their love for their daughter might extend to her choosing a mere gentleman over a viscount, you cannot possibly think that they would look upon the match with equanimity when they discover the true state of things."

Topher's nostrils flared, and his chin quivered slightly as he sat down slowly in the desk chair, resting his elbows on his knees. He scrubbed a hand over his face.

Ruth swallowed the lump in her throat and looked away. In her brother's face, she saw her own pain—the pain of admitting that what he wanted with all his heart simply could not be. She rose from the bed and stepped toward him, kneeling so that she could look up into his face.

"In less than a fortnight, we will return home to Mama." She took one of his hands in hers. "We may both return with broken hearts, but we will *not* return empty-handed. And I cannot help hoping that, when we see the relief and joy upon Mama's face, and when we watch the children delight in a full meal, it will be a bit of salve on our wounds." She pressed his hand.

They remained in silence for a few minutes, and when Ruth spoke again, she kept her voice soft. "How did this happen, Toph?"

He didn't respond for a moment, and when he did, his voice sounded heavy. "I met her that first night in Town. I'd made friends with Rowney over a hand of cards and a glass of port at a brewery not far from here, and he insisted I join him at a small party near his lodgings. I agreed—I liked the fellow, and it seemed like my best chance of spending an amusing evening. Rebecca was there—the most angelic creature I have ever laid eyes on."

His eyes glazed over with memory, and some of the pain on his face dissipated. "When an impromptu dance began, I excused myself, not knowing the figures well enough to join in with confidence. Rebecca was sitting out, of course, for she hasn't danced in more than a year. Rowney suggested we keep one another company, and so we did. And she was every bit as angelic in person as I had thought her from across the room. More so, even. I knew I would likely never see her again—we would be leaving Town soon. And that knowledge gave me confidence."

His mouth turned up in a small half-smile. "I made her laugh, asked her question after question. I wanted to know everything about her. And when she asked me about myself, I did as you suggested." He shrugged his shoulders. "I tried to forget we ever left Dunburn—answered as if she was meeting the Topher Hawthorn of two years ago—the heir of Dunburn instead of the Topher Hawthorn who shares a room with his three younger brothers." His head moved slowly from side to side. "I could see and feel the connection between us—so much that when Rowney and I returned to his lodgings after the party, I felt like I had lost my future all over again."

He let out a sigh and dropped his head. "I drank deeply that night and slept until late. Didn't want to wake up to reality, I suppose. So when you told me Oxley was willing to pay you to stay on, I was elated. I couldn't help myself—couldn't keep myself from seeking her out wherever I could. And she wanted me to, Ruth. She welcomed it."

Ruth nodded.

"But you are right." He watched his fingers twiddling in his lap. "She doesn't know me or my name—or that I haven't two shillings to rub together. She deserves better. She deserves someone like Oxley."

Ruth blinked quickly and dashed away a tear from her eye. She knew his pain. But at least Miss Devenish loved him in return. Or perhaps that made him more to be pitied—what he wanted was within reach, and that would make giving it up all the more painful. Ruth's desires were mere foolish fantasies.

Topher looked up at Ruth again. "Does Oxley love her?"

Ruth pressed her lips together. "He respects and admires her. And I think he will come to love her in time."

Topher looked away, clenching his eyes shut. Silence reigned for some time, both of them lost in the pain of the reality they faced.

"I will tell her," Topher finally said.

"Tell her what? You cannot tell her the truth."

He lifted his shoulders. "I will figure something out."

Ruth sighed. "Even if you do, there is no guarantee she will take Oxley. Not if she is so deeply in love with *you*."

His hand balled into a fist within hers, and he met her gaze, his forehead heavy-laden with soberness. "She will if I make it clear that there is no chance of a future for us—if I inspire her with dislike of me. Besides, you *can* make them love each other. It is what you do."

Ruth shut her eyes. "I don't know if I can, Topher. I am not, much as I wish I were, an unbiased observer." She lowered her gaze. "But I have to try." Her chin attempted to quiver, and she set her jaw. "They are both good people, and they stand a very good chance at happiness together."

He stood abruptly, as if her words had singed him. "I will tell her tomorrow." He stood by the door, as if inviting her to leave.

She rose slowly and walked toward him, stopping for a moment. "I *am* sorry, Topher. I truly am."

Chapter Nineteen

Philip took a dainty sip, allowing his pinky finger to stick out and watching his nieces over the top of his empty teacup. After one sip, he had made the difficult choice to gulp it all down at once, hoping to minimize the amount of time he was exposed to the questionable concoction. Apparently he was not like Ruth's father—he would rather get it all over with than draw it out.

Mary giggled in delight, and Anne smiled with approval. "I hope the tea is to your liking."

Philip set down his cup on its plate, but his pinky finger remained extended. "Indeed," he said in a high-pitched, shrill voice. "The best I have ever tasted, I declare."

More giggles ensued.

The door opened, and Alice stopped in the doorway, smiling at the scene before her. "I should rather think your tea had gone cold by now."

"Oh, no," Anne said. "This is a second batch. Uncle Phil drank the entire first batch."

He had. At great cost to himself. This second batch was worse.

Alice stepped into the room. "I hadn't any idea he was so fond of tea. I am afraid that this tea party must come to an end, though. It is time for your lessons, girls. Go on. Mrs. Morris is waiting for you."

The girls dipped into curtsies for Philip then scurried from the room. He smiled and rose from the chair he had been sitting in—a miniscule thing meant for children. It had taken considerable effort not to break it. His thighs ached from the effort of keeping much of his weight from it.

"How are things with Miss Devenish?" Alice asked.

Straight to it, then. She was never one for beating around the bush. "Well enough. We shall see, though, after the Walthams' masquerade."

"There is much you should be doing now, though, Philip, in preparation for—"

"I know, Alice. I know. And rest assured, I am doing those things."

Her brow furrowed. "It hardly seems so. You seem to be spending all of your time with that Ruth fellow."

Philip scoffed. "Does everyone track my movements, or is it just you and Finmore?"

"I am your sister. It is my business to keep apprised of your dealings. But how *did* you come to befriend such a strange fellow?"

Philip shrugged. "He is an old acquaintance. Why does it matter?"

"I suppose it doesn't. When I first saw him with you, I didn't know what to think. Those spectacles are absolutely horrid. But he seems harmless enough. What of Finmore, though? I haven't seen you with him as much of late."

Philip had to stifle a laugh. That his sister would harbor qualms about his friendship with Ruth rather than Finmore was rich indeed. No doubt her concern was whether Ruth added enough to Philip's consequence to merit the amount of time he spent in Ruth's company. But the truth was, after spending so much time on estate business, Philip hadn't even realized how much he needed a good friend. And Ruth was filling that role very well.

"Finmore had to leave town for a few days. Done up, as usual. He shall be back the moment he has a shilling to his name, undoubtedly."

"Hm. Well, I hope you know that my offer still stands to invite Miss Devenish over for dinner—and to give you a few suggestions on how to win her over."

Philip forced a smile. "You are ever helpful, Alice, but no thank you."

She sent him a dissatisfied look. "One would think you would wish to try everything in your power to ensure your success with her, not that I doubt that you will be. Successful, I mean. I have been thinking about it ever since you mentioned her as your choice, and I am of the opinion that you couldn't do better for Oxley Court than Miss Devenish. Certainly she is not from a titled family, which is regrettable, of course, but the Devenishes are nearly as ancient as the Trents, you know, and—"

"I am aware of all the things Miss Devenish has to recommend her."

She smiled. "I know you are. I just want you to be successful, Philip. Oxley Court has been far too long without a mistress, and everyone awaits news of your choice with bated breath. I am merely glad that you have made such a fine choice, and I look forward to the time when I can greet Miss Devenish as my sister."

He offered a tight smile in return. Her words were little comfort to him. She continued to assume that Miss Devenish would accept him, and the more Alice pressed him on the matter, the more annoyed he became; the more he found himself wanting to do something contrary. He quashed the immature desire.

"Thank you, Alice." He kissed her cheek. "I am afraid I must go now."

Chapter Twenty

On Friday, Ruth stepped down from the curricle in front of the house in Upper Brook Street, hurrying up the steps. She hadn't expected to spend so long with Mr. Kirkhouse. He had requested a second meeting, and Ruth had taken advantage of the time before her next appointment with Oxley to oblige the man.

He had offered her another five pounds at the end of the meeting, but Ruth hadn't accepted. Somehow it felt less like a betrayal of Oxley—as though she was merely assisting a friend rather than acting as the Swan. "You have hardly needed my help, Mr. Kirkhouse. I am quite confident that your suit would have been successful even without my assistance."

Mr. Kirkhouse had denied this, expressing how it was only after following Ruth's advice that Miss Parkham had expressed that she returned his regard. The man was over the moon and planned to address himself to her grandfather soon. He merely needed some help knowing how to present himself to Miss Parkham's guardian in the way most conducive to success.

Topher was in his room, sitting on his bed with his back against the headboard, running a finger along the brim of his hat. He glanced up when Ruth stepped into the doorway then returned his eyes to the hat.

"You saw her?" Ruth asked.

He gave a slight nod.

She crossed over to the bed with a sigh, sitting gently on the edge. "How did she take it?"

He swallowed. "She didn't understand," he said softly. "And what was I to say? I couldn't explain, for it would..." He trailed off.

"Undermine Oxley's suit and expose me."

He rubbed his forehead. "She despises me now. Thinks I was toying with her emotions. It's all I could tell her—that my feelings had changed."

"I am terribly sorry, Topher."

He looked away. "Kirkhouse is having success, it would seem."

"Yes. He hopes to receive permission from Miss Parkham's guardian."

He didn't respond for a moment, only staring at his hat. "I think I just need some time alone."

She nodded, wishing she could say something to ease his pain; wishing that everything was different.

She was late arriving to Brook Street, and she had to take an extra moment to compose herself before entering. The last thing she needed was to bring a somber mood with her.

But the moment she saw Oxley and the wide smile she had come to expect from him, her heart plummeted again. Why must he be so captivating? And so utterly out of her reach?

It was impossible to hold onto such morose feelings in his company, though. To be with Philip Trent was to feel light and full. It was to laugh and be teased. It was to have a friend like none she had ever had.

It was only when she left him that the weight set in again, that she realized what an impossible tangle she had made for herself—and for Topher.

Ruth had never been to a London ball.

Of course, she had imagined attending such events when she had lived at Dunburn. She had wondered if she might find her own love story in such a setting, standing across the set from a gentleman and meeting his gaze with that intensity she had sometimes noticed between men and women in the Pump Room.

The irony was not lost upon her that the only ball she would ever set foot in, she would attend as a man, and she would do so in the presence of the man she had fallen in love with. She would stand beside him and then stand alone as he left her side to lead other women onto the ballroom floor.

In an unexpected gesture, Miss Devenish had apparently changed her mind about when she would emerge from her mourning. She wore a blue satin gown that set her eyes on fire and made Ruth clutch at her stomach to dispel the envious ache. She was ravishing. And she showed no timidity as she danced with Oxley. Whatever she had felt upon speaking with Topher, there was no evidence that it had done anything but grant her energy.

As she looked on, Ruth felt robbed. Of what, she couldn't say precisely. Of another week with Oxley before he started courting Miss Devenish in earnest, perhaps? He hardly appeared to need her help anymore. There was no hint of awkwardness in the way he looked at Miss Devenish, his mouth stretched in a smile whenever they had the chance to speak during the steps of the dance. He had cleared the hurdle and seemed to be at ease with her now.

Ruth vowed not to tell Topher what she observed that evening. She would spare him what she herself was forced to watch: Miss Devenish in the highest of spirits, laughing with Lord Oxley as they skipped down the set of a country dance. Her lesson with Oxley on humor had apparently been successful. Success these days came with so much chagrin.

Oxley returned to her side after the two dances, slightly breathless, cheeks stretched in a large smile. She managed to return it and even offer a speaking glance.

He took a glass of champagne from the salver of a passing footman and swallowed some. "She has agreed to stand up with me for the waltz as well."

"How wonderful," Ruth said, deciding she would be anywhere but observing when it happened.

Miss Devenish stepped onto the ballroom floor with Sir Allen, and Ruth glanced at Oxley to look for any signs of jealousy. But he was looking at her, not Miss Devenish.

"Will you dance?" Oxley asked.

Ruth's heart thudded against her chest, and she blinked. She glanced down at her clothing, a stark reminder that his meaning was not what her heart had insisted on believing. He was merely curious if she would be asking anyone to dance.

"No," Ruth said, looking toward the ballroom floor as her heart slowed and twinged. "I am here on business, you know."

"I hereby release you from that obligation." Oxley set a hand on her shoulder, extending his champagne glass and making a sweeping motion with it to show the crowds around the ballroom. "Surely there is a woman here who captures your fancy, and I would wager I am acquainted with her family and could easily procure you an introduction."

Ruth was hardly aware of what he was saying, so conscious was she of his hand on her shoulder. It gripped her with the force of friendship and fraternity, in stark contrast to the way he would hold Miss Devenish during the waltz.

"Thank you," Ruth said. "But I have never been a skilled dancer." It wasn't true. She was actually quite a graceful dancer. But not as a man.

"Then I will keep you company," he said.

And he did. And Ruth could no more resist smiling in his company than she could resist breathing. Until the waltz set began forming on the floor.

"She is waiting for me," Oxley said. "Wish me luck."

Ruth watched him stride over to Miss Devenish and bow, setting

Miss Devenish's hand on his arm again, their smiles turned toward each other like reflecting mirrors.

"Mr. Ruth." Mr. Kirkhouse approached, Miss Parkham on his arm. "We are so pleased to see you here."

Miss Parkham smiled and looked up into Mr. Kirkhouse's eyes through her dark lashes.

"Good evening to you both," Ruth said with a genuine smile. Here was a success she could enjoy fully.

"I wanted to ensure that you received the first introduction to...my affianced wife."

Ruth's jaw dropped open, and she looked between the two of them. "Is it true?"

Miss Parkham nodded energetically, a becoming blush making her cheeks rosy. "My grandfather agreed just this morning."

"What wonderful news!" She tried to be less effusive than she normally would have been, taking care to keep her voice low as she took their hands in hers. "I felicitate both of you with all my heart."

"We owe a debt of gratitude to you," Mr. Kirkhouse said, setting his hand atop Miss Parkham's and looking at her with a warm smile. "And we hoped to show a measure of it by offering you a new client."

Ruth smiled nervously. "I thank you for your thoughtfulness. Truly, it is very kind of you to wish to help me, but I am not taking on any clients at this time."

"I understand you wish for anonymity," said Mr. Kirkhouse. "We have both kept things entirely to ourselves, saving a brief conversation with Miss Munroe, who has promised to be *very* discreet."

Ruth stared. "Miss Munroe?"

Mr. Kirkhouse and Miss Parkham nodded simultaneously.

Ruth shut her eyes, nausea swelling inside her. Did no one understand what discretion meant? "I am sure she will be, but unfortunately, I must still decline. I would be happy to send her a letter with the advice from my weekly column if you were to provide me with her direction. And I must beg of you to keep my identity a strict secret."

Miss Parkham nodded quickly. "Of course. We shan't tell a soul.

And we certainly wouldn't wish to make you uncomfortable. I shall inform Miss Munroe." Her eyes shifted in the direction of the long wall of the ballroom, and Ruth followed them to where Miss Munroe stood beside her brother.

Mr. Munroe's eyes were fixed on Ruth, Miss Parkham, and Mr. Kirkhouse, the same unpleasant curl to his lip that Ruth began to think was his characteristic expression.

"I am sorry to disappoint anyone, naturally," Ruth said, pulling her eyes away, "but I am very happy for the two of you. Congratulations."

They bid her good evening and excused themselves. Like a magnet, Ruth's gaze found Oxley on the dance floor with Miss Devenish, one hand about her waist, the other raised above them clasping hers, their faces only inches apart.

Ruth looked away and hurried across the floor in a stride that would have been impossible in a chemise and gown.

She squeezed through a group of matrons gossiping, passed through the French doors, and emerged onto the terrace, where the blessed, cool night air prickled at the small gap between her hair and her cravat. Her chest strained against the wrap constricting it, and she let out a slow gush of air, putting a hand to the back of her head, a lingering habit from when there had been a coiffure to grasp.

"Excuse me," said a voice behind her.

Ruth turned and found Miss Munroe looking at her. It was difficult to see any of her facial features clearly with the candlelight shining from behind, but Miss Munroe carried herself with the confidence of someone who was accustomed to having her way, chin held high and a determined glint in her shadowed eyes.

"Are you the Swan?"

Ruth glanced to see whether Miss Munroe's brother was anywhere nearby. "I think you must be mistaken, miss."

She shook her head and took another step toward Ruth. "No, no. I am quite sure. For it was Miss Parkham who told me so."

"She, too, was mistaken then, I'm afraid. If you will excuse me."

Ruth bowed slightly and moved to walk around Miss Munroe, who grabbed her arm with a gloved hand.

"I need your help, sir, and I assure you, I will make it well worth your while." There was a purposeful set to Miss Munroe's chin, and she held Ruth's gaze intently. "Please help me."

Ruth grimaced. "I am very sorry, miss, but I cannot help you." Miss Munroe's grip tightened on Ruth's arm, and Ruth looked at her in surprise, prying the fingers away.

"Unhand her!" Through the terrace doors came Mr. Munroe, fire blazing in his eyes.

Ruth's hand dropped immediately from Miss Munroe's.

"You lead my sister out here as if she were some trollop!" Munroe said, coming to stand before Ruth, nearly a full head taller than she and staring down into her eyes so closely that she could smell the spirits on his breath.

"You are mistaken, sir," Ruth said. "She followed *me*."

"Mistaken, am I?" He looked to Miss Munroe, who swallowed, the fear of her brother reflected in her eyes. "Did you follow him?"

Miss Munroe shook her head, eyes wide. "Of course not!"

Ruth's jaw went slack, but Miss Munroe avoided her eye.

Munroe turned back toward Ruth, anger and energy warring in his narrowed gaze. "You seem to have made yourself very familiar indeed with the young women in Town since your arrival, Ruth. I cannot say I am surprised to discover that you are pushing your unwelcome attentions upon them."

Ruth's words stuck in her throat. To be accused by Mr. Munroe of the exact thing he himself stood guilty of—and of something so very far from the truth for herself...it was lunacy.

"You have quite misunderstood the matter," she said, feeling her heart thrum with nerves inside her as two people appeared inside the doorway, observing. "I have not pushed my attentions on any woman, I assure you."

Mr. Munroe bared his teeth, stepping even closer. "You are up to something, Ruth. You have influenced Miss Devenish and Miss

Parkham—turned them against me. I know it. But you won't go anywhere near my sister."

Ruth's hands were sweating inside Topher's gloves, and it took everything she had not to betray just how nervous she was. She glanced at the doorway that opened up to the ballroom and saw Oxley appear there, brows furrowed, as though he had just arrived and was trying to take stock of the situation.

His presence acted as a spur, a reminder of his words in the Park. *Munroe has underestimated you, and I hope you will ensure he realizes it the next time he attempts to make you feel small.*

"Surely I cannot be blamed for your lack of address with women, sir," Ruth said, forcing her knees not to shake. She wouldn't disappoint Oxley.

Mumbling chatter spread through the gathering crowd.

Mr. Munroe grabbed her by the lapel. "What did you say?"

She looked him in the eye, willing herself to keep her courage. "I am sorry that you have found your suits unsuccessful, Mr. Munroe. But that is none of my affair or concern."

Miss Munroe had backed away from them, taking her place amongst the crowd, leaving Ruth to clean up the mess. Ruth lowered her voice slightly, ever-aware of their growing audience. "And I certainly harbor no designs upon your sister. As I said, *she* followed *me*."

Munroe snarled. "You cast aspersions upon her reputation, then?"

Oxley rushed over. "Let him go, Munroe." He took hold of Munroe's hand, and Munroe wrested his arm away.

"Name your seconds, Ruth!" Munroe said.

Ruth momentarily forgot how to breathe.

"Don't be ridiculous," said Oxley.

"This is between myself and this insolent Jack Sprat, my lord." Munroe spat out the last word.

Ruth swallowed. "A duel will change nothing, sir. I mean no offense to your sister—I merely convey the truth of what happened."

Munroe's sneer appeared. "You mean to back down. A coward, are you? Willing to lay your hands on a woman but not to meet a man to defend your honor?"

Murmurs snaked through the crowd.

"I shall say it again. I don't think much of the company you keep, my lord." Munroe sneered at Oxley.

Oxley offered a tight smile. "Rest assured the sentiment is reciprocated."

Ruth's heart ached to see Oxley coming to her defense. She was trapped—both her honor and Oxley's were now in question, and she backed down from Munroe at a cost to more than just herself.

She looked to Oxley, who watched her intently. "Will you act for me?" she asked.

"Of course." Oxley said, but she could see the troubled look in his eyes.

"Archer?" Munroe said, and a stocky man stepped out from the crowd, nodding.

"I will wait upon you tomorrow morning, Mr. Archer," Oxley said, "if you will be so good as to provide me with your direction."

The men stepped aside for a short discussion, and Ruth stood waiting, wishing that the half-circle of people would disappear back into the ballroom. Her shaking legs might give out on her at any moment, and she wanted no audience when it happened.

Mr. Munroe's gaze was fixed on her, his lip curled in a mix between a snarl and a smile. No doubt he was picturing her with a bullet hole in her chest. She shut her eyes for a brief moment. She had only shot a pistol twice in her life—both occasions many years ago when she had followed Topher on one of his mischievous expeditions with their father's pistol. If she'd had any idea that her life would depend upon her ability to shoot, she might have taken those times more seriously.

Oxley stepped toward her, putting a hand on her back. "Come, let us go inside."

She allowed herself to be ushered forward, feeling a modicum of comfort at the knowledge of Oxley's support. Her only remaining hope for avoiding the duel was that Oxley might persuade Munroe against the affair. Would that everyone was as subject to his charms as Ruth was.

"What happened?" Oxley asked in an undervoice as they stepped out of the ballroom and down the dimly lit corridor.

She let out a gush of air and lifted her shoulders. How in the world was she to explain everything to him? With her nerves fraying and Oxley the only friendly face at the ball, she couldn't face the displeasure he would feel if he knew that word was getting around about her identity as the Swan. Everyone would associate her with Oxley, and she couldn't humiliate him like that—especially not when he had just come to her defense.

"I went out for a breath of fresh air, and Miss Munroe followed after me. She had mistaken me for someone else, but when I told her as much, she tried to prevent me from leaving. It was as I tried to remove her hand from my arm that Munroe came out and misread the situation."

Oxley scoffed. "Willingly misread. He has no doubt been looking for a reason to quarrel with you." He sighed. "I will do what I can to patch things up with him, but our hopes are pinned on the unlikelihood that Mr. Archer is a more reasonable fellow than the man he is acting for. Munroe is not likely to back down." Oxley looked intently at Ruth. "Have you experience with pistols?"

Ruth smiled weakly. "Do I look like a sporting man to you?"

Oxley chuckled lightly. "I had a small hope that you had some secret, unexpected expertise with them. It wouldn't be the first time you have surprised me. But no matter. After I call on Archer tomorrow, I will come to Upper Brook Street. I know a bit about pistols." He winked.

"As much as Munroe?"

He drew back. "You offend me."

He was trying to lighten the situation, and she couldn't help but respond, putting a hand to her heart. "Forgive me for ever doubting Narcissus."

Oxley bowed ironically. "You are forgiven." He rose from the bow and looked at her intently. "Are you nervous?"

"You offend *me* now. You mustn't be deceived by these glasses. Behind my diminutive person, I hide nerves of steel."

"If your nerves are made of anything as solid as those spectacles, then I have nothing at all to fear. It was all I could do to keep from cheering when you insulted Munroe. Not just any man would show such courage."

Courage? Ruth had a few other names for it: rashness, foolhardiness, impetuosity, and above all, desperation not to disappoint Oxley. Whatever one called it, she was sure to regret it. But hearing Oxley praise her boldness warmed her heart and almost made the prospect of dying in a duel worth it. Almost.

Oxley glanced toward the other end of the ballroom. "Now, if you'll excuse me, I promised Miss Devenish a glass of champagne—it was as I went to procure it that I caught sight of the commotion on the terrace. She is no doubt wondering where I disappeared to."

"You must tell her, of course, that you were waylaid by the need to rescue a poor sapling."

Oxley frowned. "I certainly don't think highly of Munroe, but I don't know that I should call him a *poor sapling*." With a wide smile, he left her side, threading through the crowds to find Miss Devenish.

Ruth's smile faded, and she clasped her hands tightly to control their shaking.

Chapter Twenty-One

Philip had left the ball the night before with conflicting emotions. Never had Miss Devenish shown as much receptivity to his attentions as she had there. Indeed, the shift was so great as to surprise Philip mightily. Her warm smiles, her flirting, the flush of her cheeks as they danced—it was gratifying, certainly, and he had finally seemed to find his feet. He had managed to pass the entirety of the evening without making a blunder.

It was just as Ruth had said—the more time he spent in Miss Devenish's company, the more comfortable he felt. And the more he focused on the present, the less nervous he felt about the future.

And yet the evening had not passed in a rush of unalloyed victory. Philip had tried to hide his concern over the affair with Munroe—he hadn't wanted to give offense to Ruth. But the truth was, he was ill-at-ease. Munroe had killed a man in a duel before—a hushed-up affair with rumors of the authorities being paid off. He was volatile and known to hold a grudge. He was also famously blind to the exploits of his sister. Philip had had no trouble believing she had followed Ruth out onto the terrace and perhaps even made advances upon him. But Munroe wouldn't hear a word against her.

The thought that Munroe might kill Ruth made Philip feel sick to his stomach. Only now that he faced the prospect of losing Ruth did he realize how much he had come to value their friendship.

And yet, what could he do? He could try to make Archer see reason, but the fact was, if Munroe was determined to fight, there was little that could be done to avoid it. Nor did Philip harbor much hope that Archer would exercise a calming influence upon his friend. He wasn't well-known to Philip, but he had a mulish look about him that boded ill for a reconciliation between the parties.

He laid awake an hour past the time he slipped into his bed, hoping that he could instruct Ruth well enough the next day that he might get off the first shot at least. Munroe wasn't known as the best shot in London, but what he lacked in precision, he made up for with determination and cold-bloodedness. There was no chance at all of him deloping.

When he awoke the next morning, Philip's stomach churned with unease, a physical reminder of the unenviable task that lay before him. His valet assisted him into his clothes for the day, and, hoping it might perhaps quell his nerves, Philip partook of a quick, early breakfast before making his way to Half Moon Street.

Mr. Archer welcomed him with a brusk manner and stony expression, and Philip stifled a resigned sigh as they stepped into a small study off the main corridor.

Mr. Archer offered him a seat, and Philip took it, setting his hat in his lap. "I appreciate your receiving me, Mr. Archer. I come on behalf of Mr. Ruth, as you know. He has authorized me to express his willingness for reconciliation with Mr. Munroe."

Mr. Archer's lips pressed into a thin line. "I am afraid that the nature of his offense is such that Mr. Munroe is unable to reciprocate such a sentiment. His sister's reputation has been most grievously maligned, and it is his duty to seek reparations."

Philip couldn't stifle a small snort. "Forgive me, sir, but Mr. Munroe seems to be the only person who would doubt that events occurred just as Mr. Ruth said they did."

Mr. Archer stared at him, unamused. "Mr. Ruth has, from the beginning, set himself against Mr. Munroe, always using women in his attempt to do him an injury. Last night, his choice of woman passed the bounds. Such disgraceful behavior cannot go unanswered, my lord."

"Perhaps we might apply to Miss Munroe herself. Or to others who attended the ball. Surely someone must have witnessed the way of things."

Mr. Archer's lip turned up at the side in an unpleasant expression. "Is Mr. Ruth so eager to avoid a meeting with Mr. Munroe?"

Philip's nostrils flared, and he let out a humorless laugh. "On the contrary, sir. Mr. Ruth will meet Mr. Munroe at his earliest convenience."

"Tomorrow, then. Dawn at Kinham Common. By the pond."

Philip nodded. "Very well."

"Does Mr. Ruth prefer pistols or swords?"

"Pistols."

Within a few minutes, everything was settled, and Philip left Half Moon Street with a deeply furrowed brow.

Uncle Jacob's butler greeted Philip with a familiar welcome in Upper Brook Street and told him that Mr. Ruth could be found in the parlor. When Philip entered, Ruth looked up from his chair, a book in hand. He was perhaps a bit paler than usual but otherwise showed no other signs of fear. He seemed to recognize what Philip's expression signified, though, and sighed resignedly.

"I tried," Philip said, coming to sit across from him. "But Munroe *will* insist upon the duel. He has taken the position that you have maligned his sister's delicate reputation"—he widened his eyes to show what he thought of this position—"and must be brought to account."

Ruth nodded. "Thank you for trying—and for being willing to act for me."

"Of course," Philip said. "It is an honor."

Ruth smiled wryly. "You are a terrible liar. I am not foolish enough to think that acting for me adds to your consequence."

Philip waved a hand. "I have more than enough consequence."

That elicited a laugh, and Philip was grateful for the sound. Ruth was more courageous than his appearance gave one to believe, but he couldn't help wondering if his friend was concealing fear and misgiving behind his easy demeanor.

Philip stood. "Come. Let us prepare you to meet Munroe. I believe my uncle has a pair of pistols in the study. We can take them out for some practice." He turned toward the door.

"You don't have to do this, you know."

Philip stopped and looked back over his shoulder.

Ruth met his gaze squarely, his expression grave. "Surely you have better things to do than instructing a greenhorn in shooting."

Philip turned. "And *you* have surely had better things to do than instructing me on how to avoid acting like an utter buffoon in front of women."

"But you are paying me to do so. I cannot pay you for this."

Philip's brows snapped together. "I do this as a friend, Ruth. I don't precisely wish to lose you, you know. You *are* the only panda in England." He smiled. "Besides, how would I ever win Miss Devenish if I allowed Munroe to get the best of you?"

Ruth held his gaze, saying nothing for a moment. "Thank you," he said, rising from his chair.

Philip slowed his horse, and Ruth followed suit. They had come to a clearing, surrounded on all sides by tall oak trees whose leaves rustled as a breeze passed through. Philip swung down from his horse and took the pistol box from its place behind the saddle.

"My uncle used to bring me here to practice shooting," he said, glancing around with a smile. "I imagine you might see the marks from some of my bullets in the trees. Come, we will start at a close range and then draw back as we go."

Ruth had been more silent than usual on the ride there. He had chimed in every now and then with a small joke, but Philip wasn't fooled. He was trying to hide his nerves between fits of distraction, and the only thing Philip could think to do was to help him acquire more confidence by teaching him how to shoot as well as he could in the space of the next two hours.

Philip had little doubt that Munroe would shoot to kill. Why he had taken Ruth in such violent dislike, he didn't know, but the man was hardly the picture of reason or levelheadedness. The fact that he had challenged someone almost half his age to a duel spoke volumes.

"I haven't held a pistol since I was ten or eleven," Ruth said, looking at the long barrel with a frown. "Perhaps I should just delope."

"You could, but Munroe will not. And I think you stand a good chance of getting off the first shot. You are much faster than he, and his aim is not known for being very good."

"I am not sure whether that should relieve me or worry me," Ruth said with a laugh. "What if he aims for my arm and hits me in the heart?"

Philip handed Ruth a pistol, watching with a sense of misgiving at how Ruth held it. It had not been false modesty when Ruth said he wasn't a sporting gentleman.

"Here. Take a shot at that tree." Philip pointed to the widest of the trees before them, an old oak with a trunk spread three feet wide.

Ruth swallowed and took a wider stance with his feet, raising the pistol and pointing it toward the tree. There was a slight pause, and a shot rang out.

"I missed," Ruth said, and Philip laughed.

"You did, and it is no wonder. I think your bullet came nearer to hitting that little sapling a few yards to the left of the target. Here." Philip put out a hand, and Ruth set the pistol in it.

Philip busied himself with reloading. "You want to provide the smallest target you can for Munroe, which means turning your body sideways. Try again." He handed the pistol back to Ruth, who obediently turned his body sideways.

Philip frowned. The pistol looked heavy in Ruth's hands—in need of reinforcement—but Ruth couldn't stabilize it with a second hand without turning his body fully toward Munroe. It was a choice between improving his own accuracy—or widening Munroe's target.

Philip would have liked to see Munroe experience the sting of a gunshot and being out of commission for a time due to his own stupidity, but he would far rather be confident in Ruth's safety.

But Ruth deserved to make that decision for himself.

Philip hesitated. He had lost a mother and a father, but the thought of losing Ruth made him feel cold fear.

"Wait," he said.

Chapter Twenty-Two

Ruth let the pistol drop, relieved at Oxley's instruction to wait. She could feel the pistol shaking in her hands, and it embarrassed her. Who was she trying to deceive? She wasn't brave or courageous. She was nothing but a fool dressed in gentlemen's clothing.

"When I was young, my uncle taught me a couple of tricks to improve my accuracy. One is more dangerous than the other, so I will allow you to decide which you employ." He stepped behind Ruth, and she felt her muscles go tight. "Here, raise the pistol again." He reached around her, and the shaking that had affected her hand coursed up her arm and through her whole body. She clenched her eyes shut, mortified at the way her body was reacting to his proximity, when to Oxley, he was merely helping a friend avoid death. She tightened her jaw and opened her eyes, but what she really wanted was to turn around and bury her head in Oxley's chest—to seek safety in his arms.

"The first method is to aim the pistol at something specific." He moved closer, and Ruth could feel the warmth of his breath grazing the side of her neck. He had his own arm extended, his pointer finger raised so that it hovered in the air right next to her pistol. "Like the first branch on that tree. You must keep both eyes open. Are they open?"

She nodded, certain he could feel her body trembling.

"Very good. Now close your right eye."

She obeyed, and the pistol appeared to shift to the left, moving away from the tree branch she had aimed for. She blinked in surprise.

"Now open both eyes."

She complied, and the pistol moved back into its original position.

"Now close your left eye."

She closed the eye, and the pistol stayed in its place, maintaining her desired target. She turned her head, smiling.

Oxley stepped to the side and smiled back at her. "Now you know which eye to close when you take aim. The second method presents you with a choice. You must decide which is more important to you: your safety or your accuracy. If you wish to do Munroe a harm—and I would be the last person to blame you for such a desire—you have a better chance of doing so by gripping the pistol with a second hand. It is not common in duels—it is frowned upon by many—but it will give you a much better chance of hitting Munroe. To do so, you must face your body forward, offering him a wider target." He surveyed her. "Thankfully for you, you are not much wider head-on than in profile."

"I am not overly concerned with hitting Munroe"—she smiled wryly—"I cannot think that there is much chance of that, even if I *did* wish it." She bit the inside of her lip. "Do you think ill of me for it?"

Oxley's brows came together, and he shook his head. "Not at all. I have great respect for you." He put a hand on her shoulder and looked her in the eye. "I would not act as second for you if I did not, Ruth."

She swallowed and managed a smile. He respected her. There was that, at least. But how much would he respect her if he knew the truth about her?

"Now show me your stance."

She took in a breath and turned her body, letting the pistol hang at her side.

"Raise it."

She obeyed, leveling it at the same oak tree, her left eye shut. Oxley came over, putting a hand on her arm. "It is better to bend the elbow slightly, while keeping your wrist tight and steady."

She laughed nervously. "And if I am shaking like a *blancmange*?"

Oxley smiled. "Then you are at least honest about it. Only the most hardened of men—or a liar—would conduct an affair of honor without such nerves." He looked at her legs. Could he see them trembling? "You mustn't bend your knees at all, for that is expressly forbidden in the code."

She straightened, trying to keep in mind all of the things he had told her, then let out a frustrated breath. "And I have a mere second to ensure that my knees are straight, elbow bent, wrist locked, eye shut —" She blew an explosive breath through her lips.

Oxley let out a chuckle. "You will do just fine, especially after we practice more. Munroe has chosen a distance of ten paces, and Archer and I agreed that you will both fire on command. We will have a physician on hand to attend to any injuries. The physician is a personal friend of mine, and I assure you that he is very competent, should the need arise."

Ruth nodded. "Thank you." She didn't know which frightened her more—the thought of requiring a physician or the thought of being past a physician's help.

"Another thing before you fire any more shots." Oxley took the pistol from her. "I will be the one loading it, and I think you shan't have any issues, but in the event that it doesn't fire straight away, keep it pointed at Munroe anyway. If the powder is damp, it can lead to a delay, and I have heard of men blowing off their own faces when they've attempted to inspect the reason for that delay."

Ruth's eyebrows flew up. "You fascinate me."

He gave a commiserating grimace. "Rest assured, I will not load the pistol with anything but dry powder."

"I trust you." And she did.

Oxley put a hand on her shoulder and smiled bracingly. "Now, let us practice."

An hour later, Ruth and Oxley were back on their horses, riding toward Town, and Ruth couldn't help looking around the world through different eyes. How had she never taken the time to appreciate the bird song that filled the woods? The rhythm of horse hooves on soft grass? The cracking twigs that punctuated the beats? She might never experience this again—an afternoon on horseback. She might never see her family again. She swallowed painfully and blinked rapidly, hoping Oxley didn't notice.

Oxley. She might never see *him* again.

"I suppose there is a bright side to this affair," she said, trying to pull herself out of such thoughts.

He looked a question at her.

"If I die tomorrow, you shall be two hundred pounds richer." Her brows knit. "Perhaps that is only fair, for I have hardly any doubt that your suit with Miss Devenish is bound for success, and I suspect it has little to do with me."

Oxley's half-smile appeared. "Stop speaking nonsense, little fool. The two hundred pounds would go to Franks, of course. But that will not be necessary." His voice was stern as he said it, and Ruth didn't know whether he said it for his own benefit or for hers. "I admit that, at the time, it was satisfying to hear you put Munroe in his place. But I find a part of me wishing that you would have forgone the opportunity."

"And proven myself a coward?"

Oxley glanced at her. "Perhaps the sentiment does me little credit, but I find I would prefer keeping a treasured friend alive, coward though he may be, to losing him in the name of bravery."

Ruth's eyes stung, and she busied herself with rearranging the reins. "You don't mean that."

"I do."

She said nothing. If she had truly cowered before Munroe, Oxley would have lost his respect for her, sure as anything. And that she couldn't have borne. She would never have his love, but she wouldn't jeopardize what she *did* have: his good opinion.

"I feel responsible," Oxley said softly.

Ruth's head whipped around. "Responsible?"

He shrugged. "You would not have ignited Munroe's wrath had you not approached Miss Devenish in the Park that afternoon. And you did that for me."

Ruth shook her head. "That was not your fault. It was my own silly notion. Besides," she said, feigning resignation, "I am afraid it was only a matter of time before *someone* challenged me to a duel. It is my intimidating presence, you know. It threatens gentlemen."

Oxley laughed, and seeing his mood lighten lifted her own spirits.

When they came to Brook Street, though, things took on a serious tone again.

"Would you like company this evening?" Oxley asked.

Ruth met his gaze, unsure. She had no desire to spend the rest of the evening contemplating the uncertainty of her future. She would go mad, left to herself. And she had no desire to tell Topher what was afoot. He would certainly do something foolish, and her family needed him too much for that. Topher wasn't destined to live a hand-to-mouth existence. He would find a way to bring their family out of their current circumstances. He had always been enterprising.

Ruth wanted to spend the evening with someone who knew what she faced—and who could distract her from it like only Oxley could.

She nodded. "I would like that."

Chapter Twenty-Three

There was something fantastically bittersweet about the evening Ruth passed with Lord Oxley in his drawing room. It felt like a bit of stolen time—an evening painful in its perfection. And as Ruth searched her feelings, she found that, more than the prospect of death or injury, she was haunted by her dishonesty. More than once, she nearly confessed everything. What was it about Oxley that pleaded with her to reveal all—that wished so desperately to know he respected her when he knew the full truth?

But his belief in her courage was also what bound her tongue. If this was to be her last night on God's green earth, she couldn't bear for it to be full of Oxley's disappointment or disdain. God forgive her if that was cowardly.

"You *will* present yourself here tomorrow afternoon for the next lesson, Ruth. I demand it. Physical touch, is it not?"

Ruth managed a smile and nodded. Perhaps it was better that she die. A lesson instructing Oxley on such a topic would be a special form of torture.

"Get some sleep, panda," Oxley said, mussing Ruth's hair. "My carriage will be waiting outside your lodgings at five."

Ruth doubted she would shut her eyes all night, but she bid

him as cheerful a goodbye as she could muster then made her way through Grosvenor Square and on toward Upper Brook Street.

Topher wasn't home—he had spent the past two nights with Rowney, returning when Ruth was already fast asleep, as Lucy had informed her. He was hurting, and she worried for him. But she knew her twin well enough to know that only time would bring him out of such a mood.

Lucy assisted Ruth out of her clothing, falling into a companionable silence once Ruth's short, quiet responses made it clear that she was not in the mood for chatter. When Lucy left, Ruth stood in her shift and bare feet for a few minutes, eyes glazed over. There was only one lit candle in the room, but it reflected in the standing mirror beside the bed.

Ruth had been avoiding the mirror nights and mornings—the only time she wore female garments. But tonight, she glanced at her reflection and stepped toward it, forcing herself to take in the odd picture she presented.

She put a hand to her head and choked back a sudden, unexpected sob. She missed her hair—a bygone connection to her femininity. For two weeks, she had forced herself to act the part of a man, and she had done so well that she could hardly remember what it felt like to be a woman. Tomorrow, she might well die a man. And if she did, the truth would be revealed.

At least she wouldn't be alive to witness Oxley's disappointment in her.

She turned away and reached under her bed, pulling the portmanteau toward her and opening the clasps and the lid. Her dresses were neatly folded within, and she pulled one out.

She might well die the death of a man in the morning, but tonight, she wanted to be herself again. As much as she could be, at least. Just for a moment, she wanted to be the woman who, in another life, might have danced with Oxley rather than learned how to hold a pistol from him; who might have accepted a glass of lemonade from his hand instead of brandy; who might have used what she knew about love to win his heart rather than helping him win the heart of Miss Devenish.

She couldn't lace the back of the dress herself, and seeing the way the sides jutted out from her body rather than hugging her like they should have, she had to swallow down her self-pitying pain. It hardly mattered. Even with the dress worn properly, she wouldn't look the way she wished to.

"Ruth?" Topher's voice came through the door, and she hurriedly dashed away a tear and pulled the dress down around her ankles, tossing it onto the portmanteau on the side of her bed where it would be hidden from view. She tied her wrapper around her waist and rushed to the door, taking in a deep breath to steady herself before opening it.

"You're still awake," he said, stepping in uninvited. His breath smelled of spirits, and his brow was furrowed, as it had been every time she had seen him since his conversation with Miss Devenish. She wondered if it would be permanent.

"Yes," she said. "I was at Oxley's."

He trained his gaze on her for a moment, and she breathed her relief when he turned away without commenting. He hadn't said anything about her feelings for Oxley since their argument a few days ago, and for that, she was grateful. It was not a subject she felt able to converse upon without giving into mortifying emotion. Especially not tonight.

He sat on the edge of her bed. "I was thinking we might go find a doll for Joanna tomorrow, and perhaps a few trinkets for the others."

Ruth swallowed and managed a smile. "What a happy idea."

Topher glanced at her. "What is it?"

She raised her brows, trying to look like she didn't know what he meant. "What do you mean?"

"I know you, Ruth. Something is wrong."

She shook her head. "Just tired. I am having a hard time keeping up the pace being a gentleman requires."

Topher laughed weakly and rose from the bed, nudging her with an elbow. "Isn't as easy as I make it look, is it?" He sighed, his somberness returning. "Well, I am off to bed. We can go to some shops after breakfast."

Ruth followed him to the door with a chuckle. "So, one o'clock, then?"

He put a hand on her shoulder. "That's how you survive life as a gentleman, Ruthie. Lying abed late. It's the only way."

Ruth had been correct when she had suspected she would find it hard to sleep, but it wasn't for lack of trying. It wasn't until two that she gave up and slid out from under the bedcovers. She needed to write Topher a note in the event that she...

She exhaled and sat down, putting quill to paper in an attempt to express everything to her twin. She tried to keep most of it practical —advice for how to continue the column and ensure the family was cared for.

It wasn't a forgone conclusion that she would die, of course, but it was easy to forget that. She had to act under the assumption that these might be her last hours. Even if she didn't die immediately, she had heard of plenty of dueling injuries that proved fatal after the fact. She would rather it be immediate.

When she had finished the letter and sealed it, she sat for another moment, staring at the few blank sheets of foolscap in the drawer beside her. She could write a few more columns for *The Marsbrooke Weekly*—ensure a bit of money for the family—and she should certainly write to her mother. She winced in pain at the thought of leaving her mother behind.

Topher would care for her. He would rise to the occasion.

She dressed as quietly as she could, knowing that Topher slept far too soundly to stir at anything less than a gunshot. Lucy had always assisted her into her clothing, but Ruth managed to do a decent job of it on her own. She wouldn't look her best for the duel, but that hardly mattered.

The first of the servants were just beginning to stir when Ruth stepped quietly through the front door, cringing at the way the door clicked into place. Her stomach growled and rumbled strangely, confused by the disruption in the natural rhythm of her habits.

Oxley's carriage slowed to a stop just as the Watch cried the hour somewhere down the street, and Ruth climbed in to see a smile, barely visible with the light that seeped in through the window from the chaise lantern. It warmed her.

"Did you sleep?" Oxley asked.

Ruth shook her head.

"Nor I," he said. "Perhaps after all of this, we shall enjoy a large breakfast and then take a nap."

"That sounds heavenly," Ruth said, adding it to the list of plans that would never come to fruition.

Oxley kept up a stream of talk during the ride, and Ruth was grateful for his efforts to distract her. Little did he realize the havoc he had wreaked on Ruth's life since sending her that initial letter.

Try as she might to throttle it, Ruth couldn't help feeling a sliver of hope when there was no sign of Munroe's equipage at Kinham Common. But it was merely two minutes later when the sound of carriage wheels met her ears. Munroe wouldn't miss his opportunity to teach her a lesson. She had never truly believed he would.

Oxley had said that none but the most hardened of men could engage in an affair of honor without being accosted by nerves, but Munroe must have belonged to that small set of men, for he descended from his carriage and gazed around the scene as he might have upon arrival at a ball.

The sky was just beginning to lighten on the horizon, but directly above them, it stretched like a great, inky blanket, punctuated by fading bits of starlight and the sliver of a moon.

"Over here," Oxley said, leading them away from the road and toward a stretch of grass large enough to permit the affair of honor.

Another equipage arrived shortly, and a man descended from it, carrying a small leather bag slung across his shoulder. He was much younger than Ruth had expected—perhaps in his mid-thirties—with blond hair and a kindly set to his face.

"Doctor Shepherd," said Oxley as the man approached them. The two embraced, and Ruth stared at the man who might be tasked with saving her life. Doctor Shepherd's gaze moved to her, and she attempted a smile, though she was sure it fell short of conveying anything but how bleak she felt at the prospect before her.

What if she didn't die, though? What if she was merely injured in the duel? Her identity was at stake either way. She sent a prayer to God above that, if she was injured, it would be one that allowed her to remain sentient and in a state where she could at least ensure she wasn't discovered for what and who she truly was. Death might be preferable to that.

"Come, then. No reason to delay now, is there?" said Munroe, who had removed his coat and was shaking out his shirt sleeves.

With each passing minute, the sky grew lighter, yellows and oranges beginning to streak the horizon and move upward, displacing the dark night.

With Oxley's help, Ruth removed her coat, which he set neatly on the ground next to the pistol box. He and Archer inspected the pistols together and, finding them satisfactory, loaded them with gunpowder and balls.

Ruth looked away, training her eyes on the little copse of trees nearby. She wished she could disappear into them rather than face what lay before her now.

Someone nudged her. "Look there," Oxley said, indicating the pond thirty yards away from them. A white swan nestled on the bank of the pond, elegant and serene. "A good omen, surely."

Ruth quickly blinked away the stinging in her eyes. *Was* this a good omen? Or was it God's way of telling her she would be joining her father?

Oxley placed the pistol in her hands, his gaze fixed on her, forcing her own up to meet it. "It is already cocked. A few minutes, and we shall be on our way to breakfast—and then sleep."

She nodded, and he grasped her shoulder with a bracing smile before moving away. Had she made the wrong decision not to tell him everything last night?

It was too late now. The letter would have to do.

"Oxley," she said. Whether she lived or died, she needed to do what she could to stave off scandal.

He looked a question at her.

"I would prefer that the doctor see to me at home if it becomes necessary."

Oxley held his gaze, a slight frown on his brow then nodded. "I will tell him your wishes."

Before Ruth well knew what was happening, she and Munroe were back to back, his shoulders dwarfing hers before they separated to walk ten paces in opposite directions.

One...two...three...

With each step she took, Ruth tried to run through the instruction she had received from Oxley the day before.

Four...five...six...seven...

Elbow bent, wrist locked, left eye shut.

Eight...nine...ten.

She stopped and took in a deep breath.

"Attend," said the stony voice of Oxley.

Ruth turned her body sideways, pistol resting against her leg. Her heart beat wildly, and she glanced at the swan a final time.

"Present."

Ruth raised the heavy pistol, keeping her body turned at an angle and closing her left eye. She met Munroe's gaze, the smiling sneer on his lips, the glint of malice in his eye.

"Fire!"

She pulled the trigger. A deafening report sounded, and a fire burned below Ruth's rib. Her hand shot to cover it, and her eyes clenched as she stumbled back and to the ground.

The pain seared her, spreading from her side and enveloping her stomach and chest. Was she dying?

Hands covered hers, and she forced her eyes open, finding Oxley's face swimming above her. His eyes were as alert as hers were blurry, as if she had switched her glasses back to Topher's.

Whatever happened now, Ruth couldn't allow her wounds to be inspected here at the common. She tried to push herself up. "It is nothing. I am well." Her voice emerged weak and unconvincing.

"Don't be a fool," Oxley pushed her back down. "Let me see."

She shook her head. "No need. There is no need for the doctor, either. I merely need to go home and rest." If only Oxley would take her home, she could have Topher call for a different doctor—one who could keep her secret.

The doctor's face swam behind Oxley's, and Ruth blinked, forcing herself not to submit to whatever force was demanding she shut her eyes and lie back.

She rolled to the side, cringing, and pushed herself up. "See," she said, not without great effort. "I am perfectly well." She blinked to right her vision as a speaking glance passed between Oxley and Doctor Shepherd.

"I am duty-bound to see to your injury, Mr. Ruth," said the doctor.

"Go see to Mr. Munroe first," she said, jaw clenched tightly.

"Mr. Munroe does not require my assistance."

"I would prefer to be seen to at home." Perhaps she could convince Doctor Shepherd to keep her secret. Any inspection of her injury would reveal the tight cravat cloth she had wrapped around her chest. She needed to at least give the impression that her wound was not serious.

Oxley spoke. "If Ruth is not in grave danger, it might be wise for us to leave before anyone alerts the authorities."

She could have kissed him.

The doctor let out a frustrated breath. "Very well, but if I see much more blood, I *will* take matters into my own hands."

Ruth willed her body not to bleed as Oxley and Doctor Shepherd assisted her to the carriage—assistance she tried to refuse without success. She glanced around the common, hoping to see what had come of Munroe, but the action wrenched at her side and she gave up the attempt.

"I shall ride with you," the doctor said, and he shouted a command at his own chaise driver before climbing in with them.

If Ruth had had anything in her stomach, she would have lost it on the carriage ride to Upper Brook Street. They hadn't even made it out of Kinham Common when the carriage hit a particularly deep rut, and everything went black.

Chapter Twenty-Four

Philip waited in the corridor outside Ruth's room, walking back and forth across the creaking floor planks. He tugged gently and distractedly on his lip.

It was still early, and they had only encountered a curious footman upon entering. Philip knew his uncle's staff well enough to set the servant at his ease and make excuses for Ruth's condition. He didn't want word of the duel traveling around town, and he gave strict orders that the other servants be instructed not to intrude unless called upon.

Ruth had regained consciousness momentarily upon their arrival in Upper Brook Street, indicating in mumbled words that he wished to be seen to in private. Philip had been surprised at the hurt he had felt at his friend's words, but he respected them, all the same.

Doctor Shepherd had watched Ruth carefully but had not seen fit to intervene before they arrived at Philip's uncle's house. But seeing the blood seep through Ruth's dove gray waistcoat had elicited a wave of panic inside Philip, which quickly overtook his initial relief that Munroe had not managed to shoot him in the head or heart. He had known men to succumb to what had appeared to be the most superficial of injuries.

Doctor Shepherd had to save Ruth.

The door finally opened, and Doctor Shepherd slipped out. Philip rushed over to him anxiously, trying to glance inside.

"How is he?"

Shepherd cleared his throat and searched Philip's eyes for a moment. "Well enough." He glanced behind him into the room and then shut the door. His brow was furrowed and his lips pursed.

"What? What is it?" Philip didn't know what to think of the doctor's behavior, but dismay settled deep in the pit of his stomach. It couldn't be good news.

Shepherd put a hand around Philip's arm and pulled him down the corridor. "Oxley, how well are you acquainted with Ruth?"

Philip shrugged. "Our friendship is not of long standing, but, despite that, I know him better than I know most men."

Shepherd grimaced, his gaze flitting to Ruth's door again.

"What, Shepherd? What is it?" Philip was beginning to feel annoyed. If the doctor had bad news, it made it no less unwelcome to draw it out.

Shepherd's brow furrowed, and he leaned in closer to Philip. "You are aware, then, that Mr. Ruth is"—he cleared his throat again—"a woman?"

Philip's brows snapped together, and he pulled back to look at his friend. "This is no time for jokes, Shepherd. Tell me, if you please, whether you expect Ruth to make a full recovery."

Shepherd said nothing, merely looking at Philip with a grave expression.

Philip blinked. He knew Shepherd well enough to know that the man wasn't one for silly pranks.

"I don't understand," Philip said.

The edges of Doctor Shepherd's mouth turned down as he kept his gaze trained on him. "Mr. Ruth is a woman."

Philip swallowed, his eyes racing to the door of Ruth's room. "No. That cannot be."

"I am afraid there is no doubt, Oxley. My examination made it quite clear." He cleared his throat.

Philip's eyes darted around, seeking and failing to find something reliable, something to make sense of what was happening.

"I have tended to the wound—the bullet grazed her torso but did not lodge itself there—and I have administered laudanum, which should provide her with some beneficial rest. I don't anticipate any further problems, but you—or whatever servant tends to her—would do well to watch for any signs of fever."

Her? Philip couldn't wrap his mind around it. He nodded absently, and after pausing for a moment, Shepherd said, "I would stay but that I am promised to check in on Mr. Smith's son. He passed the devil of a night last night. Measles. Send for me if she shows any sign of infection."

Philip stood in the corridor as the doctor's footsteps faded. He wasn't certain whether it was seconds or minutes before more footsteps approached and a maid arrived—one unfamiliar to Philip—whose eyes were wide and alert as she approached the door to Ruth's chamber. She seemed not to notice Philip's presence.

He knew a sense of annoyance that his orders were being disobeyed, and he hurried over to bar the maid from opening the door.

"I gave an order that no one disturb us," he said, perhaps with more anger than was warranted.

"I am sorry, my lord," said the maid, her eyes still on the door. "But when I discovered that"—she hesitated—"Mr. Ruth had been brought in unconscious, I..."

That hesitation told Philip all he needed to know. The maid was already aware. Who *didn't* know?

"I think we should wake Mr...Franks," she said, with the same slight hesitation.

Anger billowed inside Philip. So they were both deceiving people, were they?

"You can abandon the charade," he said tersely. "I know that Mr. Ruth is a woman. And you might as well wake Mr. Franks...or whatever his name is."

The maid's eyes ballooned, but she nodded. "He does not like to be woken before ten, but I think under the circumstances..."

Philip nodded stiffly.

The maid disappeared into a room down the corridor.

Philip stared after her, heart thumping in his chest, hands clenching into fists. He felt...he felt...betrayed. Foolish. Angry.

The maid emerged, and behind her, a disheveled Mr. Franks. Blinking, he glanced around. "Where is she?" he asked hurriedly. "What happened?"

"In her room, sir," the maid said. "Asleep."

Franks, still in his nightshirt, pushed the door to Ruth's room open, ignoring Philip completely.

Philip's nostrils flared, and he stood his ground for a moment before following.

"What happened?" Franks asked again, kneeling by the bed where Ruth lay, sleeping peacefully. Ruth wore no glasses, and his head—*her* head—lay slumped to the side.

"A duel," Philip said, pulling his eyes away. He was too angry to look at Ruth without wanting to rouse her and simultaneously yell at her and pester her with questions.

Franks' head whipped around. "A duel? What the devil do you mean?"

"What the devil do *I* mean?" Philip thundered. "What the devil do *you* mean? The doctor informed me that Mr. Ruth is no *mister* at all! And I take it your name is not Franks, either."

Ruth stirred lightly, and Franks' lips pursed censuringly then opened as if to speak, only to close again. He glanced at Ruth, who had resumed her peaceful slumber, then stood and walked over to Philip.

"Who the devil are you?" Philip said in a voice soft but furious. Franks looked every bit a man, the stubble that had grown overnight lining his jaw and the space between his nose and upper lip. Were they a couple, then? Married, perhaps? But then what on earth was the purpose of Ruth dressing as a man? None of it made any sense at all.

Franks' lips drew into a thin line. "My name is Christopher Hawthorn. And that"—he nodded toward Ruth—"is my twin sister Ruth."

Sister. *Twin* sister? Philip's gaze flicked toward her, but he shut his eyes, still unable to comprehend, to explore the implications of it all. He wasn't yet willing to see Ruth in the way demanded of him.

"I will explain it all," Mr. Hawthorn said. He looked at his sister, a frown wrinkling his brow. "Or perhaps Ruth would rather do it. How is she? Who did this to her? What did the doctor say?"

Something in Philip—the childish part, he assumed—didn't want to answer. He didn't want to give this man what he wanted. But there was no doubt that the worry in Hawthorn's eyes was genuine. "She is expected to recover. The bullet only grazed her side. What she needs is rest—and to be watched for signs of fever."

His eyes moved back to Ruth—to Miss Hawthorn. The girl had fought a *duel*. She could have died. He felt a bit of his anger slip away, and he turned his gaze from her. She didn't deserve his sympathy. It was no one's fault but her own that she had done something so utterly incomprehensible and foolhardy.

Mr. Hawthorn let out a relieved breath. "Will you look after her while I dress?"

Philip's hands balled into fists again. Was the man serious? "I cannot think that appropriate, given what I now know."

Mr. Hawthorn grimaced and put a hand on Philip's shoulder. "I think we are well past such concerns at this point. Did you not spend the entire evening with her last night? Alone?" He half-smiled, and Philip's anger bubbled up again. It was all amusing to Mr. Hawthorn, was it?

"Yes, but I certainly would never have done so had I known the truth! I am sorry, Mr. Hawthorn, but you will understand, I am sure, when I tell you that I have little desire to stay here any longer."

Mr. Hawthorn's frown turned into a glower. "Fine. Go, then. I thought perhaps you would be good enough to ensure her well-being for a mere five minutes, even if you *are* angry. But I was obviously mistaken." He went and opened the door, standing by it in an invitation for Philip to leave.

Philip hesitated a moment, knowing an annoying inclination to stay—a desire to have everything explained to him. But to what end? What explanation could there possibly be to justify such deception? He had been duped, taken in by these siblings, made to look a fool. He had spent the entire night tossing and turning, fretting over the possibility of Ruth's death, over losing a friend who had become dear to him.

Over a fraud.

He walked through the door, jaw set tightly—too tightly to speak.

Standing on the pavement in front of his uncle's house, he stared at the pedestrians and carriages that passed where the street intersected with Grosvenor Square. There was no relief outside. Fresh air was not to be had in Upper Brook Street, with dust clouds trailing behind a passing gentleman on horseback and the din of Town all around.

Outside the presence of Mr. Hawthorn, Philip found it harder to hold so tightly to his anger. It seethed and simmered, but it didn't fully conceal other emotions that were beginning to rear their unwelcome heads: hurt and humiliation.

He had come to value his friendship with Ruth. To discover now that it was all a farce....

He should have known. He had been *paying* the Swan for his time. That was certainly not friendship—and never could be.

Scenes from the past two weeks flitted through his mind: meeting the Swan, Ruth helping him dress for church, dining together in Brook Street, accusing Ruth of trying to steal Miss Devenish's affections, helping him prepare for the duel.

And all the while, Ruth had been a *woman*. A woman who might have died that morning, and who now lay abed, wounded. Why would she do such a thing? Why would she do *any* of it?

Philip let out a breath of frustration. Doctor Shepherd would have done everything proper in caring for the wound, but Philip couldn't help the misgiving he felt. His father had died from just such a seemingly innocuous injury, acquired on an ill-fated hunting trip. All had been well—until suddenly it was not.

Philip didn't want to feel concern for Miss Hawthorn—he didn't even *know* her, for heaven's sake. What insanity had urged her to take on such a disguise? And to continue it when faced with the challenge of Mr. Munroe?

Philip's hand shot to his coat, patting at a small bulge near his chest. Her glasses sat inside. Philip had picked them up from the floor of the chaise after a large bump had knocked them off.

He pulled them out and looked at them. Hideous things they were. It had been bad enough when Philip had his first glance at the Swan, to see the man wearing silver-rimmed glasses, of all things—as if he were seventy years old rather than twenty. And then when Philip had returned days later, they had been replaced by the most conspicuous, thick-rimmed pair imaginable.

His jaw tightened at the mixed emotions the memory brought back, and he let his head fall back. His conscience urged him to go back inside, but his pride balked. How would he feel if something were to happen to Miss Hawthorn? If her wound turned putrid? She had deceived him—and grossly—but did that absolve him of the responsibility he had felt for her situation?

He didn't know what to feel anymore. He wanted answers yet wanted nothing to do with this sudden stranger.

Had it all been an act? Just how much of Ruth *was* there in Miss Hawthorn? Endless questions peppered his thoughts, and he clenched the glasses in his hand.

He let out a growl and turned back toward the house, walking up the stairs and pulling the bell.

The maid he had seen upstairs opened the door and welcomed him inside with brows pulled slightly upward. "Let me just inform Mr. Franks of your arrival."

"Yes, please inform Mr. Hawthorn," he said pointedly.

She dipped her head and curtsied, avoiding his eye, then disappeared through the entry hall and up the stairs.

Philip looked around his uncle's entry hall, feeling a wave of humiliation and annoyance. He had offered up his uncle's home for Mr. and Miss Hawthorn—welcomed them into the home of his flesh and blood—and they had taken advantage of his kindness.

Well, he would hear their story and give them the direction of the doctor, but he would not allow them to trespass upon his kindness anymore.

The maid returned and led him up the stairs and into Miss Hawthorn's room. "Still asleep," she said in a hushed voice. She looked toward the bed with a soft expression then left the room.

Mr. Hawthorn looked up from his place in the chair at his sister's side. He still wore his nightshirt, and his expression darkened upon seeing Philip. "What do *you* want?"

"I came to bring these." Philip pulled the spectacles from his coat and walked with careful footsteps to place them on the bedside table on the side opposite Hawthorn.

He set the glasses down gently and took in a breath before allowing his eyes to move to the bed.

There she was. The Swan. The woman. And she *did* look like a woman, despite her cropped hair. Her head was turned away from him on the pillow, her bare neck stretched in elegant lines, the skin soft, white, and unmarred by stubble or the harsh knob that characterized the neck of a man. Her right hand rested beside her head, dried blood on it from where she had clasped at her side after her injury.

Something stirred within Philip. Guilt, perhaps. And an annoying desire to protect her.

It was ridiculous.

"I will sit with her while you change," he said stonily.

Hawthorn's eyes narrowed. "If you mean to browbeat her, you can leave."

"I shan't do that," Philip said, walking around the bed toward the chair. How he was to browbeat someone who lay asleep, he didn't know. "Go on."

Hawthorn looked at his sister for a moment then up at Philip, suspicion in his eyes. "Very well." He rose and strode to the door, pausing to send a final frowning glance at Philip before he left the room.

Philip took his seat in the chair and let out a large breath. He looked around the room, through the window behind, anywhere but at Miss Hawthorn. But his curiosity was building, and he finally allowed his eyes to travel to her again.

He could finally see her face, and his breathing stilled. How had he ever thought her a man?

Well, no. That wasn't quite fair. One didn't go about questioning whether a man was *actually* a man.

But it was true that there was little of the masculine about Miss Hawthorn. No longer masked by thick, horn frames, her dark lashes rested at the tips of her eyelids, nearly brushing the top of her cheekbones for how long they were. Her lips were slightly parted in her relaxed, slumbering state, and, while one arm curled up beside her head, the other lay across her abdomen, pulling down at the sheet that covered her chest.

He averted his gaze. She was certainly a woman.

But his eyes roved back to her, needing to make sense of things. The hand that rested beside her face curled delicately, and his eyes followed the soft curve of her wrist, up to her elbow to where her shirtsleeves had been rolled. He had never seen her arms before, and they were certainly not the wiry or muscular forearms of a man. Her cheeks weren't flushed—a good sign—and they were clearly the cheeks of a woman. Ruth's jokes about the time saved not having to shave had been true enough.

Philip's hand stole to his own jaw. It prickled under his fingers, unshaven since yesterday morning. Though he had lain awake all night, he hadn't managed to shave before the duel. He knew an impulse to feel Miss Hawthorn's skin, to see whether it was as soft as it looked.

He sat back in the chair. She had agreed to a *duel*, this delicate woman before him. It was unfathomable. How many women would do such a thing? Would endanger their lives in such a way? Alice would have fainted clean away at the mere sight of a cocked pistol. In fact, he couldn't think of a single woman he knew who would have done what Miss Hawthorn had done that morning, and the thought elicited a begrudging admiration for her—whoever she was.

It was nearly an hour before Mr. Hawthorn returned to the room, clean-shaven and dressed in impeccably neat clothing, and his arrival took Philip by surprise. He hadn't moved from the chair the entire hour, his mind and emotions hard at work, trying to make sense of the muddle of things he thought and felt—to land somewhere.

Philip rose from the chair to cede his place to Hawthorn.

But Hawthorn stopped shy of the bed, staring at his sister with a frown. "Who in the world would duel my sister?"

Philip thought on the scene at the ball—the way Ruth—he clenched his eyes shut—Miss Hawthorn had faced Munroe fearlessly.

"It was Munroe who challenged her."

Hawthorn's head reared back. "Challenged someone almost young enough to be his child? Why in the devil would Ruth agree to it?"

Philip had the same question. "I thought you might be able to answer that. You certainly know her better than I."

Hawthorn looked at Ruth, a reluctant and fond smile touching his lips. "She probably didn't wish to disappoint you. Silly chit."

Philip's eyebrows pulled together, and Hawthorn looked at him. "She cares for your good opinion."

Philip scoffed lightly, though the words affected him more than he cared to admit. She cared for his good opinion? Not enough to be honest with him, evidently.

Hawthorn shook his head. "And she didn't say a word to me. I'll throttle her when she wakes."

"You will have to fight me for that honor," Philip said.

Chapter Twenty-Five

Ruth turned her head away from the bright light, vaguely aware of muffled voices which suddenly quieted. She shifted and winced, pain throbbing at her side.

"Ruthie." Topher's voice sounded nearby, and she tried to open her eyes, finding her lids strangely heavy.

She put a hand to her side and moaned lightly.

"Don't touch it," Topher said. "You were shot, you silly fool."

She blinked again, more forcefully this time, wisps of elusive memory traveling through her thoughts: Oxley's hand helping her grip a pistol. Walking ten paces as light traveled up the morning sky. A swan. A deafening shot.

Her eyes flew open. Topher's blurry face looked down into hers and behind him—she blinked—Oxley.

Her heart thumped wildly, and she put a hand to her face. No glasses. She needed her glasses.

"Glasses." Her voice croaked from misuse, and she cleared her throat.

"You don't need your glasses, Ruth."

She caught sight of them on the table beside the bed and made to reach for them. Topher took her hand and placed it back beside her.

"He knows, Ruth."

Her vision was clearing, and as she looked at Oxley, she could see it in his face—in the wary, hard look in his eyes. He *did* know.

A great silence stretched on as she held Oxley's gaze, until Topher's voice cut through. "I think I will give you two some time to talk." He rose from his chair and turned to Oxley, staring at him and saying nothing.

"You needn't worry," Oxley said with a hint of an annoyed smile.

Topher nodded and left the room.

Ruth tried to breathe evenly, but she couldn't bring herself to meet Oxley's gaze now. The game was up, and he held her future in his hands.

She knew the silliest desire to ask for a mirror—to have a moment to see to her appearance. This was the first time he was seeing her as a woman, and she could only imagine what she looked like.

But it didn't matter. Why would it? As if looking more feminine might lessen his anger.

More silence filled the room, heavy and thick. It felt wrong, lying down. It made her feel helpless and weak. She needed to sit.

She attempted to push herself up, but pain stabbed her side.

Strong hands wrapped around her arms and pulled her up.

"Thank you," she said, allowing herself a quick glance up into his face.

He stepped away from the bed. "How do you feel?" His words were kind enough, but his jaw was set tightly.

"Alive, I suppose? And very...heavy."

"That would be the laudanum Doctor Shepherd gave you."

His mention of the doctor brought back more memories.

"How long have I been...?"

"A few hours," he said.

She nodded. "What happened to Mr. Munroe?"

Oxley smiled slightly, but there was a strained quality to it that made her anxious. "Nothing."

She frowned. "You mean I missed entirely?"

Oxley gave a wry smile. "Only by a mile or so. But Munroe didn't do much better."

She flinched as she shifted again. "My side begs to differ."

"Yes, I cannot imagine it feels pleasant, but the bullet merely grazed you. You will make a full recovery."

She sent him an annoyed glance. "Merely, did it?"

He chuckled, but his expression soon grew more somber again.

She could only delay the inevitable for so long. "You are angry."

He fixed his gaze on her, and there was no softness in his expression. "I cannot deny it." His jaw shifted from side to side. "Why?"

She swallowed, feeling emotion rise in her throat. Did laudanum have such an effect? "Will you sit down?"

His brows drew even further together.

"It is just that, I feel a bit intimidated with you standing there, so tall and angry and uninjured."

He pursed his lips together and took a seat.

She clasped her hands in her lap and exhaled. "I never meant to deceive you. Truly. It was a series of unforeseeable mishaps that led to it." She glanced at him, and he was watching her, his eyes skeptical and stern, as if to tell her he had no intention of believing a word she said. She couldn't blame him.

"I know you have every reason to disbelieve me, and I will not fault you for doing so, but I wish to explain, and I promise to be honest with you now."

"That would be appreciated." His voice was clipped, and she felt the censure in his words and tone. She should always have been honest with him.

"I am the Swan and always have been. I write the column for our local newspaper, and Topher delivers it. I never gave anyone to believe I was a man, but it is what people assumed, and I didn't correct them. When we received your letter, requesting a consultation, I wanted to refuse. We had never done such a thing, and it felt… wrong." She felt her cheeks warm and averted her eyes. It wasn't easy to be honest about their circumstances or their behavior. "But we needed the money. It hasn't been easy since my father's death, and I couldn't subject my younger siblings to hardship when there was another option. So Topher and I decided to come to Town together—I would instruct him on things so that he could meet with you for that short consultation. But..."

She paused a moment.

"But what?"

"But you asked to move the meeting forward a day. And Topher was nowhere to be found. I thought he would return by the time the meeting was set to occur, but he didn't. We couldn't wait for your return—we hadn't the money to afford another week in Town. I was furious with him for ruining everything, for putting frivolity above the well-being of our family. And that is when the idea formed in my mind."

She stared ahead, remembering those moments with such perfect clarity that the room in Upper Brook Street nearly disappeared, and Oxley along with it. "I had cut my hair to afford the journey to London, and my siblings had teased me for looking like a boy. They have always teased me that I was meant to be one, for my parents convinced themselves they were having two boys when it was discovered late into her pregnancy that my mother was expecting twins. So when I saw the extra clothes sitting in my brother's portmanteau, I thought I would see—just see whether they fit me, whether I really did look like a boy. And I did."

She forced herself to meet Oxley's eyes—to thrust away the embarrassment of confessing her lack of femininity; to admit her ludicrous decision to this man whose opinion she valued so dearly. "I couldn't let Topher's idiocy undo all of our work, and I decided I could manage one simple hour as the Swan that people expected—as a man. And then..." She lifted her shoulders and sighed.

"And then I asked you to keep helping me. And I made you an offer you couldn't refuse." Oxley was leaning forward, elbows resting on his knees. His hands were lightly clasped, one thumb rubbing the other pensively.

She nodded slowly. "I should have refused despite that, of course. I know that now. I knew it then, I think. But I couldn't." She didn't say the next words that came to her. That it hadn't just been the money. That there had been something about Oxley himself that made it impossible for her to refuse.

She wouldn't lie to him, but she couldn't tell him the entire truth. She had wounds enough without the pain of *that* type of rejection.

He was staring at her. She could feel it. "I don't expect you to forgive me, my lord." She couldn't help herself. She reached for his hand, which he retracted slightly. She pulled her arm back and clasped her hands tightly in front of her, cheeks flaming. "But I *am* sorry. I never meant to hurt you or anger you. Indeed, I wanted to *help* you." She looked at the room around her, with its fine furnishings and freshly papered walls. The four-poster bed she lay in was finer than anything she had slept in, even at Dunburn.

And she, in her brother's blood-stained shirtsleeves, her face bare of glasses, and her head shorn of hair—she felt exposed and out of place. "We will pack our belongings."

Chapter Twenty-Six

Philip found himself hanging between two responses, both equally unpalatable. He hadn't been able to see how any explanation could suffice to justify the charade played by the Hawthorns. He hadn't been able to imagine feeling anything but anger and disgust at the excuses offered.

He had been wrong.

And every time he looked at Miss Hawthorn, his anger evaporated a little more.

She clearly expected no response at all from him, though. She was trying to reach for the bell pull but gave up quickly, wincing. She looked to him, apology written on her face. "Might you reach it for me, my lord?"

He rose and walked around the bed, frowning slightly at her form of address. If she had called him "Oxley," he might have been tempted to put her in her place—to remind her that she was essentially a stranger to him. But she had shifted the way she addressed him of her own accord.

"Certainly," he said. "You shouldn't strain yourself, you know. What do you have need of? I will see that it is brought to you."

"To have my maid gather my things."

He stopped, hand on the bell cord. "What, today? Right now?"

"Yes." She winced again and pulled the bedcovers away from herself, looking down at the place of her injury. She still wore the shirtsleeves of a man, but they were unbuttoned at the throat. She put a hand to the injury then pulled it away, inspecting her fingers with a wrinkled brow.

"What is it?" Philip moved toward her.

She pulled the covers back up to cover her side. "It is fine. Not cause for concern."

"Don't be ridiculous," he said, taking a seat beside her. "Let me see."

She hesitated a moment, watching him as if deciding whether to obey, then pulled the covers away, revealing a section of shirt that was brown with dried blood. The center was dark and wet. He reached for her hand and turned it palm up. Her fingertips were tinged with crimson.

"You are bleeding again." He looked at her with a worried brow.

"Only slightly," she said. "I will have Lucy put on new bandages before we leave."

"Don't be ridiculous. You aren't going anywhere." He put a hand to her brow, and her eyes flew to his. "You are warm."

"It is only these blankets." She turned her head away, forcing him to drop his hand. She was certainly stubborn.

"Give me your hand. I want to check your pulse."

She cocked a brow at him. "Are you a doctor now too, then? A fourth accomplishment to add to the triad?"

He tried to suppress a smile and took the wrist she reluctantly offered. Her reference to their ongoing joke acted strangely on him, as if reforging a bond. A bond he wasn't sure he wanted anymore.

He could feel a faint pulse in her soft, white wrist, and he frowned as he concentrated on its rhythm.

It quickened suddenly and strengthened, and he raised his eyes to hers. Her cheeks were flushed, but after meeting his gaze for a moment, she averted her eyes.

He let her wrist down gently, clearing his throat. "You were right. I am no doctor." He watched as the color in her cheeks abated and wondered if her pulse was slowing again.

She was genuine in her apology, and the guilt she felt was obvious. He didn't doubt that. And if he put himself in her place, he couldn't say with any degree of certainty that he would have acted differently. If Anne and Mary's health or safety relied upon such a ruse, would he not have entered into it willingly?

But that knowledge didn't rid him of the hurt or of the injury to his pride, silly though both might be.

He had the power to ruin her. He knew that. But to ruin her would be to bring his own actions under scrutiny and condemnation. And he could not afford that.

Perhaps he was a fool. But, woman or no, he still felt the bond of friendship connecting him to her. And even though it might seem justified to most, he couldn't bring himself to consign Miss Hawthorn and her brother to the devil.

Her health required her to stay put, no matter Philip's feelings. But even if she had not been injured or at risk of infection, he had questions for her—questions that he couldn't ask today. She needed rest.

And he wasn't so certain that he didn't need *her,* too. She was still the Swan. Things were looking more promising with Miss Devenish, to be sure. But they might shift as suddenly for the worse as they had for the better, and Philip wasn't blind enough to think that Miss Hawthorn wasn't responsible for any headway he had made.

"I want you to stay."

Her gaze flew to his, and she paused for a moment before shaking her head.

"We had an agreement," he said. "And I expect you to fulfill your end of it."

Her brow wrinkled. "You entered into that agreement without a full knowledge of the facts—you believed you were hiring a man to help you."

"And you are a woman."

She nodded, and her hand stole to her hair. It was a subtle movement, but there was uncertainty in it, and it endeared her to Philip in spite of himself. It wasn't the gesture of someone who engaged in deceit regularly. It was the gesture of a woman who was unused to her hair—perhaps not confident in it.

"I hired the Swan," he said. "*You* are the Swan. You told me so yourself. And I fully expect you to keep your end of our agreement. I do not claim to understand or condone what you have done. Nor will I pretend that I am pleased. I *am* angry with you. Furious, really. If it weren't for your injury, I would be tempted to call you out myself."

"And I wouldn't blame you in the least," she said softly.

He frowned. "Curse your humility. Why can you not be defensive? Or impenitent? It makes it very difficult indeed to be angry with you."

"I can try if you would like," she said with an attempt at a smile. "But the fact is, you no longer stand in any need of my help, my lord."

"Oh, you would risk having me revert to spitting lemon tart on Miss Devenish?"

A small but sad smile appeared on her lips. "I have no fear of that happening. You are well able to handle things from here."

"You have more confidence in me than I have in myself. Regardless, I insist that you keep your end of the agreement, Miss Hawthorn." The name felt strange on his lips after calling her Ruth for so long.

A tear slipped from her eye, and she brushed impatiently at it before it had time to trail down her cheek.

He smiled wryly. "You *are* a woman."

She gave a chuckle. "After weeks of wearing cravats and pantaloons, I have my own doubts on the subject." She looked at him, and her smile faded, replaced by a serious expression. "Do you really wish for my help?"

He gave a nod. "Just until the Walthams' masquerade. As we had agreed upon."

She held his gaze for a moment, and he saw the cogs turning in her head. "Very well."

On the walk back to Brook Street, fatigue began to overtake Philip, and with it, a sliver of doubt. When he had returned to his uncle's with the spectacles, it had not been with the intention of allowing his pride to be overtaken by sympathy. But that is what had happened. His anger had collapsed as he had spoken with Miss Hawthorn.

He sighed. He might well live to regret his good deed. But he contented himself with the knowledge that his suit with Miss Devenish was much more likely to prosper with the continued help of the Swan.

He waved off the servants upon his arrival home, pulling his top boots from his feet, stripping off his coat, cravat, and waistcoat, and dropping upon his four-poster bed, where he was quickly overtaken by sleep.

He woke two hours later with a grumbling stomach and wondered if Ruth—or Miss Hawthorn, rather—had eaten yet. Their plan for a large breakfast and a nap had been ruined. The thought of them both stretched out on the drawing room sofas, as he had imagined them doing, brought a frown to his face and a little flicker of revived annoyance—as much at himself as at Ruth. How in the world had he let himself be bamboozled for so long?

He had assured her that he would come to check in on her that afternoon and, while he was regretting the offer now, he was a man of his word. After dressing and ordering a belated breakfast be served in the breakfast parlor, he made his way back to Upper Brook Street.

Miss Hawthorn was sitting up in bed, partaking of bread and broth, and looking much better than earlier. The pink in her cheeks was a healthy one rather than the flush of fever, and the laudanum-induced sluggishness had gone. She used her left hand for eating, allowing her right arm to rest at her side. A silk dressing gown was wrapped around her, and the glasses lay forgotten on the bedside table.

She smiled a bit hesitantly upon seeing him in the doorway, as if she was unsure whether he had rethought his earlier decision.

"I have come to see how you are faring." He stepped into the room, leaving the door open. It was all so strange now, trying to decide how strictly to guard propriety after all the time they had spent alone together.

"Very well, thank you." She smiled slightly. "Lucy changed my bandages not long ago, and I immediately felt foolish for making such a fuss over a mere scratch."

He chuckled and sat down in the chair beside the bed. "Well, it certainly bled more than a scratch. You wouldn't allow Doctor Shepherd to examine you until we were here, so I had no idea if Munroe's bullet had found its way into you or not." His smile faded as he realized why she had insisted upon such a course of action.

She seemed to realize what he was thinking, for her smile turned into a frown as well.

"You are fortunate the ball only grazed you." He was unable to keep a hint of annoyance from his tone. "If it had found its way into a lung or one of your other organs, your insistence might have cost you your life."

She swallowed, and her voice was soft when she responded. "I was fairly certain that I was in no danger of dying."

"You might have let me know, then," he said.

"I did," she pointed out. "I even said there was no need for the doctor."

He scoffed. "Not terribly convincing, given the blood soaking your coat and the way you fainted in the carriage."

Her eyes widened and then glazed over, as if she was trying to remember. "I did, didn't I? How mortifying. And chicken-hearted."

"I don't think a woman who has played a part in a duel could fairly be called *chicken-hearted*."

She smiled wanly.

"What were you *thinking?*" he said. "Have you no regard for your own life?"

She shot him a significant look. "Oh, believe me. I contemplated making an escape more than enough times to set me firmly in the camp of the chicken-hearted."

"And yet you didn't. Why?" It was incomprehensible to him, and it frustrated him not to be able to understand. It was a reminder of how little he understood someone he had thought he knew well. Had he not told Doctor Shepherd he knew Ruth better than he knew most men?

Her cheeks gained even more color, and she took a moment before responding with a little shrug of the shoulders, avoiding his eye. "I didn't want my behavior to reflect poorly upon you."

He blinked, disarmed.

She glanced at him and rushed on. "Everyone who has come to know of me in Town associates me with you. They saw you come to my side when Munroe challenged me. Any cowardice on my part would have made you look foolish as well."

He was speechless for a moment. It had *not* been the answer he was expecting. "So you risked your life for the opinion of a host of strangers?"

She took her spoon from the bowl and slowly set it on the tray. "They are not strangers to *you*, though, are they?"

"No, but they know me well enough not to be swayed for long over such an occurrence."

The corner of her mouth tugged up in wry amusement. "Ah, yes. That unassailable reputation of yours."

"Something like that," he said with a begrudging smile.

When she spoke, there was a stiffness about her. "*You* might have survived with everyone's good opinion intact, but I would have lost yours. And I couldn't bring myself to face that." A corner of her mouth pulled up in a wry smile. "I suppose I lost it in the end despite that."

Philip found himself bereft of speech yet again, but he was spared the necessity of responding by the appearance of Mr. Hawthorn in the doorway.

He checked on the threshold at the sight of Philip. "Ah, you here again. Is he chastising you, Ruth?" He narrowed his eyes suspiciously at Philip.

She shook her head with a smile. "No, he is not." She looked at

Philip again. "Topher is returning home tomorrow. To check on the family—just for two or three days. He has refused all my begging to accompany him." She shot her brother a displeased look.

"I find myself in agreement with him," Philip said. "A bumpy journey was not in Doctor Shepherd's recommendations for your recovery."

She cocked a brow. "I may be a woman, but I am not a fragile flower. And the injury is nothing—you know that as well as I do."

Mr. Hawthorn shot Philip a glance that pleaded for his support.

Philip cleared his throat. "I am afraid I cannot forgo the Swan's services for that long."

"So you take Topher's part, do you? Traitor," she breathed.

Mr. Hawthorn laughed at his sister's antics. "She has never gone this long without seeing Joanna or George," he explained to Philip. "Don't fret, Ruthie. I will tuck them in and give them your love."

Philip watched Ruth's throat bob as she nodded with a smile. She had spoken of her younger siblings a few times over the course of their acquaintance, and her affection for them had been apparent, but the knowledge that she was an older sister somehow changed things for Philip. It made her sacrifices for them more...poignant.

Mr. Hawthorn came up to his sister on the opposite side of the bed as Philip. "I shall be back before you know it, though I don't flatter myself it's my absence that puts that look upon your face. The stage will put me back here around seven in the evening on Friday, and I expect a full dinner to be ready for me upon my arrival."

Philip frowned. "The stage?"

Hawthorn nodded.

"Don't be ridiculous. How far is Marsbrooke?"

Hawthorn shrugged. "A matter of twenty miles or so. But I am perfectly fine on the stagecoach, Oxley."

"My uncle expects you to make use of his carriage. You will take it, of course."

Hawthorn looked at his sister, as if for guidance.

She shrugged. "He can be very stubborn. And insufferable."

Philip nodded with a half-smile. "Best not to try me."

Chapter Twenty-Seven

Topher left the room to give instructions to the servants on dinner. Ruth's hunger had been teased but not satiated by the bland bread and broth Lucy had brought.

She stared after her brother thoughtfully. A journey home might do Topher good—reminding him of what was most important, of the realities of their situation. Ruth envied him in a way. She needed the reminder just as much.

But Topher leaving town provided her and Oxley with an opportunity.

"What is it?" Oxley asked.

"I was just thinking...why do we not get up a small card party here? We could invite Miss Devenish and Miss Parkham—and others if you wish. An opportunity—and an excuse—for you to have more time with Miss Devenish."

Oxley tilted his head to the side. "Hm. I suppose we could ask my sister to play hostess."

Ruth's stomach turned uncomfortably. She was intimidated by Lady Tipton, but they could hardly host a party without someone to lend it propriety. "If you think she would accept?"

"Accept? She has been begging me to allow her such a role these past weeks. I shall send a note to her this evening."

"Do you think Wednesday is too early?" Ruth asked with some hesitation. The card party needed to happen while Topher was still gone. The fewer reminders he had of Miss Devenish, the better. Ruth had even considered telling him to remain in Marsbrooke. But when she had hinted at the option, Topher had rejected it flatly.

"I'm not leaving my sister—the one who was just shot in a duel, mind you—by herself in London for that long. Who do you think I am?"

What difference three days or a week made, Ruth couldn't see, but she had refrained from pressing the matter.

"I think Wednesday is feasible," Oxley said. "If Alice accepts—which I have no doubt of whatsoever—I will instruct her to send invitations to Miss Devenish and Miss Parkham. I imagine that Miss Devenish's mother will be glad to accompany them."

Ruth nodded, trying to ignore the way her heart shrank from her task as the Swan. Somehow it felt even more difficult now that Oxley knew the truth than it had before. He might be allowing her to stay on to consult him, but she would be foolish to read anything more into it than that. He knew she had deceived him, and she could still feel a hint of coolness in his manner when any reminder of the fact cropped up.

But even if that weren't the case, she was so very far from the type of woman he would consider as anything more than a friend—or a charity case, perhaps. He employed her, for heaven's sake.

"I imagine we will have to postpone the lesson we were planning," he said.

Was there a hint of embarrassment in his expression?

She thought of her plans for the lesson on physical touch with a fluttering of her heart. Now that he knew she was a woman, it all felt different. Perhaps she could rethink the lesson so that it required less...contact. "I think we might manage it well enough." She shifted her right shoulder up and down, feeling a bit of stinging in her side.

It was uncomfortable, but nothing too prohibitive—especially if she could rework the lesson plan.

He frowned. "We shall wait until after the card party, I think."

She shook her head. "It is the perfect setting to put into practice many of the concepts we will be discussing."

He regarded her evaluatively before nodding once. "I shall come here tomorrow, then." He rose from his seat and made his way toward the door. "Oh, and Ru—" He stopped, pursing his lips. "Miss Hawthorn, I mean. It will take time to accustom myself to calling you that, I'm afraid."

She lifted her shoulders. "I don't mind if you continue to call me Ruth. It *is* my name, after all."

He considered this for a moment then nodded. "Perhaps that *is* preferable. If I am calling you Miss Hawthorn in private and Ruth in public, I stand the risk of making a mistake."

She nodded, heart betraying how relieved she was that she would continue to hear her name on his lips. "What were you going to say before that?"

He sighed. "Something related, actually. I have a request."

"Of course," she said. She hated how eager she was to grant him whatever he wanted. "What is it?"

His jaw shifted from side to side before he responded. "I understand that you will be obliged to maintain your disguise anytime you are in public. But when you are with me, I ask that you refrain from it. I wish for no more secrets. If I am to trust you, I must know who I am trusting."

Ruth swallowed and nodded quickly. "I understand. But what of the servants here? They still believe me to be a gentleman."

"I will take care of that. You needn't worry over them. My uncle is very particular about the servants he keeps on. We can rely on their discretion."

He took his leave, and Ruth watched his departure with an irrepressible sigh and a weight settling on her chest. Perhaps it was just the effect of having passed such an eventful day—or maybe it was a result of the laudanum—but she was finding her feelings for Oxley more difficult than ever to smother now that he knew the truth—now that he demanded the truth.

As Philip had anticipated, Alice was very eager indeed to comply with his request to act as hostess. She consigned her prior engagement to the devil—though in less offensive terms—and Philip knew that she would be ecstatic to have a hand in his success with Miss Devenish. If Miss Devenish accepted his offer, as he was beginning to think she just might, Alice would no doubt attribute the match to the part she played.

Ah, well. Let her have her victory. Better people believe it was Alice who had brought about the change than that people suspect the Swan.

When he arrived in Upper Brook Street on Tuesday, the maid Lucy conveyed him to the drawing room on her mistress's orders.

He hesitated before agreeing to this. He didn't feel that requiring Ruth to come downstairs to meet him would be smiled upon by Doctor Shepherd, but he could hardly suggest that the maid take him to Ruth's bedchamber. There *were* limits to what the servants would regard without blinking an eye.

He walked over to the piano while he waited, touching the keys lightly. His mother had been an accomplished pianist, and he wondered whether she had played upon these particular keys before. He could remember the sound of her voice and playing wafting upstairs when they had had company at Oxley Court, always followed by hearty applause. She was a performer at heart.

The door opened, and he glanced up, fingers still hovering over the keys.

When he had asked Ruth not to wear her disguise around him, he had been thinking of his pride. He didn't think he could continue with their agreement if he was constantly reminded of the deception she had played upon him. He didn't care overmuch if she deceived the rest of London, but *he* didn't want to be deceived, and meeting

Ruth dressed as a man while knowing well that she was a woman would always make him question whether the deception was truly over.

Perhaps it had been a rash request, though.

There was little trace of Henry Ruth in the woman who stood in the doorway of the drawing room. Her eyes were no longer framed by thick spectacles, the absence of which revealed the two sets of long, dark lashes he had noted during her slumber after the duel. The soft pink dress she wore was not of the finest fashion by any means, but it hugged her chest and revealed an elegant set of shoulders and a canvas of creamy skin that stretched from her bosom up her delicate neck until it reached cheeks tinged with pink. Her hair, while still cropped short, was not swept back as it generally had been, but rather brushed forward, so that it covered her forehead in a wispy array of brown locks.

As a man, Ruth had been thin, of shorter-than-average height, and slightly ridiculous. As a woman, she was...well, she was very much that—a woman.

She left the door ajar behind her and smiled at him with a hint of shyness and a deepening blush in her cheeks. "I am sorry to keep you waiting."

He cleared his throat and blinked, shaking his head. "Not at all. I only just arrived. How is your injury?"

She smiled. "Better. Doctor Shepherd paid me a visit this morning and is encouraged. I am grateful for his care—and his discretion."

"He is a good man—very loyal. Are you certain that you are feeling well enough to do this, though?"

She smiled. "Of course. Shall we begin?"

"Not just yet. Have a seat." He motioned to a place on the sofa.

She looked surprised but obliged him, all the same, taking a seat and setting her hands in her lap.

He sat in the chair opposite her and surveyed her for a moment. "You know quite a bit about me after spending so much time in my company, but I find I know very little about *you*—or at least, I haven't any idea how much what I have come to know is fact or fiction. I should like to rectify that before continuing."

She held his gaze, hesitating for a moment before speaking. "It may come as a surprise, but I have been very honest with you in our interactions."

"Aside from the being-a-woman part."

She nodded.

"And your name."

She primmed her lips together. "A partial untruth."

"And that Mr. Franks is actually your twin brother."

A little smile tugged at her lips. "And that."

He raised a brow. "And if I continue with the list of things I know about you, would you continue acknowledging their falsity?"

She thought for a moment. "No. Ask me whatever you wish, and I will answer you honestly."

"Whatever I wish?" He sat forward on the edge of his chair, sending her an intrigued glance.

She paused briefly then nodded. "I want you to trust me."

He twiddled his thumbs, keeping his gaze upon her. She didn't flinch from it—that was a good sign. Or perhaps she was simply a coolheaded liar. He struggled to believe the latter, though. Something about her—something indefinable—told him he could still trust her.

But he wouldn't waste an opportunity to gain a better understanding of her. She was a mystery to him—an enigma—this woman who had just spent weeks disguised as a gentleman.

What *did* he want to know? There was a whole host of questions he might ask her.

"Did you truly cut your hair to afford the journey here?" He stretched a hand toward it, rubbing a lock between his fingers. Her eyes flew to his, and he felt a jolt in his chest.

She kept her eyes on him, sitting very still. "I did."

He tried to picture what she might look like with long hair, done up in an elegant coiffure. But he found he liked it as it was. He let his hand drop. "It suits you."

She smiled. "My siblings would beg to differ. They assured me that I had finally removed the one barrier that had kept me from looking like a boy. I imagine they will insist on calling me Henry when I return until the hair has grown out more." There was warmth in her voice and expression when she spoke of her family. She looked at him with a quizzical tilt to her brow. "Of all the questions you could ask me, you choose to ask about my hair?"

He leveled a frank gaze at her. "I admit that I had wondered if you hadn't perhaps cut it *knowing* that you would be dressing up as a gentleman."

She shook her head. "I assure you it did not even cross my mind until shortly before I came to Town. It was an incredibly foolish decision, and one only made out of dire necessity."

"For your family," he said.

She nodded.

He softened his voice but persisted, wanting to understand. "If I had known, I would have paid for the journey myself."

She chewed her lip with a skeptical glint in her eyes.

"What?"

Her head tilted to the side. "You would have accepted love advice from someone unable to even afford a coach fare?"

He said nothing, taking her point. "But you clearly come of gentle birth."

A hint of humor tugged at her lips. "I was never possessed of the triad, but yes."

"What happened, then? You mentioned your father's passing as a turning point."

She swallowed and lifted her chin. "He made some unwise investments prior to his death, and we were left to subsist on my mother's small jointure when the bank failed and he died."

He frowned. "Who is *we*?"

"My six siblings and I."

He blinked. "There are eight of you dependent upon this jointure?"

"Please don't pity us, my lord."

He tilted his head. "Please don't *my lord* me, Ruth. It is Philip."

Her lips compressed into a thin line, and he smiled at the censorious expression.

"Fair is fair," he said, sitting back and crossing his arms. "I am calling you by your given name. You will call me by mine, if you please."

"And if I don't?"

He laughed, seeing the same sauciness in her that had been apparent on their first meeting. "I thought I should like to be angry with you for a while longer, but you make it difficult."

"Do I?" she said with a hint of incredulity.

He nodded. "Even the first day we met, I found it hard not to like you, much as I wished to curse your impudence and those silly spectacles you wore."

She looked at him curiously. "Had you no reservations upon seeing me?"

He reared back slightly. "Oh, I had plenty. I thought I made that quite clear."

"You did," she said with an annoyed gaze. "But what I meant was, did you not have any suspicion that I was not, in fact, a man?"

"Yes," he said baldly. "I did. I thought you were a boy. A babe in arms. But a woman? Certainly not. I don't generally question such things, you know. I have never had reason to in the past. But I imagine I shall always look suspiciously upon strangers going forward. Though"—he leaned forward again and looked at her searchingly, his head moving slowly from side to side in wonder—"perhaps I never really took the time to look at you, for now I see plenty of indications of the truth."

She smiled. "It was the glasses."

He sat back. "Perhaps it was."

"Shall we begin now? Or am I still on trial?"

"We are done for now."

She rose and extended a hand to invite him to follow. He raised a brow. "Forgetting yourself? I don't think it is customary for a woman to assist a man from his chair."

She kept her hand where it was. "And what about our relationship *has* been customary?"

He couldn't argue that. "Nothing. But my pride will not allow me to accept such assistance from a woman—and certainly not one who is injured."

She sighed and dropped her hand, and he stood.

"Now," she said, taking on the tone of a teacher. "Physical touch is one of the most effective ways to demonstrate interest and intention. Watch any man and woman in the early stages of love, and you will see them finding any excuse at all to brush arms or stand close. But touch can also be quite a delicate matter. Too much or too little can send the wrong message. It is important that you be gentle but firm in your touch, showing confidence but not tyranny."

He let out a frustrated breath. "Lovely. Another delicate balance I am bound to get wrong."

She sent him an understanding grimace. "It requires a good deal of observation, I admit. You must pay close attention to how she reacts to your touch. That is what will inform you how to adjust."

"And how exactly am I to recognize what she wishes for?"

Ruth's lips pressed together thoughtfully. "It is something that you do all the time without thinking. It is only more difficult in this case because of the emotion involved. You can tell, can you not, when someone desires to end a conversation? Or, perhaps a better example: how do you show that *you* are ready to end a conversation?"

He thought for a moment.

"Show me," she said, taking him by the arm and pulling him closer. His breath caught at the unexpected gesture, but he allowed himself to be drawn closer.

"Pretend, if you will, that I have been dominating your attention for the past five minutes, and you are eager to be done conversing because you see Miss Devenish across the room. What do you do?"

He shrugged. "I imagine I should be somewhat distracted, trying to keep track of Miss Devenish."

She nodded. "Very good. Wandering attention is an excellent indicator. What else?"

He tried to picture the scene, but he found that his attention naturally gravitated toward Ruth. He was still distracted by her transformation.

He cleared the thoughts away, instead picturing Mrs. Chesford in Ruth's place. He was always trying to end conversations with the woman.

Ruth pointed a finger at him. "Exactly. *That.* You turned away from me just now. That is a prime indication that you do not welcome my presence—that your mind is already elsewhere. And look how you are leaning slightly away from me. It is the same concept. In addition, you might give short answers to my questions, your smiles would lack authenticity, you might tap your finger or foot in impatience." She let her foot beat lightly on the floor. "Things like that. These are things that people generally do not do consciously, and that is what makes them so valuable—they are glimpses into a person's true feelings."

"So I am to look for such signs from Miss Devenish?"

Ruth smiled. "I don't anticipate she will show you such signs, as I believe she welcomes your attentions."

"So I should look for the opposite?"

"Essentially, yes."

His brows knit together as he reviewed what she had said before and then flipped it on its head. "Turned toward me"—he put a hand on both of Ruth's shoulders and turned her gently so that she faced him—"standing close"—he pulled her toward him and noted how she took in a quick breath—"genuine smiles"—he put a finger on each side of her mouth and tried to form it into a smile, an action that became unnecessary as she laughed genuinely and pulled away —"long answers to questions, and...a lack of foot or finger tapping?" He looked down at her hands and her feet. Her entire body was perfectly still, and his eyes moved back up to her face. She was very close, looking up at him, the smile he had elicited quickly fading.

He swallowed, brushing away the tension in his body. He was unused to being so near a woman. He tilted his head to the side in faux-dissatisfaction. "I will have to hope that Miss Devenish doesn't require my assistance in order to smile."

Ruth chuckled. "I am sure she won't. And don't forget her attention."

He gave a slow nod, looking her in the eye. "Not wandering."

She held his gaze for a moment then looked down, and his eyebrows drew together slightly. "And what does it mean if she does *that*?"

"Does what?"

"What you just did. Look down."

Ruth gave a shaky laugh, and her cheeks tinged with a feminine pink. "If she were to look down while you held her gaze, it might just mean she is feeling shy."

"Hm. And is that good or bad?" He didn't even know if they were still referring to Miss Devenish at this point.

"It is good," Ruth said, turning away and putting distance between them. "Has your sister received a response from Miss Devenish or Miss Parkham?"

"Yes, Mrs. Devenish accepted the invitation on their behalves."

"Wonderful," she said, standing behind the sofa and holding its back with her hands. "I will try to arrange things so that you and Miss Devenish are partnered. I was thinking we might play whist and have the two of you together, but that would mean you sitting across from one another, and that won't do." She tapped a finger. "Do you play chess?"

"Yes," he said slowly. "And you obviously do *not* if you think that chess is played next to one's opponent."

She gave him an unamused glance. "I am familiar with the rules. Perhaps we might play in pairs—two against two. It will be a good opportunity for you to give subtle indications of your intentions, just in case she stands in any doubt."

"The same subtle indications we just discussed?"

"Not exactly."

He raised his brows. "You mean to say there is more I must remember?"

She smiled.

Chapter Twenty-Eight

Ruth hesitated for a moment. This lesson was proving to be very much like torture for her, much as she had tried to reduce the amount of physical contact between her and her pupil. It was difficult to teach touch without any touching. But the better she taught him, the more likely he was to succeed—which also meant her own success and, more importantly, her family's well-being. She could steel her heart for this short lesson. She had to.

"This will be a perfect opportunity to take advantage of the unity that being on a team can foster. You will have plenty of chances for conspiring together."

He chuckled. "You have put much thought into this."

If he only knew how painfully true that was. "That is what you are paying me for, isn't it?"

There was a slight hesitation before a nod. "I suppose so."

"Very well. Some things you might try tomorrow evening"—if she said them quickly, it would be easier—"conspiratorial whispers, a soft hand on her back, small nudges—"

Philip put up a hand. "Wait, wait. You are going far too quickly. Conspiratorial whispers? Is this something I should be familiar with already?"

She shrugged. "It is just as it sounds."

He made a pained expression. "Perhaps you have forgotten how easy I find it to ruin the easiest of tasks. Don't forget what happened with the advice you gave me about maintaining eye contact. And if I found it easy to cover her with lemon tart from two feet away, I can only imagine what damage I might do at closer range."

She suppressed a smile. The thought of Philip making a fool of himself was somehow irresistible. "What would you like me to do? Tell you exactly what to say in her ear?" Oh, please no. Surely her duties as the Swan didn't extend as far as giving him the words to flirt with Miss Devenish.

"Well, I certainly wouldn't refuse such a suggestion if you were offering it," he said with a laugh. "But no. I suppose I just feel... nervous. This is new territory for me. I don't much like doing things I am not good at or haven't had occasion to practice."

She stared at him, imagining what it would be like to practice with him—to touch him intentionally. As a woman. "It is a whisper," she said blankly. "Surely you have whispered before?"

Annoyance flashed across his face—and a hint of embarrassment. "Of course I have." He put up a hand. "Forget I said anything."

Ruth felt instant remorse. She was making him feel stupid, and that was exactly opposite of what she was meant to be doing. She needed to bolster his confidence. Even if it meant...

"Come," she pulled him by the hand toward a chair. "Have a seat."

His brows were still pulled together, but he obeyed, and she took the seat beside him. "Whisper something to me."

He shot her another annoyed glance. "I am not in much of a *whispering* mood."

"Fine. I will whisper something to you, then." Perhaps it was for the best that he was frustrated. It would be a shield of sorts, knowing he was displeased with her. She leaned in toward him and clenched her eyes shut at the familiar scent of amber.

Her mind went blank, consumed with the fact that she was so close she could breathe him in. What was she going to say?

His face turned slightly toward her. "Well?"

She pulled her lips between her teeth and pulled back. "I don't know what to say."

He shot her an unimpressed look. "Allow me to try, then." He leaned in toward her, cupping his mouth with a hand, and whispered, "You are a terrible teacher." His breath tickled her ear and raised every hair on her neck.

She snorted slightly, and he pulled back.

"How was that?" he asked, a victorious cock to his brow.

She arranged her face into an expression of haughty superiority. "The delivery was impeccable, but I would advise you to choose less offensive content when you whisper to Miss Devenish."

"Duly noted."

Ruth nodded approvingly. If he wanted to play this way, she was happy to give as good as she was getting. "Now, for the hand on the back I mentioned, if you hear this sound"—she raised her hand behind him and brought it to his back with a *thud* against the solid mass of muscle. He jolted slightly, and she smiled to herself—"then you have done it too aggressively."

He turned his head toward her, the corner of his mouth trembling slightly before he managed to control it. "Very helpful," he said ironically. "Allow me to practice on you to ensure I understand." He moved toward her, and she hurriedly rose from her chair to put distance between them. He caught her by the wrist and pulled her back toward him, his mouth stretched in a smile that was a perfect mixture of promised vengeance and amusement.

She struggled for a moment to get away, and he wrapped an arm around her to keep her in place, one of his hands pressing into her back. She stopped struggling, staring up at him with a challenge in her eyes and smile. She knew he would never lay a hand on her, even in jest.

Her smile faded, though, as he stared down at her, an intent look in his eyes, as if he saw something unexpected in her face. The pressure of his hand lessened, and he took a step back, blinking.

"Your injury," he said. "Have I hurt you?"

She glanced down at her side. She had forgotten it entirely, but now that her attention was on it, it *was* stinging slightly. She shook her head.

"Forgive me," he said. "I forgot myself."

"I deserved it for goading you."

He scrubbed a hand over his face and sat down again. "You learned all of this from your father? And from watching people in the Pump Room?"

It took her a moment to respond, surprised as she was by the change in subject. She sat down in the seat beside him again. "More or less." Her observations had certainly not prepared her for how it would feel to be in love herself. It was more beautiful and more painful than words could capture.

He turned his body toward her. "And what of you?"

"What *of* me?" She tried to ignore the press of his knees against hers.

"When do you put into practice all this wisdom you have gleaned? When does the Swan get her own love story?"

Her muscles tensed, and she looked him in the eye. Why was he asking her such a question? "Love is a luxury."

"But your father married for love, did he not?"

"He did. But he could afford to do so. It was a different time, under different circumstances." She tried to give a light shrug, feeling uncomfortable at the focus on her—on the light it shone upon the gap between her and Philip. She had resigned herself to the fact that, whenever she married, it would be a practical decision. Never had that felt like more of a sacrifice than it did now.

He was frowning. "It seems unfair that someone who helps others find love should be deprived of it herself."

"Perhaps, but that is the way of the world. The artisan makes shoes he himself is unlikely to have; the servant cleans a home far superior to her own; the laundress washes linens and clothing she could never afford. We do what is necessary and use whatever talents we possess in order to survive."

He made a noncommittal sound. "Love is not only a luxury for the poor, you know."

"What do you mean?"

"There was never any talk of marrying for love in my family—at least not in a positive way. It has always been a matter of duty. Only ask my sister Alice."

Ruth kept her eyes on him but said nothing.

"What? You do not believe me?"

"It isn't that. I have no doubt that, for someone in your circumstances, there is great pressure to marry a certain type of person. But that isn't the same as love being a luxury. The fact remains that you might choose to marry for love if you wished. It might be frowned upon by some—it might not elevate your family or your estate—but it is still an option. You could marry a pauper and still have food to eat and a grand estate."

He stared at her, and she was afraid to meet his gaze. Afraid that her words would draw his pity. She met his gaze despite that, and there was no pity there, only thoughtfulness. "No. You are right, I suppose." He searched her face. "You truly believe in love, don't you? Believe in it deeply, or else you would not be the Swan. And you sacrifice your own possibilities for your family. Your hair, even." His mouth turned up into a slight smile, but there was a touch of sadness in it.

"Hair grows back," she said, waving a dismissive hand and, along with it, the tears she had cried after cutting her hair. "If you had met Joanna or George and received one of their embraces, I assure you, you would be willing to do much more than cut your hair to ensure their happiness. Besides, I am not consigning myself to misery just because I understand that my own decision to marry will have to be a practical one. There are different types of love, you know, and even if my future does not hold the ardent intensity that some people are fortunate enough to experience and pursue, I am determined that there *shall* be love between us—between myself and whoever I marry. That sort of love is a choice—a love that must be cultivated and worked at, day after day. And it is *that* type of love that a marriage must subsist on once the initial flame diminishes."

He was watching her intently, and her cheeks began to warm. "I didn't mean to lecture you," she said with an embarrassed smile, turning her legs so that their knees broke contact. "We should return to the lesson."

He drew back in feigned fear, his eyes on her hand, and she laughed. "I shan't hurt you. I have told you a few things you might try to show your interest in Miss Devenish. *Now* I hope to help you attune yourself to her reactions."

He nodded and waited for her to go on.

"There are a number of things to look for: looking up at you through her lashes, any intentional touch that mirrors your own, body turned toward you as we discussed earlier, laughter, blushing." She swallowed, realizing how many of the signs she had unwittingly demonstrated in her own behavior that very day. She only hoped he was too focused on Miss Devenish to apply his learning elsewhere.

He scoffed. "So I am to pay attention to the chess game itself, my own behavior, *and* Miss Devenish's reactions to my behavior? I am afraid you have overestimated my abilities."

"Impossible, Narcissus," she said with an ill-repressed smile. "Perhaps I am overwhelming you for no reason. I think you are comfortable enough with Miss Devenish at this point that it may all come quite naturally to you. I was in earnest when I told you that I feel you have little need of me now."

He let out a little snort. "We shall see, shan't we?"

Chapter Twenty-Nine

Philip felt surprisingly calm as he awaited the arrival of the guests in Upper Brook Street. They had chosen the day well, for the rain pattered in a steady stream outside, making the inducement of a cozy night indoors more appealing than ever.

Alice had taken on her role as hostess with alacrity and was busying herself with some last-minute instructions to the cook, while Ruth was still dressing upstairs. She and Philip had been discussing the plans for the evening when Alice's carriage had arrived—much earlier than anticipated—and Ruth had been obliged to hurry upstairs to change from a dress to the more suitable male attire that would be expected by all in attendance. The last thing they needed was to create the stir that would inevitably be caused by Alice seeing Ruth dressed as a woman. Philip wondered with a bit of curiosity whether she would even recognize Ruth as the Mr. Ruth she had met before.

As Ruth came down the stairs, Philip approached her, chuckling softly at the sight of her in pantaloons, boots, and a waistcoat.

"Good evening, Mr. Ruth," Philip said in an undervoice, glancing quickly at his sister, who was still spouting off a list of commands to the slightly harried looking servant. Poor chap.

Ruth gave an annoyed tug at her cravat. "I shall be very happy when I can say goodbye once and for all to these devices of persecution."

Philip frowned and slipped a finger between her cravat and the shirt collar. "You have tied it too tight."

Ruth sent him an irritable look. "Not all of us have valets who have perfected the art of cravat-tying, *my lord.*" She used a finger to push the spectacles back up onto the bridge of her nose.

Philip narrowed his eyes at them. "Do you even need those? You haven't worn them since"—he looked at Alice again to make sure she wasn't listening—"the duel."

Ruth gave him a wary look. "It depends upon how much the answer shall anger you."

He sighed and pulled them from her face, inspecting them with a light tap on the lenses. "Plain glass?"

Ruth looked sheepish. "They were instrumental to the disguise."

He handed them back to her with a look full of meaning. "The list of lies grows."

She lowered her head in faux meekness, and he chucked her under the chin teasingly. He had found it too easy to maintain the familiarity that had flourished between them prior to the discovery of the truth. She might look quite different to the man Philip had made friends with, but she acted very much the same. "Those ridiculous things should have alerted me that something suspect was going on."

She laughed, and he thought he saw a slight blush to her cheeks in the candlelit hall. "Well, once you had seen me with them at our first meeting, I could hardly stop wearing them. Neither could I continue wearing Topher's reading glasses."

"Is that what those were?"

She nodded. "They gave me the most oppressive headache imaginable."

"Could you see through them?"

She smiled. "Not a blessed thing. You were nothing more than an insufferable blur to me."

His laugh was interrupted by a sharp intake of breath from Alice behind them.

"They are here!" She scurried over and turned Philip toward her, straightening his cravat and smoothing his coat. "I think you should have chosen a different color of waistcoat, but I suppose there is no helping that now. We will have to hope that Miss Devenish likes that particular shade of brown."

Philip sent a long-suffering glance at Ruth, who was trying not to smile.

The bell rang, and Alice shooed them into the drawing room, following behind. "I shall endeavor to keep Mrs. Devenish occupied, and Mr. Ruth, perhaps you may engage to do the same with Miss Parkham, so that Philip and Miss Devenish can have time to…further their acquaintance." She sent them a significant glance then shushed them, as if they had been the ones speaking.

The door opened, and a footman announced, "Mrs. Devenish, Miss Devenish, and Miss Parkham."

As promised, Alice went directly to Mrs. Devenish, greeting her with a grace and warmth that reminded Philip forcibly of their mother. Watching Alice in company was much like watching a performance.

Both Miss Devenish and Miss Parkham greeted Ruth with affection, and Philip suppressed a smile. Somehow, knowing he was the only one there aware of Ruth's disguise gave him a simultaneous thrill and an interesting hint of protectiveness. He was well aware just how compromised she would be if anyone else discovered the deception.

Miss Devenish was looking striking, as usual, even more so now that she wore a butter yellow dress—Philip was still unused to seeing her in anything but blacks, grays, and purples. He quickly reminded himself of the things he and Ruth had discussed, redetermining to be observant and attentive to Miss Devenish. The image flashed across his mind of holding Ruth against him, and he pushed it—and the unexpected thrill it had caused him both then and now—aside.

The group partook of tea and a tray of sweetmeats before Alice gave Philip a speaking look and addressed herself to Mrs. Devenish. It was his cue to start the games.

Ruth sent a quick glance across the circular table in the drawing room. She sat beside Miss Parkham, who was waiting patiently in front of the chess board while Philip and Miss Devenish conferred in hushed whispers about their next move. *Chess in pairs*, Ruth had called it, knowing that it would force the teams to work together—and to do so just as Philip and Miss Devenish were now: heads huddled and eyes glancing suspiciously at Ruth and Miss Parkham to ensure they were not overhearing anything.

It was perfect. Painfully perfect. It was exactly what she had prepared Philip for, and he was doing marvelously. He looked completely natural—a far cry from the uncertain, stiff man she had watched at church a few weeks ago.

Ruth's own performance was of a different nature. She needed not only to remember that she was a gentleman—a task made more difficult by the two days she had just spent as a woman—but to also hide the misery inside her.

She had initially been worried upon Miss Devenish's arrival—the young woman was as kind and civil as ever, but Ruth hadn't missed the slightly drawn look she had. It reminded her quite a bit of Topher, and that did nothing to alleviate her qualms.

But Miss Devenish seemed to enter into the spirit of chess in pairs with enthusiasm, and even if she didn't return Philip's subtle touches, neither did she draw back from them.

Ruth and Miss Parkham had taken the first game, and the result of the current one was still very much up in the air. Philip and Miss Devenish seemed to come to an agreement, though, and the latter reached out and moved her remaining knight.

Philip looked at Ruth with a smile on his lips and a hint of anticipated victory in his eyes.

The door to the drawing room opened, and Ruth glanced up, stilling.

Topher's confused gaze flitted from Lady Tipton and Mrs. Devenish—sipping more tea on the settee—to Ruth and Miss Parkham, and finally to the backs of Philip and Miss Devenish.

Ruth tried to shoo him away, but realizing that Lady Tipton's eye had caught the action, she changed her approach, hurrying to rise from her seat. "Franks!" Ruth called out with as much pleased surprise as she could muster to cover her dismay. "Wasn't expecting your return until tomorrow."

"Yes," he said slowly, wide eyes still on Miss Devenish. "I finished my business sooner than anticipated."

"I imagine you must be quite tired from your journey," she said with a tight smile. "Wishing to rest, no doubt."

"Is this the Mr. Franks you were telling me about, Philip?" Lady Tipton asked, curiosity gleaming in her eyes.

Philip nodded. "The same. Franks, this is my sister, Lady Tipton, and beside her, Mrs. Devenish."

Topher bowed to them both.

"We are acquainted," said Mrs. Devenish with a kind smile, and Ruth held her breath as she waited to see whether Mrs. Devenish would expound upon their acquaintance. She knew a moment of panic as she thought on what the result would be if the connection between her brother and Miss Devenish became known. Her stomach flipped and churned at the realization that she was still not being fully honest with Philip.

"You must join the games, of course," said Lady Tipton, motioning for him to come further into the room.

Ruth let out a breathy chuckle and perjured herself. "Oh, Franks hates chess. I hope you don't mind if I steal him away for a moment—this business he left on, it is somewhat urgent, and it is a matter which requires a bit of consultation. You know very well what you are doing, Miss Parkham. I have every confidence that you can bring about another victory for us. Excuse us, if you will."

"Of course, of course," said Lady Tipton. "But do bring him back after. We needn't play chess all night—there are plenty of other options. And games are always more amusing with more people, I have found."

"Then it is somewhat strange that you yourself have declined to play," said Philip as his eyes roved over the chess board.

Lady Tipton waved a dismissive hand. "Oh, I am far too old for such things now."

Noting the flush in Miss Devenish's face as she looked at Topher, Ruth took her brother's arm, firmly guiding him out of the room and shutting the door behind them. She pulled him toward the library across the corridor.

"She is here," Topher said, stumbling a bit as she tugged him into the room.

"And so are you. But why? You weren't supposed to return until tomorrow."

Topher's eyes lingered on the shut door. "Mama scolded me for leaving you at all and insisted I return as soon as I had carried out business for the Swan."

Ruth dropped his arm and pursed her lips. "Of course she did." She let her head drop back with a large sigh of frustration. "What did you tell her? Does she know of my disguise?"

Topher tore his eyes away from the door and shook his head. "I didn't want to worry her."

She nodded. "How is she? And the children?"

The first hint of a smile appeared on his face. "Well enough. They miss you, though."

Ruth missed *them*. But she also felt dread at the prospect of leaving London—and Philip.

It would be for the best. In the end.

Topher's eyes traveled back to the door. "I should have let you know I was returning early, but I didn't expect...."

Ruth nodded, biting her lip. His presence at the card party could well ruin everything, and yet Lady Tipton seemed eager that he join.

"You are wishing me at Jericho," he said, dropping his eyes to the floor.

"Never," she lied. "But it does make things quite awkward. Tonight is important, you know. And it has been going rather well, though I know it is hardly what you wish to hear."

His throat bobbed, and the corners of his mouth turned down. "It is the way it must be."

Ruth sighed. "I am afraid so. You told her the last time you saw her that you had experienced a change of feelings, did you not?"

He shut his eyes and nodded. "It was the only way she would listen. She detests me. I could see it in her eyes just now."

Ruth had her doubts on the matter, but she refrained from voicing them. Topher didn't need to be encouraged to hope. Nor did Miss Devenish.

A thought occurred to her. She clenched her teeth together. It would be asking more of her brother than she felt she could fairly ask. But nothing about their situation seemed fair, and truthfully, her own situation was now requiring more of her than she felt capable of giving. She could use some help.

"Are you coming to play games?"

He shrugged. "Lady Tipton expects it. I could say I am feeling ill, I suppose. I can't imagine I will be an asset to your party, though."

"You might be," she said with a painful grimace. "But it would be terribly unpleasant for you."

"What do you mean?"

"Brace yourself," she said. "If you can manage to keep Miss Devenish at arm's length—to convince her that you regard her with nothing more than polite disinterest, it might provide a helpful contrast to her interactions with Philip." She bit her lip.

Topher's jaw was set tight, and he clenched his eyes shut. "I don't know if I can, Ruth." He shook his head.

"It is fine," she said, putting a hand on his arm. "I quite understand. But I cannot have you betraying how much you still care for her. I can make your excuses."

He nodded, rubbing his chin, and his cravat bobbed with his throat. "I can do it."

"Do what?"

"Help you. Act indifferent."

She shook her head. "I should never have suggested it."

He smiled wryly. "*You* didn't just look into Joanna's eyes and tell her you hadn't brought home a doll for her, Ruth. I did. And I am fairly certain I would do anything to ensure that we can return home with enough money to buy her that ridiculous thing." He glanced at the door again. "I *do* care for Rebecca, and perhaps if things were different, we might have been together. But the truth is, she deserves more than I can give her. And Oxley *can* give it to her."

Ruth blinked rapidly, her lashes brushing against the glass of her spectacles. "I am so very sorry, Topher." She gave a watery chuckle. "Did I not tell you we should not have accepted Philip's request? We may return to Marsbrooke three hundred pounds richer, but I fear we shall both be in a bad way."

He wrapped an arm about her shoulders. "Come. Let us go be miserable together, then. The sooner we can make this match happen, the sooner we can put it behind us."

Chapter Thirty

"Mr. Ruth shall be terribly put out when he discovers that I have lost the game for us." Miss Parkham flicked the king piece over with a resigned finger.

"Nonsense." Philip glanced at Miss Devenish beside him, who seemed to be lost in a brown study. He put a light hand on her back, wishing it felt more natural. He couldn't help remembering Ruth's demonstration the day before and smiling slightly. "The outcome would have been the same whether or not Ruth was here. Do you not agree, Miss Devenish?"

She blinked quickly and smiled. "Oh, yes. Of course. We merely needed one game to find our stride."

The door opened, and Ruth and her brother stepped in.

Philip watched her carefully for anything that might give him an indication of why she had acted so strangely upon the arrival of her brother. But she was smiling, and she came straight over to the chess table, her brother following behind.

"How did we fare, Miss Parkham?" she asked, glancing at the board.

"I am ever so sorry." Miss Parkham indicated the king.

"You likely fared better than you would have had Ruth stayed." Philip sent Ruth a teasing glance, and she shot him an unamused, false smile.

"Only a third game to break the tie will tell for certain," Ruth said. "What do you say, Miss Parkham?"

Miss Parkham let out a little laugh. "Oh, no, I couldn't possibly. I think I shall cede my place to Mr. Franks and join Lady Tipton and Mrs. Devenish for a cup of tea. I enjoy nothing more than a warm cup on rainy nights such as this one. But perhaps I shall come over and observe presently." And with that, she curtsied and made her way over to the chaperones.

Philip turned toward Miss Devenish and leaned in toward her slightly. "What do you say, Miss Devenish? Are you prepared to take on a new enemy?"

She gave a sudden, high-pitched laugh that made Philip blink in surprise. "I am quite ready." She shifted in her seat so that she sat even closer to him.

He glanced at Ruth, who was staring at Miss Devenish, her expression impassive.

Mr. Hawthorn took a seat, his jaw set tightly and his smile somewhat lacking in authenticity as he greeted Miss Devenish. What ailed him now? Had something happened at home?

All four of the players were intent on winning, though there seemed to be an extra measure of competitiveness in the Hawthorn twins.

Philip found his gaze moving to Ruth every now and then, seeking her approval for his attempts at following the advice she had given him. In fact, though, as the game progressed, Miss Devenish seemed to be the one initiating all the intimate whispers and small touches. She sat very close to him indeed, and her cheeks were flushed and her eyes bright. They seemed to be the positive indications Ruth had told him to watch for, but Philip found himself torn in response. There was something strange about Miss Devenish's behavior—or perhaps he was simply unused to romantic connection.

The game ended with another victory for Philip and her, though, and she nudged him with her elbow. "We make quite a team, Lord Oxley."

He managed a laugh and looked at Ruth, as though she might perhaps interpret Miss Devenish's behavior for him and tell him what to do next. But she was focused on gathering the chess pieces. Something was certainly off, and he wished he could have a moment alone with Ruth to see what was troubling her.

Miss Devenish was in high spirits all evening, and her manner toward Philip very promising—she had taken his arm more than once and seemed ready to be amused by his pleasantries. He felt none of the anxieties that had plagued him before Ruth's arrival and assistance, but neither did he feel the sense of victory he had anticipated he would feel given the encouragement from Miss Devenish.

Mr. Hawthorn excused himself just after eleven, pleading fatigue from his journey. His mood had not improved over the course of the games.

It seemed that he was not the only one feeling tired. Miss Devenish, too, seemed to suddenly lose some of her energy, sinking into the sofa and sipping a cup of tea with a bit of a glazed look in her eyes until Miss Parkham addressed a whispered remark to her. It was not long after that that the young women and Mrs. Devenish took their leave.

"Well," Alice said just after the door shut behind them, "*that* was quite a success, if I do say so myself. Miss Devenish was absolutely captivated by you, Philip! Well done, brother. Very well done indeed, don't you think, Mr. Ruth?"

Ruth nodded with a tired smile. "Yes, very well done."

Philip knew an impulse to take her hand but refrained, given Alice's presence. Was she feeling spent because of her wound? He should have insisted that the card party wait until she had fully recovered. It was selfish of him to expect her to orchestrate things when she was in such a state.

"I should be going," Alice said with a contented sigh. "Jon is expecting me soon. This has been amusing, though, to be sure. I will call for the carriage to be brought around for us, Philip."

"Oh." Philip hesitated. "I walked here, you know, and I had intended to walk home as well." He wanted to be sure that Ruth's injury was attended to.

"But it is raining much harder now," Alice said. "I can spare you the walk in the dark—and speak with you a bit more besides." She smiled and returned to the drawing room to gather her belongings.

Philip stared after her with a grimace then took a step toward Ruth. "Are you feeling unwell?" He nodded at the place where her injury hid beneath a coat, waistcoat, and shirtsleeves.

She shook her head. "Just a bit tired, I think."

He frowned. "It is my fault. You should be resting."

"I was the one who insisted upon the card party. Remember?"

It was true, of course, but it didn't make him feel any better. "Your brother seemed to be out of spirits this evening."

"Yes," she said, glancing toward the stairs thoughtfully. "I am afraid he was."

"I hope it wasn't for anything involving your family."

"No. They are well, thankfully. You are kind to think of them, though."

Her eyes were still cast down—behind those hideous glasses—and he put a hand on her shoulder. There had to be more to her demeanor than mere fatigue. "Ruth," he said gently, bending his head to seek her gaze. "What is it? You can tell me."

Alice emerged from the drawing room, and he dropped his hand quickly.

"Your hat, Philip. I don't wish to rush you, of course, but I assured Jon that I would return by midnight, and you know how he worries."

Philip knew nothing of the sort, but he took his hat and nodded, all the same. Ruth didn't seem inclined to speak with him about whatever was bringing down her spirits, and that simultaneously hurt and worried him.

"Perhaps we can discuss things tomorrow?" he said in an undervoice.

Ruth nodded with a weak attempt at a smile. "Yes, of course."

"I shall come then. And perhaps engage to beat you at chess again." The genuine smile he had hoped for appeared, and he breathed a sigh of relief at the sight.

"What an imagination you have," Ruth responded.

Philip followed his sister into the coach, preparing himself for her chatter and analysis of the evening. Thankfully, the journey from Upper Brook Street to Brook Street would take less than five minutes.

"Well, that was a smashing success, was it not?" She needlessly smoothed one of her immaculate gloves, looking at Philip with all the pride of someone who had just hosted the Prince Regent himself.

He nodded. "It went well." By most accounts, it *had* gone well—better than he had expected. And yet, he felt little satisfaction.

"We must arrange for another evening like it as soon as possible. Any evening she spends with you is an evening she is not spending with the other gentlemen who wish to ingratiate themselves with her." She tapped a gloved finger against her lips. "Perhaps this time we might invite her over for dinner at my house—just a small, intimate affair—for, while I like Mr. Ruth and Miss Parkham well enough, the less distractions, the better, don't you think?"

Philip stifled a smile, but his brows drew together. Why did that prospect not appeal to him? He should *want* to spend more time with his future wife, shouldn't he? He was going to ask her to spend the rest of her life with him, after all. And he liked her well enough, but...

"Alice," he said, interrupting her stream of talk. "Are you happy with your decision to marry Jon?"

She blinked at him and laughed uneasily. "Why, what a question!"

He said nothing, waiting.

She shifted in her seat. "Of course I am. Why would you even think to ask such a thing?"

"I have often wondered if you regretted giving up Vickers."

She held his gaze for a moment before looking away. "We were ill-suited."

"Were you?"

"Yes," she said firmly.

"Do you actually believe that, or did Father persuade you of it?"

The coach slowed, and Alice looked through the window. "Ah, here we are. I wish I could stay and chat longer, but Jon is waiting. I shall come by to speak with you about that dinner party."

Philip hesitated for a moment, eyes on Alice, then descended from the coach.

Chapter Thirty-One

At ten o'clock the next morning, Philip's valet Nash was helping him dress for the day when a knock sounded upon the door of Philip's dressing room. He grabbed at his shirt, which lay upon the wooden chair, wondering if perhaps Ruth had decided to come see *him* instead. She had once seen him in just such a state of half undress, and his heart quickened slightly at the memory. Little had he realized that he was subjecting an innocent young woman to such a sight.

Well, not entirely innocent. She *had* been deceiving him, after all.

"Are you going to let me in or not?"

Philip laughed his relief—and slight disappointment. It was Finmore.

He nodded at Nash, who opened the door.

"Since when do you pay calls at such an uncivilized hour?" Philip pulled the shirt on over his head, shaking out the sleeves. "Indeed, when are you even *awake* at this time?"

Finmore smiled and tossed his hat on the chair. "Wish I could say I was turning over a new leaf, but I simply wasn't patient enough to wait before seeing you."

Philip scoffed lightly, threading his arms through the holes of the waistcoat Nash held and working at the buttons. "Missed me that much, did you?"

"Heard all the gossip, more like. What's this about a duel with Munroe?"

Philip's fingers slowed on the last button. So word was getting around, was it? No doubt Munroe was parading it about that he had taught Henry Ruth a lesson he wouldn't soon forget. Philip only wished he could reveal that, not only had Munroe barely grazed his victim, the victim was, in fact, a young lady. It was hardly the victory Munroe seemed to think it.

Philip wavered over how much to tell Finmore. "Yes." He waited for Nash to bring a fresh cravat. "You know how Munroe is. He was looking for an excuse to quarrel with Ruth, and he found his opportunity."

"And you acted for him?" One of Finmore's brows was raised.

"I did."

His mouth turned up in one of his signature half-smiles. "I left you very respectable and come home to find you have embroiled yourself in an affair of honor, of all things. I must say, though, I enjoy this new side of you. Tell me, would you act for me?"

Philip chuckled, watching in the mirror as Nash evened the sides of the cloth around his neck. "No."

"You offend me." Finmore picked up his hat and sat down on the chair, leaning his back against one armrest and draping a leg over the other. "Why ever not?"

Philip cocked a brow at him through the mirror. "If you were involved, I would have my doubts about it being an affair of *honor*."

Finmore laughed. "Touché." He pulled out a snuff box. "I hear your little Ruth was injured."

"Barely," Philip said, ignoring the epithet. The thought of what might have happened to her sent a little shock of fear through him.

"I might have known Munroe was exaggerating."

"A safe assumption to make."

Nash reached for the black tailcoat that lay on the clothes press and inspected it another time before holding it up for Philip.

Finmore watched with disinterest. "By the by, did you ever discover who Miss Devenish's secret lover was?"

Philip frowned. He had forgotten about that rumor. "No, but I begin to think it another creation of the gossipmongers'."

"Hm. Well, word last night was that the man had rebuffed her."

Philip felt a niggling irritation as Nash smoothed the coat fabric across Philip's back and shoulders. "You're becoming a dead bore, Finmore, what with your neverending stream of gossip."

Finmore shrugged a careless shoulder and got up from the chair. "Thought you might wish to know."

Philip shot him a false smile and bowed ironically. "Much obliged to you."

"How *are* things going with Miss Devenish?"

"Quite well," Philip said, feeling a hint of victory at the way Finmore's brows tugged upward at his response. He didn't need to know that it was the Swan who had made such a response possible.

"I must ask, what does *quite well* mean to a man who, the last time I saw him with her, assaulted a woman with half-chewed dessert?"

Philip shot him an annoyed glance. "I am tolerably certain she shall accept my offer, if that tells you anything."

Finmore raised his brows even higher. "That is certainly more than I expected. Have you kissed her?"

Philip sat down as Nash took out his pair of black and brown leather top boots. "The girl is barely emerging from a year of mourning, Fin."

He chuckled. "That's a *no* if I ever heard one. Perhaps it is for the best, though—it gives you time to acquire some finesse in the art." He cocked a brow. "Miss Devenish will hardly wish to have the doubtful pleasure of teaching you. A bad kiss can put a quick ending to the most promising of liaisons."

Philip busied himself with tucking his pantaloons into the top of his boots, hoping it covered the niggling doubt he felt. He had never explicitly told Finmore about his lack of experience with women, but they had been friends long enough that Finmore had put two and two together. He had always excused himself from

Finmore's invitations to accompany him to places of ill-repute, using estate business as an excuse, but he knew Finmore saw through it.

Philip had assumed that, whenever he *did* kiss a woman, it would come naturally. But the assumption seemed ridiculous now. What about his dealings with women *had* come naturally?

He stood and dismissed his valet, grateful to know that Nash wouldn't relay what he had heard.

"Come with me tonight," Finmore said with a smile. "Let us give the saint some experience."

Philip hated when Finmore called him that. He wasn't a saint—just a coward who avoided things he wasn't good at. The two of them seemed unlikely friends on the surface—a rake and a "saint." But Finmore did not come from a happy home, and he drowned his problems in entertainment. He embraced where Philip eschewed. Neither of them ever spoke of the motivations for their choices, but Philip had had years to glean an understanding of his friend, and he cared for him, aggravating as Finmore could be. "You are, as always, generous in your offers to corrupt me, Fin, but I must once again decline."

Finmore shrugged and stood. "Suit yourself." He grasped Philip by the shoulder. "I shall hope for your sake that Miss Devenish is a patient teacher, for I assure you, it will not be *her* first kiss." He strode from the room, leaving Philip to wonder if Finmore spoke from personal experience with her, or if he was merely making an assumption.

He had assumed that Miss Devenish lacked any such experience, just as he did. The thought that he might be wrong was unwelcome.

Was he feeling jealous? He didn't think so. It felt more like uncertainty—like self-doubt. He had known that his abstention was uncommon among his peers, but he hadn't worried about that, thinking that at least his naivety would be matched by the woman he married.

He sighed and followed after Finmore, who led them into the breakfast room as though it was his own house. Philip regarded

Finmore's familiarity with uncustomary impatience. He hadn't planned on lingering over his food. He was anxious to see Ruth.

When Finmore finally left for his own lodgings, Philip watched his departure through the bow window in the morning room then slipped through the door to make the short walk to Upper Brook Street.

Why he hadn't wished to tell Finmore where he was going, he couldn't say precisely. The less Finmore knew of Ruth, the better. Finmore could be aggravatingly perceptive at times.

Chapter Thirty-Two

Breakfast was a quiet affair in Upper Brook Street the morning after the card party, neither Ruth nor Topher being in a talkative mood.

The small party had not been the success Ruth had been hoping for, despite what Lady Tipton had thought. She had too easily recognized the intent behind Miss Devenish's actions to feel victorious. Her sudden enthusiasm for Philip had been a desperate attempt to goad Topher to react, and it made Ruth feel sick—sick for how the shift in seemingly promising behavior had visibly confused Philip and given him hope; sick for the fact that she was still keeping things from him.

In all fairness, Ruth herself hadn't discovered what was afoot until it was too late. But what would he say or think if she told him now? It would be another bold line in the list of lies she had told him—one she didn't think their friendship could recover from.

Perhaps she needed to speak with Miss Devenish—to discover if she could find it in herself to love Philip and put Topher behind her. If she could—and Ruth couldn't imagine why she *wouldn't* be able to—then what was the purpose of dredging up a short-lived romance between two incompatible people?

Whatever Miss Devenish's feelings, Philip deserved to be loved wholeheartedly. And if Ruth could have transferred her own feelings and affection for Philip to Miss Devenish—if Miss Devenish could only see Philip the way Ruth saw him—she would have done it in a heartbeat.

"What other news did you have from home?" Ruth asked, setting aside her unpleasant thoughts.

Topher frowned, swallowing a mouthful of ale. "Not much. You know how little things change in Marsbrooke. The children miss you, of course, but they looked well enough. George was on the mend. And Mama couldn't keep the smile from her face when I gave her the five pounds from Kirkhouse."

Ruth smiled wanly. It was little comfort to know what a difference such a sum made to her family. "Did you take the columns I sent with you to the newspaper office?"

He nodded. "Yes, and I meant to tell you last night, but it went straight out of my head when..." He trailed off, brow furrowing. "In any case, when I went to retrieve our post from the newspaper office, Mr. Jolley told me he'd had someone come in asking after the Swan. Seemed to have many questions, from what Jolley said."

"What? Who?"

Topher shrugged. "He didn't say."

"And you didn't ask?"

"I did, but the man never gave Jolley his name."

Ruth sat back with a nervous breath. "I cannot think who it might have been."

Topher took a bite of toast. "It's nothing to fret over. Do you not remember the last time a strange fellow came in asking questions?"

Ruth's shoulders relaxed slightly, and she nodded.

Topher chuckled. "Found a copy of your column on the ground in High Street and wanted to meet you in person. It's a good thing, in fact—more interest means more business. Perhaps we can convince Jolley into paying a bit more every week if we can convince him of the value of the column. Maybe in our next installment, we can offer in-person consultations—take out the go-between and charge more for—"

"No."

Topher's brows drew together. "Why not? We could make a great deal more money doing it—not as much as Oxley is paying, to be sure, but certainly more than we receive from the column."

She shook her head firmly. "Once we leave London, I am done with this sort of thing, Topher. I don't wish to do it anymore. I never did." There had been too much deception involved, and it would only bring up painful memories. She didn't even know how she would go on writing the column, if she was being completely honest.

"Ruth," Topher said, "the money from Oxley will get us by for a while, but at some point, we will need more. I will apply myself to finding work, of course, but that may take time. And you know we can't live as we have been, especially not when there is an alternative."

She didn't meet his eyes. "When I agreed to come here, you assured me it was for but one hour—and *you* were to be the one meeting with Philip. And now, three weeks later, you are asking me to continue what my conscience balks at?" She paused. "I want to tell him, Topher."

"Tell him what?" He looked at her warily.

She met his gaze squarely, though her hands shook at the thought. "I want to tell him about you and Miss Devenish."

Topher stared at her. "The devil you do!"

"He deserves to know. I told him I wouldn't keep anything from him anymore."

Topher shot up from his seat, swearing softly. He paced away from the table, rubbing his forehead. "You cannot, Ruth. There is no reason to! You saw well enough last night. There is nothing between Miss Devenish and me."

Yes, nothing but a room full of tension. She sighed.

"Be honest with me and with yourself, Ruth. What is truly motivating this desire of yours to tell him? Is it some silly hope that Philip will give up Rebecca and choose you instead?"

Ruth blinked as though he had thrown a jug of water in her face. "No, Topher. It is simply that I have a conscience."

"Well, perhaps you might sit for a moment and take note of the fact that your conscience is not the only factor to consider." He tossed his napkin on the table. "By telling him, you put everything at risk that we have worked for. You think he will pay you a cent when he discovers that you have been professing to help him win Rebecca over while your own brother was courting her?"

Ruth swallowed, and the back of her eyes stung.

Topher scoffed. "Even if he didn't withhold the money, you would likely refuse it anyway. You have had qualms about all of this from the beginning."

"I have! Little though you cared for them. You cannot put a price on integrity, Topher."

"Oh, can you not?" He set his fists on the table, across from her. "Allow me to try. What about food? A roof over our heads? Money to make the journey back to our family?"

The bell rang, and Ruth and Topher held eyes for a moment, their faces both red.

"That will be Philip." Ruth rose and blinked away her tears.

Topher let out a snort. "*Philip*. You are not the only one who has made sacrifices or told lies here, Ruth. I told the only woman I have ever loved that I feel nothing for her. Try to remember that when you feel the desire to tell your precious viscount everything. I didn't sacrifice my own happiness for you to ruin all." He stormed past her and out of the room.

Philip appeared in the doorway right after, blinking and looking back at Topher. "And good morning to *you*, Mr. Hawthorn," he said in a bit of a daze. He looked at Ruth with a commiserative smile. "Still in a sour mood?"

Ruth sighed, but she couldn't help returning Philip's smile. "He is not terribly fond of me right now."

"Ah." Philip closed the door behind him. "I always suspected he was a fool." His smile widened, and his gaze wandered to her side. "How is it? Is it healing?"

She nodded. "It hardly bothers me. Have a seat. There is still some breakfast left if you would care for some."

He sat in the seat right beside hers. "I will take the seat *and* the food, if you don't mind. Finmore paid me an unexpected visit this morning and insisted on breakfasting together. The man has the appetite of an ox. Barely left anything for me." He frowned slightly as he reached for the ale. "He mentioned hearing some rumors."

Ruth's heart thumped. "Oh? What sort of rumors?"

Philip took the last piece of toast and set it on his plate. "Well, besides hearing about the duel—Munroe is apparently spreading around that he hurt you grievously—Finmore heard that Miss Devenish was rejected by a gentleman—some secret *lover*, as he phrased it." He buttered the toast with a frown. "One never knows what to believe amongst the *on-dits* that get passed around at a place like Brooks'."

Ruth forced a small laugh, but guilt was roiling in her stomach. "And does that rumor bother you?" From the way he was serving himself two eggs from the silver platter in front of him, it didn't seem to be affecting him overmuch.

He shrugged. "I told you from the beginning that this was not a love-match. I don't require Miss Devenish to fall in love with me—merely to see the sense in marrying. I hope she will respect and admire me and that, as you said, love might grow between us in time. She seemed quite willing last night—more so than ever before, certainly."

Ruth had half-hoped he had seen through Miss Devenish's behavior. But she couldn't help breathing a sigh of ironic relief that he was still set on the match, no matter what Miss Devenish's feelings were.

She let him eat in peace, taking her time to sip her tea and struggle over her conversation with Topher. No matter what she did, she would harm someone.

Philip finally set his napkin down on the table. "Thank you for that. I feel much better with a full stomach."

Ruth laughed and set her teacup down. "It would make more sense for me to thank *you* for the food. It is your uncle's, after all."

They both stood and made their way to the drawing room. "What is the lesson for today, then?" he asked.

She glanced at him. "I didn't have anything particular planned, I'm afraid. I thought I might ask *you* what you feel you need help with at this point." He opened the door, and they passed into the drawing room.

"Hm. An excellent question." They came to stand in the middle of the room as she waited for him to think, and he smiled wryly. "Finmore will have it that I cannot be sure that Miss Devenish will accept me until"—he cleared his throat—"until I have cleared another hurdle."

"What sort of hurdle?" she said curiously.

He took in a large breath, letting it out in a swift gush. "A kiss."

Chapter Thirty-Three

Ruth blinked at him, and a thought occurred to Philip. Finmore was convinced Miss Devenish was not unpracticed in such matters. Was the same true for Ruth? He knew a stirring inside himself at the thought, something akin to protectiveness.

"Oh," Ruth said in a blank voice. "A kiss." She rubbed her lips together, and he resisted the impulse to look at them and wonder what the answer was to his question. "It is certainly something we should discuss. It is always best to be prepared." She smiled, and he felt another surge of embarrassment. Was he the only person of his acquaintance who had never kissed someone?

"I await your expertise," he said, and he could hear the sourness in his own voice.

She laughed lightly. "I am afraid this will have to be more of a theoretical discussion than a lesson, as I have little to offer in the way of instruction. My wisdom comes from observation, you know, and people were disappointingly slow to kiss in the Pump Room."

He laughed—one full of strange relief. "Yes, I believe such actions are generally frowned upon in polite company. So, you abandon me here—leave me to my own devices, then?"

She cocked an eyebrow at him and turned away, walking toward the sofa. "I can't teach you *everything*. At some point, you must go out on your own into the world, little one." She shot him that teasing smile he was coming to feel belonged to them somehow. "Besides, I am not foolish enough to think you need my help on this topic." She straightened a pillow on the sofa.

He said nothing for a moment. He had caught glimpses of people kissing in dark alcoves at places like Vauxhall, had heard plenty of men brag about their conquests, but he had none of the experience she assumed he had. And he didn't know whether he wished to let her go on thinking such a thing or admit his naivety. Would she think less of him?

"And what if I *do* need your help?"

She paused, hand still on the pillow, and turned her head, wariness in her eyes, as if she wasn't sure whether or not to believe him.

He swallowed down his reluctance and fear—the things that told him that admitting his weakness would mean rejection—and forced a laugh. "You think the man who, prior to your arrival, couldn't even speak to a woman without humiliating himself is somehow experienced in this area?"

She laughed softly. "I hadn't thought of it that way. I had wondered if perhaps your lack of confidence was limited to Miss Devenish's presence—she *is* frighteningly perfect."

He grimaced. "Unfortunately I am incompetent around the opposite sex in general. I have never felt at ease around them, and I am the insufferable type of person who, rather than proving his ineptitude beyond any doubt, chooses to avoid situations that highlight it. Hence my inexperience." He cleared his throat. "Finmore seemed to think that Miss Devenish would *not* be so deficient, though."

Ruth bit her lip. "Perhaps. Perhaps not."

He let out a large gush of air. "So you are telling me I must swallow my pride and accept that I might make a bungle of it?"

"It might be good for you to have a little humble pie," she said, unsuccessfully trying to stifle a smile. "It wouldn't be fair for the rest of us if you were good at everything."

He let out something between a laugh and a scoff. "Heartless panda, aren't you? You have given me enough humble pie to last a lifetime. And what if my bungling it is the difference between two hundred pounds and three hundred pounds? Finmore insists that one kiss can make or break things."

Her smile faded slightly. "I think you are worrying more than is needful. It is the same problem you have always had—thinking too much. Forget whether you are impressing Miss Devenish or not. A kiss should be an expression of the way you feel for her, not a performance."

Philip frowned. How *did* he feel about Miss Devenish? And how did she feel for him? And if he didn't have the answer to those questions, how could he possibly convey it in a kiss? "But how am I to know if she even welcomes such a thing? The last thing I want to do is force it upon her—I have no desire to be slapped."

"I very much doubt that will happen. I think you will *know*. Much like the last lesson we had, you will observe the way she reacts to preludes to the kiss."

"Preludes?"

She shrugged with a bit of impatience. "Brushing a hair from her face, holding her gaze—things like that."

Philip could remember what had happened the last time he had tried to hold Miss Devenish's gaze.

Ruth pursed her lips and strode over to him. "Here." Her lips drew into a thin line. "You will have to imagine for a moment that I have long, silken locks of hair like Miss Devenish." She raked a few fingers through her hair, bringing the strands forward onto her forehead. The hair was growing quickly, a fair amount longer than it had been when Philip had first met her a few weeks ago.

"Now," she said determinedly, "you must—what?"

Philip was trying in vain to suppress a smile, and he put a fist to his mouth to cover it, clearing his throat and looking at her with feigned innocence. He couldn't imagine Miss Devenish looking like the disheveled woman before him—indeed, he doubted Miss Devenish ever had a hair out of place. "Nothing. Proceed."

She shot him a censuring look and folded her arms across her chest. "Do you wish for my help or not?"

He straightened and let his hand drop from his face. "I do."

She pursed her lips and uncrossed her arms. "Before you do anything, you should make sure that her attention is on you—all the things we discussed before about the unconscious language people speak with their eyes and the position of their bodies." She turned toward him, looking up into his eyes, and Philip's heart skipped a beat.

"She might show a bit of shyness—fluttering lashes, breaking her gaze away—but her attention will always return to you if she invites more intimacy." Ruth adjusted her stance, and her arm brushed Philip's.

He nodded with a swallow, trying to understand what was happening to him. He had been this close to Miss Devenish at the card party, but that had felt nothing like this—every bit of his body on alert, aware of the small space that remained between him and Ruth.

"Now what would you do?" Ruth looked at him expectantly. "Try not to overthink it. Just imagine that I am Miss Devenish, and try to focus on how you might convey your intentions without words."

Try as he might, though, Philip could see none of Miss Devenish before him. How could he, when he could see every speck of black in Ruth's brown eyes and the delicate curve of her dark lashes? The hair she had combed forward hung down, nearly reaching her eyebrows —the hair she had cut to afford the journey to London, to help her family. It was like seeing her heart on display, and he reached for it, as though by touching it, he might feel her heart.

She was still, her brown eyes looking at him intently. The air between them thickened as his hand hovered at her brow, his heart thumping so powerfully that he could hear it in his ears. His gaze moved to her lips, which parted briefly. He hardly knew what he was doing as he brushed the hair from her forehead then let his hand slide down the length of her warm cheek, bringing his thumb to her mouth and letting it graze her bottom lip and its soft, pink curves—

imagining what it would be like to feel the softness against his own mouth, to feel without seeing.

He shut his eyes, and the world went dark, but he could still feel Ruth's lips under his thumb. He raised his other hand to her cheek and wondered at the way the feel of her both grounded him and erased the trace of anything else in the world.

Slowly—more slowly than he had done anything in his life—he lowered his head, sensing the closing of the distance between them, feeling the warmth of her sweet breath grazing his face, anticipating the moment when their lips would meet.

A swishing of skirts, and cold air filled the space between them, making Philip blink and draw back.

Ruth was turned away from him a few steps away, and her hand covered her mouth. "You will do very well." Her voice was gravelly, and she cleared her throat.

Philip's heart was still thrumming, his chest rising high and falling deeply. "I…I…I am sorry." He had nearly kissed her. He *would* have, more sure than anything, if she hadn't…

She forced a smile and raised a hand to stop him, her other hand still pressed to her lips. "Don't regard it—there is no reason to apologize. You were only following my instructions. You haven't any reason to worry over your kiss with Miss Devenish." She let out a laugh, strangely clipped. "I think that is enough for today."

He nodded quickly, but the mention of kissing Miss Devenish made him frown, feeling almost as abrupt as Ruth's breaking away. "Yes, of course. Here I am, forcing you to continue with lessons despite your injury." It was a flimsy excuse. How many times had she assured him that she was fine? But, for the first time, she didn't counter his words. "I should be going. I believe Alice meant to visit today."

Ruth quickly raked her fingers back through her hair, arranging it in place. "Give her my regards—and my thanks again for acting as hostess last night."

"Certainly." He hesitated then made for the door, the quick beating of his heart still betraying what had happened. He paused again on the threshold. Why was it so difficult for him to leave Ruth without knowing when he would see her next? "Perhaps I shall come tomorrow for that game of chess you promised—after church?" Tomorrow, he would have sorted through this. Whatever it was.

Ruth smiled and nodded, and Philip took his leave.

Ruth stared at the drawing room door as it shut quietly behind Philip. She didn't move—not until she heard the muffled closing of the door to the street.

Her hand stole to her mouth, brushing at the place on her lips where Philip's thumb had last touched.

She clenched her eyes shut, as if it might erase the feeling, but his face swam before her. She had let herself be swept up for a moment, certain that he must have been feeling what she was—the electricity that made every inch between them feel a mile too far.

And she might have let it continue—indeed, she thought she might have been too weak to stop herself—had she not opened her eyes for a brief moment. Long enough to see the soft half-moon of his eyelids and to wonder whether, behind them, he was picturing Miss Devenish.

Nausea swam within her at the memory. She had *told* him to see Miss Devenish in her place. Of course that was what he had been doing. How in the world had she let herself be so carried away by her own silly wishes?

This was not what she came to London for, and only the thought that the Walthams' masquerade was in three days kept her from ordering Lucy to pack away all of her things so that she and Topher could leave London behind.

She didn't even want Philip's two hundred pounds anymore. But she needed it. And the knowledge that it would certainly be three hundred rather than two was no consolation at all.

Chapter Thirty-Four

Lucy stretched the length of a cravat in preparation for wrapping it around Ruth's chest, and Ruth took in a large breath, knowing it would be hours before she could breathe so freely again. She was sick to death of dressing in men's clothing, and the fact that Philip insisted that she not do so when in his solitary company made his company that much more desirable—if that was even possible.

Nerves made her stomach feel unsteady, and she forced herself to focus on dressing, instead of wondering what Philip had thought after leaving Upper Brook Street the day before.

As if on cue, a knock sounded on the door, and a servant informed her of Lord Oxley's arrival. Lord Oxley. If only she could think of him as Lord Oxley instead of Philip.

"Show him into the drawing room, and tell him I won't be more than two minutes."

She tried to breathe deeply again to steady herself, but the tight cravat prohibited it. She wouldn't act any differently toward Philip. Yesterday's scene had been nothing more than another lesson to him, and that's all she would allow it to be to her.

She set her glasses on her face and made her way to him.

He was standing just shy of the spot where they had nearly

kissed, with his back to her, hands clasped behind him, but he turned as she entered, blinking and then letting out a light chuckle. "I wasn't expecting you to be dressed like that. Silly of me, but this is all getting rather confusing."

She looked down at her coat and waistcoat. "We go to church, do we not?"

"Yes, yes. Though to be honest, I doubt you would be recognized if you came dressed as a woman—or even without those glasses. They could conceal anyone, I imagine."

Ruth raised her brows and removed them, walking over and handing them to him. "Let us test the theory."

His mouth stretched into a smile, and he took the spectacles from her, turning his back to her for a moment.

She smiled as she waited, ready to be amused. He whipped around, hands out to display himself. "Behold, the giant panda."

Ruth's face fell. He didn't look like a fool in them. Somehow he merely looked dignified. "Well, that is hardly fair." She stepped toward him and pulled the glasses from his face.

"What?" he said, nonplussed, hands still out.

She set them back in their place on her nose. "You don't do them justice. They aren't *meant* to make one look distinguished."

"*That* is quite obvious," he said, giving her chin a little nudge with his hand.

Philip kept his arms crossed over his chest for the duration of Mr. Gibson's sermon. He had nearly convinced himself that what he had felt with Ruth the day before was merely novelty at work—never had he allowed himself in such a situation, in such proximity to a woman. Undoubtedly he would have felt the same thing if it had been Miss Devenish rather than Ruth.

But in the Trent family pew box, he felt the same palpable awareness of just how much room there was between him and Ruth. For once, he was grateful for her disguise and the barrier it was. But while Mr. Gibson spoke, all Philip could think was how his experience with Ruth the day before was painfully similar to music—to playing all but the final chord of a beautiful song, leaving it maddeningly unresolved.

When the sermon finally ended, Philip let out a sigh of relief, rising quickly and stepping into the pathway that ran between the long rows of pews. He had spotted Miss Devenish in her own family's pew, and he felt an urgency to go speak with her. Ruth did not follow, and Philip decided it was for the best.

After he had greeted Miss Devenish and her parents, she peered around him toward Ruth. "You came with Mr. Ruth, then? And Mr. Franks?"

"Not Mr. Franks," Philip said, feeling his heart regain its normal rhythm.

"Miss Devenish!" Alice scurried over toward them, hands out to welcome Miss Devenish's, which she freely gave. "How wonderful to see you here! I was hoping I might have the chance to speak with you. Philip and I have been discussing how amusing the card party was the other night, and we thought perhaps you might like to join us for dinner tomorrow. If you are not otherwise engaged, that is?"

Philip glanced at Alice with a slight frown. She had never come the day before, so they hadn't decided upon anything together. It was like her to take matters into her own hands—something Philip had become used to over the years—but today it bothered him.

The invitation was a pointed one, especially given the superficial acquaintance level between Alice and the Devenishes. There could be little doubt on Miss Devenish's end what the meaning of it was, and Philip resented his sister's highhanded ways.

But he was being ridiculous. This was what he had been working toward, after all.

Miss Devenish looked to her mother and father, and Alice hurried to say, "We wish for all of you to come, of course."

Philip glanced back toward Ruth. She stood alone, but she offered him an encouraging smile when they caught eyes.

"It will be a small affair," said Alice, "for my husband prefers it, and I thought it would be lovely to have the opportunity to become better acquainted, given the *situation*." Her eyes flitted to Philip, and his jaw tensed. She might as well make Miss Devenish an offer on his behalf.

Details were arranged, and Philip bowed civilly as Alice said, "We look forward to welcoming you tomorrow."

As the Devenishes walked away, Philip turned to his sister, his polite smile fading.

"What?" she said.

"Did you never think to speak with me before extending such an invitation? Or consider that *I* might be otherwise engaged tomorrow evening?"

"Well, are you?"

He paused, wishing he could say he was. "As it happens, I am not, but you could not have known that."

She waved a dismissive hand. "Of course you would have cried off from another engagement if that had been the case. Naturally, this is far more important than anything else you might do." She smiled and gave his arm a squeeze, glancing at Miss Devenish. "I knew I could depend upon you to make us proud. Father and Mother would be pleased if they were here, Philip."

The buzz of conversation filled St. James's as churchgoers conversed together while Ruth looked on. She still knew so few people in Town, and with Philip engaged in conversation, she felt strangely alone.

He had rushed out of the pew after the sermon, and it had hurt Ruth more than she cared to admit—particularly since his clear destination had been Miss Devenish.

She looked away, chastising herself for ever presuming to put herself in competition with such a paragon. There *was* no comparison.

The Devenishes broke away from Philip and his sister, only to be addressed by Mr. Gibson, and Miss Devenish's gaze found Ruth. She excused herself and made her way toward Ruth, but her progress was stopped by Mr. Munroe, who had stepped away from his own circle.

Ruth tensed—she hadn't even noticed him in the church. It was the first time she had encountered him since the duel.

Miss Devenish smiled civilly and, after a few words with him, offered a small curtsy, leaving the man's smile to morph into a sneer as his gaze followed her progress toward Ruth. His expression held the same malicious glint as it had that morning at dawn, still with that hint of victory.

Ruth forced herself to look calmer than she felt.

"Mr. Ruth," Miss Devenish said, putting out a hand for Ruth to grasp. "How good to see you here." She glanced around curiously. "I thought I saw Mr. Franks with you, too. Was I mistaken?"

Oh dear. "I am afraid you *were* mistaken. He was unable to join me today."

"Oh."

Ruth glanced at Philip, still speaking with his sister, and her heart panged. Did it truly not matter to him whether Miss Devenish loved him or not? She clenched her teeth together. It was time to be more direct. "I was pleased to see you enjoying the card party the other night. You and Lord Oxley made a very good pair."

Her eyes roved to Philip. "I believe it was only owing to his abilities that we had any success, for I am not skilled at chess, you know."

Ruth smiled. "He is maddeningly good at whatever he puts his mind to." She paused a moment, wondering if she would regret her own daring. "May I ask you something impertinent, Miss Devenish? You need not respond if you would rather not, of course."

Miss Devenish looked at her with a hint of wariness but nodded.

Ruth indicated Miss Devenish's colorful yellow spencer with a nod of her head. "You have put off your mourning, and I remember you saying when I first met you that you intended to do so in order to free yourself to receive the attentions of a gentleman." She paused. "Is that gentleman Lord Oxley?"

Miss Devenish swallowed and hesitated then shook her head.

Ruth had anticipated as much. “I see. And what of the gentleman whose attentions you spoke of?”

She looked down, clasping and unclasping her hands. “Nothing. I was mistaken in believing he cared for me as I did for him.”

Ruth hurt for Miss Devenish and longed to reassure her. But the balm would be but temporary. Topher and Miss Devenish weren’t destined to be together. “I am sorry for your pain, Miss Devenish. Do you think it possible that you might be happy with someone else? That you might even come to love someone new?”

Miss Devenish looked at Ruth. “You speak of Lord Oxley, I presume.” She looked toward him. “It is a good match, and I know that my mother wishes for it—and my father too, though he would never tell me as much.”

“And you? What do you wish for?”

Her delicate eyebrows came together. “I cannot have what I wish for. But I can at least give my parents what *they* desire.”

“I do not think Lord Oxley would wish for you to be unhappy with him, Miss Devenish—to make a martyr of yourself.”

She shook her head. “I am no martyr. Lord Oxley is a good, kind man. I am not in love with him, but nor do I fool myself that he is in love with me. In that way, the match would be equal.” She let out a determined breath. “If he asked me today, I should accept him. There is no reason not to.”

Mr. and Mrs. Devenish came up behind their daughter, and her father set a gentle hand on her shoulder. “Shall we go home now, Rebecca? Your mother is feeling fatigued.”

Miss Devenish curtsied to Ruth and bid her goodbye, and Ruth frowned thoughtfully as she watched their departure, pulling her eyes away only as Philip came up beside her.

He let out a large sigh. “I think you have successfully changed me, Ruth. I cannot say I am fully at ease in her company yet, but I haven’t made a colossal blunder in some time, and that is a victory worth celebrating.”

She looked up at him. “I did not come to change you.”

He smiled down at her. “I know. You have merely improved me.”

She swallowed, and he nudged her with an elbow, a teasing light illuminating his dark eyes. “And now, are you ready to be conquered in chess?”

She scoffed, and they made their way toward the door. “I have not improved you *that* much, surely.”

Chapter Thirty-Five

Philip met Ruth's eyes over the chess board.

"A bold move," she said, and the smile in her eyes resonated somewhere inside him.

It also made him question his move.

She lowered her eyes to the board again, searching the remaining figures. Her hair was still styled in the male fashion, but she had shed her masculine garb immediately after their return to Upper Brook Street. Philip half-smiled at the conflicting sight.

The entire situation was incredible—passing a Sunday afternoon alone with a woman. The thought would have scandalized him and struck fear into his heart a few weeks ago.

But he had never felt uneasy in Ruth's company. Was it because he had met her as a man? Had skipped over the initial and most difficult parts of acquaintance?

She moved a knight three spaces and looked up at him with a cocked brow.

He blinked, refocusing on the board to determine what his next move should be. His eyebrows drew together, and he looked up again. She was biting her lip, and he found himself momentarily distracted again, reminded of how it had felt under his thumb.

"That isn't possible," he said, forcing his eyes back to the game. "I was certain I had you."

"*Certainty is absurd*, Voltaire once said." Ruth flicked over Philip's king and sat back, arms folded across her chest. She had acquired some masculine mannerisms, and Philip found them amusing.

"Another game, then," he said. "I was distracted."

She clucked her tongue. "Always with the excuses."

He sent her a glare, and they set to arranging the pieces for another game. "It is not an excuse. I am sorely regretting that card party the other day, as Alice took it as *carte blanche* to take charge of my life."

"What has she done now?"

"As good as offered for Miss Devenish on my behalf."

Ruth's head snapped up, and Philip's smile wavered. The intent look in Ruth's eyes pinned him in place, and he could have sworn he saw a flash of hurt, but it was followed by a little laugh. "You move too slowly for her."

"There is no doubt of that. I think she might take to speaking to Mr. Devenish herself if I don't do it soon. I shall have to ensure she has no time alone with him tomorrow."

"Tomorrow?" Ruth slowed as she set the final piece in place.

"Yes." Philip sighed. "A dinner party at Alice's—the invitation extended without any approval from me."

"Your move first," Ruth said. "Well, we have this afternoon for a lesson if you feel you need any further preparation. And I shall engage to keep Mr. Devenish occupied tomorrow evening if you are truly concerned about what your sister might do. I've not spoken to the man, but I have no doubt I can find a topic that will keep his attention for some time."

Philip opened his mouth only to shut it again. Ruth assumed she was invited.

At his silence, she looked up, her smile becoming less certain. "What?"

He grimaced. "Alice insists that the dinner be a *small, intimate* affair. I believe the Devenishes are the only ones she intends to invite." Philip nearly reached out a hand to take Ruth's as he watched embarrassment appear on her face. "I want you to come, believe me, but—"

Ruth waved a hand and laughed, applying herself to the chess game again. "No, no, that is wise of your sister. I am completely unnecessary at this point. It will be a good opportunity, I think. Perhaps the last step in the journey."

And then it hit Philip, square in the chest. The sum of it all—of his thoughts and feelings. He didn't *want* to spend an evening with Miss Devenish. He didn't *want* time alone with her. The only person he wanted more time with was sitting across from him, the pawn in her hand hovering over a black square.

"Ruth." Her name came out without his permission.

She looked up, the flush of embarrassment still fading from her cheeks, and he stared at her, like seeing her for the first time. Was this what it felt like to be in love? Never tiring of someone's company? Feeling able to talk about everything or nothing?

It *was.* He knew it in that moment as well as he knew anything. It was just as Ruth had said: *the sort of connection that is inexplicable and yet undeniable.*

His breathing quickened, and he felt the call of the unplucked string stretch between them again.

"What is it?" Ruth asked.

He looked at her wondering eyes, so expressive without the distraction of the spectacles she had worn at church. A small crease still ran across the bridge of her nose, fading evidence of the fact that she had been wearing them—a reminder of who Ruth was. And who she wasn't.

She was everything Philip was forbidden from wanting: poor, unknown, unimportant, with a reputation that hung upon the thin thread of her disguise—a thread that could be snapped at any moment, heaping condemnation upon her—and him. And he was falling in love with her.

He was *already* in love with her.

And still she looked at him. He glanced down at the signet ring on his right hand, worn by his father and grandfather and great grandfather. *A reminder of the sacrifices the Trent men have made*, his father had said when he had given it to Philip on his deathbed. *Now it is your turn to wear it—to remind you of the duty you owe your forebears.*

Philip twisted it on his finger then looked up at Ruth. "Do you ever tire of doing your duty? Of putting your family's needs and wishes above your own?"

She held his gaze, and he watched the hesitancy in her eyes and the emotion in her throat. She said nothing.

"You have cut your hair, dressed up as a gentleman, fought in a duel, courted danger and condemnation for weeks—all for your family. Do you never tire of it? Of making decisions that will please everyone else but you? Or are you simply so pure-hearted that such things never trouble you?"

She clasped her hands in her lap, lowering her eyes. "I am far from being pure-hearted. And duty is certainly a heavy burden at times."

"At what point, then, does it become *too* heavy? At what point does duty become tyranny?"

Ruth sighed and met his eyes again. "I don't know."

He sat back in his chair, letting his head fall back. "My entire life, I have been told that my duty lies here"—he raised his hand, and the signet ring glinted in the sunlight that streamed through the window—"with my family, my ancestors, the men who wore this ring—men I never knew, apart from my father. Time and again, my father told me of the sacrifices made by each of the men who came before me—from my fifth great grandfather, awarded a barony for services to the crown; to his son, who was granted the viscountcy. The question was always what *I* would do, what *my* contribution would be. I thought that, if I could answer that question and prove myself, perhaps I would be worthy." He interlaced his fingers, letting them rest on the table.

"Worthy of what?"

He exhaled on a shrug. "Of the title I bear? Of the power I hold? Of the respect and admiration people regard me with, which I have done nothing to merit?"

Of love. The last word stuck in his throat, refusing to be spoken, and he looked away.

Her hand came to rest on his, and she looked at him intently, leaning forward onto the table. "Duty certainly has its place. But I believe that it is most effective when it is driven by love, not wielded as a threat or a weapon. Indeed, what good is a title or an estate or a fortune if all they afford their keepers is a crushing burden of responsibility?" She touched the signet ring thoughtfully. "They are tools to be used with wisdom and not to be taken for granted or squandered carelessly, but surely they should grant as much freedom as they do obligation."

He stared at her hand on his. *As much freedom as obligation*. He had never considered the freedoms that his position afforded. But where did the obligation end and the freedoms begin?

She leaned in closer, and their gazes met. "I cannot imagine that you will be the most effective Viscount Oxley you can be if you are living under a shadow all your life—unsure if you measure up to some impossible standard, or believing that your worth depends upon meeting that standard. The title was created for *you*, not you for the title. It is largely imaginary—a simple piece of paper, is it not? But you"—her mouth turned up with the hint of a tender smile—"you are real. Flesh"—she squeezed his hand—"blood, a beating heart, a lively mind. And you alone determine how much that piece of paper defines you, for better or for worse."

He cupped his other hand over hers. He wanted Ruth, wanted her hand in his as it was now, her smile always in his sights and her laughter ringing in his ears. He wanted to finish what they had started in the drawing room.

He leaned in, eyes trained on hers, ever-aware of the soft lips through which Ruth's breath warmed his face. Her gaze remained fixed on his, the same intensity reflected in her eyes as he felt coursing through him. He reached a hand to her cheek, and her eyes shut, dark lashes fluttering lightly, telling him that she wanted the same thing he did. He narrowed the gap between them, and a chess piece clunked onto the board as footsteps sounded outside the door.

Ruth drew back, and the door opened.

"I think we might simply take the stage back to Marsbrooke on Thursday morn—oh! Oxley. Didn't know you were here. Chess again, is it?" Topher came over and looked at the board, his brows coming together. Philip's king lay sprawled upon it, knocked over by accident. "Can't say I see how Ruth won that game, but I have never been very good at chess, you know."

Philip rose from the table, heart still puttering wildly. "I shall leave you to discuss the details of your return—I have some business with my sister I should attend to." He shrugged on his coat. "I hope you know that you are welcome to use my uncle's carriage or my own. It is quite needless for you to travel on the stagecoach."

Ruth rose slowly from the table, uncertainty in her eyes and color slightly heightened. Why was it so difficult to leave her?

He gave a slight bow and left the room.

The door shut behind Philip, and Ruth swallowed down the hurt rising like the lump in her throat and the tears making her eyes burn. It was like reliving the day before—yet more bitter *and* more sweet.

"I must say," said Topher, "it is good of Oxley to offer his carriage. I would much rather that than going by stagecoach."

Ruth gathered up the pieces on the chess board. The thought of leaving Philip behind—and *being* left behind....

"You seem almost as anxious to leave as you were to come," said Ruth.

"I am."

Ruth looked at him.

"There is nothing for me here," he said. "I should have known that before I came."

They both should have known it. "If you could go back, knowing what you know now, would you have come in the first place?"

Topher tapped his hat against his leg, brows drawn together then shook his head. "No. I don't belong here—I probably didn't then, and I certainly don't now. London has everything to offer those with enough money and consequence to afford it. We have neither." He looked up at her. "Would *you* have come?"

Ruth set the final piece in the chess box and shut the lid softly. She had no answer for that question. If she had not come, she would not be hurting as she now was. Was two or three hundred pounds worth having tasted the sweetness of something that could never be? And what of her friendship with Philip? Could she truly say she would forgo that association, even with the pain it had brought?

She lifted her shoulders. "I don't know."

Topher nodded once. "Is he going to offer for her?"

Another question Ruth didn't know the answer to—hardly *wished* to know the answer to. When they had nearly kissed the day before, Ruth had easily convinced herself that it had been because Philip was picturing Miss Devenish in her place. And when Ruth had reminded him who actually stood before him—whose lips were nearly close enough to taste, he had apologized and left immediately.

But today...today he hadn't been thinking of Miss Devenish. And Ruth didn't know if she wanted to strangle or embrace Topher for his inconvenient entrance. For it was clear by Philip's abrupt departure that he had been carried away, on the cusp of doing something he *didn't* wish to do—not truly.

He might feel something for Ruth, but he did so against his better judgment. He could no more neglect his duty than Ruth could abandon her family. It was ingrained in him, and one conversation—one wishful conversation—could not undo a lifetime of training.

"I believe so."

Topher nodded once, but Ruth saw the way his jaw and throat

worked against the emotion. "And what if he does so after our departure? Shall he send the money to us in Marsbrooke?"

Ruth shrugged. She knew they needed the money. That was what all this had been about. But she never wanted to see it or touch it.

Topher looked at her for a moment then walked over and wrapped his arms around her.

Chapter Thirty-Six

Philip held the solid wood of the pistol butt in his right hand, arm extended and left eye shut. It had been some time since he had come out shooting alone, but he had needed fresh air—and something to shoot.

His eye veered away from his target slightly, landing upon one of the marks in the tree from when he had taught Ruth to shoot. He could remember the way she trembled as he stood behind her—at the time, he had assumed it was fear as she thought on the prospect of the duel. Now he wondered if she hadn't been feeling the same thing Philip felt now whenever he was near her.

He didn't doubt that she cared for him the way that he cared for her. He had seen it in her eyes over the chess board the day before, and it had been that realization which had acted like a magnet, pulling him toward her.

Opposites attract. He had heard it before, and it never resonated more than now. For Ruth was his opposite in all the ways that mattered to Society—in all the ways that mattered to someone tasked with improving the Trent legacy. And yet, never had he felt so akin to someone, like finding a piece he had never realized he was missing—a piece of him no one else understood.

He pulled the trigger, and a shot rang out. The ball barreled through a leaf on the old oak tree, breaking it from its stem and sending it fluttering to the ground.

He let the pistol drop to his side.

He knew what his heart wanted. It had taken him some time to recognize it—he had been too fixated on what he *should* do to see what was happening.

He wanted Ruth.

No, it was more potent than mere and passive wanting. It felt much more like need, like thirst, hunger, or fatigue.

His horse let out a small grunt, and Philip glanced up at the sky, shading his eyes. "I know, old boy. Time to go."

He still needed to dress for dinner before making his way to Alice's, and he cringed at the thought. The Devenishes could be in little doubt of what Philip's intentions were. He was staring duty in the face—unavoidable.

He thumbed the crest of his signet ring and walked toward his horse. How had he gone his entire life—all thirty years—only to fall in love with the very woman he had tasked with helping him win a wife?

That Ruth loved him in return was something he couldn't bear to reflect on for more than a moment. It was too good to be true—and too far out of reach now that he had finally realized it. She was a better person than he, no matter what Society believed of her. Even the worst thing he knew of her—her deception and lies—betrayed what a good heart she had.

Once home, he dressed quickly and made his way to his sister's, arriving just as the sun dipped below the top of the townhouses in Catton Street. He slipped inside, deciding against ringing the bell. Jon would be annoyed by such casual treatment of his home, but that only made the choice more inviting. Jon's self-consequence was becoming unmanageable, and, being above him in rank, Philip was in a unique position to challenge it.

A footman poked his head out from the drawing room at the sound of Philip's entrance, but, seeing him, offered a bow and ducked back into the room. Muted voices sounded from the room opposite the drawing room, and Philip approached, slowing as it became clear that an argument was taking place.

"Well, you might have asked me before assuming that I had no prior engagements! I cannot tell you how much it grieves me to have to show Lord Bolton such disrespect, only because of some insipid dinner party for the sake of your insufferable brother."

Philip was frowning at the tone his brother-in-law was using, but a smile pulled his mouth at the last words. It wasn't the first time he had been called insufferable, and the word had come to feel like less of an insult. Certainly he couldn't find it in himself to regret that his brother-in-law felt that way about him. The sentiment was entirely mutual.

"I rather thought you would be pleased with me for arranging it." Alice's voice held apology and a hint of hurt. "Tonight might well be the final chip falling into place for the match—for Miss Devenish has officially put off mourning, you know, and I think I might persuade Philip to make an offer for her within the week—before anyone else manages to do so. You cannot deny that it is a good match."

"That may well be, but why we are required to concern ourselves in Oxley's affairs is beyond me. A man in his position should surely be able to handle such things without the help of a matchmaking sister. I hope you do not expect for me to exert myself on his behalf beyond hosting the party. I have more than enough to think about with the stack of bills I received from the dressmaker today."

Footsteps approaching the door sounded, and Philip drew back, a frown on his face. He hated the way Sir Jon spoke to Alice. She was certainly not the easiest woman to deal with, but anyone who had spent more than a day in her company knew that she was desperate to please—to exceed expectations. Jon seemed not to appreciate that about his wife.

The door opened, and Jon appeared, stopping short at the sight of Philip. "Oxley," he said, his brow creasing even more deeply. "I never heard the bell ring."

Philip conjured the most genial smile he could. "It must be because I never rang it."

Jon's lips pinched together in displeasure. "If you will excuse me, I must go dress for dinner."

Philip inclined his head and watched his brother-in-law take the stairs to his bedchamber. It bothered him that Jon thought him incompetent—that he recognized that Philip required assistance in his efforts to marry. But he would far rather Jon believe that Alice was the one providing that assistance than for him to know of the Swan. The scorn that knowledge would generate....

He stepped into the sitting room, just in time to see Alice wipe a tear from her cheek. The sight tugged at his heart. He remembered when Alice had accepted Jon's offer—she had put on a smile, never admitting how it cost her to give up the future she had hoped for with Mr. Vickers. She had reassured Philip she agreed with their father that it was a much more fitting match. "Sir Jon is kind, you know," she had said. "And I think that I shall be happy with him, for I have always had such a streak of vanity that, no matter what I do, will not be overcome, and Sir Jon has promised me that I shall want for nothing with him."

Well. That promise seemed to have fallen flat. Alice would not otherwise have been shedding tears.

"Philip," she said, rising from her chair with a determined smile that twisted Philip's heart as much as her tears had.

If he and Miss Devenish married, would they be thus in five years? In a decade?

"I am glad you have arrived early," Alice said, "for I wished to discuss the plan for the evening before the Devenishes arrive." She took him by the arm, leading him out into the hall. "I think I might arrange for you and Miss Devenish to have a few minutes alone this evening after dinner. Jon and I will engage to speak with her mother and father, and you can perhaps take her for some air in the small courtyard—I have instructed that it be lit this evening, and you will be quite private there"—she pressed her lips together, though the hint of a smile peeked through—"just in case you wish to steal a few moments." She raised her brows to make her meaning clear.

Ruth's face flashed before Philip, chin upturned, lips parted invitingly, arc of dark eyelashes resting against her smooth skin.

"That will not be necessary, Alice, but thank you."

"What do you mean? Of course it is not necessary, but I assure you, I am not so prudish that I begrudge you such a little pleasure, and I rather think that it would be preferable that she know of your intent to speak with her father before you go about it—"

He put up a hand. "I thank you again for your desire to help, but I would rather you leave it to me to arrange things. The situation is more delicate than you realize."

"Delicate? How do you mean?"

How could he explain it to her? He couldn't. Ruth's reputation was at stake, and besides, Alice wouldn't understand. "I merely mean to say that I am not prepared to offer for Miss Devenish just yet."

Alice blinked at him.

"I may have been hasty in telling you of my plans before I well knew what I wanted."

"You…you mean you do *not* intend to offer for Miss Devenish? Philip, you cannot be serious! What in the world do you imagine she and her family expect after an evening such as tonight?"

"An evening I had no part in planning, you may remember."

Her mouth dropped open, and displeasure darkened her brow. "I cannot do anything right, can I?" Her nostrils flared. "And who, may I ask, do you intend to offer for if not for Miss Devenish? Who do you imagine to be her superior—more fit to take her place at Oxley Court?"

Philip gripped his lips together, unsure how to answer her question. "I am more interested in answering the question of who is fit to take the place by my side—as my wife."

Wariness entered her eyes. "What do you mean?"

"I mean," he said, "that all this time, I have been looking for the Viscountess Oxley, when I *should* have been looking for my wife."

Her eyes widened. "You are going to ruin us, aren't you?"

Philip scoffed and looked away. "Please. You are the wife of Sir Jon Tipton and the daughter of a viscount—positions that put you well above reproach."

Alice grabbed his arm. "Yes, I *am* the wife of Sir Jon Tipton, and I did *not* become such so that you could make a mockery of my sacrifice by marrying some nobody!"

Philip looked down into her eyes where anger flamed. "I never asked you to make that sacrifice, Alice. And were it not for Anne and Mary, I might wish that you hadn't done so. But I could never wish them away, and I know you could not either."

She held his gaze, her eyes watering as the bell rang. She released his arm and backed away, finally turning toward the door, where she stopped for a moment, her shoulders rising with a deep, steadying breath. Then she opened the door and disappeared.

Philip shut his eyes in consternation. He had hoped to comfort Alice, but he felt no better than Jon now.

Perhaps he was still being rash. He and Miss Devenish needn't end up like Jon and Alice. Had Ruth not said that what mattered most was the choice to love—made daily? And yet, how could he trust that Miss Devenish would make that choice? The one woman in the world with the most reason to love Philip—his own mother—had been so hot and cold toward him. Why should he expect better from someone who *didn't* love him?

He fiddled with his signet ring again. He had tried it on once when he was only eight or nine years old, on one of the rare occasions when his father removed it for cleaning. It had dwarfed even Philip's thumb, hanging loosely, a large void between it and his finger. It had seemed impossible then that he would ever be big enough or old enough for it to fit.

Now that it did, he found it uncomfortably tight, as if he had not only grown into it but also outgrown it.

Luctor et emergo. I struggle and emerge. That was the inscription inside.

Philip certainly struggled. But he had no idea how to emerge or what he would be when he did.

For a woman on the verge of contracting a brilliant match, Miss Devenish showed little sign of excitement—nor any of the willingness she had shown at the card party just a few days since.

"She can *feel* your hesitancy," Alice breathed at Philip during dinner.

But Philip was going out of his way to be courteous. In a final effort to see whether he had not perhaps fooled himself into thinking himself in love with Ruth, he did his best to open himself up to the prospect of marriage to Miss Devenish. He addressed himself to her throughout dinner, asking her questions, trying to make her smile. And smile she did. But there was no warmth in it. Only politeness. When he put a hand on her back to make a quiet remark to her, she stiffened slightly.

He wondered at it, but he couldn't help feel a bit of relief. Surely she would not have reacted so if she welcomed his attentions.

And the gesture felt wrong to Philip—like a betrayal of himself and Ruth. It was unnatural, sharply contrasted against the way he had felt drawn toward Ruth the day before, as though their hands, their faces, their souls were meant to touch.

"Miss Devenish," Alice said once the men had rejoined the women in the drawing room. "You look a bit flushed. Philip, why don't you show her out onto the terrace for a bit of fresh air? I do think it is cooler outside than it is inside." She shot him a significant look.

What Alice expected to happen during the short jaunt outdoors after what he had said to her in the sitting room, Philip hardly knew, but he was grateful for the opportunity to speak to Miss Devenish in private. He needed to understand what precisely was going on.

He offered her his arm and led her toward the two doors on the far wall of the drawing room, which opened onto one of the larger terraces offered by the houses in Town. Torches illuminated the small garden below.

Miss Devenish unfurled her fan, waving it lightly in the air. "It does feel pleasant out here, doesn't it?"

"Indeed," Philip said sardonically. "I believe my sister lit a few fires in the house to ensure it would be cooler out here. I was glad at my sister's contrivance, though, for I have been wishing to speak with you in private."

Miss Devenish glanced up at him, a wary light in her eyes.

It gave Philip the necessary confidence to be blunt. "I tend to dislike gossip, but I hope you will forgive me for addressing it in this instance, as I find myself feeling a desire to understand—and a suspicion that there is more truth than I previously supposed in what I have heard."

She looked at him, a questioning frown in her eyes. "What is it?"

He opened his mouth then shut it, directing an evaluative gaze at her as he tried to decide how to proceed. "Are you in love with someone?"

Her lips parted in surprise, and she averted her gaze. "That is not what I was expecting."

"I apologize for my forwardness, but I think it will serve us both better than the alternative. You can be fully honest with me, Miss Devenish, I assure you."

She played with the hem of her dress. "I am. Or was, rather."

"You *were*?"

She looked up to meet his eye. "I cannot tell, to be honest. At times I feel more in love with him than ever. Other times, I feel the greatest rage imaginable and regret that we ever met." She smiled sadly.

Philip frowned, watching the flickering of the torch light that illuminated only one side of Miss Devenish's face. "I see. Allow me to be even more frank still, and I hope you will oblige me by returning the favor. Do you have a desire to marry me?"

She went still, her eyes still trained on him. "I am not certain how to answer that, my lord. Sometimes, I think I should be very content with you, while at others, I think I wish to never marry at all."

He nodded. "And which of those do you feel today?"

She bit her lip.

"You can be honest. I will not take offense."

She nodded. "The latter. It is nothing against you. You are very kind and good, and I am certain that you and everyone else shall think me fit only for Bedlam when I say it, but having tasted love, I cannot find it within me to marry for any other reason."

He took her hand in his, offering a sympathetic smile. "I understand perfectly."

"You do?"

"I do. And I would never wish for you to feel compelled into a marriage you cannot enter with your mind *and* heart."

She smiled up at him with a hint of sadness. "Nor I you."

Philip glanced at the doors. "What of your parents? I fear they have come to expect a match between us, and I would hate for this to cause any problems—"

She shook her head, and he let her hand drop. "I am fortunate in my parents. They have certainly come to expect an agreement between us, but only because I gave them reason to believe it was what I wanted. They merely wish for me to be happy."

"You *are* fortunate," Philip said, a sense of envy stinging inside. He let out a large breath and smiled. "Well, then. We *do* have an agreement—just a different one from what others have come to expect." He put out a hand for a handshake, and she laughed lightly.

"We have an agreement."

Chapter Thirty-Seven

Ruth spent all of the next day with a boulder-sized weight in the pit of her stomach. She couldn't keep herself from hoping that the bell might ring or that the footman might deliver a note to her from Philip—anything to put a stop to the alternating hope and despair she was feeling.

By the time the sun was illuminating the sky with the yellows and oranges of sunset, she felt an unbearable restlessness and stepped out onto the streets. She couldn't remain cooped up in the townhouse, wondering whether Philip would emerge from the evening with permission from Mr. Devenish and a promise from his daughter—the very promise Ruth had engaged to make a reality when she had set out to help Philip.

In no part of her mind did Ruth believe that she belonged at Philip's side more than Miss Devenish did, but never had her mind been so challenged by her heart.

She returned to Upper Brook Street just in time for the last purple hues of dusk to give way to the deep blues and star-speckled blanket of a nighttime sky. She turned back toward the street once on the doorstep, taking a moment to revel in what was likely the last night she would spend with such freedom at her fingertips. She had no intention of attending the Walthams' masquerade on the morrow if she had not yet heard from Philip—indeed, she doubted she would be allowed inside without his escort—and she and Topher were set to leave the morning following it.

Silence reigned again at breakfast, as it had come to do in recent days, evidence of the humor both Topher and Ruth were in. But just as Ruth was finishing her cup of tea, a footman entered with a silver salver. He didn't bat an eye to see Ruth in her woman's garb—what Philip had said to his uncle's servants to ensure their silence and acceptance of an utterly bizarre situation was beyond Ruth, but she was certainly grateful for it. She couldn't imagine being cooped up at The Three Crowns as long as they'd been in Town, or being required to wear men's clothing day and night.

Her heart sputtered and galloped as the footman handed a letter to Topher and then one to Ruth. She felt a sting of guilt as disappointment at seeing her mother's script washed over her.

But she opened the note and smiled. The bottom half of the page contained a small, scrambled drawing from George and an attempt by Joanna to sign her name. Little notes from her other siblings filled the remainder of the space. Tears sprang to Ruth's eyes, and she gripped at her mouth to keep it from trembling. She was anxious to be back home with her family. Much as her siblings tried her patience, their sweet embraces would be balm to her wounds.

Her mother expressed an anxiousness to have Topher and Ruth home, as well as a reminder of Joanna's dearest wish to have a doll like Sophia's—as though Ruth needed such a reminder. "*Though you mustn't trouble your heads over something so superfluous and extravagant. I assure you Joanna will be content just to have you back.*"

Ruth folded the note back up and looked to Topher, whose gaze consumed the note before him hungrily.

"Who is that from?" Ruth asked.

Topher didn't respond for a moment, his eyes following the script on the page. When he had finished, he folded it up quickly, saying, "Just from Rowney. Is that from Oxley?" He indicated the paper in her hand with a nod.

"From Mama. Apparently the children insisted upon contributing." She handed it to him, and he read over the contents with a little half-smile forming as he reached the end. "George is an atrocious artist." He folded up the paper and handed it back to her as he rose from the table. "Is Oxley coming over today?"

Ruth cast her eyes down to her tea, stirring the little that remained. "I can't be certain. Perhaps not. The Walthams' masquerade is tonight, you know."

"Ah, yes. I had forgotten about that. Are you to go?"

Ruth shrugged. "I cannot think what the point would be."

Topher sent her an understanding grimace before leaving the room.

Half an hour later, Ruth stood in her room, looking at the place she had called home for the last few weeks, strewn as it was with a mixture of bonnets, top hats, slippers, and top boots. A strange scene indeed. A knock sounded on the door. "Another letter for you, miss. And a bandbox."

She opened the door with a frown, and her heart immediately leapt at the sight of Philip's script, only to plummet as she considered what news it might contain. She tried to keep her composure until she had closed the door behind her, but she set down the largest bandbox she had ever seen and hurriedly tore the seal on the letter, her eyes flying over the words within.

Little Panda,

I hope you mean to come to the masquerade tonight—I would like for you to be there for such an important occasion. I have sent along what you will need for the evening, compliments of the chest of belongings Alice has never removed from my townhouse. I meant to bring the things to you myself, but I have had some unexpected business to attend to today. Preparations and such. Both you and your brother are expected by the Walthams, under the names Mr. and Miss Franks. My Aunt Dorothea shall arrive to escort you at eight o'clock. I have taken her into my confidence, and she is thrilled at the prospect of accompanying you to the masquerade.

I can already hear your excuses and arguments against this plan, but please lay them aside. I require *your attendance this evening. After all you have done, you deserve a chance to enjoy yourself for a night—sans cravat. I shall see you this evening.*

Yours,

Philip

PS Leave the spectacles at home

Ruth reached for the large bandbox, removing the lid and uttering a sharp intake of breath at the sight within. A delicate pink dress, overlaid with lace flower embellishments, rested in the box. She pulled it out and set it gently upon the bed. He wanted her to come to the masquerade in that?

She had never touched anything so fine, much less worn it. Another glance at the bandbox revealed a silver silk domino and a black mask. She pulled out the mask and set it next to the dress, letting the silk ribbons trail off the side of the bed. The domino was the last item in the box, and Ruth smiled as she saw that it was hooded. He hadn't forgotten her short hair.

She let out a gushing breath, setting the domino on the bed. Could she go? Could she *not* go? Philip was expecting her—required her to be there, he said. *I would like for you to be there for such an important occasion.* Did this mean that he meant to offer for Miss Devenish there? It seemed so unlike him—the publicity of it. Or perhaps he merely meant that it was important because it was an ending to Ruth's and his association.

Ruth swallowed down the thought.

She ran a finger along the embellished sleeves of the ball gown, imagining what it would feel like to wear such a dress—to wear *any* dress to a ball. And to a masquerade, no less. A final hurrah.

What would she tell Topher? He couldn't go. Surely that wouldn't be wise, even if he was masked. It was too risky. The last thing they needed was for Miss Devenish to have a reminder of Topher when Philip was so close to his goal.

But Ruth discovered from Lucy that Topher had left after the note from Rowney. She frowned. Every time he went with Rowney, he either returned in the small hours of the morning or not at all. It was his last night in Town too, though, and it was his decision if he wanted to make an uncomfortable journey back to Marsbrooke due to a night of too much drinking.

Whatever he was doing, he hadn't returned by the time Ruth rang for Lucy to help her into Lady Tipton's dress. She had an uneasy feeling about the evening—maybe it was just nerves at the prospect of going about dressed as a woman—oh, the irony of it! But she found she couldn't resist Philip's plea, nor the opportunity to see him for what might be the last time. If all it did was cause her pain, at least she wouldn't leave London wishing she had gone—at least it would be the *last* painful evening she spent in Town.

Lucy worked at Ruth's hair with the container of pomade Topher had brought with him from home, and Ruth allowed her to primp and prepare her for the evening. Lucy had become quite deft at styling Ruth's hair in ways that accentuated her femininity and masculinity, depending upon what the occasion required. She deserved higher wages.

As the maid worked, Ruth traced the edge of the mask she would wear. She was becoming tired of wearing disguises, but this would be the last time.

"There. Let me see you now, miss."

Ruth stood, smoothing down the dress skirts carefully—she didn't want anything to catch on the lace embellishments. The dress was a bit short in front, but the domino would hide that well enough.

Lucy's mouth drew into a smile. "You are a wonder to behold, if I do say so myself, miss."

Ruth turned toward the mirror and went still. Her eyes stung, and she blinked quickly.

"Do you dislike it, miss?"

Ruth sniffed and shook her head with a watery laugh. "No, no. Quite the opposite. It has been so long since I felt like I looked the part of a woman, and somehow you have managed it this evening."

Lucy let out a sigh of relief. "What a shame it is that you must wear that dreadful mask and hood. But it *is* a masquerade."

Ruth clasped Lucy's hand gratefully, and the maid admired her one more time before helping her into the domino.

"If Topher returns, please tell him that I am out with Lord Oxley and shall be ready to leave first thing in the morning." She doubted Lucy would see him. But just in case.

The Walthams' townhouse was located in Grosvenor Square, making it an easy enough distance to walk. But in donning Lady Tipton's dress, Ruth had lost her freedom to walk around Town alone, and it was as the grand mahogany clock chimed eight o'clock that a carriage slowed in front of the townhouse in Upper Brook Street.

Ruth clutched the mask in her hand, nerves flapping and fluttering in her stomach. Philip said he had taken his aunt into his confidences, but what exactly did that mean? What if the woman was scandalized when she saw Ruth?

But Mrs. Barham's face was wreathed in smiles when Ruth stepped into the carriage, interest and fascination alight in her eyes.

"Miss Franks," she said, and she looked behind Ruth as if expecting someone else. "Does your brother not join us, then?"

Ruth shook her head. "I believe he decided to spend the evening with a friend."

"Ah."

Ruth took a seat across from Mrs. Barham, and that grand lady searched Ruth's face. "Marvelous! I would never have even suspected you to be the same person." She reached over and lifted the hood of Ruth's domino then smiled. "That hair suits you."

Ruth was grateful for the dim lighting as her cheeks warmed. "Thank you, ma'am."

Mrs. Barham gave the signal, and the carriage pulled forward. She continued to regard Ruth with interest, a little smile tugging at the corner of her rouged mouth. "All this time, I thought my nephew to be a pattern card of propriety, when he has been harboring the most wondrous secrets from us all." She gave a delighted laugh.

Ruth tried to keep smiling, but the words struck her conscience. Philip *was* proper, and Ruth disliked the feeling that any aberration from his normal behavior should be laid at her feet. "I am afraid that mine is a secret he has been obliged to keep—not one he would have chosen if he had known the truth from the beginning."

"Oh, nonsense." She looked through the window as they approached Grosvenor Square. "It is high time he broke free from the Trent stranglehold. He is meant for much greater things than the stuffy nonsense with which they inculcated him."

Ruth said nothing, momentarily dazzled by the light of the gas lamps which illuminated the Waltham residence. It was so very bright. Would she be recognized? Lucy had assured her that, with the hood and the mask, there was no chance at all of it, but she couldn't help the nerves fluttering inside her.

"Come, child," Mrs. Barham said, stepping down from the carriage, and the epithet made her feel cared for and protected even as she stepped into a world that was not her own. For one last time.

Mrs. Barham brought her handheld mask to her face and leaned over to speak in low tones. "I am here to do whatever strikes your fancy. My presence here lends propriety, just as Philip wished for, but you know how I feel about such things, and I assure you that I shan't be a stick in the mud. The evening is yours, and I shall be quite content to introduce you to whomever you wish to dance with, all the while delighting in the delicious fact that no one here knows you as Mr. Ruth." Her ill-stifled smile underlined her assertion, and Ruth managed a smile back, wondering what Mrs. Barham would think if she knew that the only person Ruth had any desire to dance with that evening was Philip.

Mrs. Barham gave their names to the servant at the door, and Ruth took in a steadying breath. She would do her best to enjoy herself.

Chandeliers full of tall, white candles illuminated the path to the grand ballroom, and Ruth gazed around in awe, while Mrs. Barham provided the names of various people in the room.

Even if the majority of the people hadn't been wearing masks, Ruth doubted she would have recognized many of them. She was still woefully ignorant regarding the identities of those who frequented such gatherings as this one, and her eyes searched for the familiar—they searched for Philip. She hadn't any idea what he was wearing, but she didn't doubt she would recognize him, despite that.

And she did, with a leaping of the heart. Like Ruth's own mask, his was black—dark enough that his hair looked lighter than usual in contrast. His matching black domino draped over his broad shoulders, and his mouth stretched into the contagious smile that made Ruth ache.

He seemed to be laughing in response to the man beside him, a stranger to Ruth. Though half of his face was concealed behind a white mask, the man was objectively handsome—perhaps most people would consider him more so than Philip. His dark eyes peered lazily through the narrow slits in the mask, and they held a glint in them that simultaneously intrigued and unnerved her.

"Ah, there is Philip," said Mrs. Barham entirely unnecessarily. "And Finmore with him, of course. Shall we go over to them? Finmore will wish to dance with you, no doubt."

Ruth shot a hand out to stop Mrs. Barham. "No, not just yet." If Philip wanted to see her, he would find her. But this evening was always meant to be about him and Miss Devenish, and Ruth would not ruin that. "I thought we might see what refreshments they have. This is my first time at a masquerade, and I find that I am a bit nervous, which always makes my mouth terribly dry."

Mrs. Barham patted her arm and smiled. "Of course. I quite understand."

Ruth sent another sidelong glance at Philip, and she watched his eyes move to the door, neck craning slightly to look for Miss Devenish's arrival, no doubt. Ignoring the twinge in her heart, Ruth walked alongside her chaperone toward the long tables that lined the far wall of the room. They were covered with white, lace-edged tablecloths and wreathed in flowers.

With a glass of ratafia in hand, she and Mrs. Barham found a space along the windowed wall, which looked out onto a candlelit terrace. Ruth sucked in a breath as the gaze of a masked man settled on her.

It was Munroe, and there seemed to be a glint of recognition in his eyes that sped her heart. But he turned his head away, and Ruth assured herself that she must have imagined it. She was far too much on edge.

The ballroom was filling quickly and the musicians strumming and tuning their instruments in preparation for dancing. Ruth had a feeling that Mrs. Barham wouldn't allow her to merely watch from the walls. She would find her some partner or other, and Ruth would do her best to enjoy herself. She didn't want to look back on her last evening in London wishing she had made a greater effort to take advantage of it.

She breathed in the scents of the ballroom—flowers, fruit tarts, candles, and hair pomade—and pulled her mouth into a smile. She would recount every detail of it to Joanna when she was back in Marsbrooke.

She took a sip of ratafia, letting her gaze take in the merriment around her, where couples whispered and smiled at one another, emboldened by the masks they wore. She choked suddenly, blinking quickly to focus through the water in her eyes.

Standing together in a corner of the ballroom in close conversation were Topher and Miss Devenish. He held her hand in his, just as he had done that day in the Park when Ruth had first discovered them.

How *could* Topher? And why? What could have possessed him to come? And to treat Miss Devenish with such familiarity after everything?

Ruth's eyes flew to Philip, but his back was to them—he was unaware, just as he always had been. Just as Ruth had let him be. But certainly not for long.

Philip's gaze met hers, and his mouth stretched into a smile. He took hold of Finmore's arm, saying something in his ear, and Finmore's eyes searched the room before landing on Ruth and narrowing in curiosity. He allowed Philip to pull him in their direction.

Ruth stifled the impulse to tidy her hair and dress—likely she would never rid herself of that irritating desire to look her best for Philip.

The beginnings of a waltz strung out from the instruments, and couples moved to the ballroom floor. Out of the corner of her eye, Ruth was aware of Topher leading Miss Devenish there. Panic bloomed in her chest, even as she felt her head swim with the view of Philip's smile directed toward her. His domino swished as he and Finmore came to a stop before the two women, and Ruth smelled that faint but unmistakable rush of amber.

"Aunt Dorothea. Miss Franks." His eyes twinkled at her through the black mask, as if they had needed anything to accentuate what a beautiful combination of light brown and green they were. "Miss Franks, allow me to introduce you to my friend, Mr. Julius Finmore."

Finmore stared at her with an intent, evaluative gaze and extended a hand. She hesitated a moment before offering hers to him, and he planted a kiss upon it, directing his eyes up at her from his stooped position, as if watching for her reaction to his dalliance.

She glanced at Philip, and the way he watched her, completely ignoring his friend's flirtatious gesture as his own warm eyes rested upon her, made Ruth's heart skip and stutter.

"Enough, Fin," Philip said. He bowed gracefully, eyes never leaving Ruth's. "Will you dance with me, Miss Franks?"

Ruth swallowed and glanced at Mrs. Barham, who looked on with a pleasant, indulgent expression. "Go on," she said.

Ruth put her hand in Philip's, hoping her legs would carry her to the dance floor, despite feeling as though they might give out at any second. She had never waltzed before—not in public. It would be considered fast of her, not that it mattered on her last night in London. No one even knew who she was.

"You don't have to do this," she said.

Philip looked down at her, the same warmth there in his eyes. "Do what?"

"Dance with me." She looked away. "I believe your aunt intends to force some unsuspecting gentleman of her acquaintance into taking on that task."

"But I don't *want* other gentlemen to dance with you."

She forced a laugh. What was he trying to do to her?

He led her to her place in the set and stood before her. "I am feeling selfish tonight."

He took his place across the set from her, smiling, and she couldn't help following suit, not daring to inspect his words more closely.

The dance began, and Ruth was grateful for his steadying hands —they kept her grounded, kept her near him as they turned about the floor.

He smiled down at her. "You look even more the little panda with that mask on."

"And you the giant one."

He laughed. "We are well matched, then." There was a pause as they finished the figure, and he continued. "I thought you said you weren't skilled at dancing. Yet another lie."

Her smile wavered, and his gaze moved to her lips briefly. A rueful half-smile formed on his lips. "I have been waiting to dance with you since I arrived, but now that we are here, I find myself wishing to be alone rather than surrounded as we are now."

And Ruth saw it there—the thing in his eyes which she had thought was her own feelings staring back at her, everything she had *wanted* him to feel almost since meeting him. She saw love.

They broke apart for the next figure of the dance, and Ruth caught sight of Topher and Miss Devenish on the other side of the ballroom floor. Panic dispelled the brief moment of hope inside her.

Clearly Philip hadn't seen them yet. If he did, would he recognize Topher?

It didn't matter. Ruth couldn't continue deceiving him. She should have told him long ago. It might cost her three hundred pounds, but surely being poor was better than feeling the guilt and disgust with herself that she now felt?

They came together again, shoulder to shoulder, two hands joined in front. "Would you like to join me outside?"

She swallowed, stomach swirling with sickness as she thought how he would look at her when she told him the truth. But she nodded. It was now or perhaps never.

They moved away from the floor, and Ruth was vaguely aware of all the eyes on them, frowning at the strange behavior. If she looked as sick as she felt, perhaps the audience would believe she was near to fainting.

One gaze followed their progress with especial curiosity, and Ruth's stomach clenched at the knowing glint in Mr. Munroe's eyes.

Her hand was in Philip's, and she was barely aware of anything but that fact as he led her out of the ballroom, down the stairs, through a room, and into the small garden courtyard. Cool evening air licked at the skin on Ruth's face, but it brought little refreshment.

He led her toward the side of the garden where hedges grew as tall as him. "Here." He turned to face her, still holding her gloved hand in his. "This is much more comfortable."

Ruth's heart thumped uncontrollably.

"When I saw you upstairs, I was surprised—I had been watching the door for your arrival ever since my own, but I must have missed it somehow."

He had been watching for *her*? "Philip." She forced herself to speak before her courage gave out. It would be too easy to stand here alone with him, letting him think she was better than she was. "I need to tell you something."

He nodded. "And I you." He put his other hand around hers, enveloping them as though they were small and precious.

Hesitation nipped at her, binding her tongue with the same contradictory reluctance and urgency that bound her heart.

"Wait." He pulled his mask down, redirecting his gaze at her. "I want to see you." He put a gentle hand to her head and pushed back the hood of her domino. His hand paused as his eyes roved over her hair and face, pinning her in place, then reached his hand back behind her head and gave a soft tug on her mask strings, sending shivers down her spine as the silk ribbons slipped down the bare skin of her back beneath her domino, dress, and chemise.

He let his hand cup the back of her head, and she felt every shred of power slip away as his eyes locked on her lips, the same longing in them that Ruth had been feeling for weeks.

"I have been waiting—wanting—to finish what we twice began." His other hand slipped around her waist, and Ruth struggled for the briefest moment before letting her eyes close, no longer fighting what she wanted more than anything to give into.

Muted voices from the ballroom floated above them, and Ruth felt Philip's face nearing hers, as if her body was attuned to his movements as much as to her own. The hand at her waist pulled her closer, and she ceded to it willingly.

They had touched many times, but for so long, it had been masculine—jabs with an elbow, helping her hold a pistol, bracing grips on the shoulder. But now, Philip held her like a woman, and with that first soft touch of the lips that made her shiver, he kissed her like a woman—with care and need and tenderness, his lips exploring hers gently, his hand holding her against him just as they had done in the drawing room.

Only this time, he didn't let go. He anchored her to him, where she belonged, and he kissed her. And she kissed him back, hoping that he could feel her love for him through it, just as she had told him a kiss should do.

Footsteps sounded behind Ruth somewhere, followed by voices, growing louder.

"There he is!"

Ruth and Philip broke apart, heads whipping toward the source of the interruption.

Unmasked, Munroe stood in the doorway that led from the house to the garden, the sneer of victory on his face.

Philip stood beside Ruth, holding her hand, even as unfamiliar faces gathered behind Munroe.

"What do you want, Munroe?"

Munroe's mouth tugged up on one side, the lopsided smile enhancing his smugness. "So she caught you after all."

Philip grasped Ruth's hand tighter, and she struggled to breathe evenly.

"The Swan," Munroe clarified, raising his voice far louder than was necessary to make it heard. "The woman who's been parading herself around town dressed as a man for the last month, swindling us all—and none more than you, Oxley."

Murmurs sounded, and Ruth realized that there were people on the terrace up above.

Philip laughed caustically. "Says the man who challenged a woman to a duel."

Munroe's smile faded, turning back into a sneer. "I cannot be blamed for that, surely." He looked at Ruth. "Not when she looks more boy than woman. Perhaps I should have known, though, by her cowardice."

Philip started toward Munroe, but Ruth held him back.

His chest rose and fell. "If your idea of honor is challenging women and boys to duel you, then you and I are even more different than I believed us to be, Munroe."

Munroe made a sweeping bow, looking up at the people who were congregating up on the terrace. "A compliment if I ever heard one. I admit, I am surprised to find that you knew Ruth was a woman this whole time, but I am *more* surprised to find you kissing the minx who's been leading you such a dance and making you look a fool."

Ruth's heart sank, and she pulled Philip back as he tried to lunge toward Munroe. But she was no match for his strength, and he broke away from her, reaching Munroe in two long strides and punching him in the face.

"Ruth!" Topher's voice rang out from the terrace above, and she glanced up at him. He was hand in hand with Miss Devenish.

Chapter Thirty-Eight

Philip's knuckles stung, and he clenched his hand to numb the pain. Munroe had fallen back into the arms of Mr. Archer and another man, but he threw their supportive hands off and put a hand to his bleeding nose.

He glanced at his bloody thumb then chuckled. "So you *don't* know. Then you have my sympathies, Oxley."

Philip backed up a few steps, reaching his hand for Ruth's again. If Munroe wished for a duel, Philip would gladly accept. At least this time he wouldn't be forcing Ruth into it.

"Do you want to tell him? Or shall I?" Munroe was speaking to Ruth, and he shrugged his shoulders. "He can look up there and see for himself, I suppose." He pointed lazily up above them, and Philip glanced up at the terrace, where a dozen people stood.

"Philip." Ruth's soft, plaintive voice sounded beside him, and he looked down at her. "I wanted to tell you. I should have told you."

Philip's eyebrows drew together, unease filling him at the look on Ruth's face. "Told me what?"

"Bah!" Munroe said. "Why spoil the fun and let her do it? *I* shall tell you!" He threw up his hands and shoulders, directing a pitying grimace at Philip. "Your swan has been bamboozling you, Oxley! Playing you false."

Ruth's hands clenched Philip's arm, and she shook her head, but there was desperation in her eyes.

Munroe looked at all the people gathering around, and an unpleasant smile stretched across his lips as he directed himself to the group at large. "Perhaps many of you will recognize this woman before you! She has been masquerading"—he snorted with amusement at his *à propos* choice of word—"around Town for a month now, dressed as a man. One Mr. Ruth—also known as the Swan—a poor woman who gets paid for giving love advice in a newspaper."

More murmurs sounded.

"She has been accepting money from unsuspecting gentlemen who haven't the wherewithal to handle their own affairs—who require the help of someone else to woo women." He sniggered. "Lord Oxley is one of those men."

Philip clenched his jaw, and he felt the blood pulsing in his neck, drawing the heat up into his face as his fellows looked on. Was this what Ruth meant she should have told him? That she had been discovered?

"But she has done more than cheat a few fools out of their money. She had other plans—far more ambitious ones! Didn't you, Miss Hawthorn? Far more than could be gained from helping Oxley or Kirkhouse."

Ruth swallowed, shaking her head, and Munroe sneered, the light of victory growing in his eyes. "All this time, she was helping her own brother to court Miss Devenish in secret." He pointed up toward the terrace, and Philip's eyes followed.

Miss Devenish stood there beside a masked man Philip now recognized as Mr. Hawthorn. They held hands, but Miss Devenish was frowning, her eyes trained on Munroe.

"Yes. And I must applaud the enterprise and vision of your scheme, Miss Hawthorn. Why help Oxley to win Miss Devenish's hand when you could steal him for yourself—and Miss Devenish for your brother?"

Philip's head turned slowly to Ruth.

"No, indeed," she said, and her hand tightened its grip on his. "That is not what it was!"

"Oh, but it was," Munroe said.

Nausea swirled in Philip's stomach, his hand sweating in its glove.

"I didn't know," Ruth said. "I swear. And nor did Topher. He would never have courted her if he had known it was her you wished to marry."

Philip blinked and swallowed, but Ruth's face still oscillated before him strangely.

"Mr. Ruth is a woman? And your *sister*?" Miss Devenish's stunned voice wafted down to the gardens.

"Rebecca—"

"And you...you *tricked* me into loving you?"

"No, I—"

Departing footsteps sounded, followed by Mr. Hawthorn's pleas.

Ruth reached a hand up to Philip's face. "Philip. Please let me explain."

He drew back, letting her hand drop from his and stepping backward as things clicked into place in his mind. Ruth's acquaintance with Miss Parkham and Mr. Kirkhouse—and their engagement shortly after her arrival in Town. Rumors of Miss Devenish's secret lover. The strange behavior of both Mr. Hawthorn and Miss Devenish at the card party. "It was your brother?"

Tears sprang to Ruth's eyes, and she reached a hand out to Philip. "I didn't know. And when I discovered it, they ended things."

"And you didn't tell me?" He took another step backward, remembering the list of lies he had detailed after discovering Ruth was a woman—how he had laughed as if it was a joke.

"I didn't think it mattered. Topher and Miss Devenish could never be—and you were having such success with her."

Bile rose in Philip's throat, and he stepped back again, away from Ruth's outstretched hand—the one he had been holding but a moment ago. He stumbled as his shoe hit an uneven stone, and he caught himself on the raised wall beside him, gazing dazedly around the gardens.

Pitying faces looked on, some silent, some whispering with their eyes trained on him. He clenched his eyes shut to block out the nightmarish sight.

"Philip, please."

He froze, jaw clenching at his name on Ruth's lips. She had made him look a fool—held his hand while he defended her in front of all his acquaintances—defended a person who had been secretly humiliating him.

Had she been using her own tactics against him to make him fall in love with her? He rose up to his full height and squared his shoulders. He wouldn't let her humiliate him by showing how much the knowledge hurt him.

"Don't." He turned on his heel and strode from the courtyard, pushing past a smirking Munroe and into the house.

Chapter Thirty-Nine

Ruth was vaguely aware of the tears streaming down her face as Philip left the gardens. She could feel every pair of eyes on her, hear the blaring din of whispers that shouted everywhere around her.

Munroe clucked his tongue. *"Upon my soul, a wicked lie."*

She stared at him for a moment. How had he discovered everything?

Her stomach dropped as she thought on the anonymous visit to the offices of the newspaper. Was Munroe behind that?

Ruth grabbed the mask that lay upon the bench and rushed out of the gardens. She had to make Philip understand. She was a wretch—there was no doubt about that—but she was not the reprobate he thought her. He needed to know that her feelings for him were real, even if he doubted everything else.

As fast as her skirts would allow, she ran after him, pushing through crowds of people until Philip's dark head of hair appeared before her at the door which led out to Grosvenor Square.

"Philip!"

He didn't turn but strode through the hastily opened door, disappearing into the night air. The servants made to shut the door behind him.

"Wait," Ruth said, and they pulled it open again with slightly raised brows. She hurried past them and down the steps, reaching for Philip's hand.

He stopped and swung around to face her. His jaw was sharp, his nostrils flared, his fist balled in her hand.

"Please let me explain," she pleaded.

People newly arrived to the masquerade walked past, curious eyes directed at them through their masks.

"There is nothing to say," he said, pulling his hand away. "If you are here about your money, I will have it sent around in the morning." He smiled humorlessly. "You have certainly earned it, haven't you?"

Her lips trembled, and she rubbed them together to stop it. "I don't want your money, Philip."

He raised his brows, but the gesture rang false. "Oh, you don't? Why? Because you thought you might have more than three hundred pounds if you could have me instead?"

Ruth pulled in a sharp intake of breath, hurt that he had believed something so unsavory about her. "How can you believe Munroe but refuse to listen to me?"

He scoffed and turned fully toward her, folding his arms across his chest. "Tell me, then, Ruth! What did Munroe have wrong? Were your brother and Miss Devenish courting, or were they not?"

She swallowed. "Yes, but—"

He gave a stiff nod. "Did Kirkhouse pay you to assist him with Miss Parkham, despite your assertions that I could trust your discretion?"

"Yes, but—"

"And all this when you assured me that there were no more lies between us?"

She shut her eyes, biting her lip. What could she possibly say to defend herself? She was repulsed by her own behavior. "I was wrong, Philip. I should have told you. And I wanted to."

"Then *why*? Why didn't you?"

She stared at him, chest heaving, trying to decide what to say. She could blame it on Topher. She could blame it on her circumstances and the dire need of her family. But at the end of the day, only she could take responsibility for her deceit.

She lifted her shoulders helplessly, and the night air prickled her cheeks where the tears trailed down. "I was afraid of losing you—your friendship. Your respect."

He scoffed and looked away. "Well, you have lost them. All of them."

She cast her eyes down, hoping to hide the way his words wounded her. "You have every reason to despise me. And heaven knows I don't expect you to forgive me. I only came after you because I wanted you to know one thing—to believe it, even if you can believe nothing else."

She glanced at the passing couple on their way into the townhouse, waiting until they were out of earshot. She would gladly declare her feelings before them—she had no reputation left to salvage. But she didn't wish to embarrass Philip with such a display—not after all she had already done to him.

"I love you, Philip." Her voice trembled, and she forced it to stay level as she continued. "You can hate me and think the very worst of me for all I have done—I assure you I never thought myself worthy of your consideration or of my sentiments being reciprocated—but please know that my regard for you has been sure and constant."

His jaw shifted from side to side, his eyes avoiding hers. "And what reason have I to believe a word you say?"

Her shoulders lifted. "None, I suppose. But it is the truth, all the same. You deserve far better than me, and I have no doubt that you shall have it. But you have all the love in my heart, however little it may be worth to you."

His gaze finally met hers. "I will send your money first thing in the morning." He turned on his heel and left.

Philip's hands shook as he walked away from Ruth, and he fought the desire to look back—to see whether there existed any evidence of her words on her face. It was weakness, and he hated that he cared—that, even amidst his anger and humiliation, the hurt in her eyes struck a chord in him. He had tied himself to her in a way that refused to be broken. His heart didn't want to believe what even Ruth had admitted was true—she had duped him. Again. She had pretended to help him, to be a friend to him, while the entire time, she'd had her own interests at heart.

And he had almost asked her to marry him.

Emotion rose in his throat, and he forced it back down, kicking at a bunch of flowers in a patch of grass in Grosvenor Square. He was no different than he had been twenty-five years ago—a pathetic little boy, desperate for the love of a woman who cared nothing for him.

When he arrived in Brook Street, he told Draper to inform Nash that he didn't require his assistance. He wanted to be alone.

At the foot of the stairs, he turned back to the butler. "Draper. In the morning, have three hundred pounds sent to my uncle's house in Upper Brook Street. You can wrap it in one of the papers on my desk and have one of the footmen take it."

The butler nodded. "Shall I write anything to go with it, my lord?"

"No, that won't be necessary." He hesitated for a moment, frowning and putting a hand to his temple. "And have some brandy sent to my bedchamber." He turned back to the stairs and undid the knot at his throat as he scaled them, tugging at the fabric until it came free of his neck then setting to the button at his throat.

Once he was in the silence of his dressing room, he tossed his mask and cravat onto the chair and sat to remove his shoes, eying the mask with a lump in his throat. He had thought removing Ruth's mask would help him see her clearly. What a fool he had been.

A servant entered, holding a tray upon which sat a full decanter of brandy. Philip thanked him with a nod of the head and reached for the crystal bottle and the empty glass beside it. He had a feeling it was the only way he would get any sleep.

Ruth didn't stand there long, watching Philip stride toward his lodgings in Brook Street as the summer breeze ruffled her hair and licked at her wet cheeks.

She knew a lost cause when she saw it. And her cause with Philip had been lost from the beginning.

Even if she *had* told him before—told him when she had discovered Topher's secret—it would have changed little. Their weak bond at that time would have snapped easily under such strain, just as the stronger one they'd developed had snapped under the weight of tonight's discovery.

Her hand stole to her lips. At least if she had told him before, she wouldn't be forever haunted by that kiss.

It had only been fifteen minutes since it had happened, but it might as well have been fifteen years for how distant and unobtainable it was now.

"Miss...Franks...or Hawthorn! Oh, whatever you are to be called!" Mrs. Barham took the three steps down from the Walthams' townhouse and came to Ruth, inspecting her with a grim look. She put an arm about Ruth's shoulders and attempted to guide her back toward the house. "Come, my dear."

But Ruth didn't budge. She wiped the tears on her face with the back of her gloves and shook her head. "No. Thank you, Mrs. Barham, but I am going home."

"I shall escort you there, then. Let me just call for the carriage to be brought around."

"No. I appreciate your kindness, but it is unnecessary."

Mrs. Barham stepped back and looked at Ruth with a frown. "I am your chaperone for the evening, my dear. What kind of a chaperone would I be to let you walk home in the dark?"

"It is but a street away and well-lit. The walk will do me good."

"That may be, but I must insist. I don't mind a good scandal, but danger is another thing entirely. Philip entrusted you into my care, and in my care you shall remain."

Ruth took a step backward, toward Upper Brook Street. "I have no desire to taint you by association with me—any more than I have already."

Mrs. Barham laughed. "Fustian nonsense, my dear! I live to be tainted. But if you insist upon walking home, I shall accompany you." She directed the nearest servant to have her carriage sent to Upper Brook Street and took Ruth by the arm.

Ruth hadn't the energy to resist any more than she already had. It was a short walk, at least.

"Now, my dear," said Mrs. Barham as they made their way slowly across the square. "Tell me what all this is about."

The small distance that lay between the Walthams' and Upper Brook Street took nearly half an hour to cover at the pace Mrs. Barham prescribed. Her firm hand guided them around Grosvenor Square twice before allowing any more progress toward their destination, and while Ruth had been reluctant to speak of her troubles, she found the prospect of explaining herself too appealing to resist for long.

For so long, she had held things inside, and if Philip wouldn't hear her, at least someone could understand her heart—someone could listen as she confessed her wrongs and clarified the intention behind them.

Mrs. Barham listened without a word, only nodding her head and pursing her lips from time to time, and when they finally set foot in front of Upper Brook Street, she turned toward Ruth with a sigh.

"Well, my dear." She put a hand on Ruth's arm. "It is a coil indeed, and I cannot say that I am certain it will all unravel as you or I might wish for it to." She rubbed Ruth's arm softly, a sad smile on her lips. "My nephew couldn't do better for himself than to marry you, in my opinion. But unfortunately, the Trents have always been lamentably concerned with the opinion of Society. And while he is better than his family on the whole, Philip is still a Trent. I think within a few days, you will know whether or not he intends to go the Trent way or to make his own path."

Ruth had no intention of remaining in Town to see whether Mrs.

Barham knew of what she spoke. It was impossible for various reasons, not least of which was how unbearable Ruth would find such suspense. She had no expectation of Philip's opinion of her changing. She was the antithesis of what Philip needed. And as for what he wanted? Well, he didn't want her now that he knew the truth about her. She had always known that.

"Get some sleep, child. Things look much less dreary in the light of the morning, I have found."

Chapter Forty

Philip's sheets were in an unmanageable twist when he woke in the morning, his feet bound up in a knot that evidenced how much he had tossed and turned all night.

Bleary-eyed, he reached for the pocket watch on the bedside table, blinking as he tried to read the hands. Ten o'clock. He sat up with a jolt. He hadn't slept anywhere near so late in recent memory.

The money would have already been delivered to Ruth by now. And if he knew her at all—a fact he admittedly doubted after last night—she was likely gone already, traveling home. His heart throbbed, and he put a hand to his chest. How long would it take for it to catch up with what his mind knew?

The door opened, and Nash entered.

Philip rubbed his eyes and reached to undo the tangle at his feet. "What do you mean, allowing me to sleep so late?"

Nash set a breakfast tray beside Philip and cleared his throat. "I attempted to wake you earlier, my lord, but thought better of it after the threats you made."

Philip fiddled with the sheets then threw up his hands in annoyance with a muttered oath.

"Allow me, sir," said Nash. With maddening calm, the valet set to undoing the night's work, freeing Philip's feet in a matter of seconds. "By the by, sir, Mr. Finmore is below stairs. He insisted that you wouldn't mind him coming up unannounced, but I managed to forestall him. Shall I turn him away?"

"You could try, but there is little chance of him listening to you." Philip pulled the breakfast tray onto the bed.

"I thought as much, sir."

"Send him up. And you might as well send up another tray as well. If I know Finmore, he's expecting to be fed."

Philip had little desire to discuss the night's occurrences with Finmore—or anyone—but he knew his friend enough to know it was useless to keep him from his purpose, whatever it might be.

It was but two minutes before Finmore's figure appeared in the doorway.

Philip eyed him with disfavor. "Is this a new habit of yours, then? Early morning visits? I don't particularly care for it."

Finmore smiled and took a seat in the chair beside the bed, reaching for a slice of toast on Philip's tray. Philip smacked at his hand, but Finmore ignored it, taking a bite out of the warm, buttered bread.

"Got a head, have you?" Finmore nodded at the half-full brandy decanter that sat on the other side of Philip's bed. "Must have been a bad night. It isn't like you to consume so much. Though it looks like you still needed some help." He got up and walked to the other side of the bed, taking the decanter and glass back with him to his chair.

"For heaven's sake, Fin. It's ten o'clock in the morning."

Finmore only smiled as he poured himself a glass. "So, the Swan."

Philip's brows drew together, and he stabbed a piece of ham with his fork.

"Took my advice after all, did you? And yet you kept mighty quiet about it."

"Can you blame me? I had no desire to be forever teased and mocked." He stared forward in silent consternation as Finmore took the piece of ham Philip had just cut, tossing it in his mouth with two fingers and washing it down with a swig of brandy.

"Is that why you didn't tell me? I had thought it was something else perhaps." He reached for the plate again, but Philip shifted it out of his reach.

"And pray tell what reason that might be."

Defeated, Finmore sat back in his chair. "That you'd fallen in love with the girl."

Philip slowed for a moment cutting the meat then finished the slice with fervor. "You mean to say you knew the Swan was a woman?"

"Not at all. Hadn't any idea of it."

"Well, neither did I at first."

"And yet you kept her around after discovering it, didn't you?" His eyebrows snapped together. "Come, Ox, I cannot allow you to treat that innocent piece of ham so violently."

Philip set down his utensils in annoyance. "You mean to say that, because I didn't send her packing, I must necessarily be in love with her?"

"No." Finmore reached for the unattended breakfast tray and pulled it onto his own lap. "I am saying that I have known you long enough to see that you're lovesick—and a fool besides."

"A fool! Yes, she made certain of that, didn't she?" He threw his legs over the side of the bed and pulled his crumpled shirt over his head. He hadn't even bothered to change it the night before.

"Oh, stop feeling sorry for yourself," Finmore said. "It isn't a good look. If you truly don't want the girl, perhaps I shall try my luck."

Philip whirled around. "Don't you dare so much as *touch* her."

Finmore raised a brow, a smile pulling at his mouth. "That's what I thought."

Philip turned away, opening the door of his wardrobe and standing behind it as he changed into a new shirt and pantaloons.

"Can't blame you for falling for the girl. She's a taking thing."

Philip tucked his shirt into his pantaloons, feeling his blood course through his veins at Finmore's words. "And that is your conclusion after a full sixty seconds in her company?"

"No." The fork scraped on the plate, and there was a pause. "That is my conclusion"—he spoke with a mouth full of ham—"after visiting her this morning."

Philip froze then stepped backward. "After what?"

Finmore poured enough brandy into his glass for a few more swallows, replacing the crystal top with a slight clanking. "Visiting her this morning." He said the words slowly and distinctly, emphasizing each syllable. "You really *do* have a head, don't you?"

"What the devil did you mean by doing such a thing?"

Finmore shrugged, unmoved by Philip's anger. "Thought I would see what all the fuss was about before you drove her off. Couldn't move a foot without hearing your name and hers being whispered at the Walthams' last night."

Philip clenched his jaw, wishing he could throw what remained of the brandy into Finmore's face. "You are the busiest, most gossip-hungry man I have ever had the misfortune of knowing."

Finmore only smiled. "If you want my opinion, you'll marry the girl, Ox. Never thought I would advise such a thing to a man in your position, but there you have it."

Philip inclined his head ironically. "Next time I wish for your opinion, you can be sure I will inform you of the fact." He turned away, his hands trembling slightly. He wanted to ask Finmore questions—to know what he had discovered on his visit—but his pride wouldn't let him.

"She loves you. Heaven only knows what she sees in you, but she does love you."

Philip snorted. "And she told you this, no doubt—knowing you would come relay the information to me."

"She did not. She hardly said a word, in fact. But believe me—I have spent enough time with enough women to know the look of love when I see it, and Miss Hawthorn can hardly see straight for how consumed she is with Philip Trent." He put up a hand, cutting off Philip's attempt to speak. "And don't try to tell me her regard is unreciprocated—a man doesn't look at a woman or hold her like you held Miss Hawthorn without being very far gone indeed."

Heat rose in Philip's neck and face. "How the deuce—"

Finmore sent him a commiserating glance. "I saw you from the terrace—couldn't understand why you had left in the middle of the waltz, so I went looking for you."

Philip's heart thumped and thundered as images and sensations from the previous evening flitted unbidden through his mind and body, but he focused on choosing a waistcoat. "Perhaps you missed this in the midst of all your philandering last night, but she played me, Fin. Like a flute."

"Did she?" He crossed his ankles. "Sounds to me like the girl was headlong in love with you from the moment she laid eyes on you but never thought herself good enough to so much as shine your boots—or to attempt to make you into less of an embarrassment around women, God bless her."

"She lied to me, Fin. She lied to everyone." Philip tugged his boot so harshly that his fingers lost their grip and flung him in the face.

Finmore watched with amusement. "She did. She was in an impossible situation, from what I can gather. And she will spend the rest of her life regretting it, I imagine."

"Good." Philip swallowed, keeping his head down to avoid Finmore's eye.

Finmore stood and shrugged, setting his glass down. "Very well. It is your affair, after all. But don't look to me for comfort when regret comes knocking on your door."

"It will be a sore trial, but I will endeavor to drown my sorrows elsewhere."

Finmore stepped toward the door and stopped with his hand on the knob. "Oh." He reached into his coat and pulled out a folded piece of paper. "She sent this back with me."

Philip took the note with a leaping heart, and Finmore watched him. "You're a fool, Ox." He closed the door behind him.

Philip unfolded the note hurriedly, and his heart plummeted as three hundred bills in bank notes fluttered to the ground.

Mrs. Barham's assertion that things would look less dreary in the morning had not rung true for Ruth. She had woken with a gaping hole inside—a rude reminder, along with the mask that lay on the bedside table, that it was no nightmare. It was all real.

Standing in the entry hall of the house in Upper Brook Street, she looked at the coins in her hand—all that remained of the twenty pounds Philip had given her. It was barely enough to afford the stagecoach fare to take them back to Marsbrooke. It was frightening how quickly the sum had been spent during their time in Town.

It was only another minute before Topher joined her there. His face was hard, his eyes lifeless, and the puffy bags beneath them evidence of how similar his night had been to Ruth's. Ruth didn't even need to ask what had happened with Miss Devenish.

A hackney carriage conveyed them to the inn from where the stagecoach would depart, and once inside, Topher finally spoke.

"What did that fellow want?"

Ruth looked up from her contemplation of her gloves. She had thought Topher asleep when Mr. Finmore had unexpectedly arrived that morning.

"Nothing, really." She looked through the carriage window, hoping he wouldn't ask any more questions. And he didn't. She didn't want to tell Topher she had rejected Philip's money—all three hundred pounds. She hated that, even in his anger at her, Philip had chosen to give her the full three hundred, even though she had not fulfilled the terms of their agreement. There had been no note with the money—only the monogrammed name and address at the top of the paper—and that silence had told her everything she needed to know.

Mr. Finmore had watched her as she opened the note, his eyes never wavering from her face. And though she had spent the last month playing a part, she was not a skilled enough actress to hide the hurt that filled her at the sight of the money and the blank page it was couched in.

She had looked away from it, folding it back into the paper

without allowing herself a second glance. She wouldn't take that money for all the world. She would find a different way to care for her family. She had to.

After nearly a month traveling in Sir Jacob's well-sprung equipage, the stagecoach was a jarring experience. More than once, Ruth was obliged to steady herself on Topher or Lucy as the wheels dipped into ruts made by the recent rain. She found a strange satisfaction in the jolting discomfort, though. It was no more than she deserved, and it was an unavoidable reminder of her place in life. The stagecoach was where she belonged—not the luxurious carriages and chandeliered masquerades of London.

"What will we tell Mother?" Topher said as they made their way from The Red Lion in Marsbrooke to the house.

"The truth," Ruth said, readjusting the valise in her arms. She was sick to death of lies.

A bit of silence ensued, broken again by Topher. "*The Weekly* will be expecting another column. We must get it to Jolley by tomorrow if it is to be printed with this week's edition."

Ruth shook her head. "I am done with the Swan, Topher."

"What?"

She said nothing, and neither did he.

The house came into view, and Ruth smiled as George's face appeared at the window, only to vanish as quickly as it came. The door opened soon after, and Joanna and George emerged, wrapping their arms around Ruth's legs and crying her name and Topher's.

She stooped down, wrapping her arms around them and breathing in their familiar scent. She shut her eyes on the tears that sprang there. She was home—dirty and small as it might be. Empty-handed and broken-hearted as she was. She was home.

Joanna took Ruth's face in her hands, pulling her head up so that Ruth was forced to look at her through her blurry vision. "Did you bring my doll, Ruthie?"

Ruth glanced at Topher, and he grimaced before sweeping George into his arms.

"I am so sorry, Jo." Ruth put a hand on her sister's dirt-stained face

—no doubt she and George had been playing in the small garden where the laundry hung to dry. "We were obliged to leave in a hurry, and I hadn't any money for a doll." Her voice broke, and Joanna's eyes reflected her disappointment.

"That's all right." Joanna smiled bravely. "I would rather have you than a doll. I am glad to have you back, Ruthie."

"I am glad to be back," she choked out.

Chapter Forty-One

Philip sat back in his chair, clasping his hands and frowning at the folded paper on the far edge of his desk. Aside from bringing it to his study after Finmore returned it to him, he hadn't touched it. It was the source of too many conflicting emotions he didn't feel ready yet to unravel.

It had been three days since the masquerade, and Philip was waiting for his emotions to achieve a more bearable balance. This pendulum, swinging from anger to pain and regret, was exhausting. The hurt had been poking its head through the fissures in the fury, and he thought that the anger was preferable.

A knock sounded, and Draper entered. "Mrs. Barham is here, my lord."

Philip grimaced. He had wondered if she might show her face after the debacle at the Walthams'.

"Show her in. And have some tea brought."

Draper bowed himself out, and moments later, Aunt Dorothea glided into the study. "Philip, my dear."

Philip invited her to take the seat across from him. "I was wondering when you would come."

"Yes, well"—she smoothed her skirts—"I thought I would give the Trent conceit some time to dissipate."

Philip tried to control a smile. Aunt Dorothea had never been shy about what she thought of the family her sister had married into. "The conceit is something I come by from both my father *and* mother, I'm afraid."

"Of course it is." She looked around the room with bland curiosity. "My sister was unbearable. I confess I was glad for your sake when she died—may she rest in peace—for I was certain that, between her and your father, they would raise you to be some sort of monster."

Philip hid his laugh behind a cough. "Pardon me," he said. Somehow his aunt's plainspokenness always caught him off guard. He had known that she and his mother had not been close, but he had never heard her speak so candidly about her opinion of her sister.

She nodded at the bank notes that peeked through the half-folded paper. "Is that Miss Hawthorn's money?"

Philip's smile faded.

"She sent it back, I take it."

"She did."

"Of course she did."

Philip felt a flash of annoyance at the implication of his aunt's words—as though the fact surprised her not at all. It had surprised Philip, and that sparked his guilt and his misgiving. He had hoped Ruth would take the money. It would have confirmed everything to him—it would have made it easier for him to hold onto his anger and reconfirmed that she was not for him—that he had misjudged her when he had taken her to be the goodhearted woman he'd come to think her.

But she *had* sent it back—and he knew how badly she needed it. A quick walk to his uncle's had confirmed what he had suspected—she and her brother were already gone.

And then the worry had set in. How had they afforded the

journey back to Marsbrooke? And what would they do once they were home?

"And you let her go." Aunt Dorothea sat back in her chair, fixing her direct gaze on him.

He said nothing, feeling that words were unnecessary—and perhaps not wishing to confirm the low opinion his aunt obviously had of him in that moment.

"Well," she said, rising from her chair. "Your mother would be proud of you." She paused to stare him in the eye. "And that is *not* a compliment."

Philip's eyebrows snapped together. "What am I to take from that, if you please?"

Aunt Dorothea pursed her lips. "How am I to know what you take from it? Surely you are not so incapable and reliant upon others that you require me to tell you how to interpret every single comment made to you." She lifted her chin and directed an expression of disappointment at him. "But if you *are* to base your actions upon what others think and expect of you, I will at least make my own opinion known. Here it is: I thought more of you, Philip. I *hoped* more of you. But I was wrong. You are a Trent through and through. That is all." She moved toward the door.

"Wait, now." Philip hurried to stop his aunt's progress from the room, putting his hands out to stop her. "If you are expressing your opinion, then give it full rein, by all means—but do me the service of allowing a response rather than retreating before I can defend myself."

She raised her brows. "Have you a defense, then?"

"Of course I do."

She gave a smile of faux politeness, blinking as she waited for him to continue.

He shifted his weight, suddenly feeling foolish. "You cannot truly believe that Ruth—that Miss Hawthorn—is the person I should marry."

Her brows rose even higher.

"Let us leave aside all of her deception—pretend that she had done nothing to give me a distaste for her company. She is precisely nobody. No money. No experience in Society—save a few weeks dressed as a man. And you are telling me that you think her fit to be the next Viscountess Oxley? To fill the shoes of my mother?"

Aunt Dorothea's brows drew together. "Your mother's shoes?" Her head shifted slowly from side to side in disbelief. "Listen well, Philip. I loved my sister—loved her *because* she was my sister. But I was not stupid enough to be fooled by the mask she wore in public. She may have filled the role of viscountess well, but it was the *only* thing she did well. She made your father miserable, but she was too busy pleasing herself and the rest of Society to care for such a thing. Miss Hawthorn is ten times the woman my sister was. And she may have deceived you or embarrassed you, but if the result is a bit of compelled humility on your part, then so much the better! Let me ask you this: who is more fit to hold the *unimaginable honor* of the title you offer? Someone skilled enough to appear as though the role fit her perfectly? Whose façade hides a selfish heart? Who bought the position with her wealth and then used it to appeal to her own vanity? Or someone like Miss Hawthorn, who is unassuming, selfless, and who seeks no such honors—indeed, who eschews them, but would take them on if it was what being with *you* required?"

Philip stood speechless, battered by his aunt's words.

Her face softened as she looked at him, and she let out a sigh. "You must decide, Philip, if what you want is veneer or substance—appearance or essence. You may choose a viscountess who looks the part—who brings with her all the things Society applauds—or you can choose a woman you love and respect, and who loves and respects you in return. The former will please Society, and perhaps she will please you well enough, too. But the latter...that woman will enrich your life. She will challenge you and make you a better man—and a better viscount—than you otherwise would have been. To forgive Miss Hawthorn may cost your pride for a moment. But it will enlarge your soul for a lifetime." She went up on her tiptoes to kiss him on the cheek. "Good day, my boy."

Philip couldn't stand to be in his lodgings for another minute. Restlessness and discontent were seeping into everything he did. Not even a meeting with his steward kept his mind from things for long.

It didn't matter which room he chose to be in—invariably, he found Ruth there, even in rooms she had never ventured into. His father's quizzing glass in the study brought to mind hideous horn-rimmed spectacles, and a quick and uncustomary escape into the kitchens brought his eyes to a basket of lemons. She was everywhere, and nowhere more present than in his mind, where her teasing smile would strike with no notice at all.

Nash helped him into his coat, and Philip hurried down the stairs and outside, directing the coachman to Brooks'.

More than anything, Aunt Dorothea's words had been haunting him. The fact that both she and Finmore—two people with little in common besides their disregard for Society's opinion—had called him a fool was not something he could simply ignore. He had no doubt that Ruth regretted what she had done. He had seen it in her eyes, and as he had run through the events of the masquerade, he had come to suspect that she had been on the verge of telling him the truth before he had insisted on removing her mask—and then he had been too eager to kiss her to think of anything else.

He frowned and brushed at his lips with a thumb, trying to recapture the brief moment in time when he had felt his future falling into place—when nothing had mattered but the woman in his arms. He had already made the decision then that Aunt Dorothea had spoken of—had decided that to love Ruth was more important to him than grasping for some impossible ideal that had made neither of his parents happy. He wanted to marry for love.

The revelation of her dishonesty had catapulted him backward, though, making him doubt everything and feel that perhaps he had been right about love after all—it was messy, hard, and unforgiving. It was never equally reciprocated, and it could never be relied upon.

And now that his anger was expiring, he felt rudderless. Confused. Lonely. And the minute he allowed himself to explore those feelings, a panda-shaped hole gaped back at him.

The rumbling carriage ride to his neglected club provided little distraction from the fact he was finding it harder and harder to ignore: he missed Ruth. Fiercely. He worried for her and wondered about her. He regretted speaking to her so harshly—regretted not allowing her to explain herself. He had felt justified in his anger—that he had every right to be angry—but the more he considered Ruth's situation, the less his anger had sustained him and the less clear things had become.

He had hired the Swan to help him marry Miss Devenish, and one of the first things he had explained was that he cared little for a love match. It was practical. So why was he so angry that Ruth had kept from him what she knew about Miss Devenish being in love with her brother? Had she not asked him whether he was bothered by the rumors of Miss Devenish's secret lover, and had he not dismissed them as irrelevant?

He stepped down from the carriage and into Brooks', handing his hat to the doorman. He felt a stirring of nerves as he made his way toward the large drawing room. He had been humiliated at the Walthams'. How would it feel to face the people and their opinion of him now?

As expected, when he entered the main room, all eyes turned toward him, a few whispers breaking the sudden silence. He clenched his teeth and ignored the gawking, searching the room for Finmore. But Finmore wasn't there.

Munroe approached him, his leering smile bringing pulsing blood into Philip's neck.

"Didn't think to see you venturing out in public so soon, Oxley."

"If I had known it would mean seeing you, I assure you I would not have done so."

"Oho!" Munroe said, laughing and turning toward the rest of the gentlemen in the room. "That is hardly the way to thank the man who saved you from the clutches of a scheming wench, is it?"

Philip reared back his right arm and sent his fist flying into Munroe's face. The man tumbled back and landed flat on his back, unconscious. "It is becoming a dead bore having to plant you a facer every time I see you, Munroe."

The room vibrated with stunned silence, and Philip gazed around at all the faces staring at him. There was nothing for him here. The faces were all familiar, but he found he couldn't care less what they thought of him. If any of them raised their voices against Ruth, he would have no compunction in sending them to the same fate as Munroe.

He was done deciding his future based on what they might think. He didn't need anyone else to tell him what he wanted. Or whom he wanted.

Chapter Forty-Two

Ruth kneaded the dough with her fists, brushing away a hair on her cheek, only to realize she must have imagined the hair. All that was there was flour—and now a sticky piece of dough. That was one benefit of short hair—it didn't get in the way of cooking and baking.

Mr. Jolley at *The Marsbrooke Weekly* had been disappointed when Topher had informed him that the Swan would no longer be providing content for the newspaper. He had offered them fifty percent more to continue the column, and Topher had tried to convince Ruth to accept the offer—for the sake of the family—but she hadn't yielded. She would find another way to contribute to the family's income—one that didn't elicit so many painful memories or require her to tell so many lies.

Topher came down the stairs, setting his hat atop his head. "I am off to the barrister's. Hopefully Mr. Linas will see fit to give me some honest work. He likes me well enough."

Ruth nodded with a sigh. She knew Topher preferred the adventure of smuggling to what he was seeking now, but like her, he had learned from his time in Town. The last thing their family needed was for Topher to be apprehended by one of the excisemen.

The door opened, and Ellen appeared, arms full of vegetables and potatoes from her trip to the market. Both Ruth and Topher rushed over to relieve her of her burden.

"Thank you," Ellen said. She set her hands on her hips and caught her breath. "Whose grand carriage is that outside?"

Ruth and Topher shared a confused glance as they set the food on the table.

"It was coming to a stop just as I walked in—I thought perhaps one of you was expecting one of your friends from Town."

A knock sounded on the door, and Ruth's heart thumped. No matter how she tried to tame it, it *would* insist upon hoping.

Ellen bustled to the door and opened it, while Ruth and Topher stared at one another.

"Yes, good day," said an older male voice. "Is Mr. Hawthorn at home?"

"Just a moment, if you please sir, while I see."

Topher strode over. "Never mind that, Ellen."

She moved, allowing Topher to take her place in the doorway, which he did, suddenly going still. "Mr. Devenish. Rebecca."

Ruth's eyes widened.

"C-c-come in," Topher sputtered, opening the door wider.

Mr. Devenish and his daughter stepped into the house, and Ruth was annoyed to feel the heat rising in their cheeks. It was one thing for all of London to know that she and Topher had no money—it was another thing entirely for people to see it with their own eyes.

But the Devenishes' gazes didn't rove about the room, they merely traveled to Ruth, and Miss Devenish smiled.

"Miss Hawthorn," she said, dipping into a small curtsy as her father bowed.

Ruth curtsied in return, aware of how foolish she looked, doing so in a flour-covered apron.

Topher led them into the parlor, and Ruth stared as their backs disappeared and the door shut behind them. A little pang shot through her heart, and she turned back to her dough, aware that Ellen was watching her.

"I am almost finished with this," Ruth said.

"Leave it to me, miss." Ellen came over, but Ruth stayed in place.

"No. I want to finish it. I like the work." There was something satisfying about working the dough. Ruth had offered to do it every day since their return, finding that she felt a little bit more in control of herself afterward. For a while, at least.

"Very well, miss." Ellen set to cutting vegetables, and Ruth tried not to be curious about the muffled conversation happening in the other room.

It was fifteen minutes before the door to the parlor opened again. Ruth was standing before the fire, where the bread cooked, filling the room with its scent. She turned to see Topher emerge, Miss Devenish trailing behind him. They were holding hands.

Topher's mouth stretched into a wide smile, and he led Miss Devenish over toward Ruth. "Well, sister. Will you wish me joy?" He looked down at Miss Devenish beside him, and she smiled warmly up at him.

Ruth's mouth opened as she looked back and forth between them, and Mr. Devenish emerged into the kitchen, a smile on his face, as well.

"We hope to marry as soon as the banns can be read," Topher said, gaze still trained on Miss Devenish in a way that twisted Ruth's heart with envy. He finally looked back at Ruth.

"Truly?" she asked, seeking confirmation from Miss Devenish, who nodded and moved closer to Topher.

"Yes. We can marry here in your parish if you wish," Miss Devenish said to him.

"I will marry you anywhere you choose," he responded.

Ruth embraced them both—apologizing for her state—and said everything appropriate, until the Devenishes and Topher disappeared outside, arranging details and plans for the next few weeks.

Ruth swallowed as the sound of their joyful voices became muffled and then drowned in the noise of the street. Tears burned in her eyes, and she hurried to turn back to the oven, removing the loaves of bread and sliding them onto the table.

"Miss?" Ellen's steady chopping slowed.

Ruth wiped at her eyes with the back of her hands and forced a laugh. "Bah! Those onions you are cutting! If you will excuse me..." She avoided Ellen's eye as she hurried up the stairs and into her room.

She was able to make herself decent by the time Topher called to her through the door to her bedchamber.

"Come in," she said, straightening a stack of papers on the wobbly desk in hopes that it would appear she had been busy.

He entered slowly, warily, and it made Ruth feel fragile in a way that stung her eyes again. She didn't want to feel fragile anymore, but she didn't know how to stop.

She smiled at her brother and motioned him to the chair against the wall, determined to show him the happy face he deserved.

"Well, *that* was quite unexpected," she said.

He sat down with a large sigh and a speaking look. "It was. I thought I would never see her again, much less..." He glanced at Ruth again and didn't finish.

"What happened?" she asked. "I should have asked you after the masquerade, but I thought perhaps you didn't wish to speak of it."

"I didn't." He shrugged. "She was angry—hurt, you know. She thought that it had all been a sham—that I had used your methods to trick her into falling in love with me, and that, just like everyone else, I only wanted her for her wealth."

Ruth nodded. "So, what changed?"

"Rowney. He talked to her—told her everything he knew about me. He convinced her that it wasn't all an act—that I loved her as soon as we spoke, long before I knew anything of her situation."

"He is a good friend."

"He is. Despite the fact that I lied to him, too." He sent Ruth a commiserating grimace. "I know you are trying to be happy for me, Ruth, and I love you for it. But I also know that you are hurting more than you let on, and I wish there was something I could do to change that. It feels unfair that things should happen this way, even if I *am* grateful for my own good fortune."

She pulled him up from his chair and embraced him, glad that he was unable to see the way her eyes were filling with tears. It was all they seemed to be good for nowadays. "You mustn't temper your joy on my account, Topher. I would never wish that. I am so very happy for you."

He sighed, holding her tightly. "And for our family. It changes everything, you know." He pulled away. "Rebecca has a kind heart, and she won't let our family go wanting."

"You needn't go to Mr. Linas's, then?" she teased.

He shook his head. "Rebecca's father knows someone who might be willing to recommend me for studying law."

"Well, that is good news, indeed."

He kept a hand on Ruth's arm and looked her in the eye. "We shall find someone for you, Ruthie. Don't despair." A small commotion sounded downstairs, and the familiar tones of their mother's voice reached them. "And now I must go speak with Mama. She hasn't any idea what has happened—and she is meant to accompany me to Rebecca's tomorrow. Will you mind watching the children for the day?"

Ruth smiled. "Not at all. Now go give her the good news."

Topher's mouth broke into a grin, and he hurried from the room, leaving a cloud of joyful dust behind him.

Chapter Forty-Three

Ruth pushed at her sleeve again so that it sat above her elbow, but it was too late. It was already wet. The weight of the rolled, wet fabric caused it to slip back down again, and she surrendered to the inevitable, plunging her arm back into the basin of water and rubbing one of George's shirts against the washing board.

She pulled out the small garment, twisting the excess water out and then spreading it to see whether her efforts had met with success. The same large stain stared back at her, though, just a few inches away from a hole where the seam joined the sleeve and body. He was growing too big for the shirt anyway.

She tossed it to the side, intending to make it into rags once she finished the rest of the laundry. Ruth's mother and Topher were in London for the day, and Lucy was inside, making sure that the older children stayed focused on their studies—Ruth had asked to do the laundry herself instead of being tasked with watching the children. She didn't enjoy laundry normally, but the manual labor was just what she needed to work through her emotions. Ellen was preparing dinner, while George and Joanna played at the far end of the small garden, watering the plants.

Ruth submerged her own chemise in the water and set to scrubbing it, wondering whether Topher and Miss Devenish's marriage would mean she no longer had to do laundry. She didn't feel right hoping for such a thing, but she was feeling particularly exhausted since coming home. Home *was* a refuge after the storm of London in many ways. But in other ways, it was a harsh reality—made all the more so for the luxurious interlude of the past month.

Penny stepped into the garden. "A letter for the Swan, Ruth." She held out the paper in her hand, and Ruth sighed. Topher had always picked up the post from the office of the newspaper. Now that they had ended their contribution, though, apparently Mr. Jolley was sending the correspondence directly to them. Hopefully it wouldn't be necessary for much longer.

"I thought Topher told them that we wouldn't be taking any more correspondence. My hands are wet, so I can't take it just yet. Put it on top of the dry laundry pile. I will get to it later."

Penny set the note atop the heap of dirty laundry and skipped back into the house.

A little delighted squeal sounded behind Ruth, and she turned to see one of the plant pots overflowing with water. She rushed over and took the empty watering can from George, forcing her voice to sound patient. "That is far too much water, my love."

"But you said they were thirsty," he complained.

"They are—or were, rather. But they don't need an entire pot full of water, dear, just as you don't." She directed a chastising glance at Joanna. "You know that."

"I told him to stop," Joanna said, and she tipped the horned spectacles up farther on her nose. Ruth stared at the glasses for a moment, swallowing at the memories they evoked. Joanna had been wearing them for days now, despite the teasing of her siblings.

Ruth set down the watering can and tipped the pot of plants slightly so that the excess water drained onto the stones below, then packed down the wet soil as best she could.

"Go wash up inside. It will be dinnertime soon."

With their wet clothes and dirtied hands, the two of them scampered inside, and Ruth watched them go with an irrepressible smile as she wiped her hands on her apron.

She looked at the pile of dirty clothing that still awaited her and the note that sat on top. With a sigh, she went over to it. Every time she read the Swan correspondence now, she was reminded of the short letter that had changed everything. If Topher were home, she would have made him read this one to spare her.

She frowned at the bits of soil that smeared the note as she opened it.

Dear Swan,

I write to request another in-person consultation. I understand that the rate has increased greatly, and I assure you I will provide fair compensation for your time.

Mr. O

The note trembled in Ruth's hands, and she stared at it—the familiar script, the way the clean foolscap stood in contrast to her soiled hands, the signature.

The sound of movement brought Ruth's head up, and her breath caught.

Hat in hand, Philip stooped through the doorway and into the garden, his broad figure filling the space, his gaze intent on her.

She tried to blink—to dispel the impossible view before her—but, aside from the rise and fall of her chest, every part of her refused to move.

He took a step toward her. "Ruth."

It was one word, but it lodged inside her somewhere, assuring her that what she was seeing was real.

The edge of his mouth curved up in a small half-smile. "Little panda."

Her cheeks warmed, and her vision grew blurry again.

A few quick footsteps brought him to her, and he took her hands in his. "I have been grieving you, Ruth—grieving my own stupidity and boorishness—and I needed to see you. Tell me I haven't lost you."

Her heart lodged in her throat, stopping her from speaking, and she shook her head.

He let out a relieved, shaky laugh, and his hands clasped hers more tightly. "I still need the Swan's services, but not for myself." He put a hand to her cheek. "I assure you, I need no help at all loving you. I only need to know whether *you* can be persuaded to love me again."

She covered the hand on her cheek with her own hand and pressed a kiss into it. "I never stopped, Philip. I have loved you and wanted you for myself almost as long as I have known you. But I never thought I could have you." She stared up into his eyes, hoping he could see her sincerity. "I am so sorry for keeping things from you. I was so scared of losing you that I couldn't bear the thought of giving you a reason to end what we had—the friendship that had come to mean so much to me."

He lowered his forehead until it met hers. "I understand. And I forgive you with all my heart. Please forgive *me* for being so blind and insufferably proud."

"I am used to the insufferable part," she said with a smile. "And I have a pair of spectacles for the blindness."

He laughed softly, and the sound filled some of the holes that had plagued her since he had left her standing in Grosvenor Square. "I will wear even those ridiculous glasses if it will please you, my love." He pulled back, staring down into her eyes. "I thought the reason I was always at ease with you was that I thought you a man when we met. But I was wrong. You are everything I need, Ruth. And everything I want."

She looked down, shaking her head. "I am *not* what you want, Philip. I am not Rebecca Devenish—I am nothing like her—or like any of the women you should marry. I am poor, unknown, with no reputation to speak of. I could hardly be less fit to marry a viscount."

He tipped her chin up with his finger, his brow drawn into a frown. "I *do* want you, Ruth. More than I have wanted anything in my life. I want you just the way you are"—the corner of his mouth lifted, and he put a gentle hand to her head—"short hair"—he grasped her hand and brought it up to display it—"wrinkled fingers"—he put his over her heart—"and the kindest soul of anyone I know. I want you or no one at all."

Ruth shut her eyes, letting his words soak into her, feeling her heart beat against his hand.

"Will you have me, Ruth?"

She kept her eyes shut, breathing in amber and wet soil and laundry soap, the scents of disparate worlds. She wrapped a hand around his neck and pulled his lips down to hers, bringing the two worlds into collision and melding them together as their mouths met and molded to one another. His hand moved from her heart around to the small of her back, drawing her nearer, and she ceded to it, answering his question with every means available to her but speech.

Giggling sounded, and they broke apart just as Joanna and George darted into the garden, the latter chasing after his older sister.

"He is going to get me, Ruth! Make him stop!" Joanna cried somewhere between a laugh and a scream.

Ruth caught at George's sleeve and scooped him up into her arms. He kicked and writhed, and she struggled to control him.

Philip took him from her arms, restraining the young child in an unyielding hold. "So *this* is Master George, is it?"

George attempted to free himself one more time then surrendered, looking at his captor with unabashed curiosity. "Who are *you*?"

"I am to be your newest brother," Philip said, all formality.

George's nose and forehead wrinkled. "I already have too many of those."

Philip laughed and set him on the ground.

Joanna had her head tilted to the side, her gaze moving from Ruth to Philip and back again. "Are you going to marry Ruthie?"

Philip looked down at Ruth and took her hand in his again. "I am indeed."

"But John says that Ruth can't marry till her hair grows long again, 'cos people think she's a boy!"

"George!" Joanna elbowed her brother.

Ruth sent a challenging look at Philip. "*Do* you intend to wait until my hair grows long again before you marry me?"

"It shall be a miracle if I can manage to wait to marry you until the banns are read," he said in an undervoice.

"You shall have to wait until after Topher and Miss Devenish marry," Joanna said, "for they were betrothed first. It is only fair."

Philip glanced at Ruth in surprise, and she laughed and confirmed her sister's words with a nod. "She came only yesterday with her father."

"Well, that *does* complicate things, doesn't it? For, as you said, Miss Joanna, fair is fair." Philip crouched down and beckoned the children. "But perhaps we might come to an arrangement."

George frowned and crossed his arms. "What sort of arrangement?"

Philip held up a finger. "Wait one moment."

He stood and moved past Ruth, pausing to plant a hasty kiss on her lips before disappearing inside for a moment. When he emerged, both hands were behind his back. He crouched down again in front of Joanna and George, and Ruth covered her mouth with a hand as she recognized what he held. He had remembered.

"What are you holding behind your back?" George asked, trying to sneak a peek.

"An offering," Philip said. "One for Miss Joanna"—he pulled one hand from behind his back, displaying a small, porcelain doll, with rich, brown hair and a green silk dress—"and one for Master George." He pulled out the other hand, revealing a small, wooden horse.

Both sets of eyes rounded, and their hands flung out to take the toys in hand. They tilted the gifts, admiring them from different angles, until Joanna directed her large eyes at Philip. "You may marry Ruthie today if you wish."

Philip chuckled and rose to his feet, moving back toward Ruth and wrapping his arms around her waist.

"I see you are not above bribery, my lord," Ruth said, trying to direct a quelling look at him, though her mouth betrayed her with a smile.

"One must speak in the language a child understands." He glanced at the children, who were comparing their gifts as they walked back toward the end of the garden. "Besides, it was necessary to distract them."

She raised her brows. "And why is that?"

"Because I wasn't anywhere near done kissing you."

Epilogue

Ruth could only stare. Never in her life had she seen an estate as grand as the one that stood before her—her new home, with a façade that seemed to stretch on for an eon, and a whole host of windows staring down at her.

She blinked, realizing that her husband was addressing her—and still holding her hand to assist her down from the carriage.

"Hmm?" she said dazedly.

Philip chuckled. "I merely said, 'Welcome home, my love.'" He pulled her down from the carriage, and she toppled into his arms, her awe at the sight of Oxley Court giving way to surprised laughter. Philip quickly put a stop to it with a warm and persistent kiss on her lips. She wrapped her arms around his neck and returned his embrace gladly, until she realized there was a line of servants waiting to greet them.

She pulled away, her cheeks filling with heat. "They are waiting for us," she whispered.

Philip glanced over at his staff with only faint interest. "Indeed, they are. I am paying them to do so." He dipped his head to steal another kiss, but Ruth stopped him.

He sighed and set her feet on the ground, though the corner of his mouth trembled with a smile. "Very well. We will finish that presently." He took her hand and guided her through the lane of servants, each of whom greeted her with a smile, curious eyes, and a curtsy or bow.

Ruth couldn't imagine having responsibility over the half of them. She had wondered if there might be just a bit of embarrassment or shame in Philip's manner as he introduced his short-haired, scandal-tainted bride to the staff of Oxley Court, but there was nothing but pride in his eyes, and it warmed her heart to see.

"My lord," said the butler, coming to walk beside Philip as they made their way to the door. "I hesitate to take your attention away so soon after your arrival, but I'm afraid there is an urgent matter of business to attend to in the library." He cleared his throat, donning a look of long-suffering disapproval.

Philip stared at his butler for a moment, then looked to Ruth.

The last thing she wanted was to be left alone in the grand manor immediately after their arrival. But she would have to accustom herself to the place sooner or later. And she didn't want to pull Philip away from anything urgent.

"If someone can just show me to my bedchamber..." she said.

Philip shook his head. "Will you come with me to the library? I can't imagine the matter will take long to see to, but if it does, I will take you to *our* bedchamber"—he gave her a speaking, smiling look—"myself before returning to the matter."

She smiled and nodded her agreement.

Philip guided her through the front door and down the window-lined corridor with what seemed like a dozen carved wooden doors leading off of it. He stopped in front of one of the doors and gave Ruth a significant look. "Prepare yourself."

"For what?" she asked. "A room full of books?"

He gave a grimace and opened the door, pulling her in by the hand.

It *was* a grand library, with shelf after shelf towering above. Ruth's eyes roved over them, stopping suddenly. "Oh my." Like the shelves around it, a portrait larger than any Ruth had ever seen loomed at the far end of the room. The subject was a grand, elegant woman, her hair dark and precise, eyes piercing, and a mouth that seemed to somehow smile and intimidate at the same time.

"Meet my mother, my love." He sighed. "You understand now why I tend to avoid this room." He let go of her hand and walked to the desk, where an unsealed letter sat.

Ruth tilted her head, wondering if perhaps the late Viscountess Oxley wouldn't look quite so daunting from a different angle. But no. There was no avoiding the intimidation she oozed.

"Well," she said, removing her bonnet, "I did not have the pleasure of meeting your mother, Philip, but I cannot think that even the kindest person could look anything but threatening in such a grand painting."

He chuckled as he unfolded the note. "If she overwhelms you in *that*, be grateful you *didn't* meet her when she was alive." His eyes narrowed as they ran over the missive. "Oh, for heaven's sake."

"What is it?" Ruth asked, walking over to join him.

He handed her the letter. "See for yourself."

It was short.

Welcome home, Ox. I've taken up residence in the Green Room.

Fin

P.S. You are out of brandy

"The Green Room?" Ruth asked, looking to her husband.

He opened his mouth to respond, but the door opened just then.

"Finally!" Finmore walked in, and the butler appeared behind him, an apologetic expression on his face. Finmore closed the door behind himself, though, shutting the butler out. "I wrote that note an eon ago. I thought you were only meant to be gone a fortnight." He came and bowed over Ruth's hand, the same rakish smile in his eyes as always. "Lady Oxley," he said.

Philip swatted at Finmore's arm. "We *were* only meant to be gone a fortnight." He put an arm about Ruth's waist and pulled her closer. She looked up at him, and he smiled down at her, warmth in his eyes. "We found we weren't quite ready to come home yet." He turned his gaze back to Finmore, and his smile faded. "If I'd have known what would be here to greet me, we would have stayed away even longer."

Finmore laughed as he wandered over to the liquor cabinet.

"I was quite certain when I last left here that the brandy was well-stocked," Philip said.

Finmore took out each decanter by turns, frowning at them. "Yes, well, I've been here ten days waiting."

"Ten days!" Philip exclaimed.

Finmore poured himself a glass. "When a man says he will be home in a fortnight, I believe him. By the by, did you hear about Munroe? No, I imagine not, as you've been taken up with..." He glanced at Ruth, a knowing smile on his face.

"Out with it, Finmore," Philip said. "If you mean to convey gossip, at least do it speedily. I have other things to attend to." He sent his own significant look at Ruth, and she tried to stifle a yelp as he squeezed her waist.

Finmore watched them with an expression of distaste. "I'm afraid poor old Munroe was obliged to take flight to somewhere less accessible to those who wish him ill."

"Who wishes him ill?" Ruth couldn't help asking. Philip cared little for gossip, but she couldn't stifle her own curiosity.

"Who *doesn't*?" Philip asked, tossing Finmore's letter into the fire grate.

Finmore frowned at the gesture. "Apparently, he tried to fly to the border with a young heiress, but they were apprehended by her father."

"A riveting tale," Philip said. "And now will you leave my wife and me be? I understand the rooms at the Black Boar are very comfortable."

Finmore swallowed the last of his drink then shook his head. "Not possible."

"Done up again?" Philip asked on a sigh.

Finmore gave a slight nod. "Straits are becoming quite dire. I knew I might depend upon you to house me while I rusticate a bit."

"Your confidence in the lengths of my hospitality is inspiring, Fin. But unfortunately inaccurate."

"You've plenty of space." Finmore gestured around the library. "Surely you can't begrudge a room or two."

Philip put out a peremptory hand and pulled his friend from his seat. "I assure you I both can and do. You will have to rusticate elsewhere. I have no intention of sharing Oxley Court with both you and my bride. Besides, the Hawthorns are set to arrive in a few days, and then the place shall be overrun with children."

Ruth smiled at Finmore's disturbed reaction. Oxley Court might feel crowded to Philip or Finmore, but to children who had just been living in Marsbrooke, it would feel like an entire world to explore.

"If you're so done up," Philip said, "you might consider the state of matrimony for yourself, Fin." He returned to Ruth, pulling her toward him and wrapping his arms around her without a shred of embarrassment. "Ruth might even agree to help you with a bit of advice."

Finmore wrinkled his nose at the sight of their affection. "No, thank you. Not all of us are so entirely helpless in that area as you, Ox. I shall exhaust my options before I turn to marriage to solve anything."

Philip didn't respond, merely kissing Ruth in a way that left her breathless—and a bit sorry for Finmore that he might never experience such a thing with the woman he loved.

"On second thought," Finmore said in a voice of distaste, "the Black Boar is beginning to sound more appealing by the moment."

Philip didn't give any indication of intending to stop kissing Ruth, and Finmore let out a disgusted noise. Ruth was vaguely aware of the sound of his footsteps departing and the door opening and shutting.

Philip looked up finally, smiling. "Now that I know how to get rid of him, we may well never see him again."

Ruth laughed, and he pulled her more tightly to him with one arm and ran a hand through her growing locks with his other.

He stared at her intently, and his expression softened. "I never imagined that I would share this home with a woman I admire and love more than my own life. I have lived most of my life here, but never have I felt more at home than I do right now. I know it is a bit overwhelming for you, but I hope you will give it a chance, my love."

Grasping his lapels more tightly, she pulled him down, catching his lips to hers. She had wondered of late whether she would ever accustom herself to the life she had now. She would—she knew she would. And she knew it would be her choice, too, to ensure she never forgot how fortunate she was to be with the man whose arms were now around her.

She pulled away slightly, allowing their noses to touch. "I will stand by you here"— she glanced furtively to the other side of the library and smiled—"under this utterly terrifying portrait of your mother—or anywhere you choose, Philip. And, wherever we are, whatever life brings, I promise to love you every day of it—even when you are insufferable."

He laughed softly. "And I promise to love *you* every day of it, little panda. Now, come. I believe we have some unfinished business." He raised a brow. "Did I not promise to show you to our bedchamber?"

And with that, he scooped her into his arms and carried her all the way there.

THE END

Afterword

Thank you so much for reading *True of Heart.* It was such a challenge for me to write, but a fun one. I hope you enjoyed getting to know the characters.

I have done my best to be true to the time period and particulars of the day, so I apologize if I got anything wrong. I continue learning and researching while trying to craft stories that will be enjoyable to readers like you.

If you enjoyed the book, please leave a review and tell your friends! Authors like me rely on readers like you to spread the word about books you've enjoyed.

If you would like to stay in touch, please sign up for my newsletter. If you just want updates on new releases, you can follow me on BookBub or Amazon. You can also connect with me on Facebook and Instagram. I would love to hear from you!

Other titles by Martha Keyes

If you enjoyed this book, make sure to check out my other books:

Regency Shakespeare

A Foolish Heart (Book One)

My Wild Heart (Book Two)

True of Heart (Book Three)

Families of Dorset

Wyndcross: A Regency Romance (Book One)

Isabel: A Regency Romance (Book Two)

Cecilia: A Regency Romance (Book Three)

Hazelhurst: A Regency Romance (Book Four)

Phoebe: A Regency Romance (Series Novelette)

Tales from the Highlands

The Widow and the Highlander (Book One)

The Enemy and Miss Innes (Book Two)

The Innkeeper and the Fugitive (Book Three)

Other Titles

A Seaside Summer (Timeless Regency Collection Book 17)

The Highwayman's Letter (Sons of Somerset Book Five)

Goodwill for the Gentleman (Belles of Christmas Book Two)

The Christmas Foundling (Belles of Christmas: Frost Fair Book Five)

The Road through Rushbury (Seasons of Change Book One)

Of Lands High and Low

Eleanor: A Regency Romance

Join my Newsletter to keep in touch and learn more about the Regency era! I try to keep it fun and interesting.

OR follow me on BookBub to see my recommendations and get alerts about my new releases.

Acknowledgments

Suffice it to say, I would never have had the courage—or the gall—to tackle a Shakespeare retelling without my mom. I grew up hearing and performing Shakespeare, thanks to her. She spent years—seventeen, to be exact—directing the sixth grade Shakespeare play at our local elementary school, changing many lives in the process. I owe so much to her. She helped me think through some of the hallmark elements of each play. I love her passion for Shakespeare.

My husband is always kind, understanding, and quick to make writing time possible—along with all the other tasks that come with it—whenever I need. He is better than I deserve!

Thank you to my children who have continued to nap so that I can find time to write. May the odds continue to be in my favor.

Thank you to my editor, Jenny Proctor, for her wonderful feedback—I'm so glad I have you!

Thank you to my critique group partners, Jess, Kasey, Emily, and Deborah for helping me get the book where I wanted it. I value our friendship and your input so much! Thank you to my beta readers for taking on the task of tightening things up in the manuscript.

Thank you to my Review Team for your help and support in an often nervewracking business.

Lightning Source UK Ltd.
Milton Keynes UK
UKHW012001291221
396338UK00003B/837